Karen

THE LAST SIN EATER

FRANCINE
RIVERS

THE LAST SIN EATER

a novel

Tyndale House Publishers, Inc.
WHEATON, ILLINOIS

Library of Congress Cataloging-in-Publication Data

Rivers, Francine, date
  The last sin eater / Francine Rivers.
    p. cm.
  ISBN 0-8423-3570-6 (hardcover)
  I. Title.
PS3568.I83165L3   1998   98-19967
813'.54—dc21

Printed in the United States of America

03   02   01   00   99   98
 6   5   4   3   2   1

To my husband, Rick,

With love and thanksgiving

You are God's gift to me.

ACKNOWLEDGMENTS

God has blessed me with a wonderful family and many friends who have been consistently supportive and encouraging. My husband, Rick; my agent, Jane Jordan Browne; and my editor, Karen Ball, have been heavily involved in seeing me through each project. Thank you for always being there.

Peggy Lynch: Thank you for listening to me and asking the hard questions that make me think more deeply.

Liz and Bill Higgs: Thank you for sending a box of resource materials!

Loveknotters: Thank you for listening, advising, sharing, and praying.

Author's Note

THE SIN EATER WAS A PERSON WHO WAS PAID A FEE OR given food to take upon himself the moral trespasses of the deceased and their consequences in the afterlife. Sin eaters were common in the early nineteenth century in England, the Lowlands of Scotland, and the Welsh border district. This custom was carried over by immigrants to the Americas and practiced in remote areas of the Appalachian Mountains.

This is a purely fictional story of one such person.

And Aaron shall cast lots upon the two goats; one lot for the Lord, and the other lot for the scapegoat. And Aaron shall bring the goat upon which the Lord's lot fell, and offer him for a sin offering. But the goat, on which the lot fell to be the scapegoat, shall be presented alive before the Lord, to make an atonement with him, and to let him go for a scapegoat into the wilderness.   LEVITICUS 16:8-10

"I am the way, the truth, and the life:
no man cometh unto the Father, but by me."
JESUS, THE CHRIST; JOHN 14:6

O N E

Great Smoky Mountains, mid-1850s

THE FIRST TIME I SAW THE SIN EATER WAS THE NIGHT Granny Forbes was carried to her grave. I was very young and Granny my dearest companion, and I was greatly troubled in my mind.

"Dunna look at the sin eater, Cadi," I'd been told by my pa. "And no be asking why."

Being so grievously forewarned, I tried to obey. Mama said I was acurst with curiosity. Papa said it was pure, cussed nosiness. Only Granny, with her tender spot for me, had understood.

Even the simplest queries were met with resistance. *When you're older . . . It's none of your business. . . . Why are you asking such a fool question?* The summer before Granny died I had stopped asking questions of anyone. I reckoned if I were ever going to find answers, I'd have to go looking for myself.

Granny was the only one who seemed to understand my mind. She always said I had Ian Forbes's questing spirit. He was my grandfather, and Granny said that spirit drove him across the sea. Then again, maybe that was not the whole truth because she said another time it was the Scotland clearances that did it.

Papa agreed about that, telling me Grandfather was driven off his land and herded onto a boat to America so sheep could have pasture. Or so he was told, though I could never make sense of it. How could animals have more value than men? As for Granny, she was the fourth daughter of a poor Welsh tinker and had no prospects. Coming to America wasn't a matter of choice. It was one of necessity. When she first come, she worked for a wealthy gentleman in a grand house in Charleston, tending the pretty, frail wife he had met, married, and brought over from Caerdydd.

It was the wife who took such a liking to Granny. As a Welshwoman herself, the young missus was longing for home. Granny was young then, seventeen to her recollection. Unfortunately, she didn't work for them long, as the lady died in childbirth and took her wee babe with her. The gentleman didn't have further need of a lady's maid—and what services he did want rendered Granny refused to provide. She'd never say what they were, only that the man released her from her contract and left Granny to her own devices in the dead of winter.

Times were very hard. She took whatever work she could find to keep body and soul together and met my grandfather while doing so. She married Ian Forbes "despite his disposition." Never having met my grandfather, I couldn't judge her remark on his behalf, but I heard my uncles laughing once about his high temper. Uncle Robert said Grandfather stood on the front porch and shot at Papa, not once, but twice in quick succession. Fortunately, he had been drunk at the time and Papa quick on his feet, or I never would have been born.

Grandfather Forbes died of a winter long before I was born. A heavy storm had come, and he lost his way home. Where he had been, Granny didn't say. It was one of the things that frustrated me most, only hearing part of the story and not the whole. It was left to me to piece it all together and took years in the doing. Some of it is best not told.

When asked why she had married such a fierce man, Granny said, "He had eyes blue as a dusky sky, dearie. You have 'em,

Cadi, my love, same as your papa does. And you've Ian's soul hunger, God help you."

Granny was ever saying things beyond my ken. "Papa says I take after you."

She rubbed her knuckles lightly against my cheek. "You do, well enow." Her smile had been sad. "Hopefully not in all ways." She would say no more on the subject. Seemed some questions didn't bear answering.

The morning she died, we were just sitting and looking out over the hollow. She had leaned back in her chair, rubbing her arm as though it was paining her. Mama was moving around inside the house. Granny drew in her breath with a grimace and then looked at me. "Give your mama time."

How four words could hurt. They brought to mind all that had been before and what had caused the wall between Mama and me. Some things can't be changed or undone.

Even at my young age, after a mere ten years of living, the future stretched bleakly out ahead of me. Resting my head against Granny's knee, I said nothing and took what solace I could in her sweet presence, not guessing that even that would soon be taken from me. And if I could go back now and change things so that I would not have lived through such a time of desolation, would I? No. For God had his hand upon me before I knew who he was or even that he was.

In the last year I had learned tears did no good. Some pain is just too deep. Grief can't be dissolved like rain washing dust off a roof. Sorrow knows no washing away, no easing . . . no end of time.

Granny laid her hand upon my head and began stroking me like I was one of the hounds that slept under our porch. I liked it. Some days I wished I was one of them hounds Papa loved so much. Mama never touched me anymore, nor Papa either. They didn't speak much to one another, and even less to me. Only my brother, Iwan, showed me affection, though not often. He had too much to do helping Papa with the farm. What little time he had left over was spent in mooning over Cluny Byrnes.

Granny was my only hope, and she was slipping away.

"I love you, my dear. You remember that when winter comes and everything seems cold and dead. It won't stay that way forever."

Winter had come upon Mama's heart last summer, and she was still a frozen wasteland where I was concerned.

"Spring beauties used to grow like a lavender blanket at Bearwallow. If I could wish for one thing, it would be for a bouquet of spring beauties."

Granny was ever saying the same thing: *If I could wish for one thing* . . . Her wishes kept me busy, not that I did not delight in them. She was too old to go far afield. Further I ever seen Granny walk was to Elda Kendric's house, she being our closest neighbor and near as old as Granny herself. Yet Granny's mind could travel across oceans and over mountains and valleys, and often did so for my sake. It was Granny who pointed me to forgotten paths and treasure haunts it would have taken me longer to discover on me own. It was for her pleasure I hunted hither and yon in our high mountains to collect her precious bits of memories. And it got me away from the house—and Mama's grief and rejection of me.

It was Granny who put me on the path to Bloomfield in springtime so that I could bring back a basket full of mountain daisies and bluets. She taught me how to make a wreath of them and put it on my head. She told me about Dragon's Tooth, where green rock grew just like the backbone of Ian Forbes's Scotland, or so he'd said.

More than once I'd gone there. It took all day for me to climb the mountain to bring back a chunk of that green stone for her. I traipsed to ponds filled with sunfish and hollows warm with frog song. I even found the oak tree she said must be old as time itself—or at least as old as she.

Granny was full of stories. She always took her leisure, pouring out words like honey on a cool morning, sweet and heavy. She knew everyone who came to settle into the palisades, runs, and hollows of our uptilted land. We Forbeses came early to these great smoky highlands, wanting land and possibilities. The mountains reminded Grandfather of Scotland. Laochailand Kai led them here, along with others. Elda Kendric came with her husband, dead and gone now so long that Granny forgot his name. Even Miz Elda might have forgotten it, for she was ever saying she didn't want to talk about him. Then came the Odaras and Trents and Sayres and Kents. The Connors and Byrneses and Smiths cleared land as well. Granny said if Grandfather Ian hadn't died, he would have moved the family further east to Kantuckee.

They all helped one another when they could and held together against nature and God himself to build places for themselves. And they was ever on the lookout for Indians to come and murder 'em. Those that didn't stand with the others stood alone and most often died. A few married come later, marrying in until we were a mingled lot, castoffs and cutaways and best-forgottens.

"We all got our reasons, some better than most, for sinking roots into these mountains and pulling the mists over our heads," Granny said once. Some came to build. Some came to hide. All of them did what they knew to survive.

That morning—the morning Granny died—I went to Bear-wallow for spring beauties. She longed for them, and that was reason enough for me to go. The flowers did grow like a lavender blanket, just like Granny said she remembered. I picked a basketful and brought them back for her. She was asleep in her porch chair, or so I thought until I came close. She was white as a dogwood blossom, her mouth and eyes wide open. When I placed the flowers in her lap, she didn't move or blink.

I knew she was gone from me.

It is an awful thing for a child to understand death in such fullness. I had already had one taste of it. This time it was a long drink of desolation that went down and spread into my very bones.

Something had departed from Granny or been stolen away in my absence. Her eyes stirred not a flicker; not a breath of air came from her parted lips. And she didn't look herself, but rather like a shriveled husk propped up in a willow chair—a likeness of Granny Forbes, but not Granny at all. She was gone already without a by-your-leave. I understood too much and not enough in that moment, and what I knew hurt so deep inside me I thought I'd die of it. For a while I did. Or at least I let go of what faint hope had survived the summer before.

Mama stopped the clock on the mantle and covered the mirror, as was our highland custom. Papa rang the passing bell. Eighty-seven times he rung it, one for each year of Granny's life. My brother, Iwan, was sent to tell our relatives the sorrowful news. By the next day, most of the clan of Forbeses and offshoots and graft-ins would gather to carry Granny to her final resting place on the mountainside.

Gervase Odara, the healer, was the first to come, bringing with her Elda Kendric, now the oldest woman in our highlands. Papa took the door off the hinges and set it up between two chairs. Granny was laid out on it. First the women removed her clothes, and Gervase Odara took them outside to wash. Water was warmed over the fire inside. Mama ladled some in a basin and used it to wash Granny's body.

"Gorawen," Elda Kendric said, brushing Granny's long white hair. "Ye've left me last of the first."

Mama didn't say anything. She and Elda Kendric went on working in silence. The old woman would look at Mama, but

Mama never once raised her head from what she was doing or said a word to anyone. When Gervase Odara came back inside, she helped Mama.

"She told me not more'n a few days ago that she had heard the mighty voice calling to her from the mountain." Gervase Odara waited, glancing at Mama. When she still said nothing, the healer said, "She told me it was for Cadi she tarried."

Mama's head came up then, and she stared hard at Gervase Odara. "I hurt enough without you tearing open the wound."

"Sometimes it does good to let it draw."

"This isna the time."

"When better, Fia?"

Mama turned slightly, and I felt her looking for me. I withdrew as far as I could into the corner shadows, hoping she wouldn't blame me for the women tormenting her. I bowed my head, pulling my knees tight against my chest, wishing myself smaller or invisible.

But I was neither. Mama fixed her gaze on me. "Go outside, Cadi. This is no place for you."

"Fia . . . ," Gervase Odara began.

I didn't wait to hear what she would say but cried out, "Leave her be!" for I couldn't bear the look in my mother's eyes. She was like a trapped and wounded animal. "Leave her be!" I cried again; then jumping up, I ran out the door.

Some of the clan was yet to be gathered, for which I was thankful. Had they been, I would have run into the lot of them staring and whispering. I looked for Papa and found him chopping down a cedar some distance away. I stood behind a tree watching him for a long while. It struck me how long it had been since I heard him laugh. His countenance was grim as he worked. He paused once and wiped the sweat from his brow. Turning, he looked straight at me. "Mama send you out of the house?"

I nodded.

Papa lifted his ax again and made another deep notch in the tree. "Get the bucket and collect the chips. Carry 'em back to her. It'll cut the stench in the house."

The women had already seen to that, for the doors and windows were open, a breeze carrying in the scent of spring in the mountains that married with the camphor they had rubbed on Granny's body. A tin cup of salt sat on the windowsill, tiny white granules blowing onto the floor like sand.

Mama was kneading bread dough as I came in. When she didn't look up, Gervase Odara took the bucket of cedar chips. "Thank you, Cadi." She began to sprinkle a handful alongside Granny, who was clothed again in a black wool dress. Her long white hair was cut off and coiled neatly on the table to be braided into the mourning jewelry. Perhaps Mama would add a white braid to the red-gold one she wore. Granny's poor shorn head had been covered with a white cloth looped beneath her chin. Her mouth was closed, her lips silenced forever. A second white strip of cloth had been tied around her ankles, a third around her knees. Her hands, so thin and worn with calluses, lay one over the other on her chest. Two shiny copper pennies lay upon her eyelids.

"Come tomorrow or the next day around nightfall, the sin eater will come, Cadi Forbes," Elda Kendric said to me. "When he does, ye'll take yer place beside your mother. Yer Aunt Winnie will carry the tray with the bread and the mazer of elderberry wine. The sin eater will follow us to the cemetery and then eat and drink all yer granny's sins so she wilna walk these hills no more."

My heart shuddered inside me at the thought.

That night I didn't sleep much, so I lay there, listening to the hoot of the owl outside. *Whooo?* Who is the sin eater? *Whooo?* Who will Granny see first now she's gone to the hereafter? *Whooo?* Who would come take *my* sins away?

The next day was no better as I watched everyone gather. Three uncles and their wives and Aunt Winnie and her husband had arrived. The cousins wanted to play, but I had no heart for it. I hid myself in the shadows of the house and kept vigil over Granny. When they finally laid her in her grave, I wouldn't see her anymore. Leastwise, not until I met my maker.

Mama didn't send me out again, but she sat in the spring sunshine with the aunts. Jillian O'Shea had a new girl baby at her breast, and most were gratified that the babe's given name was Gorawen. I heard someone say it was God's way to give and to take away. A Gorawen comes and a Gorawen goes.

I took no comfort in those words.

From my dim corner, I saw every member of Granny's family and all her friends come to pay respect to her. And they all brought something to share with the others be it whiskey, sweet potatoes for roasting, corn cakes, molasses sweet bread, or salted pork for the stew pot burbling over the fire.

"You've got to eat summat, child," Gervase Odara said to me halfway through the second day. I put my head on my arms, refusing to look at her or answer. It didn't seem right to me that life should go on. My granny lay dead, dressed in her finest clothes, ready for burial, but people talked and walked and ate as always.

"Cadi, my dear," Gervase Odara said. "Your granny had a long living."

Not long enough to my way of thinking.

I wondered if I would've felt better if Granny had told me herself what was to come. Thinking back, I figure she knew. Leastwise, I think she prayed for the end to come like it did, with me somewheres else. Instead of saying she was dying, she sent me chasing after spring beauties and departed this life while I was gone.

Only Iwan seemed to understand my hurt. He came inside

and sat with me on Granny's cot. He didn't try to get me to eat or talk. He didn't say Granny was old and it was her time to die. He didn't say time would heal my wounds. He just took my hand and held it, stroking it in silence. After a while, he got up and left again.

The Kai family came the second day. I could hear the father, Brogan Kai, outside, his voice deep and commanding. The mother, Iona, and her children came in to pay their respects to Mama and my other relatives. Iona Kai's son Fagan entered and went no further than Granny, viewing her solemnly in all her finery. He was the same age as Iwan, near fifteen, but seemed even older with his quiet demeanor and grim countenance. His mother had brought corn cakes and some jars of watermelon pickles to share. She gave them to one of my aunts and sat for a few minutes with Mama, speaking quietly to her.

As the sun went down, people spoke more and more quietly until no one spoke at all. I felt the difference in the house. The quiet apprehension had given way to a darkness heavier to bear. Granny's death had brought something into the house no words could describe. I could feel it gathering and closing in around us like the night, tighter and tighter as the day died.

Fear, it was.

Papa came to the open doorway. "It's time."

Gervase Odara came to me and hunkered down, taking my hands firmly in hers. "Cadi, you must listen. Do not look at the sin eater. Do you understand me, child? He has taken all manner of terrible things unto himself. If you look at him, he'll give you the evil eye, and some of the sin he carries might spill over onto you."

I looked up at Mama. She stood in the lamplight, her face strained, her eyes closed. She would not look at me even then.

Gervase Odara took my chin and tipped my face so I had to look her in the eyes again. "Do you understand me, Cadi?"

What good would it do now, I wanted to say. Granny is already gone. It was cold flesh that remained, not the part of her that mattered. All anyone had to do was look at her to know her soul had departed. How could anyone come now and make things right? It was done. Finished. She was gone.

But Gervase Odara persisted until I nodded. I didn't understand anything then, and the reckoning didn't come until a long time later. Yet, the healer's manner sapped my courage. Besides, I had learned better than to ask for explanations by then. I had heard of the sin eater, though in no great detail. One did not speak often or long of the most dreaded of mankind.

"He will take your granny's sins away, and she will rest in peace," Elda Kendric said from close by.

And would he come and take my sins away? Or was it to be my fate to take them with me to my grave, tormented in hell for what my mean spirit had caused?

My throat closed hot and tight.

Whatever secret sins had burdened Granny were betwixt her and the sin eater, who would take them from her. There would never be rest for me. There was not a soul present who did not know what I'd done. Or thought they did.

"Stand with your mother, child," my father told me. I did so and felt the slightest touch of her hand. When I looked up with a longing so deep my heart ached, she spoke softly and broke off a sprig of the rosemary she carried.

"Toss this into the grave when the service is done," she said without looking at me.

Four men lifted Granny and carried her out the door. Papa carried a torch and led the procession up the path to the mountainside cemetery. The night air seemed colder than usual, and I shivered walking alongside my mother. Her face was still and bleak, her eyes dry. Others carried torches to light our way. A full moon was up, though it was obscured by a thick layer of mist seeping in through the notch in the mountains. It looked like dead-white fingers reaching for us. Dark shadows danced between the trees as we passed, and my heart thumped madly, gooseflesh rising when I felt another presence join our procession.

The sin eater was there, like a cold breath of wind on the back of my neck.

Papa and his brothers had built a fence around the cemetery to keep wolves and other critters from digging. Granny once told me she liked the ground Papa had selected. It was a high place where those laid to rest would be dry and safe and have a grand view of the cove below and heaven above.

I entered the gate just after my mother and took my place at her side. My Aunt Winnie carried the tray on which was the bread Mama had baked and the mazer of elderberry wine. A long, deep hole had been dug and the earth piled up. Granny, laid out on her bier, was placed upon that mound of red-brown, rocky soil. Aunt Cora spread a white cloth over Granny, and Aunt Winnie stepped forward and placed the tray upon the body.

A stillness fell upon the congregation, taking such firm hold that even the crickets and frogs were silent.

No one moved.

No one breathed.

I looked up and saw Mama's face glowing red-gold in the torchlight, her eyes shut tight. When the gate clicked, those gathered turned away from Granny, keeping their backs to her. I did the same, the hair on my head prickling as I heard the soft footfall of the sin eater.

It was so quiet, I heard the bread tear. I heard him gulp the wine. Was it hunger for sin that made him eat like a starving animal? Or was he as eager to have done with his terrible duty and be gone from this place as were those who stood with their backs turned and eyes tight shut in fear of looking into his evil eyes?

Silence followed his hasty meal, and then he gave a shuddering sigh. "I give easement and rest now to thee, Gorawen Forbes, dear woman, that ye walk not over fields nor mountains nor along pathways. And for thy peace I pawn my own soul."

I couldn't help it. His voice was so deep and tender and sorrowful, I turned, my heart aching. For the briefest instant our eyes met, and then I shut mine at the strange and terrifying sight of him. Yet time enough had passed to change everything from that day forward.

Nothing would ever be the same again.

"No harm done," he said softly. His quiet footfall died away as he went out the gate. I looked toward it, but darkness had already swallowed him.

Crickets chirped again, and somewhere close by the owl hooted. *Whooo?* Who is the sin eater? *Whooo?* Who is he? *Whooo?*

Everyone breathed again, like a collective sigh of relief and thanksgiving that it was over now and Granny would rest in peace. Mama began to cry loudly—deep wrenching sobs of inconsolable grief. I knew it wasn't just Granny she was grieving over. Others cried with her as the prayers were said. Granny was lowered into her resting place. Loved ones came forward one by one and threw in sprigs of rosemary. When everything was said and done, Papa scooped Mama up in his arms and carried her from the graveyard.

Lingering behind, I watched two men shovel dirt on top of Granny. Each thud of earth made a cold thud inside me. One man looked up from his work. "Go on now, girl. Go on back to the house with the others."

As I left by the gate, I turned for a moment, my gaze traveling over the others laid to rest in the cemetery. My grandfather Ian Forbes had been first, followed by a son who had died of a

Thursday after complaining of terrible stomach pains. Three cousins and an aunt had died in a week of fever. And then there was the stone for Elen.

Halfway home, I looked down at the sprig of rosemary Mama had given me. I'd forgotten to throw it into the grave. Rubbing it between my palms, I crushed the small silvery leaves, releasing the scent. Putting my hands over my face, I breathed it in and wept. I stood like that, alone in the darkness, until Iwan came back for me. He held me close for a while, saying nothing. Then he took my hand and squeezed it. "Mama was worrying about you."

He meant to comfort, but I knew it was a lie. In truth, we both knew it.

I stayed outside on the far end of the porch, my legs dangling over the edge. Leaning on the lower railing, I laid my head down in my arms and listened to Aunt Winnie sing a Welsh hymn Granny had taught her. Others joined in. Papa and the other men were drinking whiskey, little interested in the food the women had prepared.

"What'd he mean, 'no harm done'?" someone asked.

"Maybe he meant Gorawen Forbes didn't have as many sins as she might have after such a long living."

"And maybe he's taken on so many in the past twenty years, hers wilna make much difference."

"Leave off talking about the man," Brogan Kai said sternly. "He done his duty and he's gone. Forget him."

No one mentioned the sin eater again, not for the rest of that evening while the grieving was open and unashamed.

Weary in body and spirit, I went inside and curled up on Granny's cot. Pulling her blanket over me, I closed my eyes, consoled. I could still smell the scent of her mingling with the rosemary on my palms. For a few minutes I pretended she was still alive and well, sitting in her chair on the porch listening to everyone tell stories about her and Grandfather and countless others they'd loved. Then I got to thinking of Granny lying deep in that grave, covered over by the red-brown mountain soil. She would not rise to walk these hills again because someone had come and taken her sins away.

Or had he?

Somewhere out there in the wilderness, all alone, was the sin eater. Only he knew if he had accomplished what he had come to do.

And yet, I could not help wondering. Why had he come at all? Why hadn't he hidden himself away, pretending not to hear the passing bell echoing in the mountains? Were not the sins of one life enough to bear without taking on those of everyone that lived and died in the hollows and coves of our mountains? Why would he do it? Why would he carry so many burdens, knowing he would burn in hell for people who feared and despised him, who would never even look him in the face?

And why did my heart ache so at the thought of him?

Even at my tender age, I knew.

Seventy to eighty years stretched out before me, long years of living ahead if I had Granny's constitution. Years to live with what I had done.

Unless . . .

"Forget him," Brogan Kai had commanded.

Yet a quiet voice whispered in my ear, *"Seek and ye shall find, my dear. Ask and the answer will be given . . ."*

And I knew I would, whatever came of it.

T W O

*I*T WAS THREE DAYS AFTER GRANNY FORBES WAS LAID
to rest that I met Lilybet in the forest. Papa and Iwan had been
out working, and I had been left alone with Mama's silence. I
had done my chores and sat watching her spinning wool, the
whir and click of the wheel the only sign of life from her. No
words passed between us. Not even a look. I was low and melancholy from abiding under the shadow of death.

"Can I do anything for you, Mama?"

She looked at me, and her pain was terrible to see. I had
cracked the shield of silence that protected her, and her heart
spilled out through her eyes. I knew she couldn't abide me so
close in her grieving. In truth, my presence only served to rekin-
dle her sorrow and tighten the chains around her heart. She was
held captive in her losses and found no pleasure or even solace
in my existence. I thought then it would have been better had I
died.

It was all I could think about on that sunny day, warm and
clear, with the mists burned away. I yearned for things to be different, for time to roll back, and knew it couldn't. Desperate to help
Mama in any small way, I took the basket from the porch, intend-
ing to fill it with garden sass. I knew just where to go for it, for
while Granny had still walked this earth she had shown me where

to find the savory greens and roots that added to our homegrown meals. Ramps grew aplenty under the maples in the cove; the pungent-scented bulbs added fine flavor to Mama's soups and stews. Turkey cress grew in the woods above the house. In the meadowlands below was brook lettuce, blue violet, and dock.

I had all we needed and more long before the sun had reached its high place overhead. I thought of leaving the basket like an offering on the front porch, knowing Mama would find it when she ventured outside to wash clothes or weed and water the garden. Yet hopelessness gripped me. What good would it do? Was there any offering I could give that would buy back time and undo what was done? No. I had to live with my sins, at least until I died and the sin eater could come and take them away.

If Mama would let him . . .

It was then that I turned toward the river, which was running high from the melting winter snows.

The water was cold as I waded in and so clear I could see the orange, brown, and black pebbles and ribbons of green moss on the bottom. Small fish shot past me, keeping to their hiding places in the rocks until I disturbed them. If I had a fishing pole, maybe I could catch a big one and bring it home for supper. I paused to think about it, the ache in my feet growing until they were numb. Seeing a big trout swaying in the current, I became less inclined to think of it as supper. It was beautiful, swimming there so gracefully and doing no one any harm. Besides, its death would not elevate me in Mama's eyes. It'd be food soon forgotten with the next pang of hunger.

What could I offer to earn forgiveness?

I was sore with hopelessness, grieving my own losses, and it was in that frame of mind that I began talking to myself in the wood, keeping myself company. Most of what I said was simple nonsense, just sounds to fill the void my loneliness was growing and to build my courage as I ventured further from home. I was making a decision and needed counsel. I thought then there was no other to listen but myself. Iwan could not encourage me, and Papa would not want to be bothered. Work was his salvation. So, seeking answers, I followed the river down to the fallen tree that bridged the narrows not far above the falls.

It was there my life had changed. And it was there I could make amends for what had happened.

I talked with myself as I went.

"You shudna be here, Cadi. You've been warned to keep away!"

"I have to be here. You know I have to see."

"Yes, I know, child, but it's dangerous. It's no place for little girls to play."

"I'm not going to play."

I left the basket on the flat rock and climbed on the upturned roots of that great old pine, then sat down. A sick fear gripped my throat as I held tight to the root chair. The palms of my hands were slick with sweat. Thinking of Mama spinning in silence, her face so pale and forlorn, helped me gather courage. After a little while, the river's roar seemed distant. A little longer, and it beckoned.

Closing my eyes, I imagined walking out on that rough-bark bridge. I imagined standing in the middle with my arms spread like wings. I imagined flinging myself out like a bird in flight, arching, suspended for a moment before I plunged downward into the white foam and churning currents that crashed over boulders. I imagined what it would be like dipping, rising, swirling, and being swept over the falls. I imagined going down, down into that deep blue pool below. And then I imagined my body floating onward and going wherever the river ran, never to be found again. Papa said it poured into the sea. The sea, so far away, so deep, so wide I could not even imagine it. All I knew was I would be lost forever.

Lost. And forgotten.

Granny was gone now. I was alone. There was no one left to lead me out of the wilderness of my circumstances or the blight upon my soul. There was no one to love me back from the edge as Granny had done daily since last summer. I kept thinking, *Oh, God, if only I could die, maybe then the sin eater would come and take my sins away. Oh, God, would that he could do it now while my heart beats and I still breathe, so I would not have to live with pain.*

And then she came, sudden and unexpected, like a shaft of light as the sun starts coming up over the mountain.

"Hello, Katrina Anice," she said in a voice soft and sweet.

Opening my eyes, I looked around and saw a little girl younger than me sitting beside the basket I'd left on the flat rock. She stood and came toward me.

"If you want to cross the river, there's a better place back in the meadowlands below your house. Let's cross over there."

Cocking my head, I stared at her, having no recollection of ever seeing her before. She had a cloud of golden hair that curled about her face and shoulders. And her eyes were very blue. They reminded me of what Granny had said about Ian Forbes's eyes, and I got to wondering if she was some far-off and forgotten relative. And then I wondered how she came to be sitting there with nary a warning at her coming. She just appeared, quiet as a drifting bird, and called me Katrina Anice. It was a pretty name, though not my own. Cadi. That was my given name. Simple Cadi Forbes and nothing else. Oh, but I liked Katrina Anice so much better. It sounded like a name much thought on before its hinges were set in place. Wouldn't it be nice to be someone special, someone loved? It would be a great relief to be anyone other than Cadi Forbes, even if just for a little while.

"I'm Lilybet," she said when I stayed in my solemn silence. "My father told me about you."

That surprised me. "He did?" I had no idea who her father was.

"Yes." She rose and stood in front of me. "I know all about what happened, Katrina Anice." Her expression was so tender I felt as though love reached out to encircle me in gentle arms. "I know everything about you."

Lowering my head, I looked down into the river again. "Everybody knows." My throat closed, hot with tears.

"Everybody knows something, Katrina Anice, but who knows everything?"

Lifting my head, I looked at her again, perplexed. "God knows." *God will judge.* That did not bear contemplation. *God is a consuming fire.*

She smiled at me. "I want to be your friend."

The ache inside my heart eased a little. Maybe, just for a little while, I would feel reprieved. "Where'd ye come from?"

"Someplace far away and near."

I giggled, amused by her conversation. "You are very strange."

She laughed, and the sound was like birdsong and a cleansing stream. "The same has been said of you, Katrina Anice, but I think we understand one another very well, don't we?"

"Aye, we do at that."

"And even better given time."

Retrieving the basket, I headed back with her, climbing the rocks along the river, ducking beneath low, leafy branches. Returning to the meadowlands, we sat on a warm sandy bank and skipped stones. I talked, a flood of words after a long drought. And I dreamed, too, of times ahead. Mama would laugh again and Papa would play his dulcimer and Iwan would dance.

Lilybet had called me Katrina Anice, and the name offered a new beginning. Like Granny, she seemed to love me without cause. And though I knew in my heart I was undeserving, I grasped Lilybet's offer of friendship with both hands and survived in it.

I took Lilybet home with me that first day, thinking to share the joy with Mama, but she paid Lilybet no mind, never even looking once at her. Not that this surprised me, for she didn't look at me anymore either. Papa was not comforted by her presence; he didn't like strangers about the place, and Lilybet was a stranger and inexplicable besides. She was unlike anyone I had ever met before or would ever meet again. Even Iwan was disturbed by her.

"Maybe ye shudna spend so much time talking with Lilybet, Cadi," he said several days after Lilybet first came. "Leastwise, not around Mama and Papa. Ye ken, my dear?"

I did understand and took his gentle advice to heart.

It was in Lilybet's company that I decided I must find the sin eater. The idea so fixed itself in my head that I thought of little else.

"Where do you think he might be, Lilybet?"

"He'll be someplace where no one can easily find him."

I couldn't ask Mama about the sin eater for fear of what words she might lay upon my head for more disobedience. After all, Gervase Odara had commanded me not to look at the man, and my own cursed curiosity had done me in. As for Papa, well, he had such a dark countenance most times that approaching him about anything took more courage than I possessed. Yet I was plagued about the sin eater. Finally, I sought Iwan out as he was repairing a harness.

"Why for are ye asking on *him?*"

"He seemed such a sorry old soul."

"And rightful so. He's taken enough sin upon himself to curse him for all eternity."

"But why would he do it, Iwan?"

"How should I know, my dear?"

"Oh, Iwan, why would he so forsake himself and give his soul over to hell?"

He lowered the strap of leather and looked at me grimly. "Ye shudna be asking about that mon, Cadi. Where would poor Granny be without him, aye? Ye shudna be thinking on him with pity. He's gone now. He wilna come back until he's needed again. Now, go on with ye and play. I've work to do, and it's too fine a spring day for a little girl to be thinking such heavy thoughts."

Iwan could be as firm as Brogan Kai was commanding. They both said the same thing: *Forget him.*

How could I forget him when he had looked at me and set his claws into my very soul? For every time I thought of the man, my wounded heart ached. He didn't even have a name, but was called by what he did. *Sin eater.* Dear to goodness, even thinking about him made my flesh grow cold and prickly. Yet I had to know who he was and how he came to be.

And if he could rescue me.

It got so I couldn't sleep at night without dreaming about the man. He would come to me in the darkest time just before dawn and say, "Who'll take *my* sins away, Cadi Forbes?" And he would reach out for me, waking me up in a cold sweat.

During my wanderings with Lilybet, I saw Fagan Kai, Cullen Hume, and Cull's sister Glynnis on the riverbank. They'd built a small fire and were roasting fish. Creeping closer, I watched them for some time from the green-and-pink veiling of rhododendrons and a blooming serviceberry tree. The boys were spearfishing, Fagan having all the luck.

"Why don't you go down and ask them about the sin eater?" Lilybet said, but even thinking about it made me tremble.

"I'm fine right here," I whispered. "I can hear what they're saying." And I could watch Fagan.

"He's very handsome," Lilybet said.

"Aye."

"He's a nice boy. He's a friend of Iwan's."

"They've gone hunting together." Fagan was standing on a rock in the middle of the stream, holding a spear high.

"There's a big one swimming for you!" Glynnis pointed excitedly.

"Quiet or you'll scare mine away," her brother said in disgust. "Why don't you go back and help Mama make soap?"

"You're making more noise than I am," Glynnis said, lower jaw jutting. "And besides that, you couldn't spear the cow, even tied up."

Fagan hurled the sharpened branch and gave a yelp of triumph. Stepping into the water, he raised his spear with a wriggling fish on the end.

"You did it! You did it!" Glynnis clapped and jumped up and down excitedly.

So impressed was I with his prowess, I stood, startling Glynnis, who startled Cull, who then missed his fish. "Yer lucky I don't have a gun, Cadi Forbes. I might have shot ye for an injun!" Red-faced, he waded into the water to retrieve his sharpened stick.

Fagan told him to be quiet.

"It's her fault I missed!"

Fagan waded back to shore with his catch. "I said leave her be, Cull." He looked up at me standing at a distance. "What're ye doing this far afield, Cadi Forbes?"

"Go on and tell him, Katrina Anice," Lilybet whispered, still concealed among the leafy branches behind me. "Maybe he'll help you."

"She made me miss!" Cull said, the spear gripped in his hand.

Fagan turned on him. "This is Kai land and I decide who's welcome. If ye canna hold yer tongue, get yer gear and go!" He yanked his fish from the spear and bent down to slip a thin piece of rope through its gills and out its mouth. Dropping it back into the water, he left it drifting with two others.

"I dinna say she wasn't welcome," Cull said sullenly. "I just don't like people sneaking up on me is all."

"I dinna mean to scare ye, Cullen Hume."

Cull's face darkened. "I wasna scared!"

"Yes you were," Glynnis laughed. "Yer face went white as the underbelly of that fish."

Cull turned on his sister, and with a shrieking laugh she darted away. At a safe distance, she taunted him more. "Cullen was scared. Cullen was scared." When he pitched a rock at her, she ducked. Straightening again, she stuck out her tongue at him and continued the harangue. "You missed me! You missed me!"

"On purpose," he shouted at her. "If I hit ye, ye'd just go crying home to Mama." Turning his back on her, he glared at me as though all his misery was my fault. And maybe it was, since I was the one who'd startled him in the first place and given Glynnis the ammunition for torment.

"So?" Fagan said. "What're you doing on Kai land?"

He was looking square at me.

"I wasna thinking on whose land I was. I was just following the river."

"Following to where?"

I shrugged, for I wasn't sure I could trust them with my quest. Cull seemed downright unfriendly. Though Fagan was playing gentleman, he might tire of it quick enough if I mentioned the sin eater. After a minute of waiting for an answer, Fagan gave a shrug and headed out to the fishing rock again.

"When ye going to quit?" Cull called out to him.

"When I've got me one more."

"That's what you said about the last one!"

"Cadi'll need one to roast over the coals."

I blushed, embarrassed by Cull's resentful stare. "Thank ye

kindly, Fagan Kai, but I gotta be going." I edged toward the woods.

"Stand fast. It'll only take me a few minutes." Fagan stood poised on the rock, his spear raised once more.

One didn't ignore the command of a Kai, be he the father, Brogan, or one of his three sons. Even this one, the youngest and least, commanded deference. I stood as I'd been told, wishing I had never let myself be seen, while at the same time glad to have gained some small bit of attention from one so important in our mountains. I had always been drawn to this boy. He measured up to Iwan.

Fagan cast his spear and leaned forward quickly. Grabbing the end, he lifted it high, sporting a writhing fish on the end. I expected him to give a yelp of triumph as he had before, but this time he returned to the riverbank with an air of dignity.

Glynnis came back, giving over her badgering of her brother. She admired Fagan's catch with fulsome words and then turned a jaundiced eye upon me. "Does yer mama know where ye are?"

"She doesna mind my wandering."

Cullen gave a short laugh. "I heard she ain't been right in the head since—"

I ran for the woods. Fagan called out to me, but I didn't stop. I was not going to stand and hear the rest of what Cullen Hume had to say, Fagan Kai or no Fagan Kai.

Diving into the leafy branches, I raced between the trees heading up the hill and along the wooded hillside.

"Cadi!"

Ducking into some thick bushes, I crouched down, out of breath. Sitting as far back in the leafy cave as I could, I drew my knees up tight against my chest and waited, scrubbing the tears from my eyes.

"Ye canna let words hurt ye so," Lilybet whispered.

Words could be sharper than a two-edged sword. They cut

deep and left me bleeding. I tensed and held my breath as I heard footsteps coming my way.

"Cadi!" Fagan stood not far from my refuge. He looked around slowly. "Cadi, where are ye, girl?" He stood quiet for a long moment, his head cocked slightly.

Like a cornered rabbit, I remained still.

"Cullen's sorry. He dinna mean anything. He's just sore because he ain't caught a fish today. Come on out, Cadi. Ye must have a good reason to be so far afield."

"Say something, Katrina Anice. Maybe you and Fagan and the others can find the sin eater."

"I'm your friend, ain't I, Cadi Forbes?"

"Are you?" I said from my hiding place.

He turned sharply, looking in my direction, but I could tell he hadna seen me.

"Go out, Cadi," Lilybet said.

"Be silent," I whispered to her.

"Go on out to him."

"No."

"He may know something that would help."

"What could he know?"

"Ye won't know until ye ask, now will ye?"

Pushing the branches aside, I stood up. He grinned at me. "Ye run faster than a deer, you know?"

Pressing my way through the shrubs, I stood in front of him, my cheeks hot. "Ye dinna have to follow."

"No, I dinna," he said and nodded his head in the direction of the river. "Come on back."

We didn't say anything to one another on the way, and I began to regret taking Lilybet's advice. Cullen and Glynnis were roasting fish.

"I didn't mean nothing," Cullen said and handed me a long stick with a trout. It had been gutted and cleaned. I thanked him and sat down to roast it. Glynnis talked about helping catch the fish by scaring them toward the boys holding the spears.

"Fagan's done it before," Cullen said. "He's teaching me."

"You'll do better next time." Fagan tossed a fish head with skeleton attached into the brush. "I learned from my brothers. They used to plague me something awful about my aim. Took a sight of time to learn just when and how to throw. You'll catch on, Cullen."

"What're you doing so far from your house?" Glynnis looked at me with curious interest.

Taking a deep breath, I let it out slowly, hoping my heart would slow down and drop back into its rightful rhythm. "I'm trying to find out about the sin eater."

Cullen swore exactly like his father. "The sin eater! What're you doing wanting to find out about the likes of him?"

"He's a monster." Glynnis's eyes were wide. "He has fire red eyes like the devil and long fangs like a wolf. And his hands are claws."

I knew that was not so but said nothing about it. Glynnis would want to know how I knew, and I was loath to admit I had looked at the acurst man when he was taking Granny's sins upon himself. I had seen no fangs, but that didn't mean he had none. He had surely eaten like a ravenous wolf. "Who told you these things?"

"My mama did."

"He must've been a man once," Fagan said.

"A man who gave himself to the devil," Cullen said. "He loves sin. He spends his whole life looking for it so he can feast on it."

"Maybe that isna so," I said. "He sounded so awful sorrowful after eating my granny's sins. And he called her 'dear,' as though he cared for her."

Fagan, Cull, and Glynnis said nothing for a long moment.

Fagan was staring off toward the mountains, frowning slightly. "I wonder where he lives."

"No one knows." Cullen shrugged. "Only time he ever comes into the cove is when the passing bell rings for somebody."

"I'd be afraid to go looking for him," Glynnis said.

"He must be somewhere close enough to hear the ringing," Fagan said, still contemplating the mountains. "Maybe up there somewhere." He pointed toward the highest mountain to the west. "My father's always told me to keep away from those mountains."

"Could be he lives up one of them hollows."

Glynnis shook her head. "Couldn't hear nothing if he did."

"Well, maybe someone tells him when someone's died. Who says he hears the bell?" Cullen said.

"Who'd it be?" I said.

"Gervase Odara maybe." He shrugged. "She's the one who'd know if someone was dying, her being the healer and all. Maybe she tells him."

I thought about that. Maybe I could talk with her when she was visiting with Elda Kendric. She was there every few days with a remedy to ease the old woman's swollen joints. "She used to come by our house and visit with Mama, but that was a long while ago."

"Your mama don't make people welcome no more," Glynnis said. "Mama said she's so deep in grieving over her dead that she ain't got time anymore for the living."

They all looked at me. I wasn't comforted by their attention. I hadn't come for pity but to find out anything I could about the sin eater. It appeared to me they didn't know much more than I. Everything they'd said so far was guessing, and I could do that all by myself. I looked up at the mountains to the west and wondered if he was up there somewhere. "Seems a lonely place..."

"Maybe he ain't far away at all," Cullen said.

Fagan got up and washed his hands in the river. "Cullen could be right. Who's to say the sin eater stays up on a mountain. Maybe he comes down and watches people."

"He could be watching us right now." Glynnis shuddered and looked around, face paling. "I wish you hadn't said that, Fagan. I ain't going to sleep nights now wondering if he's peering in our windows."

"Maybe he knows when someone's going to die." The thought clearly troubled Fagan.

Cullen tossed his fish bones into the fire. "Maybe he's like the wolves sensing when an animal's sick. He can smell death coming and prowls around until he can feast on it."

"He dinna come when Elen died," I said.

Fagan sat down again. "There was no need. She wasna old enough to have done anything wrong."

That was not the only reason, of course. But he was kind enough not to say it.

I blinked back tears. "Granny told me once that all of us are sinners. They taught her that back in Wales."

"If he dinna come, it must mean she dinna have any sins big enough to need eating." Fagan's tone was soothing. "He knows when he's to come, Cadi. The night of your granny's funeral, Mama said the sin eater knows when he's needed."

Did he? Was he out there somewhere watching us? Were his eyes fixed upon me?

"You going to eat that fish?" Cullen said to me. I handed him the stick with the half-eaten fish.

"Why don't we look for him?" Fagan said.

Cullen's head came up. "If he so much as looks at you with his evil eye, you're dead."

"No you're not," I said before I thought better of it.

Three pairs of eyes turned on me, wide and questioning. I blushed and put my head down on my knees.

"You looked at him, dinna ye?" Fagan said.

I'd opened the door to more grief and disregard. Would he tell my brother first chance he had?

Glynnis drew back slightly. "Dinna ye know you're not supposed to look at him, Cadi Forbes? Dinna anyone tell ye?"

"I cudna help myself! He sounded so sorrowful."

"He gave you the evil eye, didn't he?" Cullen cringed back. "Oh, you're in it now. You're in it."

I jumped up, standing over them. "He dinna have red eyes. And his hands were fine and clean, not claws at all."

"And his teeth?" Cullen leaned forward. "What about his teeth?"

"I dinna see his teeth." My passion was spent and I looked away. "He was wearing a hood with eyeholes and a flap over his mouth."

"He was probably hiding them," Cullen said and sank his teeth into the rest of my fish.

"He must be a monster for all the sin he's eaten," Glynnis said.

"That must be why he covers his face," Fagan said. "Whoever he is, he's been the sin eater since before I was born."

Glynnis shook her head. "Could we talk about summat else?"

"Now who's scared?" Cullen said smugly.

"So what if I am? You ought to be, too." She looked at me warily. "You shouldn't talk about him at all, Cadi Forbes. Summat terrible could happen to you."

"Talking about him ain't going to bring him down on her head," Fagan said.

"Who's to say?" Glynnis looked at him. "You don't know what could come of it!"

"And you do?"

"I know enough to know he's evil and no good can come of even thinking on him."

"Why don't you run on back to Mama?" Cullen taunted.

"If I do, I'm going to tell her what you're talking about!"

"And I'll tell her you're a liar!"

"And she'll take a switch to both of you," Fagan said.

I sat silent, feeling the prickles of fear rising. Why had I trusted them? If Glynnis went home and told her mother we were talking about the sin eater, her mother would want to know how they dared. Cadi Forbes, that's who dared. And Cadi Forbes hadn't just dared talk about him. She had looked at him. Oh, I had sins aplenty on my head and here was another. I could not go through a day without committing another grievous error.

"Glynnis is right." I hoped I hadn't done them harm. "I'm sorry I said anything about him. Just forget it." It was my trouble and I would sort it out.

"You'll have to pray," Glynnis said. "Pray hard to almighty God that the evil don't take hold of you."

"I know." I had done a lot of praying over the past year, but I didn't think God was listening. I held more hope in Granny's prayers on my behalf than anything I had said on my own. And Granny was gone. There was no one to intercede for me now.

I didn't linger with them long after that, but made my excuses and headed back. Lilybet met me on the trail. "They don't know any more than I do," I said to her.

"Are you going to give over looking for the sin eater?"

I considered it as I headed home. Maybe it was a poor idea trying to find someone who was so much an outcast. Yet wasn't I? Not an outcast from the community but from my mother's heart. And maybe Papa's, too, for that matter, though he didn't make it as apparent. He could talk to me without that heart-split look in his eyes. Maybe men didn't feel as deeply as women.

Yet, feeling as I did, I could not leave it as it was. I had to seek the man out, whatever the cost. Lilybet seemed pleased that I had not given up my quest. "Do ye know what ye'll ask him when ye meet?"

"I've not thought that far ahead."

"Think it through then, Katrina Anice. I think ye'll come upon him sooner than ye think."

When I looked at her, hoping for an explanation, she just smiled at me, her eyes alight with promise.

THREE

Gᴇʀᴠᴀsᴇ Oᴅᴀʀᴀ ᴄᴀᴍᴇ ʙʏ ᴛʜᴇ ʜᴏᴜsᴇ ᴀ ꜰᴇᴡ ᴅᴀʏs later. When I came in from doing chores, she and Mama were sitting inside near the hearth, Mama staring at the flames. "Good day, child," the healer said as I stopped in the doorway, unsure of whether to enter or wait outside until her departure. It seemed providence that she appeared, having been the one to warn me about looking into the sin eater's eyes.

She put her worn hands on her knees and pushed herself up. "I just come by to visit with your mama awhile. I'd best be getting on to Elda Kendric, or she'll wonder what's become of me."

"How's she doing these days, ma'am?" I remembered how much stock Granny took in the old woman. She always said they were good friends who had come through many a hardship together.

"She's in a lot of pain though she doesn't like to let on. Why don't you come along with me? It would cheer her up to see Gorawen Forbes's granddaughter." She cast a look at Mama. "Unless you've things for Cadi to do for you, Fia."

"She can go," she said dully, not looking up from the fire.

"Bring a shawl then, Cadi. It's clouding over."

I was weary from my chores and would have preferred stretching out on Granny's bed, but what Lilybet had said came back to me. If anyone would know anything about the sin eater, it was Elda Kendric. Except for Granny, she had been around the longest. If I went to visit her, I'd soon learn where the sin eater lived. The hope of that enticed me into obedience.

The healer and I walked a ways in silence, she thinking and me not knowing what to say. Then she paused along the pathway. "Here's pennyroyal. It's good for fevers." She picked leaves and put them into the basket she always carried. Granny used to say she was born with it dangling from her arm. "Over there's bleeding heart. Pull the smaller plant, dearie, and take it up gentle so as not to break the root. That's the best part."

I hastened to do her bidding, eager to please. I had a long liking of the healer, for she was kind and given over to the care of people. She had been one of Granny's dearest friends and often came to pass time. They would talk about the mountain people and cures for their ailments. I liked sitting by and listening to their rememberings, though they sometimes seemed cautious in my hearing. Often it was in my mind to be a healer like Gervase Odara. She was held in high regard in our small community of families, nestled as we were in the mountain coves and hollows. And so I ran to do her bidding.

My knees sank into the deep leaf fall. It lay so thick on the ground it was like a newly stuffed mattress. I drew the bleeding heart carefully from its growing place, thankful and pleased it came up easily. Brushing away the dirt, I carried the prize back to Gervase Odara, hoping to earn her good pleasure.

"Thank ye, child." She smiled and tucked the plant into her basket, then brushed the hair back from my shoulder as we began walking again. "Your mama says you have a new friend."

I clasped my hands behind my back and said nothing. My happiness was dampened knowing it was not my company she had sought after all. Mama had put her up to it.

"Lilybet, she says you call her."

I made a sound that could have been taken for yea or nay.

She stopped to cut some bark from a red oak tree. "Why don't ye tell me about her?"

"Nothing much to tell, ma'am."

"Where'd she come from?"

"Far away, she says, ma'am."

"Far away o'er the mountains? Or further away than that?"

"Across the sea, I reckon."

"That far? Maybe she comes from closer than you know, aye?"

I was not sure what she meant by that, but it had an ominous sound. We came out of the woods to the stretch of highland meadow. Yellow daisies and purple lupine and white lace were growing. I didn't want to talk of Lilybet anymore and ran my hands along the flowers as we walked through them. They were damp from dew. The sky was clouding over, and thunder rumbled in the distance as we headed uphill toward the trees.

"It'll rain before we reach Elda's," the healer said.

"Yes, ma'am, but only long enow for the earth to have a drink." Granny had always said that. It pleased me to think about the things she used to say, and I knew that Granny had said it often enough that the healer would remember also.

"Aye, my dear." She laughed at my fair imitation. "And true it is." Her smile turned wistful. "Your granny was a wise woman, my dear, and we all sorely miss her. You most of all." She looked at me intently. "Aye?"

"Papa, too, I'm thinking," I said to be polite.

"As should he, her being his mother and all. But your papa ken what was coming, I reckon. It's harder for the young to understand an end when they're just at the beginning with a long living stretching out ahead. That's the way of things, dearie. We're only allotted a certain number of years to walk this earth, and then our time comes. Your granny passed on and another enters in. Jillian O'Shea had her baby two mornings before we laid your granny to rest."

"There was room aplenty for a new baby without Granny leaving."

"I know, child, and let there be no misunderstanding. She dinna die so that the babe could come. I mean only that her passing isna the end of everything. Life goes on. And your granny will rise again on Judgment Day. Most likely, she'll see Jesus coming down from heaven from where she's resting high on that hill. No, my dear. It ain't her I mean. It's the living concerns me most. Your granny's resting easy now, sleeping until the end of time comes upon us all."

"Because of what the sin eater did for her."

She gave me a sidelong look. "Aye, that's true enow. She'll have no sins to make her walk these hills, but we've other things to talk about, you and I. Important things. Has Lilybet any folks?"

I saw she meant to keep me from speaking more of the sin eater and fix on Lilybet. I was greatly uncomfortable with the set of her conversation. "She mentioned her father." I hoped for another opportunity to learn more about the sin eater once we reached Elda Kendric. Being so old and near the grave herself, Elda Kendric was not afeared of anything.

"And have ye ever laid eyes upon her father, dearie?"

"No, ma'am."

"And where'd ye meet Lilybet?"

My heart started in pounding. I thought to tell her I'd met Lilybet in the meadow at the west end of the cove, but everyone knew Gervase Odara could tell when someone was lying. She stopped at my silence. Taking hold of my shoulders, she turned me to face her. "Tell me, child."

Her pale blue eyes were so fixed upon me that I blurted out the truth. "At the river."

She straightened with a start, releasing me. Afraid of what was coming, I darted away, calling back over my shoulder. "Miz Kendric might like some flowers." I retreated to the top of the meadow to gather some, thinking Gervase Odara might go on without me and I would catch up when she reached the old woman's house.

She waited. Both arms looped through the handle of her basket, she waited and watched. "Where by the river, Cadi Forbes?" she called after me.

I could feel the heat coming up my neck and filling my face and then washing away as quick as it come, leaving me cold as winter snow inside. "Does it matter?"

"Aye, it matters, child. Now, come on back. Elda's waiting."

I did as she bade me, bringing a bouquet of flowers with me. They would cheer the old woman and give me something to hold on to.

"Where did this Lilybet come upon ye, child?"

I knew she would not give over until she knew all she had set her mind to know. "Above the falls."

She looked troubled. "Near the tree bridge?"

I nodded once, slowly, my eyes filling with tears. Sucking my lower lip, I bit down, awaiting her pronouncement upon me.

Gervase Odara's mouth became pinched with dismay. Cupping my chin, she lifted my head and waited for me to look at her. "Ye must be careful, Cadi Forbes. Ye must listen hard to me, my girl, and do as I say. Close your heart to this Lilybet. Do not let her near to ye again. This is most important. I ken you're sorrowful and hurting for what happened, dear, but ye mustna let those feelings be a road into your soul." She stroked my tears away, looking as aggrieved as I was feeling. "Oh, child, thar's things in these mountains even I dunna understand, but I know enough to leave alone. And ye must do the same. This Lilybet is not what she seems."

Every way I turned, I faced a mystery. Oh, I understood rightly enough that she was warning me against having anything more to do with Lilybet. What I didn't ken was why. What things were in these mountains? What things should be left alone? And what was wrong with Lilybet, who had been only kind to me? And now I must forsake her when she was my only true friend? Gathering my courage, I asked the healer about all this, but she shook her head and would not say more. Even as young as I was, I understood that she was afeared of something and talking about it made that fear grow. For my sake, she tried not to let it show, but I sensed it all the same. Death has a smell that permeates. She was not frightened by what she knew but by what she didn't understand.

Why was it so? And did it have to stay that way, ever being afraid of what was beyond our understanding?

In my heart I knew that Lilybet was opening a door for me. She was giving me a glimpse inside. But inside what?

I didn't know. All I had in response to my questions were more questions.

Elda Kendric was in sore spirits and sorry condition when we reached her place. She hollered from inside her house for us to come in. Gervase said right off she could see the old woman's joints were swollen. In fact, Miz Elda was aching so fierce she couldn't even rise to greet us. She tried, but her grimace turned to a growl. "I was wishing for ye to come two days ago."

Gervase Odara made no explanations, but went to Elda Kendric's cabinet and took out a jug of whiskey. She poured a goodly amount into a mug and stirred in honey and vinegar. "Thar's a small pouch in my basket, Cadi. Bring it o'er here if ye please." I did so and watched her open it and add two pinches of powder to the drink. "A bit of rhubarb'll help the poor dear." She pulled the drawstring and handed the small pouch back to me, then offered the drink to the old woman. Elda Kendric downed it right quickly, clearly craving ease. Then the healer took a jar from the shelf and went outside.

"She'll be back soon as she's caught some bees," the old woman said. "Why don't ye sit awhile and keep me company?" She smiled through her pain. "I don't bite too hard, especially since I lost my teeth. Pull up that stool."

Here was my opportunity if I had the courage for it. I sat close to Elda Kendric and tried to think of a way to ask about the sin eater without being found out. She looked at me, a small smile playing on her lips. Granny used to get that look sometimes, as though she knew very well what I was thinking. Or thought she did.

"Those are pretty flowers ye're holding thar. Did ye pick them for your mama?"

"No, ma'am. I thought ye might like them."

"I do indeed. Yer granny was partial to blue beauties, but I've always liked daisies best."

I placed them in her lap and watched her finger the blossoms. "They come from the meadow below your woods, ma'am."

"Thought so. Last time I walked through that meadow was on the way to yer granny's funeral." She looked up from the flowers. "Lyda Hume came to visit yesterday and said her young'uns had seen ye."

"Fagan was spearing fish."

"Jest like his daddy. Ain't happy unless he's killing something."

"Ma'am, I was wondering . . ."

"Wondering about what?"

"Well, about who ye'll want to come to your funeral."

She cackled. "Land sakes, chile, what a thing to ask a poor old woman. I ain't dead yet."

"Yes, ma'am, but what good'll it do to wait?"

The healer returned. Two bees buzzed angrily in the bottle she carried.

I moved back as Gervase Odara knelt. Forsaking modesty, the old woman pulled her skirt up past her knees. Angering the bees by tapping the jar, the healer removed the first one with wood tweezers. Elda Kendric drew in her breath sharply as she received the first sting.

"Time was I could have gone out and caught these bees myself without waiting on yer convenience," Miz Elda said, brushing away the dying honeybee that had just dispensed the poison that eased her pain. She sucked in her breath sharply as the healer put a second bee on her other leg. When the treatment was done, Miz Elda laboriously pushed her skirt down again. "The chile was just asking who'll be invited to my funeral."

Gervase Odara looked at me with dismay and I blushed.

"I reckon I'd want everyone invited who'd like to come," Miz Elda said, leaning forward and patting my hand. "I'd like a wake just like yer granny had. Plenty of good food for the women and whiskey for the men."

"And the sin eater? Will ye want him to come, Miz Kendric?"

"Oh, indeed. I'll have sore need of him."

"And how'll we find him for ye?"

"Ye won't need to find him. The passing bell echoes in these mountains," Gervase Odara said. "He'll most likely hear it."

"Is that where he is? High on the mountaintop?"

Gervase Odara frowned as Miz Elda answered. "Reckon so." She rubbed her aching legs. "No one really knows where he lives, except maybe—" The healer cleared her throat. "Hmmm," Miz Elda said, meeting her glance. She looked at me again. "Could be he's living in a house he built or a cave he found, but he ain't so far removed from us that he won't know when he's needed. Don't ye worry yourself about it."

I knew to leave off asking where to find him and tried another track. "How did he come to be the sin eater?"

"Why, he was chosen, of course."

"Chosen? How?"

The healer turned while mixing another mug of medicine for Miz Elda. "It isna good for a chile to be so fixed in her mind about the sin eater." She came to us and handed the mug to the old woman.

"I was just wondering what to do if Miz Elda died and—"

Elda Kendric snorted. "Just because yer granny has gone on her way don't mean every soul past seventy is going to chase right on after her." She drank the remedy, shuddered, and held out the empty mug to Gervase Odara. "Thank ye kindly, Gervase." She moved easier, shifting in her chair. "I'm feeling a wee bit sleepy."

"Soon as we get some vittles into ye, we'll put ye to bed. I'll come round tomorrow and see how ye be." The healer had brought bread, berry preserves, and a jar of thick soup, which she was warming over the fire she'd stoked.

"Let's just visit awhile. I'll eat after ye go."

"Ye'll eat now, Elda."

The old woman looked at me, eyes twinkling. "She doesna trust me."

Gervase Odara cracked an egg and stirred it into the soup she was heating over the fire. Pouring it into a bowl, she brought it back and put it on the table.

Elda Kendric took the proffered spoon in her gnarled, misshapen fingers. "Nothing tastes good anymore." But the bread and berry preserves were to her liking, especially when washed down by tea brewed from the green bark of a wild cherry tree. The healer sat by her, making sure she ate every bite and drank every drop. They talked about others in the cove. Mercy Tattersall was in a family way again, seven babies in eight years, and the woman is done in from the last. Tate MacNamara shot the painter that had been killing his sheep. Pen Densham's son Pete fell from the hayloft and broke his leg in two places.

Not once did they mention the sin eater.

"Thar now, dearie, ye sleep well," Gervase Odara said, having seen the old woman to her bed and covered over with a quilt. "I'll come by tomorrow."

"Cadi," the old lady said sleepily. "Ye come by anytime, dearie. We'll talk about yer granny. I miss the old soul."

"Thank ye, ma'am. I hope ye'll be feeling better."

She took my hand and held it strong as Gervase Odara turned away to tidy up the cooking things. "We can talk about other things, too."

It fixed in my mind that she was talking about the sin eater, and it was all I could do not to press her right then and there with questions. But she was already dozing off, the healer's remedies sitting well with her and easing her poor body of its pain.

Lightning split the gray sky with white as we were on the way home. "We'll keep to the trees," Gervase Odara said as the deep rumble rolled. She was afeared, and rightfully so, with the sky brightened again. I heard of a man once who was running for home and got struck dead in the meadow just below his house. Granny said she reckoned he had done something real bad to rile up God like that.

Another jagged shaft of light struck in the distance, and I thought sure it was coming for me. A wind came up as the thunder rolled again. Closer and closer it came. Granny had told me God's voice was like the thunder, and he lived in the dark clouds. She had learned all this when she was very young in Wales and had attended services every Sunday with her mother and father. "He is fire and wind," she'd said.

"Is God speaking to us, ma'am?"

"Shouting more like it," Gervase Odara said as the thunder rolled again, so heavy and loud now the hair stood up on my head. "Stay to the trees, Cadi, and move along. The skies'll open afore we can make shelter the way ye're dawdling."

As the lightning flashed, I thought I saw someone standing in the trees above us. The light blazed hot, and there he was in his tattered clothes and hood.

"Sin eater!" I cried out and then the light dimmed and so did he.

"Hush now!" Gervase Odara snapped, having glanced sharply up the hill. "Thar's nothing there." She caught hold of my hand and pulled me back and along with her through the woods. When I looked back over my shoulder, he was gone.

Mama sent me for firewood as soon as we arrived home. Lilybet was waiting beside the pile of oak Papa had chopped.

"The healer says you're not all ye seem to be," I told her. "And she told me I shudna open my heart to ye."

She smiled sadly. "Do ye think I mean ye harm, Katrina Anice?"

"No."

Her eyes softened and she came closer. "You must trust your heart in this. Heed what it tells you."

My heart ached within me, ached for something I could not define. Looking into her eyes, I believed she knew what it was I longed to have, and if I but trusted her, she would show me the path to finding it. I thought the sin eater was the key. I wanted to tarry longer and tell her about my visit with Elda Kendric.

"Go back for now, Katrina Anice," she said. "We've time to talk tomorrow when you're out and about in the sunshine and the meadow."

I stacked one last piece of firewood on my arm. Glancing up again, I saw she was already gone. Straining under the burden I carried, I returned to the house.

Gervase Odara was leaving as I came in, the rain having already stopped. She tipped my chin and told me to remember what she'd told me.

Mama was making preparations for supper when I dumped my heavy load into the woodbin. "Put another log on the fire, Cadi," she said dully. She didn't say another word to me for the rest of the afternoon.

Papa and Iwan washed up outside and came in near dusk for supper. Plowing, tilling, and cultivating the fields had been done in Aries. Now that the fruitful sign of Taurus was upon us, planting had begun. Papa always said crops planted in Taurus and Cancer would stand drought.

"What've ye been doing all day, little sister?" Iwan said to me, ladling out another helping of Mama's stew.

"I went to Elda Kendric's with the healer."

"And how's the old soul?"

"She's in terrible pain, but doesn't reckon she'll be dying soon."

Iwan grimaced and said nothing more. I saw by his expression that I had said too much already. Mama ate slowly without speaking to anyone. Papa looked at her several times, like he was waiting for something from her. After a while his face hardened, and he didn't look at her again. He finished eating in silence, pushed his plate away, and stood. "I got work in the barn." He went out the door.

Iwan went outside and sat on the porch while I cleared and washed the dishes. Mama left me to it, sitting at her spinning wheel again, retreating into her solitude. When I finished, I went outside to be near my brother. He was the only one who had not been undone by our tragedy. I sat on the edge of the porch and rested my head in my arms on the railing. We didn't say anything. He was tired and I was sad, and both of us were looking toward the barn where the lantern light shone through the open door.

FOUR

AS SOON AS THE SUN CAME UP, I SET ABOUT MY CHORES, in a hurry to be finished and free to return to Elda Kendric. She was working in her garden when I arrived out of breath and with another bouquet of mountain daisies. She didn't pause from her labors, but I could tell all was not right with her.

"You paining again, ma'am. I could fix you another remedy."

"And likely poison me. What do ye know about remedies?"

"I was watchful of Gervase Odara. Honey, vinegar, and whiskey."

She gave a snort of disgust. "Gave me a headache."

"And bees." I dreaded the thought of catching them and trying to hold them properly while they bestowed their healing stings upon the old woman, but I would do it if it would give her ease. And gain her goodwill.

She kept hacking at the soil with her ancient hoe. "Work . . . will . . . ease . . . the . . . pain . . ."

"Why dunna ye let me do the hoeing, and ye con walk around in the sunshine?"

She paused a moment, thinking. Handing me the hoe, she set off. She kept such a distance between us that I couldn't ask her anything about the sin eater. I worked alone until Lilybet came to keep me company.

"Do ye think she knows anything about the sin eater, Lily-bet? It's said she tells stories that ain't always true."

Lilybet nodded, sitting on a patch of green and watching me work. "Oh, yes, she knows. She's the oldest lady in the cove. She's lived a long time. If anyone knows anything about the sin eater, it will be Miz Elda."

"She'll have seen him at other gatherings, I reckon. But how do I ask her?"

"Straight out."

Turning, I called out, "Miz Elda, what do you know about the sin eater?"

She stopped from her meanderings and turned to stare at me. "What do ye want to know about *him* fer?"

"Tell her the truth," Lilybet said. "It's more likely she'll help you if you do."

The way Miz Elda was staring at me, I was fair to certain that Lilybet was right. The old woman knew very well why I wanted to know about the strange man and his doings. "I need his help, Miz Elda." And, mortified, I started to cry. I didn't know the tears were even coming until they were upon me. Head hanging, I clung to the hoe and turned away, ashamed.

Miz Elda limped to me and put her gnarled hand on my shoulder. "Aw, chile. I could feel yer hurt yesterday when ye wuz here with the healer. It fair pours out of yer eyes. Anyone with a lick of sense would know yer sorry for what happened."

"Being sorry don't help much."

"Time heals wounds."

I shook my head. "Not this kind," I would have said if I could have gotten the words past the lump in my throat. Some sins can't be covered up or talked away. I longed to have the evil I had done *removed*. And it seemed the sin eater was the only one who could do it. "I have to find him, Miz Elda. I have to find him *now!*"

48

"He canna do a thing for ye, chile. Dunna ye see? Let it go. What's done is done. Ye gotta live yer life through with what happened. Ye just weren't thinking. That's all. Things happen when people ain't thinking. Do good to others from here forward, and ye'll only have the one black mark at the end."

"I've need of the sin eater, Miz Elda."

"Ye've a long time yet before ye've need for the sin eater. He ain't coming for ye 'til ye've breathed yer last."

"I wish I was dead, and then it'd be over." I dropped the hoe, ready to run.

Miz Elda caught hold of me and turned me back again, gripping my shoulders in her clawlike hands and shaking me slightly. "Dunna ye be too quick with yer wanting to die. God might hear ye and take ye at yer word. Ye hear me? He's done it before. Donal Kendric used to moan about his troubles and say he might as well be dead, and God took him at his word. Ye hear me? Ye tell God ye're sorry for such foolish talk. Tell him!"

"I won't."

"Ye tell him!" She shook me again.

"*I won't!*" Pulling free, I lashed out in despair, railing at the poor old soul though none of it was her doing. "Why must I wait? Why must it ever be that way? Why can't the sin eater take my sins away *now?*"

"Because it ain't the way things've been done, dearie."

"Well, who made things that way?"

"Laochailand Kai," she said wearily. "He said he had need of one as he lay dying, and God knows he was right about it. Well, we all made sure he had one." Expression closing, she headed back for her porch.

I followed close behind, wondering if I understood her rightly. "Thar were none before then?"

"Aye, thar were, back across the sea where we all come from, in Scotland and Wales and England. The sin eater then was usually a poor peasant who lived well away from everyone else. I remember the sin eater who come to our house when my mother died. He stank with the sins he'd taken on himself and wore rags like a beggar. My mother was a good woman given to kindness to any who came for help, and that sin eater drank *three* full glasses of wine and demanded more bread as though she'd been the meanest sinner in the district."

"Maybe he was jest hungry."

She stopped and looked at me, frowning slightly. "Well, now, I never thought of that."

"Please, Miz Elda. Can't ye tell me where our sin eater lives so I could talk to him?"

She shook her head. "It won't do ye no good to know where he is, chile, if'n he doesna want to be found." She walked laboriously up the steps, clinging to the railing. "Fetch me my pipe and rabbit tobacco. It's on the table inside." Groaning, she sank into her willow rocker and rested her head against the back.

Blinking back tears, I did as the old woman asked. I had sins enough upon my head without plaguing the poor old dear to death. She looked ready to die right then, and if she did, it would be another sin upon my head for riling her up so. Thinking of Granny, I tapped down Miz Elda's rabbit tobacco and lit the pipe myself. When I put it in her gnarled hand, she thanked me and commenced to draw the smoke deep, sighing as she released it. "The weeding ain't done yet."

"I'll finish up afore leavin'."

"Finish now and give a poor woman rest."

With a heavy sigh, I relented. "Yes, ma'am." I went back to my labors in her garden.

Lilybet was waiting. "Don't be discouraged, Katrina Anice. Keep looking. You'll find him."

The sun rose high and hot as I worked. Soon the sweat was beading on my face and dripping down the back of my neck. I kept on, determined to finish what I'd started. Going down on my hands and knees, I pulled the weeds that threatened to choke out Miz Elda's crop of carrots, okra, and corn.

"That'll do!" Miz Elda called. "Come and sit awhile." She seemed quite mellow now, drowsy from smoking her rabbit tobacco and comfortable with her face in the porch shade and her body in the sunlight. She rocked slowly. "The sin eater lives up on Dead Man's Mountain."

It made perfect sense. It was the one place Granny had never sent me. But Iwan had gone there and never seen him and I said so.

"Maybe he just never said."

"He would have told me."

"Did he go to the top?"

"He said so."

"Well, do ye see every deer in the forest?"

"No, ma'am."

"The sin eater's like that. He keeps himself hidden away until he hears the passing bell." She rocked and smoked and added with a sly look at me, "Or gits the call."

She was hinting at something, and I was about to ask her what when Fagan Kai came unexpectedly from the woods and helloed the house. He had two dead squirrels tied together by the feet and slung over his shoulder, and he was sporting a black eye.

"Come on up," Miz Elda said quick enough. "Have a fight, did ye?"

"No, ma'am," he said solemnly, his mouth tightening.

"Kais are always fighting," she said in an aside to me.

With scarcely a glance in my direction, Fagan addressed the old woman sitting on the porch and smoking her pipe like she was royalty. "Thought ye might like some fresh meat, Miz Elda," he said as his dog flopped down in the shade near the steps.

"Might if'n they was dressed and skinned," she said, the pipe between her teeth.

Red-faced, Fagan turned away and took the dead squirrels off into the woods, his dog trailing after him. She cackled softly and puffed away contentedly while I tried to get the conversation back to where it had been before his untimely intrusion. She would have none of it, and to add to my frustration, Fagan soon returned.

"Here they be, ma'am," he said.

Miz Elda eyed the dressed squirrels disdainfully. "Too small for roasting," she pronounced, bringing high color into Fagan's cheeks again. "And I prefer possum." His smile flattened out. "Or bear meat." There was a definite twinkle in her blue eyes. "Don't reckon ye've shot a bear yet, have ye, boy?"

"No, ma'am. Not yet. Haven't seen one yet this spring." His response implied he had the courage but lacked the opportunity.

Miz Elda cackled loudly this time. "Well, when ye do see one, I hope ye're armed with more than yer slingshot, or the bear'll be having ye for supper." She pushed herself up from her chair and took the dressed squirrels inside.

Fagan turned and looked at me square on. "How ye be, Cadi Forbes?"

"Fair enough."

"What ye lookin' at me like that fer?"

"I was here first."

"There's room enough for two, ain't there?" He came up the steps as though he owned them.

Lilybet was looking at me and I lowered my eyes, ashamed of my ill temper. "I was talking with her, that's all."

"So go on and talk. I ain't stopping you." He leaned back against the rail and crossed his arms over his chest. "I know why you're here. You still looking for the sin eater, ain't ye? Ye're asking Miz Elda about him."

"Maybe I am and maybe I ain't."

"Your face is red as a boiled crawfish. You're asking her all right."

"So what?"

"So you ought to leave well enough alone is all! You shudna be looking for the sin eater!"

"I con look for anyone I please."

His face darkened. "You say? You owe me and you'd better listen. I asked my father about the sin eater like you wanted, and he knocked me off the porch." He pointed to his blackened eye so I'd know it was my fault. "My pa said if I ever mentioned him again, he'd take the skin off my back."

Pulling my knees up, I put my head down. After a moment, I looked up at him through a blur of tears. "I'm sorry." It seemed no matter which way I turned or what I said, I did wrong.

"Pa said just mentioning the mon brings evil into a house."

Remembering the sin eater's eyes, soulful and sad, gazing at me from behind the leather mask, I shook my head.

Fagan frowned. "Why won't you believe what you're told, Cadi Forbes?"

"Because it don't seem right!"

"What don't?"

"That the mon who takes away sins should be so hated."

"Ye dunna ken what you're saying. He takes sin *into* himself. He *eats* it, doesn't he? So it becomes a part of him, don't it? And he's been at it so long, thar ain't nothing left of whatever he was before."

"Then why did he sound the way he did?" I said, the tears coming again. "And his eyes—"

"Ye looked at him, did ye?" Miz Elda said from the doorway, and Fagan straightened guiltily. "Did ye, chile?"

I hung my head. "Yes, ma'am."

"Were ye told not to?"

"Yes, ma'am."

"Then what made ye do it?"

My mouth trembled. "It was the way he spoke of Granny. As though he had pity on her and loved her."

"Aye," Miz Elda said. "He had good cause."

"What cause?" Fagan said.

She came out onto the porch. Leaning on her cane, she stared off toward the valley so long I didn't think she'd answer. She must have been considering what to do, for she said finally, "I don't see the harm in telling ye." Turning, she looked at me square. "For a long time after your Grandpa Ian died, yer granny'd go visit his grave. And every time she did, she'd take summat with her. Half dozen ears of corn, a bundle of carrots, a small sack of potatoes, some eggs. She went right on through the worst of winter taking with her some smoked pork or dried venison, a string of leather-britches beans, a jar of preserves. She'd leave those things on Ian Forbes's grave for the sin eater."

Turning slightly, she looked at Fagan Kai. "Most people give the sin eater a glass of wine and a loaf of bread, then give not a thought about him or what he took on himself for the sake of their loved ones. They don't give a thought to what he'll do for them someday neither." She looked back at me. "Yer granny was different, Cadi. She looked out for the sin eater. She let him know she hadna forgotten what he done."

Lowering her aching bones into the rocker, she placed her cane over her lap. "Now, Cadi here has a reason for wanting to find the mon and dunna ye go talking her out of it, Fagan Kai."

"But my pa said—"

"Maybe your pa has a reason for wanting to stay clear of the mon."

"What reason?" Fagan said.

"Who's to know excepting maybe the sin eater himself?"

"Are you telling us to go looking for him?" Fagan challenged.

"I ain't tellin' ye to do nothing that ye haven't set your mind to already."

"He's been telling me not to look for him," I told her.

"Because he's figuring on finding him hisself, ain't ye, Fagan Kai?"

"I never said so."

"Dinna have to. It's in yer nature. Anyone tells ye not to do summat, ye're bound and determined to do it. Ain't that right? Especially when ye've taken blows over it."

Fagan's mouth tightened.

Miz Elda leaned back and closed her eyes. "Dinna yer pa tell ye to stay away from *me*, boy?"

He turned his head away, but I'd seen the look in his eye that confirmed everything the old woman said.

"Yer pa still holds a grudge again' me for summat done years ago. He's got the longest, meanest memory of anyone in the cove. Ever tell ye why he dunna want ye or any of yer kin to have nothing to do with Elda Kendric, hmmm?"

"No, ma'am."

"No? Well, then I ain't goin' to tell ye neither. Maybe someday it'll all come out by itself. Likely kill him if it does. Or someone else if'n he has anything to say about it."

Fagan glared at her. "Don't talk about my pa that way."

"I can talk about Brogan Kai any way I want, boy. You're on my porch. Ye dunna like the track of my conversing, ye con leave."

He looked hurt and undecided. Loyalty won out. With a troubled frown, he went down the steps and headed for the woods.

"Thank ye for the squirrels, Fagan," Miz Elda called. "Ye've yer mother's good heart and yer father's aim."

Watching him stride away, I felt sorry for him. Glancing up

at Miz Elda, I saw tears in her eyes. "Ye like him, don't ye, Miz Elda?"

"Aye, I like him more than all the rest. Problem is he don't know who he is yet."

"Who is he?" I said, having no ken to her meaning.

"Time'll tell, dearie." She stood, leaning on her cane and watching Fagan disappear into the woods. "Time'll tell." She turned to me. "Ye've got hours of daylight yet," she said in an odd tone. "And thar's a heap of climbing to reach the top of Dead Man's Mountain. If ye're of a mind to go, ye'd better start now."

I got up quickly, feeling free and eager to be on my way. "Yes, ma'am." I was off her porch and down those steps faster than a cat chased by a pack of dogs.

"Cadi Forbes," she said firmly, halting me in my tracks. "It's the only reason ye came, ain't it?" She stood there staring down at me, old and proud, her chin slightly tipped, her mouth disdainful, her hand white knuckled on her cane. "Ye come here just to find out about the sin eater. That was it, weren't it? No other reason than that."

I thought of lying and knew it was no use. She would know just like Granny always knew things about people. And of a sudden, I found myself wishing Miz Elda was blood kin and closer bound. I'd done a terrible cruel thing coming to her for my own uses and not thinking of her needs. She had been my granny's dearest friend in the world, and I had had no thought to her grief. Now, looking up at her, she reminded me of Granny. She was getting so crippled up that she wouldn't be able to do much of anything soon. Except die. My heart clenched tight at the thought.

Company. That's all she craved. Someone who cared about her feelings. A friend who came to see her for her sake and not to dispense cures for a fee or find out about the sin eater. For all her pride and prickliness, she was lonely, though I was fair sure she'd rather die than say so.

Well, I knew all about loneliness and being separated from those ye love.

Meeting Miz Elda's eyes, I saw myself and was ashamed—ashamed into my very soul. "Yes, ma'am," I said truthfully, tears burning. "That were my reason."

"Go on then," she said with a jerk of her chin. "Go on about yer business."

"Go on now," Lilybet said softly from the base of the steps. "Go on and do what's in your heart to do, Katrina Anice. And do it quickly, for it needs doing."

I raced back up the steps before I lost my nerve and slipped my arms around Miz Elda's waist. "It won't be my reason next time."

She gave a soft gasp of surprise, and then I felt her hand brush my hair lightly.

That slight touch made something open inside me, something that hadn't opened in a long, long time. She was all angles and soft flesh and she smelled not unpleasantly of rabbit tobacco and whiskey. Remembering her aching bones, I eased my tight hug and backed off a little.

She tipped my chin. "Tell me what ye find," she said and then set me back from her. "Go on with ye, chile." Her words were filled with tenderness this time, and her faded blue eyes were filled with moisture.

I hadn't gone more than a hundred feet into the woods when Fagan Kai caught hold of my arm and swung me around. "Hold on thar!" he said when I came at him tooth and nail. "Hold on!"

He grunted in pain when I kicked him in the shin. Letting go of me, he hopped one way while I collapsed on the ground with a yelp, holding my smarting toes tightly between two hands. "See what ye done!" I railed at him.

"You kicked *me*. Don't blame me if ye broke your foot."

"Sure, I kicked ye! What'd ye expect grabbing me like that, scaring me to death?"

"I had to run after ye once before. Remember? I didn't like the prospect of doing it again!" Hunkering down, he watched me massage my toes. "Ye break any?" He was smiling, taunting.

I flexed them cautiously. Wincing, I glared at him. "No." The stinging pain was easing off and I stood up. I walked around and around until my foot stopped paining and I knew nothing was seriously wrong.

"Good as new," he said, grinning now.

"Yep." Turning sharply, I punched him as hard as I could in the stomach. He let out a great *oooff* and doubled over. Grabbing his hair with both hands, I pulled with all my might. How the mighty fall! Triumphant, I leaped over him and ran for my life, screaming back at him, "Don't ever do that again!"

I was ever doing things I later regretted, relishing the moment without thinking of the outcome. And I regretted that, for I didn't figure on him following me so fast.

Seeing as he was Brogan Kai's son, I guessed my life was over. I was a rabbit, and a wolf with bared fangs was chasing me. I looked for a hole to hide in, but Fagan was coming too quick for me to see much of anything but a blur of green slapping my face when a branch caught me hard above my right eye. Fagan ducked. I felt him getting a hold on the back of my dress. The seam tore in my struggling, and I managed another blow or two before he let me loose.

Trying to beat him across the meadow was a mistake. He took me down less than halfway across and knocked the wind clean out of me. I lay on my back like a banked fish, gasping for air, while he, on hands and knees beside me, did the same.

"You crazy or what?" He was red-faced, though whether

from temper or running I weren't sure. As soon as I got my breath back, I figured on tearing out of there before I found out.

I dragged in badly needed air and let out a sob, scrambling back from him.

All the heat went out of his eyes. "I didn't mean to scare ye, Cadi. Cross my heart and hope to die." He made the sign of the cross over his chest and held his hand up in a solemn oath. "I just wanted to talk to you is all."

I figured he was telling the truth, for his wind was back and he wasn't strangling me or pounding me into the ground.

Sitting back, he plucked a blade of grass and chewed on it. "Ye ought not to run like that. Ye could step on a copperhead and be bit without even knowing it. It's a slow, mean way to go."

His uncle had died of snakebite before I was born. Granny had told me the story. The uncle, Brogan's brother, had been bit while hunting. He'd cut and bled himself right after it happened and made it back to the house. Gervase Odara applied plasters, but it hadn't done any good—the poison had gone into his blood. Once that happened, there weren't nothing to do but wait for the end.

I sat up slowly, keeping my feet under me so I could run if I had to. I didn't say anything but kept my eyes fixed upon him to judge his mood. I figured Fagan would say what he wanted as soon as he was ready. But it better be quick or I'd lose my nerve and run for it.

He tossed the blade of grass away and looked at me with his solemn blue eyes. "Ye hadn't oughta go looking for the sin eater, Cadi. I ain't never seen my father afraid of nothing. But he's afraid of *him*."

I stared at Fagan, surprised. Everyone in the valley knew that Brogan Kai was afraid of nothing. Why would he fear the sin eater? "Maybe your father was just angry at ye for speaking of the mon."

"Sure enow, he was mad, but he was scared, too. I'm telling ye, I saw it in his eyes. For just a second, he went so white I could feel my hair stand up. The sin eater must be the devil himself, Cadi."

"He wudna hurt me."

"Maybe he's hurt you already and ye dunna know it."

"How so?"

He frowned, scratching his head in frustration. "Well, your mind is fixed on him, ain't it? Ye looked at him once, and ye ain't been able to get him out of your head since. That ought to tell you summat. He's laid a curse on ye just like ye were told he'd do if ye looked."

His words seemed sound and troubled me greatly, but they didn't break my resolve. If anything, they made it all the more important to find the man. If Fagan was right, then what else could I do but find the sin eater and try to undo what had already been done? If the sin eater had cursed me, who else but the sin eater could undo it? I did not try to explain this to Fagan, thinking he'd see it for himself once he thought it over. Besides, it didn't matter. I was cursed already, my sins heavy upon me.

I didn't say that to Fagan, either. He would want to know the full reasons behind my thinking, and what I had done was too shameful a thing to talk about. The people only knew the half of it—what had happened, not what had brought it on. Even Mama and Papa and Iwan didn't know. But God did. God knew. I didn't want Fagan Kai to think the worst of me. Better he come to his own conclusions. Wrong as they might be, they would be a whole sight better than the whole truth.

Besides, Fagan was adding to my burdens in other ways. His father had knocked him off his porch on my account, and that smote my conscience something fierce. I wondered what trouble I had brought on Glynnis and Cullen.

Then I decided it didn't do any good wondering and worrying. If I was going to change anything, I had to climb Dead Man's Mountain and find the sin eater. I didn't have time to sit around thinking on it. Sitting and thinking too long might eat away my nerve. I had to do it while my courage was still with me. I stood up and brushed myself off. "I'm sorry your pa hit ye on my account."

"You're still goin', ain't ye? Ye won't listen to reason."

Ignoring him, I kept walking. Jumping up, he caught up. "I'm going with ye."

"I dinna ask ye to."

"Where'd Miz Elda say he was?"

"Dead Man's Mountain," I said. He turned pale but kept on. Grabbing his shirtsleeve, I pulled him to a stop. "Your pa knocked ye off the porch just for asking about the sin eater. What do ye think he'll do if he finds out you're helping me look for him?"

"He won't find out."

"Your pa knows everything that goes on, Fagan."

He knew that was true enough and thought heavy on it as we walked together. "He wouldn't do nothing to you, Cadi. I'd make sure of that."

What could he, a boy of fourteen do? But that wasn't the worst of it. "He'd do summat to *you.*"

Fagan stopped and looked at me. "I've got my own reasons for wanting to find the sin eater, Cadi. It's got nothing to do with you anymore."

He set off again in the direction of Dead Man's Mountain.

F I V E

For the next week, Fagan and I spent our afternoons on Dead Man's Mountain. We found no signs of the sin
eater. Worse than that, we had barely covered any territory by
the time the sun was sinking toward the ridge of the western
mountains and we had to come back down again. It would take
a lifetime to explore the meadows, forest, thickets, and rocky
crags, and we still might never find him.

"We won't give up," Fagan said at my despairing countenance. "We'll keep on."

"What good's it gonna do? He doesna want to be found." I
sat down and fought back the tears as I stared up at the great
mist-shrouded peak. "There must be a thousand places for him
to hide up there."

"I guess we'll have to figure out a way to flush him out."

"Using your old hound?" I looked doubtfully at the rangy
beast with his muzzle fur gone white. He flopped down, lay
back, and went to sleep in the grass.

"No," Fagan said flatly. "He's too old." He sat down and
rested his forearms on his raised knees. His face was set in con-
centration. "A snare, maybe."

"The sin eater ain't as dumb as a rabbit."

"Do tell," he said, in no better humor than I after all our

hunting and nothing to show for it. "He's probably watching us from somewhere up there and keeping a distance between us. Only time he comes down off his mountain is to eat sin."

"What about the vittles in the graveyard?" Lilybet said from where she sat in the midst of some ferns a few feet away.

My head came up. "What'd ye say about vittles?"

Fagan glanced at me. "I dinna say nothing."

"Not *you.*"

Lilybet got up and walked over to me. "The sin eater came down off his mountain for the food Granny left for him."

"He did, didn't he?"

Face pale, Fagan was looking at me funny.

Jumping up, I laughed. "Remember what Miz Elda said about Granny leaving gifts for the sin eater? We can do that. We can put gifts on Granny's grave, and he'll come."

Looking around, Fagan gave me a curious stare. "Put out bait, you mean."

"Like the rabbit you trapped for Miz Elda."

His eyes flickered as he grasped the thought and made it his own. "He con trap rabbits for himself. And he can find his own garden sass. It has to be summat that'll tempt him down off his mountain. Can ye steal some preserves?"

"No. Mama keeps count of the jars she puts up. I'd be found out."

"Molasses, then, or cornmeal. They won't miss a cup or two."

"What con ye offer him?"

"Only thing we have plenty of is whiskey, and Pa's the same with it as your mama with the preserves. He sells it to settlers over the mountains."

"How'll the sin eater know we're doing it? It's been weeks since Granny died."

"Miz Elda said no one ever thought of him before your

granny did, and he found the gifts she left for him. I reckon he'll come around and find out about ours, too."

I looked up at the mountain and wondered about him all the more. Did he creep down in the dead of night and peer in windows and walk through graveyards? Did he sleep all day while the sun was up and rise in darkness, walking by moonlight?

Three sharp whistles sounded in the distance. Fagan jumped to his feet, stuck two fingers in his mouth, and made an earsplitting whistle back. "I've gotta go. It's Cleet's signal." Cleet was his older brother. "You'd best get home, too. Sun's going down." He ran off, leaving me at the foot of the mountain with only Lilybet for company.

I heard a crack. It was the same sort that echoed when my father was chopping wood. Startled by it, for no one was supposed to live near Dead Man's Mountain, I stayed longer, craning my neck and tipping my head to hear it again. *Crack!* The sound echoed once more. Thinking my luck had changed and it might be the sin eater, I ran toward the west, forgetful of the dipping sun.

"Time enow tomorrow, Katrina Anice," Lilybet said, keeping pace with me. "Ye'd best go on home, now. It's getting late in the day."

Closing my ears to her, I kept on.

The burbling stream drowned out the sound, and I moved away from it, pausing to listen again. One last crack sounded, and then there was silence. Through a veiling of laurel, I saw a small cabin set back against the base of Dead Man's Mountain, a thin spire of smoke rising from the chimney. A slender woman with a long, blonde braid was carrying an armload of firewood up the steps. She disappeared inside the house, leaving the door open.

I wanted to stay longer, but the sound of crickets was growing louder as the sun was slipping behind the western mountains. I had to go.

As I made my way through the heart of the valley, I was made uneasy by the mists rolling in. They was seeping through the trees and approaching fast. If not for the moon, I'd have lost my way.

Just then, a sound like a woman's scream split the night, making the hair stand up on my neck. I knew what made that sound. A painter, it was, and close enough to have my scent. Thinking to keep the stream between me and the beast, I splashed across, slipping twice and soaking myself from the waist down. I didn't care how wet I got as long as I put distance and obstacles between me and that great prowling cat of the night.

When the crickets stopped chirping, I knew it had leapt across and was stalking me. Whether it was behind or before me, I didn't know. Too afraid I might run the wrong way, I stood frozen, staring into the growing darkness.

No insect rasped.

No owl hooted.

My heart picked up speed, pounding harder and faster with each breath. I heard a twig snap behind me and my breath expelled. I burst forward, running as fast as my legs would carry me. All I could hear was the pounding of my own heart and the sobbing breath escaping my lungs.

Why hadn't I listened to Lilybet? Why hadn't I started for home before the sun dropped past the horizon? A thousand thoughts raced through my head as my feet pounded the grassy earth. Not even the rosy glow remained, and the sky grew darker with each minute that passed.

Lungs burning, I stumbled. Catching myself up before I fell, I lunged on. Something was coming fast, bounding behind me, catching up. I could hear it gaining ground. The thump and rustle of leaves warned me of its swift advance. Turning, I saw a dark shadow streaking toward me. I had never seen an animal move as fast as that big cat did. My thoughts froze; I couldn't move. Its sleek body bunched and then stretched out long as it leaped.

And then it let out a fearsome scream, for something struck it. I heard the thud and saw the beast spasm in midair and fall clumsily. The beast rose again, nervous and snarling viciously. Crouching, it crept closer to me—ears flattened, fangs bared in a deep roar. There was another thud, and the beast gave a sharp cry of pain, swinging to the side to face its hidden attacker. It let out a scream of rage as it was struck a third time, then bounded off into the forest again.

Panting, heart racing, I didn't move.

"Go on home now, Cadi Forbes," came a low voice from the dark shadows of the forest.

I knew that voice. I had heard it once before in the graveyard the night Granny was buried.

All reason fled. With a cry, I ran. I raced as fast as my legs could carry me across the meadows. My breath came out with each step, my heart pounding in my ears. Clambering up the hill, I bumped and scraped myself. Bounding up the steps of the cabin, I burst in the door, slammed it, and threw my body back against it.

Papa was standing near the fire with Mama, the rifle tucked under his arm, barrel down. They both glanced around sharply at my entrance. Mama took one long look at me up and down, shut her eyes, and turned away. Head down, her shoulders shook. Papa slammed the rifle back into its mount and came toward me. His relief was short-lived. "You're all wet."

"I slipped in the creek, Papa." It was a lie, but if I told him I was on the other side of the river, he'd use the belt on me. I was still shaking from what had happened and scared enough to lose water. I didn't need more torment.

He was not fooled. His mouth pulled down, his eyes narrowing in anger. "Adding lies to everything else, are ye, Cadi girl?"

A cold chill washed over me at the tone of his voice.

"Go wash up, Cadi," Mama said, her back still to me.

"And after ye do that, ye con go to the woodshed and wait for me thar."

Shoulders slumping and still trembling, I went back outside. I took a long, slow look around before I went down those stairs. I wondered if the sin eater was still out there in the darkness and mists watching me. There was wash water in the bucket. Staring off downhill toward the woods, I splashed some on my face and arms and then washed my hands. Shivering, I went to the woodshed and closed myself in. Sitting in the darkness, I waited for Papa.

He came with his belt. I could tell the anger had gone out of him. "I take no pleasure in this, Cadi."

"I know, Papa."

He disciplined me without another word. I didn't cry for his sake. "I'm sorry, Papa," I said when he was done.

"Being sorry ain't enow," he said grimly. "Ye ought to know that by now." He left me alone.

I cried. Oh how I cried and pondered my sins. Seemed every day they grew heavier and harder to bear. They seemed to master me for I could not understand myself at all. I wanted to do right, but nothing I did turned out that way. I always ended up doing the wrong I hated. And even as I was doing it, like looking for the sin eater in spite of all warnings against it, I knew perfectly well what I was doing and did it anyway. I couldn't help myself. It seemed sin was inside me making me do wrong. No matter which way I turned, I couldn't make myself do right.

And it was going to get worse because I wasn't going to stop looking for the sin eater. I was going to keep on until I found the one who could help me. And I was going to steal some of Mama's preserves to try to draw him down from his mountain hiding place.

"I want to stop doing wrong, Lilybet, but I can't," I said, tears running down my face. "Even when I want to do what's right, I do what's wrong." I knew how Mama would feel about me taking a jar of her preserves, but I was going to take them anyway. And leather-britches beans, and molasses, and corn-meal, and whatever else it took. More wrongs to try to make things right. I was more miserable now than when I'd started the quest after the man I thought could save me.

But he had saved me, hadn't he? From the painter, at least. Trouble was, could he save me from all the rest?

"Keep looking, Katrina Anice," Lilybet said. "Don't stop where you are. Keep on and you'll find who it is you're looking for."

"The sin eater was there, Lilybet," I whispered. "Right there. He must've been following me."

"Yes. The man helped you, Katrina Anice."

"He hit that devil beast three times without a miss. Hit him hard enow to change his mind about eating me. He must have a slingshot, like Fagan. That must be how he hunts."

"He's but a poor man."

"I was so scared, Lilybet. I've been looking for him days and days, and then, when he was right there, I *ran*." I cried harder. "I'm a fool, a pure, cussed fool!" My chance had presented it-self, and I had lacked the courage to grasp it.

Someone tapped on the door. "Come on back inside, Cadi," Iwan said.

"Papa said—"

"Papa sent me. Now come on out."

The dishes were cleared away. My stomach tightened at the aroma of the meal they'd shared without me. Iwan's hound was eating my portion. I felt no tinge of resentment. I'd rather lose a meal than have Papa still mad at me. I'd deserved the lashing he'd given me. Maybe if he'd beaten me more, I'd feel cleansed instead of miserable.

Papa glanced at me. "Go on to bed." He looked so tired and worn down.

"Yes, Papa." I'd been to bed without supper before, but Granny had always slipped me something. I knew there'd be nothing tonight, and I was resigned to waiting until morning to feed the wolf in my belly.

I slipped beneath the covers on Granny's cot and pulled the quilts high over my head, burrowing down and curling up. Hunger pangs gripped my stomach. I'd had porridge for breakfast and then been too busy hunting for the sin eater to think much about eating. Six afternoons I'd been up on Dead Man's Mountain with Fagan Kai and seen nothing of the sin eater. Six!

"Go on home now."

He was there all the time, close enough to be watching us!

Oh, why had I run away? Why hadn't I stood my ground and called out to him? He had been no more than twenty feet away, hiding in the night shadows, and I had run from him like he was death itself. I was ashamed for my cowardice. Had the man wanted harm to come to me, he would have let the painter make me his supper.

It was a warm night, and Iwan went out on the porch to sleep in the hammock. Mama went to bed after cleaning up the dishes and doing mending. Papa sat a long while, staring at nothing and then followed her. I heard them mumbling. He sounded gruff; she was softly plaintive.

"I canna help it," Mama said.

"Ye can and you know it. How long's it gonna go on?"

"I never want to go through it again."

"Do ye think I do?"

"I can't bear it."

"There's the truth of it. Ye want *me* to bear the load."

"I never said that."

"Ye dinna have to. Every time ye turn your back on me, you're saying it."

"Ye don't even try to understand."

"Then *make* me understand. Explain it to me."

"It shudna have been Elen!"

"Ye'd rather it'd been Cadi. Is that what you're saying?"

Mama started crying soft, broken sobs.

"Fia," Papa said, his tone changed. I could tell by it that she was tearing his heart out with her grief. "Fia, ye canna go on this way." His voice softened so that I only heard the gentle murmur as he tried to console Mama.

She would not be comforted.

It should have been me and not Elen. That was the thing of it. I knew it would have been right had it been me. For in truth, it was my doing, the tragedy that had befallen us. Leastwise, I could have prevented it. Miz Elda tried to excuse me because I was a child and I was thoughtless. Would that it were that simple. I hadn't intended harm to come to Elen. I had simply wished her away.

Long after Mama and Papa were sleeping, I lay awake thinking about my sin, troubled into my soul, held captive by the terrible guilt. I wanted to tell Elen I was sorry. I'd been so happy when she'd been born, but hated her when she took Mama's love away from me. It only got worse.

"Take care of Elen, Cadi," Mama would say. "Watch out for our little angel." And when Elen would cry, "Give her your doll, Cadi. It won't hurt to let her play with it awhile."

My throat was tight with sorrow. I sat up for a long while whispering to Lilybet. "Do ye think she con hear me, Lilybet? Papa said being sorry ain't enow, but I'd like her to know. She never done nothing terrible wrong, and I was mean. I dinna want her following me. And that morning—"

"Who ye be talking to, Cadi?" Papa asked from across the room.

Looking over, I saw the large, dark shape of him sitting up in bed. "Lilybet."

"Tell her to leave."

My breath came out softly and I hung my head. "She's gone, Papa."

"I don't want ye talking to her anymore. Do ye ken what I'm saying to ye?" He was angry.

Tears welled. "Yes, Papa."

"Never again. Do ye hear?"

"I hear, Papa." And I knew even as I said it, I didn't mean I wouldn't do it.

"Time ye stop acting like ye're crazy. Now, go to sleep."

Burrowing beneath the blankets once more, I closed my eyes.

"He doesn't understand, Cadi," Lilybet said softly. "Someday he and your mama will understand all of this. And so will you."

Clinging to that promise, I closed my eyes and went to sleep.

S I X

$\mathcal{P}$APA WAS UP BEFORE DAWN. HE WENT OUT TO MILK the cow, awakening Iwan when he came back in. Mama filled them with porridge before they left to work in the fields, leaving me to clean up the dishes while she went out to work in the garden. I finished quick as I could and stole a jar of berry preserves from the back of the shelf. Setting it on the table, I rearranged the others so it wouldn't be missed. I peered out the door to make sure no one was looking, then ducked out. I hurried down the steps, slipped around the side of the house, and darted up the hill into the forest. I hid the jar among some ferns where I could fetch it later.

After I fed the chickens, Mama set me to work pulling more weeds while she went down to tote water for washing. Papa had set up the big iron pot outside for her. She poured in bucket after bucket of clear creek water, then dipped each article of clothing until it was soaked. Rubbing soap onto the soiled spots, she scrubbed each garment up and down on her washboard. I toted water up the hill and poured it into the rinse barrel.

The sun was well up before the clothes were rinsed and the pot and barrel emptied a bucketful at a time around the seedlings coming up. Mama pulled up some potatoes, carrots, and onions and put them in her basket, which she held out to me.

"Wash 'em in the creek while I get salt pork." Soon as I took it, she headed off for the springhouse where Papa kept the meat.

Mama had the pot over the fire and the salt pork soaking by the time I got back from our creek. She was punching down the bread dough she'd made that morning before doing the wash. I set the basket on the table and stood watching her, wishing for a kind word. She glanced at me as though my presence discomforted her and dabbed beads of sweat from her brow with the back of her hand. Summer was just outside the door, heating up fast. Papa and Iwan were likely done with the fieldwork and fishing by now.

"Go on with ye," Mama said, still not looking at me.

I fetched the jar of stolen preserves and headed straight for the family cemetery. Filled with dread, I entered the gate. My fears soon departed in the quiet. Green grass had already sprouted on the mound of rich earth over Granny Forbes. A smooth, multicolored river stone the size of a large pumpkin had been placed at the head of her resting place. By Papa, I reckoned. Putting the jar of preserves on it, I sat, raised my knees, and buried my head in my arms. Most of the time, my grief was tolerable. Then, sometimes unexpected, it welled up until it fair choked me.

Lilybet came and sat next to me. "She wasn't afraid to die, Katrina Anice. She was tired."

"It was too hard living in a house filled with sorrow and silence. She wanted peace. Now she has it."

"Yes, she does," said Lilybet.

"Only I wish she hadn't gone."

"She couldn't help you."

"Remember that last day when she was so quiet? She was thinking back over her life, wasn't she? She missed seeing the spring beauties at Bearwallow for herself."

"She missed more than that, Katrina Anice."

Weary, I lay down beside the earthen mound and ran my hand over the sprouts of grass coming up from the earth blanket that covered Granny. I wondered what it would be like to sleep for eternity. Would she dream? Some nights I went to sleep so tired; then I woke up without a remembered thought for the hours that had passed. Was death like that? A dreamless sleep from which no one awakened until Judgment Day? Would time pass like a blink of an eye the way a dreamless night passed? Or was death a troubled sleep, filled with confusing dreams?

"What is it like, Lilybet?"

"I don't know anything of death, Katrina Anice. I only know life. Turn your heart toward that."

"Death is all around me. It's right here with me." Not just inside the gate of the cemetery, but all around us.

"So is life. You must choose."

Lilybet bewildered me. Sometimes she seemed a child much like me, and at other times older than even Miz Elda. There was something she was trying to show me, something important, something that would change everything, but I could not grasp it no matter how hard I tried. And I was tired, too tired from the night before to want to do much serious thinking on anything anyway. I thought perhaps she didn't understand my meaning about death, for it was a feeling deep inside me. Even down in Kai Valley meadowlands, with the sun shining upon me, I could feel the dark forces surrounding us all. The sin I had committed was terrible, but there was more—so much more beyond my understanding. Part of me wanted to find whatever it was I was looking for, and another loathed the mere thought of changing anything.

I likened it to the gathering of clouds and the heavy air pressing down before the skies opened up and the jagged shafts of light struck the mountains. Sometimes the air was so full of power, my hair would stand on end and my skin tingle. God was in it, but there were others, too. Taints and demons, Granny always said. And I stood betwixt—hell so close I could feel the blackened pull of it, and heaven so distant . . .

Somehow, someway, the sin eater held the answers to all of it. If only I could find him.

Leaving the berry preserves behind, I went out the gate and hid among the ferns where I could see the sin eater when he came, but he would not see me.

And there I waited.

And waited as the day grew warmer and warmer.

Yawning, I lay on my back, knees up and hands behind my head, and gazed through the canopy of green to the blue sky beyond. Birds flitted from branch to branch, chirping and twitching this way and that before swooping off. And the heat came down through the trees, weighting my eyelids. Curling on my side toward the cemetery, I bent one fern frond down so that I could see through to where I'd left the jar of preserves. If the sin eater came, I'd see him straightaway. All this from the comfort of my soft, forest bed.

I awakened a long while later when a stream of light touched my face. Disoriented and still drowsy, I wondered what I was doing sleeping on the ground. Then remembering, I clambered to my knees and leaned forward, parting the ferns cautiously. The jar of preserves was still where I had placed it. Dejected, I let the fronds snap back. It was a vain hope that the sin eater would come so soon. If he came at all.

I left my post and went to Miz Elda.

"Any luck?" she said from where she was sitting in the shade on her porch. I didn't have to ask her what she meant.

"No, ma'am. It's a mighty big mountain, and he don't want to be found."

"So ye've given up already. God made the world in six days, and ye can't even find one measly soul on a mountain in eight."

"I ain't giving up. I put preserves on Granny's grave just like she done."

"Stole 'em, did ye?"

I hung my head.

"If it ain't yers, it ain't much of an offering. Just like when ye brung me flowers from me own meadow."

The heat of shame came up in my face, burning plain for her to see. My eyes felt hot and my throat tight. "I don't have nothing to give," I said in my own defense.

"Ye just ain't thought on it much yet." Leaning back, she closed her eyes and rocked slowly.

My spirit was cast down within me. I walked the rows of her vegetable garden, plucking a weed here and there, and then wandered off again. Without even thinking on it, I ended up back at the river and followed it right up to the Narrows and the tree bridge where I'd been forbidden to venture.

I could not seem to help myself. For as long as I could remember, the place had drawn me. The trail out of our valley lay on the other side. To get to it, you crossed over the river in Kai Valley where it shallowed. The Narrows was a deadly place, but beautiful, too. The rush and tumble of the water swirling over the rocks and pouring down into the deep pool below the falls had always beguiled me. Iwan was the first to show me the Narrows and the falls, though Mama was terrible angry with him for doing so. It was dangerous, and it was also "the doorway to the outside world." Being good, Iwan never took me back again. He didn't have to, for I went on me own. I'd lay on my stomach and peer over the edge, my heart racing at the sound of the water's roar.

I had long wondered about the trail on the other side. The first time I'd ventured across the tree bridge had been the year Elen was born. I was six and Mama had no time for me. To my way of thinking, I'd been loaded down with her chores as well as my own while she cuddled and cooed over my baby sister. I had never been so scared as that day when I inched my way across the tree bridge. I imagined myself falling into that swirling torrent, tossed around and pulled down to smash against the rocks before plunging over the falls. I was shaking so bad I sat straddling the tree and worked my way across that way.

The second time, I was eight and showed more courage.

I crossed over the Narrows dozens of times after that, venturing down the trail to the pool below the falls. It was a magical place with ferns, azaleas, rhododendrons, and towering pine. The pool was deep and blue, the water cold and clear. Gathering in the rocky basin, it surged over more rocks, turning to the south and racing on. To the sea, Papa said. Our river, like all others, ran to the sea.

Papa and Iwan had followed that river last year. They were gone five days and came back with nothing to show for their journey.

The air was heavier still, the clouds darkening. Lightning flashed in the distance, followed by a roll of thunder. It would rain soon, as it often did on sultry afternoons. The rain never lasted, just fell long enough to drench the mountains and raise a mist come morning.

Standing above the falls, I saw someone below kneeling on the mossy bank and bending over the water for a drink. Drawing back, I hid myself among the low-hanging blooming serviceberry tree. I thought he was an Indian at first, for I'd heard they wore their hair long and dressed in buckskins. Then he leaned back and straightened up, and I saw he was tan like Papa and wore a beard. He wiped the moisture from it and cocked his head as he looked up in my direction, like he sensed I was there. I drew back quickly, but not so far I couldn't watch as he headed up the steep trail that would bring him into our valley.

Curiosity made me scamper across the tree bridge and dive

into the thick bushes on the other side. Who was he? And why was he coming? Other than Lilybet, I'd never known a stranger to enter our cove, and I wanted a closer look.

The stranger came up the steep incline. As he came up the trail, head high, I could see his lips were moving. When he reached the top, he paused and looked down at the falls and then up along the course of the river through the Narrows. I could hear him then, for he spoke loudly, his right hand stretched out above and before him.

"The voice of the Lord is upon the waters: the God of glory thundereth: the Lord is upon many waters. The voice of the Lord is powerful; the voice of the Lord is full of majesty. The voice of the Lord breaketh the cedars! Yea—" he turned away from me, his hands rising as he looked up. His voice rose again, and gooseflesh rose upon me—"The voice of the Lord shaketh the wilderness . . . the voice of the Lord maketh the hinds to calve, and discovereth the forests; and in his temple doth every one speak of his glory. . . ."

Shuddering, I shrank back further into the fronds and cascading branches, crouching there, holding still. My heart pounded. Could this be God come to our highland? And if not, was he someone sent by the Almighty himself?

Turning, the man started along the path toward our valley, his voice coming on stronger with each step. "The earth is the Lord's, and the fullness thereof; the world, and they that dwelleth therein." He moved away so that I could not hear. I crept through the brush above him, straining my ears, terrified to get too close lest his eyes turn upon me.

"Lift up your hearts, O ye gates; and be ye lifted up, ye everlasting door and the King of glory shall come in! Who is this King of glory? The Lord strong and mighty! The Lord mighty in battle! The Lord of hosts, he is the King of glory!"

The wild-haired man stopped and thrust his hands high.

Head back, his voice rose again. "Hear me when I call, O God! Lord Jesus, hear my prayer! Hearken unto the voice of my cry, my God and King; for unto thee and thee alone I pray. You are a God that hath no pleasure in wickedness, and there is wickedness in these mountains. Oh, yea, Lord, neither shall evil dwell with thee. The foolish shall not stand in thy sight. Thou hatest all workers of iniquity. Thou shalt destroy evildoers!"

Lightning flashed close by, making the hair on my head rise and chills course down my body even as the sky rumbled an answer to the man. Retreating, I pressed my way as quickly as I could through the undergrowth above the trail.

He must have heard, for he called out, "Who's up there?"

Terrified, I hastened my flight. Leaping to the trail, I ran for the tree bridge. I must have made plenty of noise in my flight, for he followed after me. I thought sure he would send a lightning bolt to strike me dead.

"Child, *wait!*"

I leaped nearly as high as my heart did. Four bounding steps took me across the tree bridge to the other side, another four plunged me into the forest. I hid there in the shadows, shaking and watching fearfully as he stood on the other side of the Narrows. His lips moved. Perhaps he was calling down some curse of God upon my head. Panting, heart racing, I closed my eyes and clutched the tree behind which I hid and waited for the lightning to strike.

It didn't come.

When I finally dared open my eyes again, the stranger was gone.

I ran all the way to the cemetery. The jar of preserves was gone. For one instant, I felt a rush of hope until I saw the footprints. My heart sank. I didn't want to go home to what I knew was waiting.

The rain came, pelting me with icy drops as I stayed the day in the forest. I knew the storm would pass soon. When it did, I went and sat in the midst of the meadow below Miz Elda's house, dry-ing in the afternoon sunshine. It was warm enough that steam rose from my thin dress as I picked mountain daisies, shook off the raindrops, and spliced stems together to make a wreath. I laced in bluets and Queen Anne's lace and mountain laurel.

When I finally came home, Mama was sitting in Granny's chair outside. Her face was pale and rigid. I had never seen such a look in her eyes before and was afraid. Papa and Iwan hadn't come in from fishing yet, and we were alone. I held out the crown of flowers for her. A year ago she would have taken them and kissed me. Now, she just looked at them, winced, and rose. Turning away, she went on into the house. I followed her and saw the jar of preserves sitting right in the middle of the table.

"If it ain't one thing, it's another, Cadi. Ye've always been contrary. Right from the first when it took me two days birthin' ye. I almost died . . ." She drew in a sobbing breath. "Ye've al-ways been a child going where ye oughtn't go and doing what ye oughtn't do. And now ye're a thief besides, stealing from the mouths of your own family."

There was no defense against her words, the first she'd spoke to me in a long time. They came in a rush, pouring out hot and heavy. She grabbed my arms, shaking me so hard I thought my neck would snap. "What're ye doing in the graveyard?" Her fin-gers dug in painfully, jerking me back and forth. "Ye never think before ye do summat, do ye? Ye never think of the evil that can come. Ye just do what comes to ye without a care!"

Letting loose of me, she grabbed the flower wreath from my hand. "Ye think flowers can undo what's been done?" She broke it. "Ye think to fix grief with *these?*" She tore at it with trembling hands until the flowers were scattered at her feet. "Ye think being sorry's enow? It'll never change nothing. I wish . . . I wish . . ." She stopped, her face white of a sudden when wailing filled the room.

My hands gripped my head, and the sound continued. I'm not sure when I realized I was doing the wailing, but I couldn't stop. The sound come from down deep inside where something was broken. All I could do was stand there and look at the shredded wreath and Mama and wail.

Trembling, she took a step back from me, her face contorting. She looked down at the floor. "Ohhh . . ." Dropping to her knees, she gripped her head and rocked back and forth, and I fell silent.

"What goes on in here?" Papa said from the doorway. Seeing Mama, he came in quickly and yanked me away from her. "What'd ye do now, Cadi? Go on outside. Go on, I say! Get out of here!"

I didn't have to be told again.

It was Iwan who found me sitting in the quiet of the barn. "Mama's fine," he said as he sat down beside me. "She dinna say what ye'd done to get her so upset. Ye want to tell me?" When I shook my head, he ran his hand gently over my hair. "Mama says to come in for supper."

"I ain't hungry."

"Ye sick then?"

I gave a shrug and looked away, toying with the straw. Aye. I was sick. Heartsick.

He plucked a piece of straw from my hair. "Mama said hungry or not, ye're to come in and sit with the rest of us." He took me by the hand.

No one said much of anything. Even Papa didn't seem to have much appetite. He said he was going to have to make a trip down to the trading post for more shot and powder, and if Mama would tell him what she needed, he'd see to it. When I got up and cleared the dishes, Mama sat looking at me for a long moment. I could feel her eyes on my back. She got up quietlike and went outside to sit in Granny's chair. She stayed there the rest of the evening, just staring up at the darkening sky. I was in bed long before she came back in.

Head covered with Granny's quilt, I could hear her moving about while Papa snored. She went to bed once and then got up again. I could hear her moving things about on the shelves and wondered if she was counting the jars and cans again, wondering how much else I might have stole. I burrowed down deeper.

"Cadi?"

I stiffened, but it was no use pretending I was sleeping. I drew the quilt down slightly, afeared of what more she would have to say to me.

"Take 'em." She put the jar of preserves next to me. "I *want* ye to have 'em." Her voice broke softly. She stood a moment longer. Reaching out, she made to touch me and then withdrew again, padding back to bed.

Come morning, I put the jar of preserves back in the cemetery.

SEVEN

BROGAN KAI AND TWO OF HIS OLDER SONS CAME TO talk with Papa. I shucked corn on the porch while Mama sat inside, spinning. She had heard the hound barking and asked me what was wrong. Once told, she went back to her own thoughts, not plagued by curiosity. Like it was most days, her mind was elsewhere. Somewhere in the past, I reckoned, where Elen still lived.

Fagan's father was the fiercest looking man I ever seen. He had dark hair and eyes, and he was taller than Papa by a head and built thick and hard. Just seeing him put fear in most people, and Cleet and Douglas took after him. I wondered how Fagan dared defy his father, being small by comparison to the rest of his clan. Fagan had blue eyes like his mother. Iwan said once that Fagan was like a falcon born into a nest of eagles.

All three Kais shouldered guns that morning. I figured they were out hunting again. They were always hunting. Once a year, they took pelts outside our highland valley, though they never seemed to come back the richer for it.

I found it disturbing they talked so long to Papa. Kai men were not much for visiting. The only time you ever saw them all together was when someone had died and they came to pay their respects.

Or when there was trouble.

I reckoned the latter by Papa's stance. Soon as the Kais left, Papa came up to the house. "There's a stranger in our highlands, Cadi. If ye see him, get away. Hear me?"

"Yes, Papa, but why?" I hoped he could put my fears in words, but he glowered at me.

"Don't be asking why. Just do like you're told. Ye've shucked enow. Go on and play. But stay close, ye hear? Your mama will call ye back when she's ready."

He could have just said straight out he wanted to talk to Mama without me around to eavesdrop. Setting the bowl aside, I went down the steps, making to leave. Soon as he went inside, I darted around and squatted beneath the window Mama always left open while she spun. I had to know what the Kais had said about the man of God. I was willing to take whatever came, even a lashing and dark hours in the woodshed if need be.

"An outsider's come," I heard Papa saying. "The Kai says the mon's camping in the center of the valley by the river and claims he's come in the name of the Lord."

The click of her spinning wheel didn't stop. "What would God want with us?" I could hear the bitterness in her voice, as clear as her laughter had once been.

Papa didn't say nothing for a minute, then went on. "The Kai says he's crazy. Talks about all of us being rotten and needing redemption. The Kai says to stay away from him."

It seemed an odd warning since Mama never ventured down the hill anymore. She couldn't bear to go near the river or even look at it. It didn't seem likely she'd be crossing it to listen to some stranger from the outside world.

"If he's dangerous, why don't they run him out now?"

"Brogan's given the mon the word and time to think on it. Figures he'll go on his own if no one pays him any mind."

"And if he doesn't?"

"The Kai'll deal with him. Outsiders have come before. They dinna stay long."

I could not remember a single outsider entering our valley and reckoned Papa must be talking of times before I came to be. I wondered if Iwan would remember.

"If he ain't dangerous," Mama asked, "where's the harm in letting him stay?"

"The land's all taken up. We ain't got room for more."

"That's not the reason, and you know it."

"Reason enow. Ye want people coming and bringing their own ideas about how things oughta go? The Kais and Forbeses and Humes and all the rest came up here to these highlands to get away from all that. We have our ways, Fia. Ye ken that. And they be tried and true."

"*Our* ways? Seems to me Brogan lays down the law harder than—"

"Dunna be speaking again' him, Fia."

"They did what he wanted, dinna they? And now we're cursed for it!"

"We're not cursed. Dunna talk such foolishness."

"Three children dead, Angor. What do you call that? *Three.*"

I could hear her weeping.

"Others have lost children to fevers and such, Fia. Ye oughta be counting your blessings instead of wallowing in your grief. We've had enow! We've got Iwan and Cadi." His voice softened some. "Think on them for a change."

"Iwan's good as gone. Soon as he's old enow he'll be taking his leave. And Cadi? What comfort is she, mad as she is?"

"She isna mad!"

"What do ye call it when she talks to air all the time?"

"Maybe the healer's right and she's keeping company with a taint."

"Don't say that!"

"It oughta bring ye comfort, Fia," he said in a cold, cruel voice. "It could mean Elen's not gone from us after all."

Mama wept harder, and my guilt grew intolerable. It was what I'd done that had them at each other's throats. I sat down, back against the wall and my hands covering my head, hearing them go on at one another.

"Just stay away from the mon like I'm telling ye," Papa said. "Ye believe in God, same as I do. We don't need anybody saving us, and we sure don't need no one laying more burdens on our backs. We got more than enow already."

"How do ye know that's what he's about?"

"The Kai heard him out and says so. That's good enow for me."

"Brogan has his own ax to grind."

Papa was silent for a moment. "If the stranger comes, I'll warn him off."

"And if you and Iwan are off hunting?"

"Bolt the door and dunna give him so much as a by-your-leave. Iwan will do the same if I'm gone."

"Ye told Iwan? When? I thought he was off hunting."

"He was at Byrneses' when Brogan stopped by."

"What was he doing there?"

"Cluny's growing up. Or haven't ye noticed?"

"Cluny?" Mama sounded sad.

"Take comfort in it, Fia. She may be the chain that binds him to this valley. He mightn't leave at all."

I heard Papa's footsteps cross the room and go down the steps. Mama was weeping. Pushing myself up, I ran into the forest. I kept running, branches lashing my face, until I was too tired to go on. Sinking down, I leaned against the trunk of a great pine, my chest heaving for air, wishing I could die right there and never hear them tearing at one another again.

After a while, the birdsong and the wind in the trees com-

forted me. I wandered down the mountainside and sat in the
sunshine among the yellow-faced daisies stretching their faces
heavenward. Lying back, I stared up at the clouds moving
slowly across the sky. Shapes changed, shifting billows of
white. One looked like a hound sleeping. Another was like
someone sitting on grass, one arm stretched out toward the
horizon.

I started thinking on the man of God, wondering what he
had come to say, wondering, too, why the Kai was so determined he not be heard. I reckoned it must be my contrary nature
rising in me again, for what else could it be that made me rise
and head down toward the valley floor despite the fear I had of
both men?

The questing spirit in me, I reckoned, ever seeking what it
would never find: a way back to the time before—

I cut off the thought, turning my mind away. The Kai had
given his command, and Papa said heed it. So why did something deep down inside me gnaw at me to hear the man out?
God had sent him. Who can stand against God and not come
out the worst for it? Didn't God see and hear everything and
bring judgment? Was I not already condemned?

I went down until I stood at the edge of the trees looking out
across the valley floor. A curl of smoke rose into the morning air
and a man sat close by, roasting a fish. My heart beat faster, and
taking a deep breath, I sneaked closer, finally going down on my
hands and knees. Swallowing my fear, I crawled through the tall
grass until I reached the shrubs that lined the river. Inching
closer, I peered down the bank and across the ripples to where
he sat, head bowed. He ate, rose and washed his hands, then sat
again, head bowed.

"A day in the presence of the Lord is better than a thousand
lived without him," came a soft whisper.

Glancing behind me, I saw Lilybet standing close by. Afraid

she'd be seen, I motioned her to sit down and be silent. She came closer, stretching out on her stomach beside me.

"He knows we're here, Katrina Anice."

"I was very careful."

"And intent."

"Is that so wrong?"

She smiled. "You're not far from the truth."

"How long have you been here?"

"Since the day you saw me at the river."

Sometimes there was no talking to her and making sense of it.

The sound of rustling made my heart leap in fear. Copperheads sometimes slithered among the brush and rock of the riverbank. I looked about me, muscles tense. Fagan appeared, briefly startled at the sight of me. He had crawled on his belly through the grass, same way I had.

"What're ye doing here?" he growled low, a look of pure disgust on his face.

"I could ask the same of you!" I whispered back, resentful of his presence.

"Dinna my father tell ye to stay away?"

"Same as he told you, I reckon."

His mouth tightened. He got that look on his face that he was going to do what he wanted no matter what and started crawling forward again, using his elbows and snaking his body along until he came up alongside me where Lilybet had been. Bold with me, she was shy of others. And strange beyond my ken.

In truth, I was glad of Fagan's company and didn't mind him knowing so. "I seen him when he first came up the trail through the Narrows."

"And?"

"He was talking to God. And God answered."

"You're crazy."

"I am not!"

"Shhhh!"

Tears pricked my eyes as I glared at him.

"Has he said anything?" Fagan said.

"No."

"Done anything?"

"Ate a fish he roasted."

"Maybe he's sleeping now," he whispered. "Can't tell nothing from this distance." He edged closer and one of the branches snapped back, smacking me in the face and drawing a startled cry of pain. The branch waved and shuddered over my head as I ducked and covered my stinging cheek.

"Well, now ye've done it." Fagan's voice trembled.

I looked up again, and my heart bounded around in my chest like a rabbit before a hound, for the man had raised his head. His bearded face was cocked to one side, like an animal alerted that an enemy was near. When he rose to his feet, my heart stopped and then began beating again so fast I thought it was coming up into my throat. I could scarcely draw breath.

"He's looking this way," Fagan whispered.

"I con see. I con see."

"Don't move. I don't think he's seen us."

The man came a few feet closer to the edge of the river. "Blessed is the one that walketh not in the counsel of the ungodly," he called out, "nor standeth in the way of sinners, nor sitteth in the seat of the scornful!"

He was looking straight across the river toward us, and I moaned. Fagan shimmied back quickly and clamped a hand over my mouth, his fingers digging in. "Shhhh!"

"And the one who delights in the word of the Lord and meditates on it day and night shall be like a tree planted by the rivers of water, that bringeth forth his fruit in his season. His leaf also shall not wither; and whatsoever he doeth shall prosper."

Fagan's grip eased as he watched the man.

"The ungodly are not so!" the man shouted. "They are like chaff which the wind driveth away!" He waved his arms and stepped closer. "Therefore the ungodly shall not stand in the judgment, nor sinners in the congregation of the righteous. For the Lord knoweth the way of the righteous: but the way of the ungodly shall perish!"

Fagan let go of me, fascination on his face, and I took the opportunity to edge back further into the thick brush and out of sight of the man of God.

"Where ye going?" Fagan said.

"He wants to kill us," I whispered, keeping my head down.

"How so?"

"Can ye not see? Can ye not hear? He comes in the name of the Lord."

"That's the reason I want to hear."

"Ye've heard."

"But not understood."

"So ye'll stay until he calls lightning down on you?"

"He dinna strike ye dead the first day, did he?"

"I dinna give him the chance!"

The man came to the very edge of the river. "Hear the word of the Lord!" he called out so loudly that his deep voice carried across the waters. "Take heed what ye hear! With what measure ye mete, it shall be measured unto you; and unto you that hear shall more be given. For ye that hath, to ye shall be given: and ye that hath not, from ye shall be taken even that which ye hath!"

"What does he mean, do ye think?" Fagan said.

"He's saying what I done will be done to me and more." Unless I found the sin eater first. If I could talk him into taking my sins away now, maybe then I could come back and get close enough to hear what the man of God had come to say and not fear being struck dead in the doing.

Fagan was pale but determined. "I'm staying."

I left him to his own conscience, figuring he didn't have the sins on his head that I had on mine. I made my way cautiously back through the tall grass and then darted into the cover of forest as fast as I could. Ducking behind a tree, I looked back around the trunk to see if my departure had been noted. No dark clouds or rumbling in the heavens. The man was still standing near the water, looking toward the place where Fagan was hiding. And he was talking, though not as loud as before. Leastwise, not loud enough so I could hear him.

Thankful Fagan was keeping the man's attention fixed, I climbed a tree where I could see more clearly what was happening. Sitting high in my leafy bower, I watched the man pace and raise his arms. It was a long time before he stopped talking and sat down again. Fagan had never once come out into the open, and he was in no hurry to leave his hiding place now that the man was finished saying whatever he had to say. I wondered why Fagan was staying put. Maybe he was too scared to move. Maybe the man had cursed him so he couldn't.

I was gathering my courage to go check on Fagan when I saw him wriggling on his belly through the tall grass. By the time he reached safety and could get up and dust himself off, I was there, waiting. "Why'd you stay so long?"

"I wanted to hear more."

"What'd he say?"

"Lot of things."

"Like what?"

"Go listen for yourself," he snarled. When he raised his head and glared at me, I saw the tear tracks down his dusty cheeks. Before I got over the surprise and had the sense to ask why he'd been crying, he'd already run off, leaving me standing in the shadows with my mouth open.

Fagan's tears over the man's words filled me with a lethal curiosity. I wanted desperately to hear what the man of God had come to say but knew I'd better find the sin eater before daring it. We'd never had anyone like this stranger in our highland valley before, and I was in terrible haste because I didn't know how long he'd stay. God could call him away anytime, and then I'd never hear what the Lord had told him to say.

So I set off to find the sin eater again. He hadn't come for the preserves. They were still sitting on Granny's headstone. Maybe he didn't like blackberries. Maybe he didn't like me.

Soon as I fed the chickens and collected the eggs the next morning, I left. All along the river, there were places to cross over, but I waited until I saw the creek that came down from Dead Man's Mountain running into it. Looking up at the craggy peak, I was filled with despair, wondering how I was ever going to find a man who didn't want to be found. There must've been a thousand hiding places up there.

"Talk to the lady," Lilybet said, having kept me company.

I found the small cabin again with no trouble and took up watch in a cascade of mountain laurel, trying to gather my courage. The lady was out working in her garden and looked harmless enough. But who was she? *What* was she that no one even mentioned her?

"Come on," Lilybet said, standing out in the open and beckoning to me. Rising from the thicket, I stepped out into the open. "Call out to her."

"Hello!" I called out.

The woman straightened sharply, staring at me.

"Hello," I said again.

"Go away!" She backed a step and looked over her shoulder toward the mountain. "Go away, I tell you!"

I'd come too far to retreat now. "I'm looking for the sin eater."

She hesitated, lowering her hoe. "Ring the bell."

"No one's died."

She cocked her head in surprise. Her stance relaxed some. "Why, ye're Cadi Forbes, ain't ye?"

"Yes, ma'am."

"Well, go on home, child. Ye dunna belong at this end of the valley. This is no-man's-land and no place for you."

"Then why are you here?"

"I belong here."

"Please. I want to find him. Can ye help me?"

"Leave the mon be! He's got sorrow enow without ye adding to it. Now, go home. Go home and stay away from here!" Rather than return to her gardening, she went inside her cabin and closed the door.

I stood for a few minutes longer, waiting and hoping she would come out again. I didn't go home. I went back into the cascade of mountain laurel and sat down to watch and wait upon her. She came out after a long time and returned to her work.

Who was she? And why was she living so close to a forbidden place? Why was she all by herself? Everyone in our valley had family aplenty, even Miz Elda's who'd chosen to go over the mountains. Maybe that was what happened. Maybe this woman's kin had gone on to Kantuckee or back to the Carolinas.

She straightened once and wiped the sweat from her brow with the back of her hand. Leaning on her hoe for a few minutes, she gazed toward the mountain again. She stood staring up at the peak for a few minutes and then went back to work. Once or twice, she seemed troubled by something and glanced my way. I supposed she was like an animal that sensed the presence of an enemy. I was not her enemy, but she didn't know that. Not yet, at least. If she'd only let me get closer, I'd tell her myself.

When the sun was high and hot, she took up her weed bucket and carried it to a burn pile where she dumped it. The rake and hoe she took inside. When she came out again, she was carrying an empty jar. She headed straight to the bee gums standing near a sorrel tree. There were four of them, big and active with bees. Granny had always robbed our hives at night and used smoke to put the bees into a stupor before raising the lid. This lady opened a hive in broad daylight without the least sign of fear. I thought for sure she would be stung unto death, for I could hear those bees from where I was hiding in the curtain of laurel. They came swirling out and around her in a gray, humming cloud.

She stood perfectly still and calm, arms hanging limp. They covered her hair, shoulders, and part of her face, resting upon her like a great bee-shawl, sagging her with their weight. Covered like that, she leaned over slowly and lifted one of the combs out, holding it over her jar. The amber honey drained into it until it was glistening gold in the sunshine. Laying the comb atop the jar, she replaced the bee gum lid and started slowly back toward the cabin. The bees lifted away like smoke above her, swirling and humming and returning to the hive. By the time she neared her garden, all had gone from her. Lighter of foot, she went up the steps and disappeared inside her cabin.

Entranced, I sat back on my heels, amazed at what I'd seen. Leaning forward, I peered through the tangle of leafy vines wondering what more magic this woman could perform.

I saw her a while later, leaning out the side window. Cupping her hands, she whistled, a high melodic sound like birdsong. She placed something wrapped in a cloth on the sill and drew back inside where I couldn't see her.

I waited a long time to see what would happen next.

Nothing did.

She leaned out twice more to whistle that melody. The day wore on until I knew I had to leave. Creeping away, I glanced back once and saw her framed in the window, leaning out and looking up at Dead Man's Mountain.

EIGHT

"CHARMS BEES, DOES SHE?" MIZ ELDA SAID. "NEVER knew that about her, but it dunna surprise me much. She always was fey."

"Ye know her? Who is she?"

"Her name's Bletsung Macleod. No one's had much to do with her for years. Or maybe that ain't right. Maybe it's the other way around." She got her thoughtful expression, staring off toward the mountains. "Macleods never were much for company." She looked at me. The troubled look gave way, and she got a set one instead, as though she'd made some kind of decision about something I didn't ken. "Her father died of a sudden."

"How?"

"No one knows how. Not that anyone cared. The man was cold cruel. When he was dead and buried, his girl stayed as much to herself as he ever did, though not for the same reasons, I reckon."

"What reasons?"

"Ye're full of questions, ain't ye?" She leaned back, rocking her chair slowly in the cool morning sunshine. "Douglas Macleod dinna like people much. Had no trust for them. His daughter was the only thing he cared about, if care is a proper way of putting it."

"Did she have a mother?"

"Aye, she had a mother. Rose O'Sharon was her name. She up and died of a spring. By her own hand, some say. No one really knows for sure, just like no one really knows how Douglas Macleod died. But it got people worrying. Some were already saying they'd seen Rose O'Sharon's taint wandering the hills, and they were afeared when Douglas Macleod died, there'd be two haunting our highlands by night. Summat had to be done about it." She sighed, leaning her head back. "And summat was."

"What?"

"We chose the sin eater."

Chose? I sat up straighter, surprised. "I thought he was always here."

"Seems like, but that ain't the truth of it. It was Brogan Kai's father, Laochailand Kai, who brought us back to the old ways." She stopped rocking and looked at me. "Ye see, we had sin eaters in Scotland and Wales. It were a custom I thought well left behind, but the old Kai wanted it otherwise. So the men threw lots into a mazer, and all the women stood by praying it wouldn't fall and be one of their own." She closed her eyes as though the memory pained her. "The man whose name was drawn left that very night with Laochailand Kai's sin upon him, and that of Rose O'Sharon and Douglas Macleod as well."

"Then what happened?"

She looked at me with impatience. "Nothing happened. He went to live on Dead Man's Mountain, and no one has spoken his name aloud since."

"Will ye tell me his name, Miz Elda?"

"No, child, I will not. It would do ye no good. The man knows his place and keeps to it. It was God's will he be chosen, and he accepted that."

She seemed so troubled, I leaned closer. "Should he not have been the one?"

"What a fool question." She let out her breath and turned her face away. "It was a long time ago, Cadi. Too long ago to be undone."

"It burdens her," Lilybet said, sitting on the bottom step and looking up at us.

I could see she was right. "Did he have family, Miz Elda?"

"Aye, but they're all gone now."

"Dead?"

"No, dearie. Except for his mother, that is. She died a few years after the lottery. Of a broken heart would be my guess. I dunna think there was a day after his leaving that she dinna weep for him and what he'd become. As for the rest, his father and brothers and sisters, they couldn't abide one of their own being a sin eater. They was so ashamed of him, they went on to Kantuckee and we ain't heard from 'em since."

I felt the prick of tears and bowed my face so the old woman would not see. It seemed the more I knew of the sin eater, the closer I felt to him. Oh, I knew shame. I knew what it was to lose the love of those I held most dear. The lot had fallen upon that poor man, but it was my own sin that had fallen upon me and was crushing me still. Yet, the sin eater was more than I, for he knew and accepted his fate while I fought hard against mine.

Why had he accepted it so readily and just gone away to live on that lonely mountain? "I have to find him, Miz Elda."

"I know, child, but I don't know what good it'll do ye. Or the rest of us. Except bring more trouble down on us."

"You've never tried to talk me out of it."

Reaching out, she ran her hand gently over my hair. "I'd go with ye if these old legs were strong enow to carry me past the meadow."

I took her old gnarled hand and held it between mine. Her skin was so soft it felt like the thinnest leaf. The blue veins stood out. "Do ye think if he takes my sins away, Mama will forget?" When she didn't answer, I looked up and saw the tears running down her wrinkled cheeks.

"No, child. She'll never forget, but maybe she'll be able to forgive."

I couldn't sleep that night and crept out of bed. Sitting on the steps, I looked up at the night sky with the sparkling stars and the full moon. An owl hooted and crickets chirped. There was no wind and the air was refreshing cool. I looked toward the valley where the man of God was.

"You want to go down there, don't you?" Lilybet said, sitting down beside me.

"He's probably sleeping."

"No, he isn't. His heart is as burdened as yours, Katrina Anice."

"How do you know?"

"He hasn't done what he came to do."

"And what's that?"

"He'll tell you if you let him."

"I'm afraid of him."

"It's not him you fear, Katrina Anice. It's God."

"Shouldn't I be?"

"You can't run from him forever."

"Who ye talking to, Cadi?" Iwan said from behind me, startling me something terrible. I jumped.

"Easy, girl," he said and sat down where Lilybet had been.

"I was just thinking."

"It's too late to be thinking out loud."

"Can't help it."

He leaned forward and clasped his hands between his knees. With a sigh, he looked slowly around the yard and along the porch, his troubled gaze finally coming to rest on me. "Were ye talking to Elen, Cadi?"

"No."

"Ye sure?"

"I'm sure."

He frowned, searching my face in the moonlight. "Ye still looking for the sin eater?" he whispered.

I shrugged and looked away. A lie might have set his mind at rest for a time, but it wouldn't have convinced him.

He was silent for a long time, looking off toward the valley.

I broke the silence between us. "Do ye ever think about hearing what that man has to say, Iwan?"

"I've thought about it, but I'm leaving well enow alone."

"Because the Kai told everyone to stay away?"

He turned his head and gave me a sad look. When he looked away again, I could see the muscle working in his cheek. "Ye gotta have order, Cadi. The Kai's only trying to protect us."

"But the man's from God, Iwan."

"So he says. That don't mean it's so."

I told him in a hushed whisper about the thunder and lightning. He looked less certain after that. "Do ye think the Kai would change his mind if he knew that?"

"It's hard to say, Cadi. He's set against him."

"I don't think that man's gonna leave, Iwan."

"He'll leave, all right."

"What if he doesn't?"

"He'll die."

My heart dropped at his words, and tingles of gooseflesh rose on my arms and legs. Would they really go that far?

Iwan turned his head and looked at me. When his eyes met mine, he frowned. "Winter's not so long away. He'll go of his own by then. The snows'll drive him away."

I knew that wasn't what he thought. Shivering, I shook my head, afeared what would happen. "You've got to talk 'em out of it."

"He's come to stir people up. The Kai's just trying to keep us together. And he's right, Cadi. No one's got the right to come into our mountains and tell us what to think and how to live. No one."

"Is that what he's doing?"

"The Kai says he's come to set sons against fathers and fathers against sons, and we ain't gonna let that happen. The Kai's right. The old ways have held us together."

"All he done is talk."

"So far. His voice carries," he said grimly. "Now, come on." He took my hand and stood. "Time ye were back in bed and asleep."

I lay awake on my cot, listening to the night sounds and thinking about the man of God down in the valley. What Iwan said was true. There was more to him than a loud voice. His words stuck like burrs on wool, pricking and making me uncomfortable. Nothing he had said had blown away with the wind and been forgotten.

Dreams plagued me, fiery dreams of men with torches surrounding the man of God. He made no effort to fight back or run away. "Ye've come out as against a thief with your weapons for to take me, and I sat here daily by your river trying to teach ye. Why did ye not listen to the word of the Lord?" The Kai struck him in the face. Blood trickled from a cut, and the man stood firm, looking back at him grimly. "This is your hour, and the power of darkness."

With curses of rage, the men took hold of him and beat him and rolled his lifeless body into the river. I watched as he was swept into the currents of the Narrows and awakened just as he went over the falls.

It was barely sunrise. Papa was not in bed. Throwing off my quilt, I hurried outside, looking for him. When I didn't see him, I ran straight down the mountainside through the forest to the meadow without a single thought as to what I was doing. Lungs burning, I ran on through the high grass. Birds burst from the ground and winged into the air, startled by my mad race. I didn't stop until I reached the riverbank. Panting and holding my aching sides, I hid behind a stand of brush and peered over.

Smoke curled up from a small fire by the riverbank, but the man of God was nowhere in sight.

The terrible dream had been true. The man of God was dead and gone. I just knew it, in my heart, I knew. So sure then was I that Papa and Iwan had brought the blood guilt upon themselves that I cried out in despair, sat down, put my head in my hands, and wept. We were lost. We were all lost. I was not the only one on the road to hell, and it grieved me sorely.

"Who's there?"

Fear and relief can marry in a start, and so they did when I heard the man call out from across the soft rippling waters. Heart stopping, my head came up and I saw him rising from the ground. Why had he been lying facedown in the dirt so far from the warmth of the fire?

Looking around, I saw there was no escape without being seen. Crouching lower, I kept myself hidden from his sight, wondering what to do now that sunrise was coming upon us. Would I have to sit here all day until night came again before I could creep away to the safety of the woods and mountains again? Oh, why had I come? Did I really think my father and brother could kill a man who was doing them no earthly harm?

"Who has come?" the man said again, loud enough this time to make the hair stand on the back of my neck.

"'Tis only I, sir," I said, afeared he would bring the thunder and let the whole valley know I'd gone against the Kai's command.

"Do ye hail by a name?"

"I dare not tell ye, sir."

He came closer to the river's edge. "A child ye are by the

sound of your voice." He cocked his head. "Are ye the girl who ran from me when I was on the path above the falls?"

I hunched lower, face hot, heart racing. He was like a hound. Should I lie and throw him off the scent? I didn't have the chance, for he spoke first.

"Cross the Jordan. Come into the Promised Land. Come hear the word of the Lord."

"I can't!"

"Can't or won't?" he called back without hesitation.

"I *can't.*"

"What holds ye back?" He came closer still, his feet touching the cleansing stream, craning his neck from side to side trying to see me.

"Don't look this way! Please don't look for me."

"Are ye afraid of God?"

"Yes!" Cringing, I lowered my head and covered my face.

"'The fear of the Lord is the beginning of knowledge.'"

Shuddering, I raised my head slightly, peering through the branches, hungering and thirsting to hear what he had come to say and yet afraid to do so, knowing I was not worthy. "I want to come. I do. But I can't. Not yet."

"Don't wait. You never know what the morrow will bring."

"I have to find the sin eater first."

"Who did ye say?"

Sniffling, I backed away. "Look away. Please look away so I won't die."

"Child . . ."

"Please don't call down the lightning on me."

"I'm not God." He said more, though I couldn't hear clearly enough to make out the words. Lowering his head, his shoulders slumped, and I thought for an instant he was crying. I stayed no longer than that. Before I had gone far into the forest, someone grabbed me from behind and yanked me around.

"I saw ye out there," Brogan Kai said, his dark eyes glowing like hot coals. "Going against me. Going agin' your pa." He slapped me, holding my arm so I'd not fall.

"I dinna—"

"*Liar.*" He slapped me again, harder this time, so that I tasted blood in my mouth. "Deceitful child. Vile. It's *you* who's brought this upon us!"

"No!" Struggling to get away from him, I screamed. Grabbing my throat, he cut off the sound.

"Cadi!" Papa's voice shouted from somewhere higher on the mountainside. "Cadi, where are ye?"

The Kai leaned down, his hot breath in my face. "If ye go out there again, I'll kill you. I swear it on me own soul. Better one should die, than all suffer." His hand tightened, cutting off my air, cutting off the blood. When blackness started to pull me down, he let me go and disappeared into the woods.

"*Cadi!*" Moments later Papa turned me over and held me in his arms. "Who did this to ye? Who did this?"

Crying, I clutched his shirt, my throat hurting so much I could scarcely draw breath let alone tell him anything. Nor did I dare. I had never seen such a look on my father's face before. Death was in his eyes and hell coming after. "It was the stranger, wasn't it?"

"No," I croaked out, shaking my head, crying harder.

Papa looked toward the valley floor and then dismissed the idea. Even I knew the man could not have come so far so fast and returned again to his place across the river. Papa looked at me again. "Was it the thing who keeps ye company?"

Thing? What was he talking about? What *thing* did he mean? Dizzy and feeling the shadows closing in, I shut my eyes, drifting in pain.

Lifting me in his arms, Papa carried me home. "Go for Gervase Odara," I heard him say as he came through the door.

Vaguely, as in a dream, I saw Mama rise from her spinning. "What's happened?"

"Do as you're told, woman, unless ye'd like to lose another child!"

I heard nothing after that.

NINE

"DRINK, CADI. COME ON NOW, CHILD, DRINK. THAT'S it."

My throat ached.

"Tell me what happened, dearie. Tell your old friend, Gervase." She dabbed a cool cloth on my forehead and smiled down at me tenderly.

"It wasn't him," I whispered hoarsely. It hurt to speak, but I had to make her understand. "It wasna the man of God."

"We know that, my dear. He has not moved from his place by the river." She continued to dab my face gently. "Tell me who it was."

If I told her, she would tell Papa, and Papa might want to do something. He might even try. If I said anything, I knew something terrible would happen, and it would be on my head. I looked away from Gervase Odara's all-too-seeing eyes.

"You're safe now, Cadi. You con tell me what happened."

Safe? Who could be safe from a man who held power in the palm of his hand? Everyone bowed to the will of the Kai. Everyone did as he told them to do.

Except me, and I hadna been thinking.

And Fagan.

Fagan! What had become of Fagan? I hadna seen him in days.

"Ease now, my dear. Lie back and rest awhile."

"I want to go."

"Go where, child?"

I couldn't tell her. If I blurted out Fagan's name, she'd wonder why I wanted to see him now, what had brought him to mind. And then the truth would come out, and disaster would follow. Weeping, I sank back onto my cot. Gervase Odara leaned over to me, speaking gently, stroking me with the cool cloth. My head felt fuzzy and my eyelids so heavy I could scarcely keep them open.

"Rest awhile, my dear. That's it. Close your eyes and sleep."

"Did she tell ye who attacked her?" I heard Papa ask softly.

"No, but I think I know what it is," she whispered and stood, moving away from my cot. "Summat tried to choke her to death."

"The taint?"

"It's a child keeps her company. The bruises on her neck weren't made by a child, but the child's master."

"The devil himself, ye're saying?" Mama whispered fearfully.

"Who else could it be? Nothing like this has ever happened in our valley before."

"What about Macleod?" Papa said, almost hopefully.

"Long since departed, and Rose O'Sharon with him. No, their souls was put to rest years ago by the sin eater. This canna be laid at their doorstep. Nor even Laochailand Kai's. Summat dark is at work upon your Cadi."

"What's to be done about it?"

"I con make her a talisman, but I'll need Gorawen's hair. Fia?"

I thought of the necklace of hair Mama had braided with Granny's white hair. She wore it every day, touching it now and then in fond memory. Maybe it took her back to better times, times long before I was born.

"Could ye not use summat else?" Mama said. "It's all I have of her."

"And ye'd not spare even a strand of it for your own daughter?" Papa said. "A curse on ye, Fia! A curse on ye for your unforgivin' soul."

I heard a door close with a hard thud and Mama crying. "He doesna understand what I feel and I canna tell him. I canna tell anyone . . ."

Gervase Odara spoke soft words of comfort, but they did no good.

It was several days before I was allowed out of the house, even to do chores. Mama had given up her mourning jewelry after all, and the beautifully braided white-hair necklace now hung around my neck. With a child's wisdom, I knew it would do me no good against the Kai. Or anything else for that matter. And it had not kept Lilybet away, for she had come to me each day and sat on the cot with me, keeping me company while Mama was out and about her chores.

"Do not be afraid of the truth, Katrina Anice. The truth will set you free."

"The truth will get Papa killed."

"Oh, my dear, trust in the Lord and lean not on your own understanding."

"It's ye who dunna understand. The Kai . . . the Kai is all powerful."

"The Kai is but a man. A poor, broken, frightened man who needs the truth as much as you do."

I remembered the look in his eyes, the feel of his hand gripping my throat. I did not understand where she got such foolish notions.

"Seek and ye shall find, Katrina Anice. Ask and the door shall be opened."

"Go away. Ye're giving me a headache."

And she went, quietly, just as I asked her to do.

The first place I went when I was free again was down the mountainside to the edge of the forest so I could look across the meadowlands to the river. The man of God was still there. And, like a pestilence, avoided by all.

Except Fagan, perhaps.

What of Fagan?

I went looking for him, and found Glynnis and Cullen instead, picking blackberries near the creek. "Ain't seen him since yesterday," Glynnis said, popping several plump berries into her mouth and picking another to drop in her bucket.

"He was fishing," Cullen said.

"Where?"

"In the river," he said with a smirk.

Rolling my eyes, I looked at Glynnis.

"Down where Kai Creek runs in." She picked another blackberry and ate it.

"Quit eating 'em or we'll be here all day!" Cullen yelled at his sister. Turning, she gave him a simpering smile, spilled the contents of her bucket into her hand, and ate them all. Uttering a growl, he started after her as she shrieked with laughter. She hopped out of the blackberry briars and raced for home. "I'm telling Mama you made me spill 'em!"

Fagan wasn't at the creek. Climbing a tree, I looked toward the copse of bushes near the man of God, but he wasn't there either. At least my mind was at ease about some harm coming to him. If he was out and about yesterday fishing, it was a sure thing his father had not killed him yet.

After wandering around for the better part of the morning looking for him, I gave up and went to visit with Miz Elda, and there, plain as the nose on my face, was Fagan sitting on her front porch, chewing straw and passing the time of day. "I've been looking for ye hither and yon!" I said, fit to be tied and locked away in a woodshed.

He blinked. "What for?"

"To see if ye was all right, that's what for!"

His expression darkened. "Why wouldn't I be? You was the one attacked. Not me."

What could I say to that without blurting out it was his own father who'd done it?

"By the devil himself, I heard," Miz Elda said. I blushed, avoiding Fagan's steady, if somewhat bemused, gaze. The old woman sat staring at me. "Got nothing to say about it?"

"What's to say?"

"Tight-lipped. Now, there's a change."

I sat glumly on the bottom step and kept my back to her. Her chair creaked as she began rocking again. "No flowers today, Fagan. She must be carrying a grudge agin' me for something."

I glanced up at her, annoyed. "What reason would I have?"

"No reason. But then, most folks don't need reasons for holding grudges, leastwise not up in these mountains." She rocked some more. "Since that ain't what's bothering her, Fagan, I reckon she must've thought I was dead and buried."

"I did not!" I turned to stare up at her, appalled at the suggestion.

"I don't see no flowers."

I turned away again.

"Well?" she said after a long pause.

Tired and frustrated, I got up and marched off. I half expected Fagan to catch up with me, but he stayed put. The old woman was growing more cantankerous every time I saw her. Returning with a bouquet of mountain daisies, I held them out to her.

"What am I going to do with 'em out here? Put 'em in some water."

When I went inside, I saw the flowers I had brought her last time still in the mason jar. The stalks were wilted, the petals dry and scattered upon her table. I thought of Mama tearing up the flowers I brought her, and here was Miz Elda keeping 'em until they was long dead and should be thrown out.

"*Fresh* water!" Miz Elda called from outside.

All the hurt and frustration seeped out of me. I made the trek to the creek, scrubbed out the slimy mason jar, filled it with fresh water, and carried it back. Smiling, I arranged the daisies, swept the dead, dried petals into my hand, and went back outside. I sat on the top step this time, just opposite Fagan, and leaned back, making myself more comfortable. I felt more at home on Miz Elda's porch than with Papa and Mama and Iwan.

Miz Elda fixed her rheumy, blue eyes on me. "Now, what happened to ye, child? And tell us the truth."

I pinched pleats in my dress and avoided her gaze. "I don't rightly remember."

"Ye remember all right. Ye just ain't willing to say."

I looked at Fagan and then away.

Miz Elda caught that look, and her eyes narrowed. "Where was ye coming from when it happened?"

"I'd just been down by the river, where the man of God's camped."

Fagan's head came up, his quiet gaze more intense. "Thought ye was scared of him and never going back."

"I dreamed he'd been killed."

"And?" Miz Elda said. She stopped rocking.

"He ain't dead," Fagan said.

"I was asking Cadi."

"He's hale and hearty," I told her. "He was lying on the ground on his face when I come up on the other side of the river, but he got up fast enow and started in talkin' to me."

Fagan leaned forward. "He *saw* you?"

"No, but he heard me."

"What'd he say to ye, chile?"

"Nothing I could understand, Miz Elda. He kept telling me to cross the Jordan, wherever that is."

"The Jordan," she repeated, leaning her head back. "The Jordan. Where have I heard that before?" She made a sound of disgust. "There are times when things tickle my mind, and I can't scratch 'em out."

Fagan frowned. "What kind of things?"

"Things just out of reach. Things my mother said to me when I was but a wee chile. I can half remember 'em sometimes when I'm dozing, and then they just slip away like flour through a sifter. Frustratin' as all get-out. It's like having a buzzing gnat in your ear. I can't swat 'em dead without deafening myself in the process. Ain't even sure why they're comin' on me now, after all these years and me so near the grave. You'd think an ol' woman like me'd earned some peace in her old age." She sighed heavy. "Sure do wish I could hear that man down there."

She rocked again and looked at Fagan. "It'd give me pure pleasure to have him come up for a cup of elderberry wine."

"Don't look at me! I ain't askin' him. Pa's warned everyone to stay clear of him."

"Oh, your pa. Ain't stopped you before."

Fagan turned his head and glared at me.

"Don't go looking at me, Fagan Kai. I dinna tell her."

"No one had to tell me. Plain as the nose on his face."

"What is?" Fagan said belligerently, testing her.

"Ye telling me I'm wrong?"

Pressing his lips together, he didn't say anything.

"You and Cadi got a lot in common."

"We ain't got nothing in common," he said, annoyed with both of us.

She cackled, enjoying his discomfort. "Well, you're both listening to voices other than your ma and pa's."

"What voices you talking about?"

"Well, now, if I knew that, I'd be a whole lot wiser than I am, now wouldn't I? But I'll hazard a guess. Cadi's been listening to her heart, and you've been listening to your head, and neither one of you are getting anywhere that I can see."

Fagan gave me a look to say she was just an old woman who was rambling on, but sometimes I wondered if there weren't more to Miz Elda's words than what she said. Sometimes I had the feeling she was testing us both. Or prodding. Hadn't she been the one to point the way to Dead Man's Mountain? Not that it had done me much good.

Now she was pointing toward that man by the river.

"Ever thought of asking your pa why he's so dead set against him?" she said to Fagan.

I jumped to Fagan's defense. "Why would he want to do that when asking about the sin eater got him knocked clean off the porch?" By his glance, I could tell he did not appreciate my help.

"Pa said he dinna want anyone going near the man," he said, looking away. "That was the end of it."

Miz Elda gave a snort. "That's enow to start things off."

Fagan threw his straw away. "Why do ye hate him so much?"

"Hate's a mighty strong word. I don't hate him, boy. It's just that he takes too much on himself. Always did. Ye canna think for people. They gotta think for themselves."

There was more to Brogan Kai than wanting to think for people, but I didn't want to talk about the look in his eyes or his hand squeezing off the air to my lungs and blood to my head.

Miz Elda sighed. "Sure do wish I could hear that man. I ain't for this world for much longer, and it sure would be nice to know what the Lord has to say afore I have to go and meet him face-to-face." She looked between the two of us. "If one of ye was brave enow, ye could extend the man an invitation to visit a poor, sick, old woman with one foot in the grave and the other on shaky ground."

"Don't say that, Miz Elda! Why do ye have to talk about dying all the time?"

"Why wouldn't I talk about it? I'm old and it's the way of all flesh. No getting around it."

"Sometimes ye sound like you're in an all-fire hurry!"

"Well, there's nothing holding me here. My family's all gone over the mountain, and my friends is all dead."

"What about us?" I fought back tears.

"You've got each other."

"You shudna talk about death so much, Miz Elda. It upsets Cadi, and she just lost her granny not a month ago."

"See what I mean?" she said with a faint smile, looking between us. Then she grew serious. "Fine and dandy. We won't talk about me dying anymore. We'll just sit and listen to Fagan tell us what that man's been saying while he's been hiding in the tall grass and bushes."

Fagan blushed. "I don't always hear everything he says 'cause of the river."

"Just tell us what ye have heard."

He let out his breath and scratched his head. "First time I heard him, he said the sins of the father are visited on the sons to the fourth generation."

"Reckon that's why we have ourselves a sin eater," Miz Elda said, watching Fagan's face. "So trouble don't rise up to haunt us."

"And then he said, 'I will proclaim thy name to my brethren, in the midst of the congregation I will sing thy praise.'"

"Well, if that don't beat all."

"Yesterday he was talking about a rock and swallows."

"A rock and swallows," she said, thinking. "Maybe he meant the cliffs where the swallows build their nests, the ones near the Narrows."

"And he was talking about building houses on sand."

"That's pure foolishness," Miz Elda scoffed. "Anyone knows better than that. What would he say a thing like that for?"

Fagan shrugged. "I heard him say, 'the stone which the builders refused is become the head stone of the corner, and this is the Lord's doing.'"

"A rock and swallows, houses built on sand, and a rejected cornerstone," Miz Elda said and shook her head. "Maybe your pa's right and ye ought to leave him alone. He sounds crazy." She started rocking again, slowly, gazing off toward the valley as she sometimes did. "You two go on now. I need to rest awhile."

It wasn't rest she wanted. It was time to think on the things Fagan had told her. I wished she would tell me what was in her mind, but reckoned she was probably harkening back to a time past and trying to remember what it was she had forgotten.

"Did the sin eater ever come for the preserves?" Fagan said as we was walking down Miz Elda's path to the meadow.

"Never did. The jar's probably still sitting there." A sudden idea came to me, and I started running.

"Where ye going?"

"To the graveyard!" I called back over my shoulder.

The jar of preserves was still there. I took it up and dusted the jar off with the edge of my dress.

"What've ye got in your head to do with 'em now, Cadi Forbes?" Fagan asked, panting from the run.

"I'm going to give 'em to the bee charmer."

"What bee charmer?"

"The woman who lives in the cabin at the bottom of Dead Man's Mountain."

"The crazy woman?"

I glanced at him. "Who said she was crazy?"

"My ma. I told her I'd seen the cabin, and she said to stay far away from it. The woman living there is crazy."

"I don't believe it."

"Ma said she murdered her own mother and father."

"Miz Elda said Rose O'Sharon killed herself, and no one knows how Macleod died."

Fagan blinked in surprise and then his jaw set, his eyes darkening. "Just stay clear of that woman, ye hear. My ma wouldn't lie to me."

"I never said she lied."

"Yes, ye did."

"Miz Elda's older than anyone else on these mountains, and I reckon she knows more than anyone. Even your ma."

"Maybe ye oughta stay well away from Dead Man's Mountain, too! Chasing after the sin eater'll get ye nothing but trouble."

"Ye sound just like your pa," I said, angry now. His face reddened. As I came out the graveyard gate, he blocked my way.

"Ye're not going, Cadi." When I tried to pass, he snatched the jar of preserves and hurled it against a pine, shattering the glass and splattering Mama's blackberry preserves in all directions. "Now, what're ye going to do?" Fagan spread his feet.

When I threw a punch at him, he caught my arm and swung me around, pinning me back against him. I twisted and jerked, trying to kick at his shins with my heels, to no avail. "Listen to me, you stupid girl! I did it for your own good!"

"People gotta think for themselves!"

"Ye gonna repeat everything that old woman says?"

"Are ye gonna choke me just like your father did?"

His hands tightened briefly in shock, and then he shoved me away from him. "What'd you say?"

I spun around, glaring at him. "I hate you, Fagan Kai! I hate you, and I hate your father! Did ye hear that?"

His expression fell slightly, and I knew every word struck hard and deep. "I heard you."

The look on his face dissolved my anger and made me cringe. Feeling guilty, I tried to defend myself. "Ye shouldn't have broken the jar. It wasn't yours to break!"

"It was Pa?" he said in a small voice.

He looked so hurt, I wanted to take the blame away. "He caught me coming back from the river. Said I was going against him." My conscience smote me something fierce and I felt sick. My tongue had been like a fire, and I feared it had burned up our friendship. Seems like when you destroy something, you realize too late how much it meant to you in the first place. "Nobody knows, Fagan. I swear. I dinna tell my pa or anyone. And I won't. Cross my heart and hope to die. I wouldn't've told you if ye hadn't broken the jar!"

"What're *you* crying for? It's *me* who'll burn in hell."

"Burn for what?" I said, sniffling and rubbing my nose.

"For every mean thing my pa's ever done. Just like that man says. The sins of the father'll be laid on the sons."

"That ain't fair! Ye must've heard wrong."

"I heard him right."

"Ye said the river—"

"I heard him plain, I'm telling ye!" His eyes teared up, and I remembered the day he'd come back from the river crying.

I came closer. "Then I reckon we could both use the sin eater."

"And what good would it do to find him? We ain't dead yet."

"Maybe we could ask him to take our sins now."

"Why would he want to do that?"

"I don't know! But it's worth asking him, ain't it?"

He chewed on his lip, thinking. "All right," he said, looking grim. "Tomorrow. I'll meet you where Kai Creek joins the river. We're going hunting."

TEN

HIDING BEHIND A CURTAIN OF MOUNTAIN LAUREL, Fagan and I watched the crazy woman's cabin, waiting for some sign of her. Neither of us was brave enough to hello the house and bring her out, nor willing to admit our fear. It was early yet, and we used that ready excuse as we waited for the sunlight to spill over the valley floor and chase the shadows away. Both of us sat, getting wet with the heavy dew that dripped down from the leaves.

"I went down to listen to the man last night," Fagan whispered.

"What'd he say this time?"

"He kept calling out for us to come to him and hear the word of the Lord, and we'd have rest for our souls."

"We'd be resting, all right. In our graves after being struck dead."

"It dinna sound that way to me, but I wasn't going to walk across that river. Pa or one of my brothers would've seen me. They've kept watch off and on."

"I'm afeared of the mon, too, Fagan."

"I ain't afeared of *him*. I'm afeared what he'd *do*." He raked his hair back, frowning. "I don't reckon even Pa would do nothing to a man come from God."

I didn't say anything to that, for I was troubled in my mind remembering my nightmare. Besides that, Brogan Kai had looked able to do anything the day he had me by the throat. I reckoned Brogan Kai thought he was God. In this highland valley, at least.

A deer with her two fawns came into the open, grazing in the shadows not far from where we were hidden. Fagan sat up straighter, his attention fixed not on them but further on toward the forest. "Will ye look at that?" At the awe on his face, I looked to see a huge buck standing among the trees out of the edge of light, his antlers a majestic crown for a proud head. "Never seen one so big. Wish I had a gun."

"How con ye say that? He's so beautiful!"

"He'd feed a family through winter."

I glared at him, thankful all he had was a slingshot.

When the cabin door opened, the doe's head came up sharply, and she bounded away, the fawns on her heels. The buck melted into the forest. Fagan and I both leaned forward, peering through the dangling vines and waiting for Bletsung Macleod, the crazy woman, to appear.

She came outside in her long white nightgown, blonde hair curling down over her like a golden cascade clear past her waist. Stretching, she put the back of her hand to her mouth as she yawned. She walked along the porch and stood there at the end, gazing up at the mountain. She whistled like a bird and waited for a long moment. Then she whistled again, waiting once more.

"There it is," Fagan said. "Did ye hear it?"

"Yes," I whispered, for a whistle had come from the forest above.

"It's not like any bird I've ever heard before."

After that, Bletsung Macleod went back inside her house.

"Why don't you make her something, Katrina Anice?" Lilybet said, sitting not far away.

"Such as what?"

"I dinna say nothing," Fagan said, glancing back at me.

"It was Lilybet."

"Don't start acting crazy on me!"

"I'm not acting crazy!" Hurt, I got up.

"Where ye going?"

"Down to the creek to find some flowers."

"Flowers? *Now?*"

"To make a garland for her, Fagan. She might take more kindly to us coming to her place if we have summat for her. And since ye took it into your head to break the jar of preserves . . ."

"Go on then and get the flowers. I'll keep watch."

I picked my way through vines and briars and reached the water. "Why can't he see you?" I said to Lilybet. I was tired of her mysterious answers.

"You know why."

"Because ye don't exist. Because you're in my head."

Lilybet merely smiled as she sat on a moss-covered boulder, her blue eyes clear and filled with knowledge of me.

"Gervase Odara thinks you're a taint," I said stubbornly.

"She thinks I'm worse than that."

"But it's not fair."

"Life isn't fair. It's difficult. From the moment you draw your first breath to the last."

"Why does it have to be that way?"

"Because men are stubborn. They wanted their own way, and God allowed them to have it."

"And so Fagan and I must suffer."

"As all suffer. It's one long test of faith, refining you for what you were meant to be."

"And what's that?"

"Find out."

"Why can't I know now? Why can't ye just tell me?"

"Because you're stubborn, too. You still refuse to understand, even when the truth is all around you in everything you see from the depths of the earth to the stars in the heavens."

All the anger went from me, and my throat tightened with grief. "I don't want to be stubborn, Lilybet. I want to understand."

"You will find all the pieces, and God will bring them to light."

"When will that be?"

"In his time."

It didn't take me long to find all the flowers I needed, and Fagan was where I'd left him, peering through the vines. "She's still inside. She's stoked up the fire. See the smoke?"

I sat and worked quickly, making splits in the stems and tucking others through until I had made a garland for her hair. I kept thinking about all Lilybet had said to me, making sense of none of it. I looked at my handiwork and hoped Bletsung Macleod would like it better than Mama had. "It's done."

"It's a fine thing, Cadi." His words pleased me enough to make me blush. "Did your ma teach ye how to do it?"

"Granny taught me."

Gathering our courage, we went out into the open at the base of Dead Man's Mountain and approached the small cabin. "Hellllooo!" Fagan called and I held the wreath so that Bletsung Macleod would see it. When she didn't come out of her house, Fagan called out bolder, *"Heelllooo!"*

My heart jumped. "The curtain moved."

"Come on then. Don't hang back." Fagan motioned to me as he walked toward the house. "We brung ye summat, ma'am!"

"I don't want nothin'. Go away!"

"We're just being neighborly!"

"I said, 'Go away!'"

My shoulders drooped, but Fagan stood his ground, jaw tense. "We ain't leaving until ye come out and talk to us!" He sounded more like his father than I had ever heard him before.

"Fagan," I whispered, mortified. There was enough on my head without him making it worse.

"I told ye to stay away, Cadi Forbes, and now ye come back and bring this rude boy with ye! Git on! Git out o' here!"

Fagan blushed dark red. "I ain't meaning to be rude, ma'am, but we—Cadi and me, that is—need to talk to ye. We don't mean ye no harm." He nudged me. "Tell her!"

"We mean ye no harm, ma'am!" I called out to confirm his declaration. "And we brung ye summat."

After a long moment, Bletsung Macleod opened the door and came out onto the front porch. She was now dressed in a worn dark skirt and faded blue shirtwaist, her hair gathered into a hasty braid. "Why can't ye leave well enow alone, Cadi Forbes?" she said in a despairing tone. "Why can't ye stay away from this godforsaken place?"

"I gotta put the pieces together." I knew as I spoke that it made no sense to anyone, not even me. Fagan looked at me quizzically, but didn't say nothing.

Bletsung Macleod stayed in the shadows, standing near a post. She reminded me of the doe, ready to bound away at the first hint of danger. And it seemed odd, her being growed up and all. Seeing her like that made all my own fears seep away, and I was filled instead with a strange tenderness and pity toward her. "She's afeared of us, Fagan."

He sensed it too. "We'll go slowly."

As we came closer, she glanced quickly toward the forest, her movements tense of a moment. I looked toward the forest, too, wondering if she had seen something like a bear or a painter, but nothing was there out of the ordinary that I could see. So Fagan and I kept acomin' ahead until we was standing to the right of her front steps. I laid the flower garland on the porch at her feet and then backed away.

Bending, she picked it up and looked at it. She touched the

purple flower petals, then gazed at me, perplexed. "Thank ye, Cadi." It sounded almost a question. Her gaze moved to Fagan, studying him with a faint frown. "What be your name, lad?"

"Fagan, ma'am. Fagan Kai."

If anything, she grew more wary. "Brogan Kai's son?"

"Yes, ma'am."

"Ye dunna look like him."

"No, ma'am. People say I look more like my ma."

Tilting her head, she studied him. "Aye, 'tis true. Ye have your mother's eyes." Her mouth tipped sadly. "How be Iona these days?"

"She don't complain."

"Reckon she wouldn't." Bletsung Macleod glanced toward the forest again and then stepped forward, one slender, work-worn hand resting lightly on the rail. "She got what she wanted." She sighed and looked down at us again. She didn't ask why we had come. She wasn't going to make it that easy.

Fagan forgot all about the sin eater. "How do ye come by knowing my mother?"

"Everybody knows everybody in this valley." Her voice was heart-weary.

"I never heard of ye until a few months ago."

I wondered if Fagan knew how belligerent he sounded.

Closing her eyes, Bletsung Macleod lowered her head.

"Why ye saying things to hurt her?" I whispered fiercely.

Fagan's face jerked with pain. "I ain't trying to hurt her. I just want to know the truth." He looked up at the woman on the porch. "People say ye might have killed your own ma and pa."

She raised her head and looked at him, blue eyes dark with pain. "That so? What else do they say?"

Convinced Fagan had made a fine mess of our visit, I clutched his shirtsleeve, hoping the feel of my hand might give him pause. It didn't.

"Some say ye're crazy."

She just stood silent now, looking between us.

"Cadi here says ye're a bee charmer, and she thinks ye might know summat about the sin eater."

I could feel Bletsung Macleod's gaze fix upon me then. Troubled, she searched my face. "How old be ye, Cadi?"

"Ten, ma'am."

"Are ye ill? Do ye have a tumor or summat that's drawing the life from ye?"

"No, ma'am."

"Then go on home and forget about the sin eater."

"I can't."

Fagan stepped forward. "She has to talk to him, and so do I."

"He won't let ye near him."

"I have to ask him summat."

Her eyes flashed. "Questions! Sticking your nose in where it's none of your business. And what for? So ye con carry more rumors like your folks? Well, I won't help ye!" She started to turn away.

"I reckon if ye won't help us, we'll find the sin eater for ourselves," Fagan said, chin jutting.

Bletsung Macleod turned to us again and leaned forward so that the sun shone on her face. She did look half crazed. "You leave him be! Stop hunting him like he was an animal with no feelings!" She looked square at me. "For the love of mercy, Cadi Forbes, he's taken the sins of your granny on himself. Ye near got done in by a painter once, dinna ye? And he would have taken all your sins on him then, too. Can't ye be thankful for him and leave the mon be?"

Covering my face with my hands, I sobbed. Fagan put his arms around me, holding me close like Iwan sometimes did. "Ye've no call to talk to her like that and make her cry!"

"You're her friend, Fagan Kai. Make her see reason," she said wearily and went back inside the house. Both of us heard the bar drop heavily into place.

Fagan tried to cheer me up on the long walk home, but some feelings have to ease on their own. You can't talk them out or forget. Sometimes you can't even make sense of them. You just gotta walk on through.

I was not of a mind for hunting with Fagan. I didn't care to fish or pick flowers or do anything else but what my mind was determined to do. So when we come to Kai Creek, I told him I was going home.

As I walked through the woods, it came to me like a blinding flash of summer lightning: The only way Bletsung Macleod could've known about the painter was if the sin eater himself had told her.

Fagan went back with me three days running and then balked and went hunting. "She don't know nothing about the sin eater."

I followed after him for a while, hoping to change his mind, and then went back, taking up my vigil again behind the curtain of mountain laurel. I dozed off in the heavy moist warmth of the afternoon. When I woke, I saw Bletsung Macleod leaning out her window. I moved closer, wondering what she was doing talking to thin air.

Then I saw him. A man, sitting below her window.

Bletsung Macleod didn't look down at him, and he sat low down, head bowed. Was it a hat he was wearing? No, it was a hood!

My heart quickened, and I slunk along the edge of dense greens, careful not to set anything moving.

Bletsung looked out toward the mountains as she spoke. Though I was able to get closer, I was too far off to hear anything. She spoke and then listened. I wished I could hear what they were saying to each other. They seemed in no hurry to end their conversation. No one had died, so it was for certain she wasn't telling him he was needed at another funeral.

Heart thumping, I watched, intrigued by their camaraderie, wondering at it.

Bletsung Macleod stopped talking and listened a long while. Her lips moved again, and then she leaned further out the window, reaching down to him. He raised his hand toward hers. Their fingers were the barest inches apart when he withdrew. He stood and started quickly toward the forest. I saw he was slipping away again, and it was no telling how long it'd be before he came back now he knew I was watching for him.

"Sin Eater!" I cried out. I was through the vines and running. "Sin Eater! Wait! *Wait!*"

The man ran.

"Cadi, *no!*" Bletsung Macleod intercepted me, catching me before I reached the woods. "Cadi, no. You mustn't . . ." Tears were running down her cheeks. "Oh, child, child . . ."

Struggling and kicking, I gained my freedom and ran into the shadows, chasing after him, crying out for him to stop, to wait for me.

He would not.

I kept running, pushing through the tangled branches until I was utterly lost in the rhododendrons. Out of breath, I stopped and looked around me. I listened, hoping to hear some sound from him as he climbed higher, hiding among the crags above me.

Nothing.

"Sin Eater, where are you?" My lungs were burning, my heart racing.

Silence.

"I ain't going back until I talk to you!" I kept on, forcing my way through the snarls of green. Higher and higher I climbed, crying, lost and frightened. And determined.

Panting, I stopped again. "Please. I have to talk to you!" A streak of white lit the gray-clouded sky, and my skin tingled. The patter of rain splattered the leaves and thunder rolled. "Sin Eater! Sin Eater!"

"I'm here."

I turned sharply toward the sound of his voice lost somewhere in the heavy rhododendrons. He was close, so close. "I can't see you." I pushed my way through several branches.

"Ye can talk from where ye stand."

I stood still but a moment. "I left some preserves out for ye on Granny's grave, but ye never came back."

"I dinna know of your kindness toward me."

"They ain't there anymore. Fagan broke the jar. I'll get ye more if ye want. Mama has a shelf of jars. She won't miss one."

"No, don't do that. I'm not in want."

No, he had fresh bread and honey from Bletsung Macleod. "Jam goes good with bread."

I heard the rustling of branches and knew he was the same distance from me as he had been before. Each step I took, he was a step further off, maybe two.

Sorrow gripped me. "Ye talk to Bletsung Macleod. Why won't ye talk to me?"

"We're talking, ain't we?" There was gentle humor in the words.

His voice came from another direction now. Turning again, I kept on. I paid no heed to the direction I was going, and only vaguely noticed that the going was easier. "Would ye take my sins away, Sin Eater?"

"Ye know I will, Cadi. When the time comes. Unless I'm gone. Then there'll be another to take my place."

"I mean *now*."

"It ain't done that way, darlin'."

I stopped, heartbroken. "But why not? What con I do to show I'm sorry? I'd do anything." He was silent so long, I thought he had left me there alone. "Is there no forgiveness for one such as me, Sin Eater? What con I do to make up for what I did?"

"Ye con do right from here on, Cadi. That's what ye do. Ye help other people without thinking about the cost to yourself. Ye live your life to please God Almighty. And ye hope, Cadi. Ye hope and ye pray that in the end he'll forgive you. Ye try to get by on that."

He sounded so grievous sad, my throat and chest tightened. "I try, Sin Eater, I try so hard, but that don't change what's been done already."

"No, it doesn't."

"I'm sorry to be asking ye to take on more, Sin Eater, but I don't know who else con help me. And I canna go to the man of God with my sins upon me."

"What man of God?"

"The stranger who's come into the valley. He's down by the river. He came up by the Narrows and speaks in the name of the Lord." The sin eater said nothing for so long, I called out to him again. "Where are you?"

"I haven't left ye, Cadi, my dear. Be still and hear me out."

"I'm listening."

"If I try and take your sins away, will ye do summat for me in return, Cadi Forbes?"

"Anything!" My heart raced. "I'll do *anything!*"

"Tomorrow, ye come back. Bletsung Macleod will show ye the path. Bring me what's necessary for the ceremony. I'll eat the bread and drink the wine and say the prayer, and we'll see what God will allow."

I began to shake, emotions suddenly at war within me. Hope. Joy. Fear.

"And whatever happens, Cadi, ye have to promise me ye'll do whatever I ask of ye. Will ye now?"

"I promise."

"I've your word on it?"

"Yes! I promise! I cross my heart and hope to die, Sin Eater. I'll do whatever ye ask."

There was a still quiet for a long moment, and then he spoke softly. "Keep walking, Cadi. A few more steps. Do ye see the path?"

"Yes."

"Until tomorrow then, and God have mercy on us both." I heard him no more after that.

The path led me down the mountain to Bletsung Macleod's small meadow. It went straight to the space beneath her window. She was framed there, watching for me. As soon as I appeared at the edge of the woods, she came out to meet me. I thought she meant to take me to task for hitting and kicking her. She had the right.

"He let ye speak with him?"

I raised my eyes and saw no anger. "Yes, ma'am. I reckon he figured I'd never leave off following him unless he did."

"Do ye feel the better for it?"

"Some, ma'am, but I'll feel even better tomorrow."

"Tomorrow?"

"He said to come back with bread and wine."

"Oh." Lifting her head, she gazed up at the mountain, troubled.

"I'm sorry I kicked ye, Miz Macleod. I had to talk to the sin eater. I just had to . . ."

She looked down at me again and ran her hand gently over my hair. "I forgive ye, Cadi. I understand." Her eyes grew moist with tears. "We all have to do what we must do. You go on home now." As I walked away, she called out to me. "Cadi? Ye con come down to the cabin tomorrow, if ye like. After ye talk to the sin eater. I'll have honey cakes ready for you."

Her invitation surprised and touched me deeply. "Thank ye kindly, ma'am." I raced off happily. All I needed now to complete my quest was the necessary things for the ceremony. And I knew who might be called upon to give them to me.

"Now, what would ye be wanting wine and bread for, I wonder," Miz Elda said with a dry smile. "Think ye've found the sin eater, do ye?"

"I have! He lives on Dead Man's Mountain, just like ye said he did."

"Don't go spreading around who told ye. Brogan Kai'll take offense at my meddlin'. Did Fagan see him, too?"

"Fagan gave up and went hunting."

"More's the pity, but then again, maybe that boy'll bring me another plump squirrel for my cook pot."

"I could bring ye some salt pork and smoked venison, if ye'd like."

"Ye could, aye? Ye gonna ask permission this time or just steal it out from under yer mama's nose like ye did those berry preserves?"

I blushed. My sins were ever before me. "I'll ask. I promise."

"Ye could ask 'em for wine and bread, too."

The heat drained from my face. "No, ma'am, I couldn't."

Miz Elda took my hand. "Maybe askin' 'em would give 'em a sign how deep ye hurt inside."

"They know." Mama must believe it was right for me to suffer. But I could see she was suffering, too, and it was a suffering I had brought upon her.

The old woman patted my hand tenderly. "Reckon they got their own guilt to carry, Cadi."

I frowned, wondering at her words. "Mama and Papa ain't never done nothing wrong."

"You don't think so?"

I pulled my hand from hers. "I know so."

"Honey chile, ye dunna ken nothin' yet about this valley or the people in it." She looked away from me, leaning her head back and closing her eyes. "Don't matter though. No matter how deep the truth gets buried, it always comes to light."

I left the house before daybreak, careful not to awaken anyone. The moon was full and cast a glow over the meadowlands. I wondered about the man of God down there by the river as I hurried along the pathway to Miz Elda's cabin. Her lantern was burning. When I tapped at the door, she called for me to come on in and said, "I been up all night thinking about ye. Everything's ready, dearie."

On the table was a half-filled jar of blackberry wine, a small loaf of bread, and a white shroud.

I hugged her. She returned the embrace. As I drew back, she cupped my face. "Ye tell the sin eater that Miz Elda Kendric sends him a fond hello. Will ye do that for me, Cadi?"

"Yes, ma'am."

"And tell him summat else for me, too, Cadi. Tell him I ain't never forgotten his name."

"Will ye tell it to me, Miz Elda?"

"It's for him to say, honey chile." She smiled sadly and released me. "Fagan gonna meet ye there?"

"Fagan doesna know I'm going. This is between me and the sin eater."

"And God. Don't ever forget God's the one who'll say yea or nay to us in the end."

"I've never been able to get him outta my mind." It was fear of him that drove me. I wanted desperately to be cleansed of my sins so I wouldn't be judged too harshly and spend eternity burning in hell.

"I'll be thinking of ye, Cadi. I'll keep ye in mind until ye come back and tell me all about it. So don't leave me wondering. Ye hear?"

I promised, took the shroud, the wine, and the bread, and hurried on. My goal was just within reach. My soul would at last be at rest within me.

The path behind Bletsung Macleod's dark cabin wound upward to the heights. I was tired by the time I got there, hurrying so far. It was a goodly distance from our end of the valley. Pausing to rest, I lifted my eyes to the mountain. From whence shall my help come? Wondering if I'd have to climb clear to the top before I found the sin eater again, I set off, determined to find my salvation.

The sin eater came to meet me. "I'm here, Cadi." His gentle deep voice came softly from the forest. "Ye need climb no further."

"I brought the wine and bread, sir. Miz Elda gave it to me." My heart was thumping wildly. I was sore afraid of him. "She said to tell ye she thinks fondly of ye and she hasn't forgotten your name." I turned full circle and still could not see him.

"Thank her for me," he said softly from the trees on the steep slope above me.

"Will ye tell me your name?"

"I have no name anymore. I'm lost to all I was and ever hoped to be."

I bit my lip, wavering. "I'm sorry I'm asking more of ye."

"Lie upon the earth, Cadi, and put the white cloth over ye. And then set the bottle of wine and bread upon your chest."

I did so, shaking violently. Setting the jar and bread at my side where I could feel them, I lay back on the cool earth and drew the shroud up, covering myself from my feet to the top of my head. Feeling for the jar and bread, I placed them on my chest and held them there so they wouldn't fall.

Trembling, I heard the sin eater come from his hiding place in the forest green. His footsteps were soft. As he came very near, I heard him sigh.

"Do ye want to tell me what ye did that grieves ye so, Cadi Forbes?"

The heat of shame filled me. "Do I have to? Did Granny tell ye all her sins? Or any of the others afore they died?"

"No."

"Did ye know what they were after ye took them upon yerself?"

"Some of their sins I knew, Cadi. Like everyone else knew. Some sins are plain as day. Others are hidden deep into the very heart. Those are the worst. The secret sins are like a cancer to the soul. I never know what they are. I just . . . take what's given."

"I don't want to speak aloud of what I done." I was trembling and kept my eyes tight shut. "I don't want ye to know."

He took the jar of wine and small loaf of bread from me. He was careful not to touch my hands. I reckoned he didn't want to stain me further with the sins he already carried. And then he spoke. "Lord God Almighty, I am willing to take Cadi Forbes's sins upon myself . . . if ye are willing."

My throat ached with tears. He sounded so sad, so deeply burdened. I listened to him eat the bread and drink the wine and felt ashamed. I waited, scarcely breathing, praying my sins would be taken away. I waited for my burdens to be lifted so that my heart would not feel so heavy within me, like a stone pulling me down into darkness.

Nothing happened.

"I give easement and rest now to thee, Cadi Forbes, dear child, that ye walk not over fields or mountains or along pathways. And for thy peace I pawn my own soul."

I lay still as death, waiting and waiting. Relief did not come. I felt heavier than I ever had before, so heavy I thought I might sink into the earth itself and be swallowed up. I had listened to the gentle voice of the sin eater and heard him partake of the meal of my sins. I had not felt ease at all, but a terrible consuming anguish and pity for the man beside me. He had tried—and failed—to save my soul.

I knew I was doomed.

"Why do ye weep so, Cadi Forbes?"

I had come to the end of my struggling, and my fate was before me. God knew me for the sinner I was. God would decide what he would do to me. I knew what I deserved: death and a fiery pit of eternal torture and damnation.

Curling on my side, I bunched the shroud about my face and wept. "What must I do to be saved?"

The sin eater sighed. "I wish I knew, Cadi. Oh, how I wish I knew." He rose, moving away from me a ways and standing in the shadows of the forest. He waited there, letting me cry myself out. "Ye said ye would do whatever I asked no matter what happened, Cadi. Do ye remember?"

"I remember." I raised my head against the dullness that swept over me. He moved behind a tree, hiding himself from me.

"Will ye keep your word to a sin eater?"

"I'll keep my word to ye." I needed no more sins upon my conscience.

"Then this is what I ask of you."

I knew after he told me that my life would soon be over.

ELEVEN

"*H*OW LONG HAS SHE BEEN LIKE THIS?" PAPA ASKED
from where he stood looking down at me on my cot.

"Since she came home." Mama stood behind him.

He knelt down, touching my forehead. "Did ye eat summat
in the woods?" When I shook my head, he frowned. "She ain't
feverish."

"She's gone all day long, every day. Disappears right after doing her chores."

"Where does she go?"

"I don't know."

Papa's jaw clenched as he stroked my hair back from my face.
"Where do ye go, Cadi? Why do ye stay away so much?"

Lip quivering, I turned my face to the wall. I could've told
him what ailed me. Plain old fear—gut deep and spreading
through every part of me. The sin eater had told me what he
wanted and reminded me I'd given my word. Oh, that I hadn't
been so desperate and reckless to promise before knowing what
he'd expect. And now, it was too late to back out. But telling
everything to Papa would only bring trouble on others, and I
had enough trouble of my own.

Papa glanced up at Mama. "Did she tell ye where she's been
going?"

"I dinna ask."

Papa rose, angry. "Why not? Don't ye care?"

"Ye canna change her nature, Angor."

"So ye let her run wild? Ye let her make friends with taints?"

I glanced around as Mama turned her back to him. "I saw she was feeling poorly and told her to go to bed," she said in a thin voice.

"Seems to me, ye could've asked her how she came to feel so poorly."

"I doubt she'd tell me."

"A ready excuse."

"What's the use in trying to make ye understand!" She walked across the room and sat down before her loom. She clenched her hands in her lap and stared straight ahead. "Do ye really think so little of me, Angor? Do ye think your harsh words canna hurt me?"

He followed, back rigid. "No more than ye hurt others with your silence. Elen's gone! She's *dead!* Are ye not afeared of losing Cadi, too?"

"I lost her a long time ago." She raised trembling hands to her work. "Both at once."

"Ahhhh—!" Papa cut the air with a disgusted wave of his hand. "I'm getting Gervase Odara."

The healer made me drink a tonic. It was not honey, vinegar, and blackberry wine. It was vile-tasting stuff meant to purge whatever poisons were sickening me. And purge they did, adding to my travail. She stayed with me through the day, holding my head and later bathing me. I was wrung out.

When evening came, Gervase Odara dozed in the chair beside my cot while Papa sat outside on the porch and Mama sat before her loom. Her hands lay idle in her lap, and she stared silently out the window.

I felt like a lonely bird on the housetop. My heart was withering like burning grass within me. I lay upon my cot, knowing the first breath of God upon me was going to blow me straight to hell.

I ate the bread Gervase Odara gave me though it tasted like ashes, and I swallowed tears, mingled with the fresh warm milk Iwan brung me. He sat with me awhile, not talking about anything in particular—leastwise nothing I remember.

By evening, I was resolved. I'd keep my promise to the sin eater, come what may.

"She seems better," Gervase Odara said, for if one could eat, she reckoned they were on the mend. I could not tell her that it was my last meal before I was done to death. She put on her shawl and headed for home. Papa, relieved of worry, went to bed, snoring as soon as his head touched the straw mattress. Iwan did likewise on the cot on the porch.

Only Mama sat in the moonlight awhile longer, her lovely face like a pale white mask. She rose after a while, took her hair down, brushed it out, and braided it for the night. Then she came to me and sat for a long while beside my cot, her shawl held tightly around her. Leaning forward, she placed her hand on my brow. I held very still, pretending to be asleep, my throat closed tight, aching.

"I don't know how to make things right between us, Cadi. I reckon God himself will have to do it."

I reckoned God would make things right by morning. By then I'd be dead.

Oh, how I craved Lilybet's company. Where had she gone? Why did she not come to me when I needed her? And Granny. How I missed her and ached to talk with her again. I remembered the night she was buried and the first time I'd laid eyes on the sin eater. He had come to take her sins away. But had he? And even if he had, what good was having your sins taken away if you were already dead and in the grave?

"Eagles fly higher in a storm. . . . Trees grow strong in stiff winds. . . . Our mountains and valley drink water from the rains of heaven." Lessons from Granny. And I couldn't help but wonder. Would I remember those I held so dear when I was no more?

When all were in bed asleep, I rose from my cot and went down the mountain path to keep my promise to the sin eater.

Moonlight shone on the ripples as I stood on the bank of the river, looking across at the camp on the other side. The man of God was there, sitting in the open, forearms resting on his raised knees, his head bowed. I could not tell if he was awake or sleeping. Truth was, it didn't matter. Fear gripped me so tight I wanted to turn and run away as fast as I had before. I wanted to be far away from this place, from this man.

"I want ye to go hear the word of the Lord, Cadi Forbes, and then come back to me."

I had given my word and could not go back upon it. "I have to keep my promise," I whispered under my breath, trying to give myself courage. "I have to keep my word."

"Cross the river to the Promised Land," the man from God had called out once. *"Cross the river . . ."*

As I stepped into the biting cold water and started across, the current pulled at my legs. It was a wide stretch across slippery, round pebbles. Whenever I'd crossed the river before, it had always been further up where I could jump from rock to rock and never touch the water. The river here was as high as my knees. I wondered what it would be like to slip and fall and be swept along to the Narrows and down over the falls. A few moments of terror and then darkness.

Justice.

When I saw the man of God raise his head, I stopped midriver, my heart lodging like a flapping bird in my throat. I was in the open where he could see me plain in the moonlight. Closing my eyes, I waited for the lightning to strike me dead. A moment passed, then another, then another. I opened one eye cautiously. He was still sitting, still looking at me. Silent. Waiting.

I came ahead slowly, feeling my way with my cold-numbed toes. Shivering, I walked slowly up the bank and stood before him, waiting for the end to come.

"You're but a child." He sounded disappointed.

Hanging my head, I remained silent, ashamed of my sins and sorry others hadn't come instead of me. It should have been Papa or Mama or Gervase Odara or any number of others to come hear the word of the Lord. It should've been Brogan Kai himself leading the people of our highland valley down to hear what God had to say to us. What shame this, that I, least worthy, should be the one? *A child.* Oh, no. I was more than that. I was a frightened coward, a vessel of sins, a girl cast so low there was only judgment left.

"Sit," the man of God said and I did, Indian fashion, hands clasped tightly in my lap. I could feel him studying me. "You're shaking." He reached out and picked up a dark wool coat.

"I ain't cold, sir." It was pure terror had me trembling so.

He cocked his head slightly, as though seeing me better. He put the coat aside. "'Fear of the Lord is the beginning of knowledge.'"

My throat was closed tight, pulse throbbing. I remembered those words. He had said them before.

"Why do you come?"

I swallowed hard. "To hear the word of the Lord, sir." Plunging ahead, I pleaded before he had time to say no. "I ken the word of the Lord ain't meant for the likes of me, sir, but there's another who craves the words ye've brung and canna come near." Like a whisper in my ear, I remembered Miz Elda. "Nay, not one, sir. There are two."

"The boy who hides in the bushes?"

I had forgotten all about Fagan. "Two others," I amended yet again.

"And what keeps them from coming of their own free will?"

He sounded so stern, I had to work my mouth to get enough spit to speak. "Miz Elda is too old and frail to make the trek down. She says ye con come up and see her if ye like."

"And the other?"

"He ain't supposed to venture into the valley unless someone's died. Reckon there'd be big trouble if he did."

The man of God said nothing for a long moment. He bowed his head and remained that way, as though deep in thought. I wondered if he was asking God's permission to speak to me. The palms of my hands grew damp. I closed my eyes, hoping hard he would be permitted—and I wouldn't be laid out dead where I sat.

He raised his head slightly. " 'The Lord is nigh unto them that are of a broken heart, and saveth such as be of a contrite spirit.' "

His deep voice was so gentle, my heart slowed its mad pace. I found I could breathe again.

"It is the Lord who giveth wisdom. Out of his mouth cometh knowledge and understanding. And he who dwells in the shelter of the Most High will abide in the shadow of the Almighty. The Lord redeemeth the soul of his servant and none who trust in Him shall be desolate."

He spread his hands and lifted his face to the heavens. The faint sheen of moonlight showed me his features. His expression held a strange rapture. "O Lord, thou art a shield for me; my glory and the lifter up of mine head. I cried unto thee. I laid down and slept and awaked again, for the Lord sustained me against those who have set themselves against me round about. And ye have brought one to hear thy word everlasting. O Father, the Spirit of the Lord God is upon me because the Lord hath anointed me to preach good tidings unto the meek. Ye have come to bind up the broken-hearted, to proclaim liberty to the captives and the opening of the prison to them that are bound; to proclaim the acceptable year of the Lord and the day of vengeance of our God; to comfort all that mourn; to give unto them beauty for ashes, the oil of joy for mourning, the garment of praise for the spirit of heaviness; that they might be called trees of righteousness, the planting of the Lord, that he might be glorified!"

Aggrieved, I tried to soak it all in, every word. But how could I remember what made little sense to me? I waited until he stopped talking. Trembling, cold with fear, I craved under-standing more than life. "If ye'll pardon me beforehand, sir, might I ask ye summat?"

"Ask and ye shall receive."

"What's a prison, sir? And what captives do ye mean? Only ones I've ever heard tell of was taken by Indians years ago and never heard of again."

"These are not the things of which I speak."

"I want to understand. I do."

"Lord, give me thy words. Open this child's heart and mind so that she might hear the word of the Lord and carry it with her. You know I've never been around children . . ." His voice grew quieter until it was but a mumble—perhaps even a grumble.

I closed my eyes in despair. Miz Elda and the sin eater would've done better coming themselves. This man was not eager to impart the word of the Lord to such as me. And if he did, it seemed fair clear to me that it was not likely I'd understand it anyway.

He sighed heavily and raised his head again, looking at me.

I waited, determined not to move until I had something to take back to the sin eater.

"Listen and learn, child. When the world was fresh and new, having just been spoken into existence by God, he created a man and a woman and placed them in the Garden of Eden. He loved them and gave them everything they needed, and gave them free-dom in all things except one. They were not to eat the fruit of one tree. But one day, in the midst of Paradise, a serpent, Satan, came to the woman and deceived her so that she did eat of it and then gave the fruit to her husband to eat as well. Because of what they did, God cast them out of the Garden of Eden.

"Though they repented, the damage had already been done. Sin and death had been brought into the world. With each gen-eration, sin grew like a weed until the very heart of man was evil. In time, God gave laws so that men might know what manner of evil they did and turn to God for deliverance. But they were stubborn and stiff-necked and would not trust him. Those he had rescued from Egypt rebelled against him and worshiped idols. So God made them wander in the desert until they all died and then brought their children across the river Jordan and into the Promised Land.

"Still, man did not change. They sinned and sinned again. God would punish them, and they would repent and cry out to God for deliverance. And God would forgive out of his gra-ciousness and mercy, his loving-kindness and compassion. They would grow prosperous once more and reject the Lord for other gods and idols. Generation upon generation."

I understood, for was he not speaking of me? No matter how hard I tried, I still sinned. Evil preyed upon me, and I did the very things I didn't want to do. Elen. *Oh, Elen.* I closed my mind to thoughts of her, knowing the choking grief would keep me from hearing anything more.

"Yet God had a plan, even from the beginning of time. He knew all that would happen, and he knew how to make the way for man to return to him. For man can do nothing for himself. Yet with God all things are possible."

He paused briefly, then rose, pacing. After a while, he came back and hunkered down. "Far from here is a place where civilization began, and it is called Judea. One thousand, eight hundred and fifty years ago, in the days of evil King Herod, God sent his angel Gabriel to a city near the Sea of Galilee called Nazareth to a virgin girl set to wed a man named Joseph. The virgin's name was Mary. The angel told her not to fear for God favored her. The Holy Spirit would come upon her and give her a child, and she was to name him Jesus."

I looked at him, eyes wide. "I've heard of Jesus."

"What have you heard?"

"My granny said Jesus was betrayed and nailed up on a cross to die."

"And?"

"He rose up from the grave and went to heaven where he sits at the right hand of God. And he'll come back on the last day and judge us all."

"Did she teach you anything else?"

"She said we must do as much good as we can while we breathe, for we'll all be judged by how we've lived. If we do enow, when Jesus comes back, he might take us to heaven."

"And ye think people can do enough good to undo the evil done?"

I thought of Elen. I thought of dozens of wicked things I'd thought and done before that terrible, fateful day, and I thought of the dozens of sins I'd committed since then. And I knew. Nothing—absolutely nothing—would be enough to undo the sins on my soul. Bowing my head, I put my face in my hands and cried.

"Ah, child, you are heavy burdened."

"There is no hope. Not for me."

"Do not weep, child. God *is* your hope. He did not send Jesus to condemn the world. He sent him so that all who believe in him might be saved and have eternal life."

"But I do believe! I do! And I'm not saved."

"You believe Jesus lived. You believe he was crucified and

went to heaven. Hear the word of the Lord. Jesus was born of a woman, became strong in spirit, performed miracles, and never sinned. Not once in thought or deed did Jesus disobey God the Father for he was God the Son incarnate. He went willingly to the cross to die and took all our sins upon himself."

"Oh!" Something tight within me flowered. Could it be I understood rightly? "You mean he's just like our sin eater!"

"Your what?"

"The sin eater. He comes after people die, and he eats the bread and drinks the wine and takes all their sins upon himself so that they can rest in peace."

"And you believe this?"

"Everybody believes. Well, almost everybody. I don't know anymore what I believe. I went to him and asked him to take my sins away. And he tried."

"No man can take away your sins. Only God."

"But Granny said God canna even look on sin. That's why we've got to have the sin eater."

"And how did he come to be?"

"I reckon he was chosen."

"How?"

"I don't rightly know, sir."

"What's his name?"

"I don't know. Miz Elda said as soon as he was made the sin eater, he had to leave his family and live off by himself, and nobody was ever to speak his name aloud again. And no one's to look at him when he comes down to eat up the sins."

"And what becomes of him?"

"I reckon when he dies, he takes all the sins with him to hell."

The man of God lifted his head and looked to the heavens. "And one of the enemies of Jesus named Caiaphas, being the high priest, said, 'It is expedient for us, that one man should die for the people, and that the whole nation perish not.'"

"That's the way of it, sir. Is it wrong?"

"It is wrong, and you must have a care for the man himself."

"I do, sir. He was kind to me and has cared for us."

"And he's been deceived and sorely used. If you've come for the truth, child, hear and receive it. Only Jesus Christ, the Lamb of God, can take away sins. This man you call the sin eater is being used by Satan to stand in the way of truth. He is a scapegoat. He has no power in and of himself for any good thing."

Sorrow filled me until I thought I would perish of it. How could I tell the sin eater this without grieving his heart to death?

The rosy hint of dawn was on the horizon, and I knew I must go before Papa or Iwan awakened and I was missed. I rose, hands clasped tightly. "Thank ye kindly for speaking with me, sir."

"I am not finished speaking with you, child."

"If I dunna go now, I'll be missed and there'll be trouble. Can I come back?"

"I will stay here until God tells me otherwise. But don't wait long. We've not much time left."

I started toward the river and paused to look back. "Sir, I must warn ye. There are some who would see you dead and gone."

"The Lord is my strength and shield."

Feeling foolish, I remembered the lightning and reckoned God could take care of him if he wanted.

The man of God sat watching me as I waded back across the river. Safely on the other side, I looked back and raised my hand. When he raised his hand in response, I felt a tiny spark of hope. Ducking into the forest, I raced for home.

T W E L V E

$\mathcal{A}$ STRANGE EXCITEMENT FILLED ME. I COULD NOT GET out of my head what the man of God had told me. I was bursting to talk about it all with Miz Elda, but Mama was of a mind to keep me about the home place all day. When I said I was well enough to be up and about, she said I did look better and sent me to gather eggs and pick peas to snap on the front porch. I worked quickly, eager to be away. Oh, how I yearned to talk over what the man of God had told me, but I dared not speak a word of it to Mama. She'd only tell Papa, and then I'd likely spend the rest of my days locked in the woodshed for going against the Kai.

When the peas was all snapped, Mama handed me the broom and set me to sweeping out the house and sweeping off the porch. Finishing that, she called me to help her with the wash. She was slow and thorough in all she did, so slow and thorough I was tensed up through and through. I felt so tied up inside that I feared something might spring loose.

"Ye're fidgeting worse than a dog with fleas," Mama said, scrubbing one of Papa's shirts against the washboard. I tried to stand still, but it was near impossible.

Mama paused and straightened, wiping some curling strands of dark hair back from her sweat-beaded forehead. "Ye do it awhile." She stepped aside, her eyes barely brushing mine. She watched me from a few feet away. "Ye used to chatter like a magpie. Now ye say nary a thing from morning 'til night."

It was a strange thing for her to say to me, considering her long silences. She only spoke to me to tell me what to do, never wanting a peek at my thoughts.

"Gervase told me ye've been spending time with Miz Elda." She looked away toward the valley.

Nervous and perplexed, I glanced at Mama, a little afraid of what she might be thinking. Why was she talking to me now after so many long months of silence? Why was she asking questions? I wished she'd look at me, look straight into my eyes and hold still long enough for me to get a feel of what it was she was feeling and trying to say.

She sighed. "Reckon ye miss Granny."

I did, indeed, but I ached to tell Mama I missed *her* more. My eyes pricked with tears. I had missed Mama long before the fateful day her last small bit of love for me had died.

Mama did look my way then. She met my gaze, but in an instant hers skittered away, dropping and holding to my idle hands. "Dunna forget to scrub the collar."

Dipping Papa's shirt in the washtub, I rubbed hard against the metal board, trying to scrub away the pain in my chest. I must be terrible indeed for Mama to wince so. She walked a few feet away and stood in the shade, face averted. Once she raised her hand and brushed her cheek. I knew she was crying again. Silent tears for Elen, for Granny, for those she'd loved and lost.

Fagan came by our place next day. Iwan met him as he came up the hill and talked with him a short while. Then Fagan went off toward home again, and Iwan went back to work. I was helping Mama peel and core apples and cut them into quarters to fill a ten-gallon wooden tub for bleaching with sulfur. When Iwan came up to the house for nooning, he didn't say anything about Fagan's visit, not until I asked straight-out why he'd come by.

Iwan shrugged. "Dinna say." He tore off a hunk of bread and dipped it into his bowl of stew. "Reckon he wanted to go hunting, but I dinna have time today." He ate his bread. "Said Miz Elda was asking about ye though."

"What about her?" Papa said, brows coming down.

"Said she hadn't seen Cadi in days and wondered if summat was wrong with her."

I looked at Mama. "Can I go for a visit, Mama? Please."

"Ask your father," she said tonelessly, picking at her food but not eating much.

"Papa?"

He looked at me hard and long, though what he was searching for I could not even guess. "Ye can go to Miz Elda's and nowhere else. And be back home before sundown. Hear me?"

"Yes, sir." I cleared my dishes and lit out the door like a mouse avoiding a cat's stare. I ran the whole way to Miz Elda's cabin and found her sitting and rocking on her front porch.

She took her pipe of rabbit tobacco out of her mouth. "Thought ye got lost on Dead Man's Mountain."

"Sick." Panting hard, I waited for my lungs to stop burning. "Saw him."

"Did he take away your sins?"

I shook my head. Still too out of breath to speak, I gestured.

"What're ye pointing to the valley fer?"

"Saw *him.*"

"Down there? The Kai hears he's coming down from his mountain and there'll be hell to pay. Settle down, child. I don't know what ye're trying to tell me. Now go on down to the crik and get yourself a drink of water. Ye ain't making a lick of sense."

Dropping on my knees beside her stream, I splashed water on

my heated face and cupped more in my hands to drink. I had run so hard I was afraid I would lose what I ate. I waited a few minutes until my wind was back and my stomach settled, then hastened back. "The sin eater made me promise him I'd do whatever he asked even if he couldn't eat my sins and take 'em away."

"And he dinna?"

"He tried, Miz Elda. He tried real hard. He ate the bread ye gave me and drank the wine and said all the right words. And I felt the worse for it."

"Worse?"

"All I could think about was him and how sad he sounded and what I was asking him to do for me. And it dinna work. It was all for naught."

"Ye said he made ye promise to do summat for him whatever happened."

"He told me to hear the word of the Lord from the man of God camped down in the valley and come back and tell him what was said."

"And ye went?"

"I went. Night before last. I thought the man'd strike me down with lightning sure, but he let me come across and sit with him. And now, I don't know what I'm going to tell the sin eater."

"Tell him what you was told."

"I can't, Miz Elda! It'll hurt his feelings summat fierce."

"Why?"

"'Cause that man of God says the sin eater ain't got no power to take away sins. Fact is, he's standing in the way of God. He called him a scapegoat and said Jesus Christ is the Lamb of God who takes away sins, and there ain't no other who can do it. He said he had more to tell me, but I had to get home before daybreak or get tanned and locked up 'til I'm old as you."

"Are ye going back and hear the rest?"

"Soon as I can. Only Mama is keeping me so busy doing chores, I ain't got time to go nowhere."

"Ye're here, ain't ye?"

"Papa said I could come, but I have to be back before sundown. That don't give me much time. I can't go out there and hear the word of God in daylight. If someone sees me, the Kai will hear and that man'll get himself shot dead."

"Well, then, ye go on back home and tell yer pa ye're needed by an old woman who's been feeling poorly of late."

"Are you?" I looked her over, worried. She didn't look no worse than usual.

"Quit looking at me like I had one foot in the grave. Go on home and ask yer mama if ye can stay a few nights with me. Tell her I'm needing help and would be gratified if she'd loan ye to me for a few days. That oughta give ye time to hear the whole piece that man's got to say. Ye reckon they'll have any problems with that?"

"Mama won't care. It's always Papa wanting to know what I'm doing and where I've been. And I think the only reason he's interested is 'cause he thinks I'm keeping company with a taint."

Miz Elda gave me a droll look, her pipe clenched between her teeth. "Now what would make him think a crazy thing like that?" She waved her hand in dismissal. "Quit yer bellyaching and git on home and ask."

"They'll likely tell me to fetch Gervase Odara for ye."

"Tell 'em I already seen her and been taking her cures, but I crave a bit of company and someone to fetch and carry for me. Don't give me that look, child. Say it exactly like I tell ye, and if yer pa wants to come take a look for himself, let him come."

"He'll see ye looking healthy and ornery as ever."

"Think so?" Miz Elda took her pipe from her mouth, sagged in her rocker, and let her mouth hang open and her eyelids droop. She looked about as bad as a body could get without being put in a grave. When I giggled, she straightened up in her rocker and glowered at me same as always. "Now, go on, afore I come to my senses and tell ye to stand wide and clear of that prophet down there."

Papa did go over and talk with Miz Elda. He left me home while he was about it, and it was near dusk when he came back. Mama was raking coals off of the Dutch oven when he came in. "Miz Elda don't look so good and sounds even worse. The poor ol' soul ain't long for this world."

"Ain't surprising." Mama hooked the handle and dragged the oven onto the hearthstones. As she lifted the lid, the rich aroma of venison stew filled the cabin while I set the table.

"After supper, Iwan'll walk Cadi over."

"Thank ye, Papa!" I said, excited and wishing I was on my way already.

Mama glanced from me to him. "What good's Cadi gonna be to that sick old lady?"

"Miz Elda likes her company. Says she takes pleasure in listening to her chatter. Says it's been a long time since she's had children around, her own going over the mountain the way they did."

Mama straightened, her hands at her sides. "She sent 'em away."

"So's they'd have a better life."

"And she ain't never heard from 'em since. Is that for the best?"

Papa leaned toward her slightly, like a bull ready to butt horns. "Reckon Elda Kendric knew to put her children's needs above her own wants." At Mama's stricken look, he turned his back on her and looked at me. "Go on out and get washed up, Cadi. And fetch your brother for supper."

"Wait, Cadi," Mama said sternly. "Who'll do her chores while she's gone?"

"I told ye to go on," Papa said to me. "Now go!"

At his tone, I did as I was told. But before I was out the door I heard him turn back to Mama and snarl, "Leave off making mourning jewelry out of Granny's hair and weaving that blanket in memory of Elen, and I reckon ye'll have *plenty* of time."

I found Iwan in the barn working over a harness.

"Papa wants us to wash up for supper."

"Is that all? Ye look like ye had summat important to tell me."

"I'm gonna be staying with Miz Elda for a while."

"How long a while?"

"Couple of days, maybe more."

"Ye don't look unhappy about it," he said with a questioning frown.

"I don't mind." I wanted to tell him why, but knew he'd feel obliged to tell Papa. It wasn't in Iwan's nature to go against him in anything. And he'd never in his life consider bucking the Kai. If I told Iwan I'd been down to hear the man of God and was going again so's I could carry what I learned to the sin eater, he'd make certain I never made it out of the yard. "She's a nice old woman."

He laughed. "Nice! I hear Miz Elda's as cantankerous as a hedgehog."

"Only when her bones're aching. Besides, she was Granny's dear friend."

"She was that."

Mama and Papa didn't say a word to each other through supper. "Take some smoked venison with ye," Papa told Iwan, "and a few jars of preserves. Miz Elda ain't been well enow to do much for herself."

"If it's all right, Pa, I'll go by Cluny's on the way home," Iwan said. "Moon's full enow tonight to see my way home."

Papa smiled knowingly. "Do that. She's a pretty little gal and growing up fast. Take the gun with ye. Ye might run into the painter that's been killing sheep."

The evening was filled with frog song and fireflies dancing. Iwan walked cautious, the gun tucked secure under his arm, barrel down, the hound sniffing along the trail ahead of us. "What's your hurry?" he asked me with a wry glance.

I slowed my pace, wishing heartily he'd hurry his. "Just thought ye'd want to get on to Cluny's soon as ye could."

"Cluny ain't going nowhere. Her pa never lets her go much beyond the porch after the sundown anyway."

I liked Cluny better than any of the other girls in the highlands. Everyone had their own ideas about what happened to Elen and took pleasure in discussing it among themselves, especially if I was around. Cluny was the only one who treated me same as before. "Ye going to marry her someday, Iwan?"

"Dunno."

"She'll say yes."

"What makes ye so sure?"

"Granny said a girl blushes when a boy she loves comes close, and Cluny blushes every time ye're anywhere near her."

He grinned at me. "Ye mean like ye do whenever Fagan comes round."

"I do *not!*"

He laughed. "Don't get all het up! And come on back here and walk with me. I was only teasing."

Face hot, I fell into step beside him again. As we crossed the highland meadow together, he grew more serious. "What's going on between you and that old woman anyway?"

"Nothing."

"I can always tell when ye're lying, Cadi."

"She lets me talk is all."

"Talk about what?"

"Just things."

"What sort of things?" He was pressing harder than usual. Had Papa put him up to it?

"Whatever comes to mind," I said, hoping he would be satisfied with that.

"Ye used to talk to me about things."

"Ye're all the time busy working for Pa and mooning over Cluny."

"That don't mean I don't have time for ye. Come on, Cadi. Why won't ye trust me?"

"Who said I don't trust you?"

He pulled me to a stop. "So prove it. Tell me what's going on between you and that old woman and Fagan Kai."

"Why do ye think summat's going on?"

"Fagan ain't in the habit of asking after people, especially ten-year-old girls. Add to that his father telling him to stay clear of Elda Kendric. If he'd been staying clear, he wouldn't know the old woman's been wondering where ye've been. And now we're about it, why would she be saying she missed ye if ye hadn't been over there often enow for her to get used to ye? Tell me that."

Flustered, I tried to pull free. "How should I know? Ask him."

"I did ask him. He dinna give me an answer that satisfied."

"He's *your* friend, Iwan."

"I thought he was, but he don't have the time of day for me anymore. Any spare time he's got, he's spending with you. It don't sit right is all."

"What don't sit right?"

"Look here, Cadi. He's near as old as I am. So what's he see in a baby like you?"

"Mayhap we're both interested in the same things."

"*Things* again. Name a few."

"Fishing," I said lamely and jerked free. I started walking again.

"Ye've never shown an interest in fishing before."

"And trapping."

"Trapping what, I'd like to know?"

I bit my lip, afeared I'd slipped. "Fagan brought a squirrel to Miz Elda."

"The Kai'd sooner see her starve."

I stopped and stared back at him. "Why, Iwan? What's he got against her?"

"I don't know, but he's been dead set against her as long as I can remember."

"That dinna keep Granny away."

"No, and I reckon it ain't gonna keep you away either." He whistled sharply, turning the hound back from his wanderings. "I got a gut feeling you and Fagan and that old woman are in for a heap of trouble."

When he asked no more questions, I knew he was letting go of me. Things had changed between us. I hadn't wanted it to be that way, but telling him what I had to do would have put stumbling blocks in my path. It made me sad I couldn't trust my own brother. A part of me wanted him to press harder, to dig deeper, to draw the truth out of me, while another part of me was afraid of what he'd do if he knew what I was planning. I stopped and waited for him, wanting to build a bridge between us and not let the gap widen further. "I'm just trying to set things right, Iwan. That's all I'm trying to do."

He stood looking at me. "And the old woman's helping you?"

"She's my friend."

"And Fagan?"

I lowered my head, embarrassed at what he might see in my eyes. "Fagan's got troubles of his own."

Iwan tipped my chin. "All well and good, Cadi, as long as he doesna drag ye into 'em." He walked on without speaking after that. The hound fell in beside him, panting and grinning when my brother scratched his head.

Miz Elda was sitting on her porch, waiting. Iwan helloed the house and waited for her to call back before he came closer. He slung the gunnysack off his shoulder and onto her porch. "Greetings from the folks, ma'am. Sorry to hear ye're feeling poorly."

"Tell 'em thank ye kindly for whatever ye brung in the sack."

Iwan nodded and strode off without a backward glance. Miz Elda watched him go.

"That brother of yours ain't much for socializing."

"He's on his way to the Byrneses' to see Cluny."

"Ahhh. No wonder he's in a hurry. Cleet's had his eye on the girl, I heard."

"Cluny likes Iwan better."

"That's never mattered to a Kai," Miz Elda said grimly, then gestured. "What's in the sack?"

"Smoked venison and some of Mama's preserves." When she looked down her nose at me, I stared back at her. "I dinna steal 'em. I swear. It was Papa's idea."

"Reckon I can believe that since it was Iwan who brung the sack," she said with a wry grin. "Go on now and cut off some of that smoked venison and put it to soak."

"Iwan shot a young buck, Miz Elda, not an old stag."

"I don't doubt that, child, but that meat'll have to soak a month of Sundays before I can chew it. I've only got a few teeth left."

We sat on the porch together, Miz Elda rocking, me just staring off into the darkness toward the western mountains. We didn't say anything. I don't rightly know what Miz Elda was thinking about, but as for me, I was trying to think over what I'd say when I faced the man of God again. It was hard going. The crickets were chirping and the frogs croaking so loud a body could hardly think for all the noise.

"Have ye changed your mind about going down there again?" Miz Elda said.

"No, ma'am."

"Well, it's dark, ain't it? Ye best get going. Time's awasting."

My heart started thumping. "Just because the man let me across the river once doesna mean he'll welcome me again." I could feel the sweat of fear breaking out on the back of my neck all over again. What a coward I was! I could practically feel the yellow streak spreading on my back!

"If God wanted to strike ye dead, Cadi Forbes, I reckon he could do it right here and now on this very porch."

"There's a comfort, Miz Elda," I said in a tone that near matched her own.

"That's the spirit," she chuckled. "Go on, now. The longer ye worry a matter, the bigger it grows."

Watchful, I headed down her hill. I only had a few more days before the moonlight would be but a mere white crack in the night sky. Mountain darkness was black as pitch before the new moon, and I wouldn't be able to use a torch without the whole valley knowing my comings and goings.

The man of God rose as I waded across the shallows. Shivering, I walked up the bank and stood uneasy before him. "So you've come again."

I blinked, uncertain, heart melting. "Where else can I go, sir, when ye be the one who's come in the name of the Lord?"

"Sit then, child, and we will talk more." He sat near the small fire. Glancing around, I hesitated, knowing firelight could be seen at a great distance. The man of God raised his head and looked at me. He had blue eyes, intense and burning. "Is it shame or fear that holds ye back?"

Biting my lip, I looked up toward the mountains round about and then hung my head. "Both, I reckon." I dared another look at him. "My coming could bring harm to ye."

"The will of God prevails."

I crept closer, trying to hold somewhat to the shadows. "What is the will of God?"

"That you open your heart to Jesus Christ."

I shuddered slightly, thinking of the sins I carried. Lowering my head, I couldn't look at him. What would he think of me if he knew what I had done? Would he say God offered me salvation then? Or would he send me away before I heard all he had to say?

"The Lord longs to be gracious to you. He waits on high to have compassion on you."

I shook my head, unable to believe mercy would be given if all was made known. Tears trickled down my cheeks, and shame held me silent.

"They that sow in tears shall reap in joy," he said gently. "The sorrow that is according to the will of God produces a repentance without regret, leading you to salvation. You are here, child. What holds you back?"

"I'm unworthy."

"No one is worthy. All have sinned and fallen short of the glory of God. Only Jesus is blameless and holy. Only he was never stained by a single sin. And he died for you. He died for all sinners so that we might be saved through faith in him."

"But you can't have sinned like I have. God sent you. You can't have done anything so bad."

"Before the Lord called me, I was a man of unclean lips. I was a man with an insatiable hunger for the treasures of this world. I sailed the seas in search of it and took bloody lucre as I could. I drank and brawled in watering holes in a dozen ports. I used women and left them and had not a care for anyone but myself. And then the Lord spoke my name. In the midst of a storm, he struck me down so that I could not move or speak. The ship's purser put me in the care of one of the captives who had no value for ransom, a man of the cloth named Brother Thomas. He fed and bathed me and read aloud from the Bible from Genesis to Revelation, and my soul drank the living water of Jesus Christ. God carved his Word into my heart and mind. When the ship made port in Charleston, my strength returned and God spoke to me again. He said, 'Leave this ship and go into the high mountain valleys and speak the word of the Lord.' And so I'm here, and here is where I will remain until God says otherwise."

His story gave me hope. Perhaps I could tell this man the truth. Perhaps he would understand. Perhaps he could tell me what to do to make things right.

"Trust him," Lilybet said, and I saw her standing just behind him. "What have you got to lose but the sins and sorrow that have plagued you for so long? Tell him what troubles your heart."

"If I tell you—" my eyes filled with tears so that I couldn't see his face or his expression—"will you promise not to hate me?"

"As the Lord has loved me, so will I love you."

I bowed my head, anguish and guilt overflowing me. I was not sure of God's love at all. Was it loving to send a man who sailed the seas up to the mountains to speak the word of God when all around him wanted him gone or worse? But I had reached the end of my road and knew no other way to go. And Lilybet was standing there, knowing all about me, and telling me to go on with it.

"I killed my sister."

When he said nothing, I rushed on, the sins I had committed and kept locked within me tumbling out like water rushing through the Narrows and pouring over the falls. I could not stop them. "It was a cursed day from beginning to end. Elen wanted my doll, the doll my granny made me. She was crying and carrying on summat fierce because I wouldn't let her play with it. She grabbed it and tried to pull it away from me, and I hit her. Mama said I should share, and I dinna want to. It seemed like no matter what I was playing with, Elen wanted it and I told Mama so. Mama said I was selfish and mean. Her saying that hurt my feelings so bad. It'd all been filling up and boiling in me—the resentment. I was so angry, I said I hated her and I hated Elen and I wished they was both dead. Mama slapped me. She ain't never slapped me like that before. Slapped me so hard my ears were ringing and then she yanked my doll away. She said I dinna deserve to have it and gave it to Elen. She said I was old enough to stop playing with dolls anyway."

I stared off into the darkness, remembering that horrible day and my anger so vividly it might just have happened.

"I ran away. I went to the river. And Elen followed me. I could hear her calling out to me. She said I could have my doll back. She said she was sorry. 'Cadi,' she kept saying, 'Cadi, where are you? Where are ye, Cadi?' And I wouldn't answer her. I wanted to be as far away from her and Mama as I could get. So I went to the Narrows. I'd been told never to go there, but I'd been there lots of times. Whenever I was mad or wanted to be away from my sister that's where I'd go. And I wanted to be alone that day. So I went across the tree bridge. When I got to the other side, I went down the trail you came up that day you came to our valley. And I sat by the pool below the falls."

I swallowed hard, my mouth dry with the shame of telling.

"I never figured she'd follow me there or try to come across. But she did. She come after me. I looked up once and saw her standing in the middle of the tree bridge. I just looked up and saw her there. And I was still so mad, I wished she'd fall. I wished she had never been born. I thought maybe Mama would still love me . . . thinking if she was gone . . ."

I couldn't say more. My throat closed up tight, my heart so

heavy and cold, remembering Elen screaming, remembering Elen falling.

"It was my fault she fell. I wished it to happen! When I saw her fall, I stood up and screamed, but it was too late. She came down over the falls and went under them. I kept on screaming and screaming her name, hoping she'd come up, but she never did."

The man of God rose and came around the fire. He sat down again and lifted me into his lap, his strong arms coming around me and holding me close as I sobbed.

"She fell and it was my fault! I wished her dead and she died. I wished Elen dead."

He held me close and rocked me gently, and as he did, I found the strength to tell him how Papa and Iwan had dived into the pool, searching for Elen until they were exhausted, all the while Mama stood on the bank crying, her face like death. For the next few days, they walked the river, searching. They were gone a week. When they came back, Papa said they couldn't find her. They gave up hope after that. Everyone knew Elen was dead. She was gone, and my family would not even have the smallest comfort of burying her body.

Papa had found my doll washed up on a bank. He gave it back to me. With no body to bury, there was no funeral and no stone for her in the family cemetery. So I found one I thought pretty. It took me days to roll it from the river and up the hill and inside the burying place.

Drained, I looked up at him. "Will ye tell God how sorry I am? Will ye ask him to forgive me?"

"You've only to ask him yourself, child. The Lord does not despise a broken and contrite heart. The Lord is compassionate and gracious, slow to anger and abounding in loving-kindness. You've confessed your sins. Now, will you trust in him?"

I thought about it but a moment and decided. "Yes."

"Well done. What's your name, child?"

"Cadi Forbes."

"Well, then, Cadi Forbes, do you accept Jesus Christ as your Savior and Lord?"

"Yes, sir. I will."

"And will you give up and let go of your sins and leave them at the cross of Jesus? Will you let yourself be washed clean?"

"Please."

"So be it." He lifted me from his lap, stood, and held out his hand. "There's one more thing to be done, and God will have the firstfruits of this valley." He led me to the river, walking into a pool until the water was midway up his thighs. I had to hold tight to him or be swept away. "Lean into my arms, Cadi, that I might baptize you in the name of the Father and the Son and the Holy Spirit."

The icy water closed over my head, shocking my body briefly, before the man raised me up and set me on my feet again. I shivered with cold and exhilaration. My body felt charged like the air after a lightning strike. I wanted to shout but held quiet, knowing I'd only bring trouble down on our heads. The current was strong, and I held tight to the man of God as we made our way back to the bank.

"I have to go now."

"You've more to learn."

"I'll be back." Trembling with cold and excitement, I flung my arms around his waist and hugged him before I hurried back to the shallows and splashed my way across the river. As soon as I reached the other side, I ran. Blood pumping, legs pumping, I raced across the meadow and up the hill through the woods. I wanted to laugh, to shout, to sing out a song of deliverance.

Miz Elda was sitting in her rocker, waiting for me. "Well?" she said as I came panting breathless to the porch.

"It's done!"

"What's done?"

Clambering up the steps, I laughed breathlessly, tears running down my cheeks, and hugged her. "I've been saved, Miz Elda. I've been washed clean."

"Ye're wet is what ye are! Have ye lost yer senses swimming in the river at night? Leave go, child. Ye're soaking me through."

"Oh, Miz Elda, Miz Elda—"

"Leave go, I say!" She pushed me away and rose from her chair unsteadily, her eyes bright. "Now come on into the house and get those clothes off. Get a blanket around ye before ye catch yer death and end up in heaven before I do. Ye can tell me everything when ye're bundled up."

"Everything's all right now, Miz Elda. Everything's going to be fine."

But it wasn't fine. Not right away, anyhow. I'd run off so fast, I hadn't heard everything the man of God had tried to tell me, and I wasn't prepared for what was to come.

I didn't realize I was entering a battle—one I could win only by trusting in the Lord. And trust, for me, ain't easy to do. It's a learned thing, comin' one step at a time. I knew nothin' of the world and who'd been let loose upon it. But I had been so desperate for help, filled with sorrow, drowning in guilt.

I never once figured on God using me the way he did.

THIRTEEN

𝓕AGAN CAME BY MIZ ELDA'S CABIN THE NEXT MORN-
ing. "What happened? You look different."

"How so?" I couldn't help wondering if I looked as good on
the outside as I felt on the inside. I stood on the porch, balanc-
ing a basket of dirty laundry on my hip the way Mama sometimes did.

"You're smiling. Ain't seen you smile much. You look
pretty."

I felt shy of a sudden, wondering if I looked foolish to him
with the heat coming up in my face. I was mortified, especially
after what I'd told Iwan.

"What ye turning all red for?"

I might have gained some semblance of calm if he hadn't
gone and said that! "Nothing." The shine clouded over.
"What're ye doing here so early?" I said, wishing he'd stop looking at me like I was some new bug he'd found.

He held up a string of trout I hadn't noticed. "Thought Miz
Elda might like some fresh fish. She up and about yet?"

"Nope."

"Late for her. She's an early riser."

"We talked near all night."

"About what?"

"As if it's any of your business." I came down the steps.

"Why're ye so het up of a sudden? What'd I do?"

"If ye gotta know, I went down and heard the man of God last night. That's what we talked about."

Fagan's face tensed up, and he gave a quick look around. "Ye shouldn't talk about him so open like. Ye can't know who's around to hear ye. Do ye want these or not?" He held out the fish.

"She'll be much obliged, I'm sure." I set the basket down and took the fish. "I'll put them in some water." I went back up the steps and inside, not reckoning on Fagan following. He stopped just inside the doorway and looked around. It was a dank-smelling, small, mean cabin, but some improved from my sweeping and washing the table and dishes and opening the shutters to let some air in. I ladled water into a bowl and laid the fish in it.

"Your folks know ye went down there?" he said in a whisper.

"Nope. If it weren't for Miz Elda, I wouldn't have been able to go. She's helping me out."

"How so?"

"I couldn't go nowhere without Pa asking where I went and what I was doing. And then Mama started asking questions. So Miz Elda said she was feeling poorly and wanted me to stay with her awhile and help her out. So here I am."

He glanced toward the bed where Miz Elda was sleeping. "She sounds pretty bad."

"She always sounds that way when she's sleeping." We stood a moment and listened to her snore and wheeze and whistle. I giggled. "She makes more noise than Papa and Iwan put together."

"Don't reckon you'll be getting much sleep as long as ye're staying here," Fagan whispered, grinning.

"Don't matter." I headed for the door. I wanted to talk more to Fagan and dinna want to wake Miz Elda. "I was doing some chores for her," I said when we were on the porch. I went down the steps and picked up the basket. "I already swept out the house and washed the table and dishes. Her clothes ain't been washed in a week of Sundays and neither has her bedding. I figured on doing that and restuffing her mattress as soon as she gets off it. There's hay and dried clover in the barn."

"What's got into you?"

"I gotta do summat until nightfall. Makes the time pass quicker to be busy, and it'll help Miz Elda. She ain't been up to it in a long time. You want to help? Her vegetable garden needs weeding and watering."

"That's woman's work."

"Well, then, I guess ye can't be bothered hanging around here, can ye? I'll tell her ye brought the little fish."

"Cool down." He followed me. "If ye tell me what that preacher said to you last night, I'll chop wood to last a week."

I told him, leaving not the smallest detail out. I knew by the look on his face that I'd have company that night.

Miz Elda came out past noon, a ragged blanket wrapped around her, her gray hair sticking up all over her head. "Cadi Forbes! Where in blazes are my clothes?!"

I ran and took her dress and undergarments off the line and ran to her with them. "I washed 'em, ma'am. I've been so busy, I forgot to put 'em back inside for ye."

"Busy doing what?"

"Weeding and watering your garden." She was staring across at Fagan stacking firewood. "He brought some trout for ye this morning. They're in a pan of water on your table."

"Too small for Brogan most likely."

I took offense for his sake. "Fagan cares about you, Miz Elda. Else he wouldn't go against his father and come see ye at all." I nodded toward him. "He's chopping ye firewood."

"I can see that. I ain't blind yet." She eyed me dolefully. "Pretty quick to his defense, ain't ye? How long's he been here?"

"Since just after sunup."

"That long? I suppose ye spilled the beans to him about last night."

"Fagan's going with me soon as he can sneak out."

She frowned. "Think what ye're doing, Cadi Forbes."

"It was his own idea to go, Miz Elda. I dinna ask him."

"Ye're fanning a fire in that boy that could burn him up and send him straight to kingdom come."

"Maybe he'll get saved just like me."

"That's fine for the hereafter, but as for now he's still got to live with his pa."

"He might get a tanning for going down there, but once they hear—"

"Maybe ye're the one who needs eyes to see, Cadi, girl. Have ye never noticed the marks that boy bears or asked yerself why he's away from home from dawn to dark? Brogan's beaten the spirit out of his mama and brothers, but there's summat in Fagan that won't be conquered."

There was an odd look in Miz Elda's eyes when she spoke of Fagan—part pride, part despair. She stood watching him a moment and then looked at me again. "Go careful or reap the whirlwind!"

Fagan came back shortly after dark. His father and older brothers had said they were going coon hunting. "Thought he'd leave Douglas home, he was so mad."

"Why?"

"Douglas put too much powder in his gun again. Pa said he's going to blow himself to kingdom come yet if he don't pay more mind to what he's doing. Ma went to bed."

"She sick?" Miz Elda wanted to know.

"Just tired." He looked away. "She gets real sad sometimes. Don't say why."

The old woman stared off into the darkness. "Comes of getting what you thought you wanted and finding out it ain't what you thought it would be."

Fagan looked at her, something flickering across his face.

Miz Elda seemed more troubled as time went on. "I've been remembering things from long past. I dreamed about my mother last night," she said. "She was sitting before the hearth looking so young. She was sewing and I was a little girl again. She said, 'The eyes of the Lord are in every place, Elda, watching the evil and the good.' And I asked her why he dinna do nothing to make things right."

I leaned forward. "What did she say?"

"She said he was waiting."

"Waiting for what, ma'am?"

"Well, now, if I knew that I wouldn't be so troubled by the dream, would I?"

"She was just asking, Miz Elda."

"Always asking questions," Miz Elda said. "Always looking into what's none of her business and going where she shouldn't ought to go. That's her trouble, and now she's gone and got us both doing it and no telling where it'll end!"

"You're just afeared for us, Miz Elda, and ye don't gotta be." I was too eager to hear more from the man of God to be upset or dampened by her misgivings. "I'm going before it gets any darker."

Fagan got up, as ready as I was.

"God help ye both," Miz Elda said, hands tight folded in her lap. "God help ye."

"Hold up," Fagan said as I ran ahead. He could not keep up with me for I fair flew o'er the ground. I had waited all day to run down the mountainside, across the meadow to the river. I waded in without hesitation, arms outstretched to keep my balance. On the far shore, the man of God arose, ready to speak.

"Fagan's come with me, sir. He wants to hear what God has to say, too."

The man stood his ground, a black shadow against a starlit sky. "Have you heard the name of Jesus Christ, boy?"

"Only in a curse, sir." Fagan's voice shook.

Heat poured into my cheeks. "Not from me, sir," I said quickly.

"Not from her." Fagan took my hand. His palm was sweating, and he was trembling.

"Be still," the man said softly. He stretched out his hands in welcome. "Sit and I will tell you of the coming of the Lord."

He had lit no fire, and as he spoke night wrapped us in a protective blanket. We paid heed to nothing but the sound of his deep voice as he took us back to the creation of the world and the fall of man, the law brought by the prophet Moses, who talked with the Lord face-to-face, and then on through the prophets who called for repentance and were killed for their faith.

"And then, in the days of Herod, the king of Judea, a far-off country, lived a priest of the Jews named Zechariah and his wife Elisabeth. And they were both righteous before God, walking blameless in the commandments and ordinances of the Lord. And they had no child . . ."

I listened intently, drinking in his words. The angel Gabriel had appeared to the priest as he served before the Lord, telling him his wife would have a son named John. When he didn't believe the angel, he was struck mute until the child was born. God also sent the angel Gabriel to a city of Galilee named Nazareth, to a virgin named Mary espoused to Joseph, a good and humble carpenter. Both were descended from the house of David, from which all knew the Anointed One of God would come forth.

"And the angel said unto her, 'Fear not, Mary: for thou hast found favor with God. And behold, thou shalt conceive in thy womb, and bring forth a son, and shalt call his name Jesus, God is salvation! He shall be great, and shall be called the Son of the Highest: and the Lord God shall give unto him the throne of his father David; and he shall reign over the house of Jacob forever; and of his kingdom there shall be no end.'

"When Mary was great with child, a decree went out from Caesar Augustus that all the world should be taxed. Joseph took Mary to Bethlehem. When her labor pangs began, there was no place for them to stay, so Joseph found shelter for them in a stable. Mary gave birth to Jesus, the Messiah, the Son of God, God the Son Almighty. She wrapped the babe in swaddling clothes and laid him in a manger. The angel of the Lord appeared to the shepherds and told them of Jesus' birth, and the heavenly host praised God.

"The angel of the Lord appeared to Joseph in a dream and told him to take the young child and his mother and flee to Egypt, for King Herod wanted to kill the child. Determined to kill the Messiah, Herod sent forth men and slew all the children two years old and younger who were in Bethlehem and in all the cities and towns.

"In time, Herod died, and an angel of the Lord appeared again to Joseph in a dream and told him to take the child and his mother and return to the land of Israel. So Joseph took Jesus and Mary to Galilee and lived in a city called Nazareth. There, God the Son grew and walked among men. God, the Creator of all the universe, led the life of a common carpenter until he was thirty years old.

"Then came John the Baptist, preaching in the wilderness of Judea and calling people to repent, saying the kingdom of heaven was at hand."

Fagan and I sat transfixed, envisioning all as the man of God's voice rose.

"And Jesus, when he was baptized, went up straightway out of the water: and, lo, the heavens were opened unto him, and John saw the Spirit of God descending like a dove and lighting upon him. And lo a voice from heaven, saying, 'This is my beloved Son, in whom I am well pleased.'"

The man bowed his head and fell quiet so long, Fagan and I looked at one another. It was Fagan who spoke. "What happened then, sir?"

"Then was Jesus led by the Spirit into the wilderness to be tempted by the devil." He raised his head, and I knew he was looking at us. I could feel his intensity. "The same devil who holds this valley prisoner and wants to keep it in darkness; the same devil who will come against you."

The hair on the back of my neck stood up. I'd known all my life of the existence of evil. I wanted to forget it existed in the world.

"The same devil dared test the Lord God, Jesus Christ, our Savior and Lord. Satan is his name, and he is the great deceiver, full of pride, a murderer, and the father of lies. He tried to deceive Jesus, but the Lord prevailed against him. Only the Lord prevails.

"When Jesus returned from the wilderness, he dwelt in Capernaum by the Sea of Galilee and there began to choose his disciples among the simple, hardworking fishermen. Twelve men he called, common men all, with nothing to hold them together but the Lord.

"And God the Son, Jesus Christ, made the blind see, the deaf hear, the crippled walk, the dumb speak. He cast out demons and cleansed lepers. He stilled a storm and walked on water and brought the dead back to life.

"And then the powers of darkness gathered. Men plotted against him, and one of his own betrayed him. He was taken while in prayer, tried in the middle of the night, spit upon, beaten, scourged, and mocked.

"And then Jesus was crucified."

The darkness around us was so quiet, my ears rang. "Crucified?" I whispered. "What does it mean, sir?"

He stretched his arms out wide. "They nailed his hands and feet to a cross and stood it up before the people where all could see his shame. And they left him there between two thieves to die a slow and agonizing death."

"But *why?*" Fagan said, his voice choked with emotion. "He dinna do anything wrong!"

"He was despised and forsaken of men, a man of sorrows, and acquainted with grief. He was pierced through for our transgressions, crushed for our iniquities. The chastening that should fall upon us fell upon him, and by his scourging we are healed. We are all of us like sheep that have gone astray. Each of us has turned his own way, but the Lord has caused the iniquity of us all to fall upon him. Jesus rendered himself the guilt offering for our sins. He poured out himself to death, numbering himself with the transgressors, bearing our sins so that we might be saved."

"Is that the way of it then?" Fagan said grievously. "Must we suffer for the sins of others?" He put his head down and wept.

I had never seen him cry before and didn't know what to do. The sound of his brokenness made me ache for him.

"They took him down from the cross, and a rich man laid the Lord in a tomb hewn out of a rock. A great stone was rolled over the doorway, and Roman guards stood guard round about so that the seal might not be broken and the body stolen away."

The man of God stood, his arms held up exultantly as dawn's first light edged over the mountains to the east. "And an angel of the Lord came! And the Roman guards fell upon the ground in a faint. The angel rolled away the stone, and Jesus arose. *He arose!* Death could not hold him in the grave!"

Fagan fell forward on his face.

The man of God paced, the excitement spilling from him as the words of the Lord spilled forth from his lips.

"Jesus appeared first to Mary of Magdala and then to his disciples and to hundreds afterward. He walked upon the earth for forty days and then ascended into heaven to take his place at the throne of God."

Goosebumps rose all over my body. My hair stood on end. Trembling, I found myself clambering forward to my knees, murmuring praises to the Lord and weeping.

"The Lord God, Jehovah Roi, reigns forevermore!"

My heart swelled within me until I thought it would burst. "He reigns." Morning light pushed back the darkness. "He reigns!" My mind did not fully grasp it all, but my heart responded along with the Spirit dwelling within me.

The man stood arms held high, head thrown back, his face alight, his eyes closed. Fagan drew back, sitting on his heels and gazed up at him, watchful, waiting, face pale and wet.

My trembling ceased and I sat back upon my heels, feeling content and peaceful. I never wanted to leave this place. The man of God lowered his arms to his sides and looked down at us. He smiled tenderly at Fagan. "Do you believe that Jesus is the Christ, the Son of the Living God?"

"Yes, sir."

The man held out his hand to him. Clasping my hands together, I followed them to the river. I was filled with joy as I watched Fagan be baptized. There were two of us now—two who had heard the word of the Lord and believed. When Fagan came up out of the water, I knew he'd been washed clean of sins and he wouldn't have to worry anymore about bearing those of his father.

And then I saw his eyes as he came toward me. They burned with an inner light not so different from the man who walked beside him—and sudden fear pricked my soul.

Oh, what would happen to us now with Fagan looking the way he did? He looked near aglow, on fire inside. Two of us had been buried and raised in Christ, two out of a hundred souls in our highland valley. What would Brogan Kai do when he found out what his son had done?

The three of us stood together. Fagan fairly trembled with some inner verve while I stood by looking at him and wondering how he could go home without everyone seeing the change in him. What had I done? I'd brought him down to the man of God thinking it would be our secret, something that would bind us together.

And so it would in ways I could not have guessed.

The prophet put a hand on each of us. "Go now. Rest. Speak to no one except the old woman of what's happened here and been said. I have more to tell you before you go out into the world but not much time left." He took his hands from us.

Go out into the world . . . not much time left?

"What do you mean?"

Fagan took my hand firmly and pulled me away. "He's said we're to go."

"But, Fagan, wait! I want to know—"

Fagan didn't give me time or breath to say more. He pulled me along the river to the brush and rocks, hurrying. "Come on!" Letting go of me, he hopped from one to another, pausing once to look back and make sure I was following. "Hurry!"

"You hadn't ought to have pulled me away like that. What did he mean?"

"He'll tell us when he's ready. I'm going on ahead now," he said when I reached the other side. "I've got to get back before I'm missed. Go on to Miz Elda's and do like he said. I'll see ye tonight." He headed quickly up through the trees.

Not much time left . . .

I could not get those words out of my mind. Dread filled me, for in the pit of my stomach I knew exactly what the man meant.

F O U R T E E N

"*I* HAD A DREAM," MIZ ELDA SAID BEFORE I COULD tell her a word about what was said the night before. "A strange and terrible dream." I was out of breath from running and so had no time to tell her my news before she went on ahead with her own. "That man down there was speaking, and fire was coming from his mouth. And he was setting everything ablaze, clear up to the mountaintops."

"And destroying everything?" I said, puffing, afraid of what I'd done and what was coming.

"No, and there's the strangeness to it. The flame grew until everything was within it, like sunlight when it's so bright ye can't see what's in front of ye."

"I'm terrible scared, Miz Elda."

"Ye look it."

"I should not have taken Fagan."

"Why? What happened?"

I told her. The amazing part was I could remember everything the prophet had said, every detail, as though by his telling it the word of the Lord had been carved into my heart and head. The Cadi Forbes I'd been two nights ago was changed. I wasn't the same. And neither was Fagan.

Nothing was going to be the same, and the fire Miz Elda had dreamed of was going to come down and burn us all.

"Try to rest now, chile. Ye're done in."

I didn't think I'd be able to sleep, but as soon as I lay down upon the cot, I sank into a dreamless sleep so peaceful I might as well have been laid beside Granny. I didn't know time passed until I awakened to Miz Elda shaking me.

"I've fixed some porridge for ye, Cadi. Come eat."

It was late in the afternoon, the sun dipping. My heart thumped fast and hard as I realized how short time was. Fagan would come soon.

Not much time left . . .

Miz Elda put a bowl in front of me as I sat at her table. Picking up a jar, she poured a thick stream of honey over the chopped hazelnuts and raisins she'd sprinkled on top of the cooked oats, barley, and wheat. "I had me a visitor today." She plunked the jar of honey down right in front of me.

Heat poured into my cheeks and then drained away just as quickly, leaving me cold. "Bletsung Macleod."

Miz Elda eased her aching bones into the chair across from me. "She says the sin eater's been waiting to hear from ye. He's holding ye to the promise ye made."

I blinked, biting my lip, and bowed my head, ashamed. "I forgot all about him."

"Well, ye'd best remember him. He's the one who sent ye down there in the first place. If left to yerself, Cadi Forbes, ye'd still be holed up inside yerself, living alone with yer guilt and shame. The way that man is now, poor soul."

Remorse filled me, and sorrow, too, for what I had to tell him. "Did ye tell her I'd come?"

"I told her ye've been going down into the valley and hearing the word of the Lord just like ye promised ye would. Ye've only one day left, and then ye'll be ready to carry the message to him."

"Is that what ye think the man meant when he said we had not much time left?"

"Don't rightly know for sure what he meant, chile, but I reckon ye'll know by tomorrow." She gestured. "Go on and eat. Ye'll need your strength."

I didn't think I could, but after one bite, my mouth fair watered with appetite. I'd never tasted anything so good. I tucked into the savory dish and scraped the bowl clean.

"Where'd ye get the milk, Miz Elda?" I said, drinking down the mug full.

"Your mama brought it by just past dawn."

"Mama?" I said, surprised. Why would she do such a thing? "Ye should be drinking it, then, not me." Mama was sure to be angry that I was drinking milk meant for an ailing old woman.

"I've never had a taste for it," she said and sat down again. "I've summat I want ye to give the man when ye go down to him tonight." She put a piece of parchment on the table and rolled it carefully. Her hands trembling as they always did, she tied a string around the parchment and pushed it across the table to me.

"What is it?"

"Well, if it's any of yer business, it's the deed to this place."

"What're ye giving him that for? Where ye going to live?"

"Right here. If that man wants a place to stay, I've room aplenty in the barn. Way I figure it, I'm not long for this world. He could stay here until I pass on, then take it all. Maybe build a church." Her mouth curved in an odd smile as she looked away, thinking again, going back in time. "That'd make Laochailand Kai roll over in his grave."

"Laochailand Kai?"

"Only God can undo what's been done," she said, not listening to me. "If God'll have anything to do with those of us who let it happen."

"What happened, Miz Elda?" I reached across the table and put my hand on hers. "Miz Elda?"

She looked at me again and sighed. "Ye just give the man God sent the parchment there, and ye tell him this is everything I own and the inheritance I'd have passed on to my children if they'd stayed to collect it."

I was purely frustrated and brimming with questions. "Mama said ye sent your children over the mountain."

"Aye, I did. I told 'em to go and never look back."

"Did ye not love them?"

Her eyes grew fierce. "It's cause I loved 'em I sent 'em away, chile." Shaking her head, she turned her face away. Closing her eyes, she sat still for a moment. No matter how still and silent she sat, I could see she was struggling inside herself. I was surprised when she spoke. "What happened to that boy who lives on Dead Man's Mountain could've happened to any one of my own three sons." She looked at me, and I saw tears gathering in her eyes. "They were friends, ye see, my sons and . . . the one who became the sin eater."

"How was it done, Miz Elda? How was he chosen?"

"By lot, that's how. It was Laochailand Kai's plea before he died." She gave a mirthless laugh. "So it is with hard men given to cruelty. The fear of God comes upon them at the end. They know they're going to come face-to-face with their Maker. Laochailand had sins aplenty upon his head. He said he needed a sin eater, and Brogan set about getting him one. Some of us argued against it, but Brogan said his father swore upon his deathbed that he wudna stay in the ground unless one came to take his sins away. The thought of Laochailand Kai walking our mountains 'til the end of time as a taint put the fear of perdition into us. No one dared gainsay Brogan after that threat. And so it was done as he demanded. Each man past thirteen placed his mark on a piece of bone, and the lots were put into a mazer. One was drawn and it was all settled. Except we never figured on it being who it was. We all thought it'd be one of Laochailand Kai's own."

"Why?"

"Because Brogan said God was sure to choose the one who was the worst sinner among us. We never reckoned on God choosing whom he did. I'll never forget the look on his face." She lowered her head. "Oh, there was a heap of crying for days afterward, and none of it was for Laochailand Kai, though he died the very night the sin eater was named. And the boy came and did like he was supposed to do. And it's been that way ever since." She was silent a moment, grieving, I guessed, though I didn't know the depth of it. "That was twenty years ago, twenty long years."

More than twice the years I'd been alive that poor man had been alone on Dead Man's Mountain. "At least Bletsung Macleod's been his friend."

"And there's the worst of it," she murmured softly.

She would not tell me more, and we sat upon her porch watching the sun go down and the stars come out. We listened to the crickets and the old hoot owl. The night wind rustled the trees, raising gooseflesh on me. Time passes terrible slow sometimes, especially if you've someplace you want to go.

Where was Fagan? What was taking him so long?

I longed to go down into the valley and cross the river again to the man of God, for his words delighted me more than the savory dish Miz Elda had made for me. Everything within me blessed the Lord, who had redeemed my life. As far as the heavens were above the earth, so great was the mercy God had shown me. For as far as the east is from the west, so far had he removed my burdens. I was dust and the Lord God Almighty himself had made me his own child.

"I canna wait longer," I said. "Fagan knows the way."

183

As I hurried down the mountainside, I felt a strange foreboding. It was as though there were evil forces gathering in the darkness, watching me as I hastened to hear the word of the Lord. I paused at the edge of the forest, catching my breath. I was sure no one was following me, and I ran on, careless now in my haste. Shoving vines back, I pushed my way through the leafy curtain near the river.

Someone grabbed hold of me, clamping a hand over my mouth to cut off my scream. When I tried to bite the hand, Fagan hissed in my ear. "It's me! Now, hush, will ye? Ye've made enough noise coming down here to rouse the dead. Ye gonna be quiet?" When I nodded, he released me.

"Where've ye been?" I said, furious with him for scaring me so. "I waited for you!"

"I'm here, ain't I? If I could've come to Miz Elda's, I would've. Ye ought to know me well enow by now."

"What happened?"

"I ain't wasting the time to tell ye. Come on. But be quiet about it!"

The man of God was waiting. He laid hands upon both of us in warm greeting. As we sat on the ground together, he spoke to us the words Jesus had said to his disciples. He told us the Lord had gone up on a mountainside near a great lake and talked to a multitude. "Blessed are the poor in spirit. . . ." It was there also that he fed five thousand people with a few loaves of bread and fishes.

We heard the story of a son who took his inheritance and left his father to live an unrighteous life. When he realized his sins and turned from them, his father was waiting to embrace him and celebrate. And I knew in my heart that the man was telling us what God was like. He told us, too, of a farmer who sowed wheat and of the enemy who sowed tares among the wheat. He spoke of a mustard seed and how even a little faith is enough, for God will make it grow. Best of all, he told us Jesus would return. Yet mingled with the joy of that thought was fear, for the sun would be darkened and the moon would not give light and the stars would fall from the heavens. Everyone would see Jesus coming in the clouds with great power and glory. Everyone. Even those who had never believed he existed at all.

"When will Jesus come back?" Fagan said. "Will it be soon?"

"Verily, I say unto you, that this generation shall not pass, till all these things be done. Heaven and earth shall pass away, but the word of the Lord shall not pass away. Yet, the hour and the day knoweth no man, no, not even the angels in heaven, nor the Son. Only the Father. Take ye heed, watch and pray, for ye know not when the time is. Be ready."

"Would that it were now," Fagan said grimly, gazing up toward his mountainside.

The man of God bowed his head, looking weary. His hands rested, palms up on his knees as he sat Indian fashion. "It is done, Lord. May thy word be a lamp unto these small feet and a light unto these great mountains."

Fagan and I looked at one another and then back at him. "Done? You've only just started teaching us. You aren't leaving now, are you?" I was distressed at the thought of his going. There was still so much I wanted to know. "Where will we go to hear the word?"

Truth be told, I could've sat there forever listening, but God had other work in mind.

"God set you apart, even from your mothers' wombs, and called you both through his grace to be his own. He has given you the Holy Spirit. God himself is your teacher, not I. My time with you is at an end."

Tears came quick as fear, and the aloneness gripped me. "But I can't hear God the way I hear you!"

"*Listen.*"

"But how?"

"Be still. Know the Lord. He is God and there is no other."

"What of me?" Fagan said solemnly. "Nobody cares what Cadi does, but my pa would have my hide if he knew—"

"Do not walk in the counsel of the ungodly, nor stand in the way of sinners, nor sit in the seat of the scornful. Delight in the Lord your God. Be like a tree planted by the river that brings forth fruit in season. Those who despise the Word of the Lord will not stand in the day of judgment, for the breath of the Lord will blow them away like chaff."

Fagan was shaken. "My father . . . my brothers . . ."

"Only fear the Lord and serve him in truth with all your heart, Fagan Kai. For all the laws and the prophets were summoned up in Christ when he said, 'Love the Lord your God with all thy heart and all thy soul and all thy might. And love one another as you love yourself.'"

I clambered to my knees, beseeching him. "You can't go. We need you!"

"I am not the Lord, child. Do not lean upon me. Lean upon the one who called you out, for they who wait upon the Lord shall gain new strength. They shall mount up on wings like eagles. They shall run and not grow weary. They shall walk and not grow faint."

I was no eagle. I was a grounded sparrow, shuddering in fear. I looked at Fagan for help, but none was forthcoming. He had his own troubles.

He edged closer, looking disturbed. "Sir, we came. We listened. We accepted everything you've told us as the truth. What's going to happen to us now?"

"Satan will come against you."

Agitated, we both began speaking at once. "Satan! How do we fight against him?"

"Why dinna ye tell us before?"

The man held his hands up to quiet us. "They that trust in the Lord shall be like these mountains which cannot be removed," he said calmly. "As they are round about us, so the Lord surrounds you. He will go out before you and stand as your rear guard."

"I can't fight my father!" Fagan said.

"I'm but a child!" I looked fearfully out into the darkness.

"The Lord is God."

I wished at that moment I had not come back after the first night, when relief and happiness had spilled over me. All the goodness and mercy were forgotten. The exhilaration I had felt evaporated. The Lord had drawn me out of a black pit, and now it seemed the devil himself was coming up after me. I was sore afraid. And angry.

Jumping to my feet, I stood with my fists clenched. "Why did ye come here at all? Why did ye make me think everything was turned to rights?"

"Be warned, Cadi Forbes," he said in a tone that made me feel God himself was speaking to me. "Satan wants to sift you. Do not think that because you have given your life to Jesus and been saved that the battle is over. The Lord himself went out into the wilderness, remember? And so it has begun. Satan will prey upon your doubts and fears and try to drive you away from the Lord your God, for it is your heart he wants and your mind he will attack. Remember that he is the father of lies and a murderer."

Shivering, I looked out into the darkness. "I will hide."

"He will seek you out wherever you are."

"I wish I'd never come here! It's gonna be worse than it was before. I wish I'd never listened to ye!"

"Be quiet, Cadi!" Fagan said, disgusted. "You're such a coward."

"You don't have to be scared," I said, turning on him. "You've got the Kai to fight your battles."

The man of God looked between us with sorrowful eyes. He stood slowly, looking out across the river. "They come."

Turning, I saw three flickering spots of fire on the riverbank opposite us. Men were crossing over.

"It's my father!" Fagan said. "Ye've got to run, sir! Ye've got to hide!"

Unmoved by Fagan's plea, the man stood with grave dignity, waiting.

"Don't ye hear me?" Fagan said, grasping his arm and pulling at him. "You've got to *go*. I'm telling you. *He'll kill you!*"

"Do not fear the one who can kill my body, but the one who can destroy the soul."

"*Fa . . . gan!!*" came a deep voice filled with wrath. "I warned ye, dinna I?"

Terror filled me and I fled into the darkness, hiding among some shrubs where Brogan Kai and his sons could not see me. Fagan stood his ground, putting himself in front of the man of God.

"He's done nothing wrong, Pa! Leave him be!"

"Ye dare stand against me?" Brogan Kai strode up the bank and grabbed his son by the throat. "Who ye gonna believe? A stranger from across the mountains or your own pa?" He squeezed tighter so that Fagan clawed at his hands for release. "Ye gonna listen to someone who rants and raves like a madman about summat he says happened eighteen hundred years ago and not listen to me?" Brogan's face was wild with rage as he shook Fagan.

"Let the boy go," the man of God said quietly.

"*Ahhhhh . . .*" Brogan cast his son aside. "Sniveling little rat! *Betrayer!*" He spat on Fagan who lay choking and crying on the ground.

"The kingdom of heaven belongs to such as he, Brogan Kai."

Brogan's head turned, his eyes narrowing coldly. "The kingdom of heaven, ye say?" He gave a mocking laugh. "Well, mon, I'm gonna send ye to Hades this verra night!" The first blow knocked the man back, but not off his feet. "I warned ye to leave my mountains or I'd kill ye! I should've done ye in the first day. Instead, I showed ye *kindness*. I showed ye *hospitality*. And ye've turned my own kin against me."

"God made you upright, Brogan Kai," the man said straightening, blood trickling from his mouth, "but you sought out many devices!"

"These are *my* people!"

"The ways of a man are before the eyes of the Lord, and he watches all his paths. *Repent and be saved. . . .*"

Brogan Kai came at him in black fury.

"Nooo . . . !" Fagan cried out, stumbling to his feet and trying to stop his father. "Pa, don't!" Cleet held him back.

Cowering behind the bushes in the darkness, I covered my face, hearing the poor man's grunts and groans of pain as our clan leader hammered him with his fists. When the man fell to the ground, Brogan used his boots. The sounds coming from Brogan Kai were like some wild animal.

Finally, no sounds came but the rasping of breath from the Kai. "I warned ye what I'd do, dinna I? Ye had it coming." He gave the unconscious man one last, vicious kick and turned away to look at Fagan. "So much for the power of *his* God." His face shone black with triumph.

"I hate what ye are!" Tears streamed down Fagan's face. "And I hate that I'm your son!"

Emotion flickered across the Kai's face. Pain? Desolation? What had I seen? He strode to Fagan, whose arms were clamped tightly by his two brothers. "Ye dare say that to me? Yer own flesh and blood?"

Cleet and Douglas let go of Fagan and drew back out of the way as their father unleashed his fury on his youngest son.

Sure the Kai was going to kill him, I scrambled over the ground frantically, finding a smooth stone. I hurled it as hard as I could, and it struck Brogan Kai on the back of the head. Shocked at what I'd dared to do, I ducked back into my hiding place as the Kai released Fagan and stumbled. Shivering in terror, I watched as he touched the back of his head. His hand came away bloody.

"Who's out there?"

I held my breath, cowering, praying God would hide me.

"Ye want us to go look, Pa?" Cleet said.

The Kai touched the back of his head again, wincing. As he peered out into the darkness, a look I'd never seen before came over his face. "Stay where ye are. He's a dead aim with that slingshot of his." His back was to the others so they didn't see what I did: *Fear.* It was there just for an instant, but real and plain enough for me to see. And then his face hardened again and he swore. "This has got nothing to do with you! Ye hear me?"

"Who is it, Pa?"

"Never mind," he said, his expression shuttered. "Let's go."

"What about that prophet? He ain't dead yet, Pa."

"He will be by morning," Douglas said, straightening. "He's bleeding from his mouth, Pa. I think ye done caved in his ribs."

"Ye want I should carry Fagan, Pa?" Cleet said, eager to do his father's bidding, whatever it was.

"Leave him where he lay. He'll come home with his tail between his legs soon enough."

"He's bad hurt."

"I said *leave him.*"

"What're ye gonna do about Cadi Forbes?" Cleet said and my heart stopped. "She was here."

"Forget her for now. She's probably still running. I'll talk to her pa again soon as it's daylight. If he don't do summat about her right quick, I will."

FIFTEEN

THE TORCHES HAD BECOME MERE FLICKERS FROM across the river and among the trees on the mountainside before I crept out of the bushes and scrambled over to where Fagan lay. He groaned when I rolled him over. Crying, I lifted him against my knees. The sky had lightened enough that I could see his bruised and swollen face. One eye was almost shut, and there was a lump on his jaw the size of a goose egg. Tears streaked his dirty face.

"Is he dead?" he whispered through bleeding lips.

"I don't know." Swiping the tears from my eyes, I looked back over my shoulder at the man lying still a few feet away. "I think so, Fagan."

"Go see." Fagan gritted his teeth and struggled into a sitting position.

I crawled across the space to the man of God and leaned over him. He was breathing, just barely, and I could hear a horrible gurgling sound deep in his chest. His lungs were filling with his own blood. "I'm sorry, sir! I'm sorry they done this to ye."

"Is he alive?" Fagan said, moaning as he tried to get up.

"He's dying, Fagan." I choked back a sob. "What can we do?"

The man's eyes opened, and I drew back slightly, pressing my dusty fists to my mouth. He looked at me, and I remembered the terrible things I'd said to him and felt ashamed into my very bones. Doubt had been born. I was helpless and afraid. "Why dinna God stop him? Why did he let this happen to ye?"

His lips moved. His eyes beseeched. Leaning down over him again, I tried to hear what he wanted to say.

"Re . . . mem . . . ber . . ." His breath came in a long sigh, and he said no more. His eyes were still open, seeming to look straight at me.

Shivering, I drew back and inched away from him. For some strange, inexplicable reason, I felt the man of God had passed the chore on to me.

"Cadi?" Fagan said.

I shut my eyes so that I wouldn't have to look into the man's. "Oh, God," I whispered under my breath. "What am I gonna do?" I was shaking with fear.

Fagan's groan made me turn. Bad hurt as he was, he was struggling to rise. "We got to get him some help." He held his ribs, panting against the pain. "Gervase Odara—"

"It's no use, Fagan. He's dead." I couldn't run and tell Miz Elda. What could she do, old as she was? I couldn't run to Papa because he'd do nothing, knowing he'd be going against the Kai if he did. And Mama? She'd lay another stone on my back for my disobedience.

Fagan was on his knees, hunching over in pain. He wept. "Oh, Jesus, I'm sorry. I tried to stop him. I did."

"What am I gonna do?" I whispered. "Oh, God, what am I gonna do?" Who would dare to help us, knowing we'd gone against the Kai?

"Katrina Anice," Lilybet said softly, and my head jerked up. She was standing a few feet from me, the faint sunlight lifting beyond the mountains at her back. "Take Fagan to Bletsung Macleod."

I didn't hesitate. Seeing dawn's light on the horizon, I knew we had to get away from here as fast as we could. I hurried over and drew Fagan up again, helping him rise. Grinding his teeth in pain, he held his feet and leaned on me. "Pa'll look for me at Miz Elda's," he rasped.

"I ain't taking ye there."

"Where then?"

I told him.

Fagan was too done in and too heavy for me to get up the steps. I left him half-conscious on the ground and hurried up to the door, pounding. "Miz Macleod! Miz Macleod! Come help. Please!" I pounded again, harder, louder. "Help us!"

"Cadi, what on earth are ye doing—*oh!*" She came out the door and down the steps, not the least concerned that her blonde hair was streaming down her back and over her shoulders. She hunkered down beside Fagan, touching him and looking him over. "Help me get him into the house, Cadi." Slipping an arm around his waist, she nodded to me and we rose together.

The inside of Bletsung Macleod's small cabin come as a surprise to me. I'd expected it to be dark, dank, and dusty and filled with spider webs—that seemed to go along more with what people said about her being mad and a witch and all. But it was swept clean, with no dust to be seen, and the windows were open to let in the cool morning breeze.

She had few furnishings: a table with two straight-backed chairs, a cabinet, and a large bed in the back corner. Beside it was a small table. A long work shelf was beneath one of the windows that looked out over the garden. Under it was a crockery bowl, two jugs, and several small storage barrels. Hanging on the wall to the right of the window and table were her cooking utensils. Several pots and pans hung on hooks near the fireplace, and a big iron pot was suspended over the smoldering coals of a banked fire. She had a spinning wheel and a loom.

All plain and simple . . . except it wasn't. There were touches of beauty everywhere I looked. The chair backs were carved with doves in flight, the cabinet with grape leaves and grapes. Every piece of furniture had been polished to a sheen with beeswax. Dried vines had been carefully knotted into intricate and delicate patterns that draped across and along the sides of each window. A cracked pitcher filled with flowers sat on one sill. One shelf had a row of jars filled with pure amber honey. A bowl of apples sat upon the worktable, their sweet scent mingling with that of the herbs she'd hung from the rafters and the pie tin of dried rose petals.

Everywhere I looked were beeswax candles. Several of various sizes were placed on the mantel among pine bows, one graced each side of the worktable, three at varying heights were set upon the commode, and four in a candleholder suspended above the dining table.

Most wondrous of all was the porcelain teapot with painted flowers and graceful curves that sat in the center of her table on top of a colorful, delicately woven woolen scarf that draped over the sides. I'd never seen anything so pretty.

"Help me get him onto the bed." She bore more of Fagan's weight than I could. I lifted his feet while she gently shifted his body onto the rope bed. The mattress was thick and rustled with cornhusks. Even the old, worn quilts upon her bed had color and pattern to please the eye.

Fagan sighed deeply as Bletsung slipped her arm from beneath him.

"Is he dyin'?"

"No, dearie. Fetch some water, Cadi. Quick now." She placed her hand on his forehead. "The bucket's there by the door." I ran to do her bidding.

She'd stoked the fire, added wood by the time I came back. Taking the bucket from me, she poured half the water into a pot hanging over the fire. "Near as I con tell there's no bones broken except maybe a cracked rib or two."

"Should I run and fetch Gervase Odara?"

"It'd do no good, Cadi. We've done as much as she could do. And no use telling his mama. There are precious few who'll come near this cabin, and she ain't one of them." She looked at me solemnly. "Was it Brogan Kai?" When I nodded, she sighed softly. "Then we're in this alone."

I knew what she meant. Even my father was afraid of him. Why else would he bend so easily to the man's will? One visit and a few words was all it took. Everyone did the Kai's bidding.

Except for the man of God. And look what'd been done to him!

I started to cry—deep wrenching sobs. I jerked slightly in surprise when Bletsung Macleod put her arms around me. "Now, now, child," she said tenderly, and I let her hold me close. She stroked my back, murmuring comforting words to me the way Mama once had when I was but a wee bairn. Before Elen . . . "Shhhhh, dearie, Fagan'll be all right. Ye'll see. Were ye two with the mon in the valley?"

"Aye, and he's dead. The Kai killed him. Beat him to death."

"I dinna think he'd go so far . . ." I felt Bletsung Macleod's body give a shudder, and then she let out her breath slowly, relaxing. "So that's the way it stands."

Raising my head, I saw tears streaming down her cheeks. She gazed forlornly toward the window that opened out toward Dead Man's Mountain. "It doesn't do any good to hope for the moon, Cadi. Ye just have to make the best of what life gives ye."

What hope had we now?

"Trust in the Lord, Katrina Anice, and the power of his strength," Lilybet said from the doorway, the sun at her back.

I turned at the sound of her voice. "What strength has God when the Kai could kill his man like that?" Moving out of Bletsung Macleod's arms, I beseeched Lilybet for answers. "He just stood there! He just took the blows! And God dinna do nothing to stop the Kai! Why dinna he strike him dead? *Why did he take our hope away?*"

"Every messenger God has sent to man, even his own Son, Jesus, has been rejected. But heed the word of the Lord, Katrina Anice. *Remember.* 'God so loved the world, that he gave his only begotten Son, that whosoever believeth in him should not perish, but have everlasting life.'"

"What of the man?"

"He's but a breath away, my dear."

Gooseflesh rose and I shuddered. "Are we going to get killed too? Is that what ye're saying?"

"The truth has set you free, beloved. Now you must choose to walk in it."

"Easy for ye to say, but what of the Kai? Is he going to let us walk anywhere at all now he knows we went against him?"

"Believe on him who saved you, Katrina Anice."

"I want to believe. I do."

"Then believe."

"I try to believe."

"*Believe.* Set your mind and heart upon Christ and obey the word of the Lord. Stand firm, Katrina Anice. God himself is going to fight for you."

Though I didn't understand her full meaning then, I felt the despair lift like the clouds being burned away by sunlight. The Lord would fight for such as me? How could I believe such an amazing thing? Yet, I did. My soul drank in her words, and the cold fear melted away. New strength poured into my veins until I fair trembled with it. The Lord, the Lord *my* God, would fight for me.

"Remember," the man of God had said.

And I did. Every single word he had said. Turning, I was bursting with hope. "God will protect us."

Bletsung Macleod stood against her worktable, a hand pressed to her heart, her face pale as birch bark. "And they say *I'm* mad."

"I ain't mad, ma'am. I swear I ain't."

She looked past me to where Lilybet had been standing. "Then who was ye speaking to like that?" Frowning, she looked at me again, waiting for me to explain.

What could I say to that? I worried my lip, not knowing what to tell her about Lilybet. It would not set her mind at peace if I told her Lilybet had appeared to me when I was planning to jump off the tree bridge, ending my life over the falls where my sister had lost hers. She'd think Lilybet was Elen come back from the dead just like everyone else did.

The cornhusks rustled as Fagan roused. "She ain't crazy, Miz Macleod," he said faintly. "She's just a little odd. Likes to talk things over with herself."

Bletsung Macleod considered his words and sighed. "Well, I reckon I've done a bit of that myself. Lie back and rest, boy. Ye'll do yourself more harm moving around."

"I can't stay here. I'll bring trouble on ye."

"Ye'll bring nothing on me that ain't been at my door for years already." She pressed his shoulders back. "No one'll find ye here."

"Pa'll track me straight to ye, ma'am."

"Brogan Kai will not bother ye as long as ye're under my roof. Shhh, now. Just take my word for it. Ye're safe with me."

As I stood at the foot of the bed looking at Fagan's swollen face, Bletsung reached out and lifted the parchment dangling from a string around my neck. "What's this? A lucky spell or summat?"

"Oh!" I'd forgotten all about the parchment I was supposed to give to the man of God. Mayhap it was a good thing I'd forgotten, for had I handed it over, it might even now be in the Kai's hands. "Miz Elda's going to wonder what's happened. If I don't go back soon, she might worry herself to death."

Miz Elda was not alone when I reached the edge of the woods near her cabin. Brogan Kai was standing on the porch leaning down over her and talking while his sons stood at the bottom of the steps. Miz Elda was rocking the chair back and forth, slow and easy, looking off toward the valley and not saying a word to him. He raised his voice once, and though I could not hear his words, his tone and demeanor spoke loud enough. He went down the steps and jerked his head, his sons following after him.

They took the path that led to my father's house.

As soon as they were out of sight, I ran the distance to Miz Elda.

"What're ye doing here, child?" she said, none too pleased to see me. "Brogan's looking for ye. Ye can't stay."

"The Kai killed the man."

"Brogan's making no secret of what he done," Miz Elda said. "Told me straight out about it and claims he did it for our own good. He said that man was trying to lead us astray. Where's Fagan?"

"Bad hurt. Cracked rib and all bloodied. Bletsung Macleod's taking care of him."

"Stood with the mon, did he?"

"Yes, ma'am." I unlooped the parchment from around my neck and held it out to her. "I'm sorry, Miz Elda."

Her lips pressed together as she looked at it. "He didn't want it?"

"I forgot is all."

She gave a bleak laugh. "Might be a blessed thing ye did." She looked off the way the Kai and his sons had gone. "Seems nary a thing goes the way we plan. Well, enow." Frowning, she looked at the rolled parchment in my hand. I could see she was thinking hard again. "Keep it with ye, girl. Put it back around your neck and tuck it inside yer dress where nobody'll see it. And when my time comes, give it to Fagan."

"Fagan?"

"Ye heard me. Don't tell him about it yet. He won't understand my reasoning, and if I was to explain, it'd only make more trouble for him."

"How?" I could make no sense of what she was saying.

Her face looked bleak and despairing. "Sooner or later, things are going to have to come to rights."

"What things're ye talking about, Miz Elda?"

She waved me away impatiently. "Go on back to Bletsung now. Go on, I tell ye. Longer ye stay around here, the more chance of trouble."

I stood on the edge of her porch, heart breaking. I didn't know when I'd be able to come back and see her. What if she died while I was gone? "I'll miss you."

Her eyes filled. "God's bringing all this pain on us for what we done."

I could tell her heart was broken, too, not by my leaving but by whatever dark secret she'd held so deep inside herself all the years. I came back and knelt beside her chair, putting my arms around her frail body one last time. "No matter what ye done, Miz Elda, I love ye and I always will." Hadn't I sinned and been forgiven?

With a sigh, she rested her cheek against my hair. "It ain't what I did that haunts me so, dearie. It's what I didn't do, and each year that passes makes it all the worse." She was weary with regret. "I reckon now that the mon's dead, we'll have to stay by the old ways 'til the mountains tumble down on us."

The words came to my lips of their own accord. "Cast thy

burdens upon the Lord Jesus, Miz Elda. No good thing will he withhold from ye if ye love him."

"Did the mon in the valley tell ye that?"

"Yes, ma'am. And he said Jesus washes our sins away and makes us white as snow." I told her the best part of what the man had said to me; the gift of grace he'd poured on me I poured on her. And her dry, old body soaked it in like rain on parched soil.

"Can it be that easy?"

"It was for me."

She touched my cheek gently and smiled. "That's because most of what ye did was in your own mind, child."

"Wishing's doing. The way God sees it."

"Maybe so. Only I want ye to know your granny and I never thought for a moment ye pushed Elen into the river."

"Mama did."

She didn't deny it. "Ye'd best go now, Cadi, before Brogan comes back this way and sees ye."

"Is he gone to my father?"

"I'm afraid so. He was none too happy ye were down in the valley with his son. He'd like to lay the whole blame at your door."

"It was my doing."

"No, child. There's a hand bigger than yours in all this. Ye've stirred up words my mama said to me years ago back across the sea. But I'm remembering more. As to the rest, in time, we'll see whether God means to lift us up or crush us down. Now, go!"

Kissing her cheek, I went quickly down the steps.

"Cadi. One more thing."

"Yes, ma'am?"

"Tell Fagan I'm right proud of him."

Bletsung Macleod greeted me as I came through the door she'd left open for me. "He's sleeping sound," she said with a smile.

The cabin was filled with the mouthwatering aroma of fine cooking. My stomach cramped with hunger, but I was so tired I could scarce hold my feet. "Sit there, darlin'." She nodded to the table as she ladled a goodly portion of stew into a bowl. Setting it before me, she poured water into a pewter mug. "Squirrel stew and biscuits." She took a cloth from a small basket. "Ye like honey?"

"Yes, ma'am!"

She took a bottle of amber from the shelf and opened it. "Split a biscuit and put it on the saucer." I did and she poured honey in a thick golden stream until the biscuit was covered. Mama had never done such a thing, and I stared at the golden stream, sticking my fingertip in and tasting it. Laughing, she set the jar down.

"I never tasted anything so good." Not even Granny's hives had produced such sweetness as this.

"I always set my bee gums near the mountain chestnut. Can't get better honey."

She sat down opposite me. "Eat your stew, Cadi. Ye're sorely in need of a little meat on your bones."

Bletsung Macleod was as fine a cook as I'd ever visited, better even than Mama. I finished the bowl of stew and the biscuit, easing the thick sweetness with the cool mountain springwater. Full, I struggled to keep my eyes open. Unable to fight it any longer, I pushed the bowl away and put my head in my arms, going straight to sleep right there at her table.

I awakened to the sound of voices and found myself tucked next to Fagan. He was still sleeping soundly from the pain elixir she'd given him.

"The mon's dead," Bletsung Macleod said, and half asleep, I didn't think much about her talking to herself. "Aye, I'm sorry to tell ye. Brogan was the one who done it. I reckon he left the mon alone as long as people stayed clear of him."

The wind stirred the leaves outside her window, and I heard a soft, deep voice.

"Cadi went back to Elda's after helping the boy here," Bletsung Macleod said. "I was surprised she come to me. Don't know what made her do it considering what most people think of me. She's the only child who's come near this cabin, her and the boy. She's a strange one, she is, given to talking to herself." She laughed softly. "When she first got here, she started in talking like someone was standing in the house. Scared me clean out of my wits, I con tell ye. I thought she'd brought a taint with her. But the boy said that's just the way she is. Reckon it comes of being heartbroken and cast out. . . ."

Again, that soft, deep voice.

"Purely so. I was surprised when she came back instead of going home to her mama and papa."

I heard the response clear this time. "She's been staying with Elda."

Who was speaking? Bletsung Macleod perched on a stool next to an open window. She went on talking, all the while keeping her head up and looking at the mountain as she spoke. And then, with a sharp quickening of my heart, I knew who was sitting below her window.

The sin eater.

Fagan moved, the rustling of the cornhusks like thunder in my head. I closed my eyes quickly, heart pounding, as Bletsung Macleod fell silent. He was here, all right. If I let them know I was awake, he'd want me to talk to him, to tell him what the man of God had said. And how could I tell him the truth without causing him more grief? So I pretended to be asleep when Bletsung Macleod left her seat by the window, came across the room, and leaned over us. She tended to Fagan first, rinsing a rag and dabbing his bruised face, tidying the quilts. She brushed some hair from my forehead. "Cadi?" Determined she not catch me out, I moved slightly, giving a soft moan and pulling the quilt up higher. Then I held still as a sleeping mouse in its hidey-hole, not moving again until I heard the soft scrape of the stool by the window.

"They're still asleep."

The sin eater spoke softly in question.

"She dinna say anything about what the mon said. She'll likely sleep the day away."

"Ye'll be glad of the company," I heard him say quietly.

"Aye, I am that. I'll do whatever I can for them. The boy's a brave one, going against his father the way he has. Brogan never had the courage to do it. And Cadi's Gorawen Forbes's grandchild. That's for sure. The woman was kind to ye. I'll treat Cadi like my own child."

Again, he spoke.

"Well, it ain't my doing," Bletsung Macleod said, sounding distressed. "I dinna tell them to come." A pause and the gentle, calm voice. "No, I won't take 'em home." Her voice was low and fierce. "If ye could but see what Brogan done to his own son, ye wouldn't suggest it. People who treat their children the way these two've been treated don't deserve to have 'em at all. And besides that—"

"Bletsung, my love, would ye have it so if it were you?"

My love?

"We've no right to judge."

Bletsung Macleod was silent so long I wondered if she was angry at the man for his gentle reprimand. Cautiously, I opened my eyes just enough to see her still sitting, pale and pensive, by the window. She was staring up at the mountains. Perhaps the sin eater had gone away again.

"I reckon you're right." She sighed. "Oh, sometimes I can't help thinking what might have been." Closing her eyes, she bowed her head sadly.

"There ain't a day goes by that I don't think about what I

done, Bletsung, and what's come of it. I thought I was sparing ye from suffering, and instead I've brought it on ye twenty years and more. Ye should've gone o'er the mountains with my kin and started afresh somewhere else."

"How could I leave when my love is here?"

"Ye'd be long married with children of your own by now."

"I only wanted yours."

They both fell silent. The maple leaves rustled, and I heard the plaintive sound of a mourning dove.

The man spoke softly, and Bletsung rose from her stool. "Oh, please, stay awhile longer. Ye don't have to say nothing. I just like knowing ye're close to me."

"I'm always close."

She eased back onto the stool again, running her hand along the windowsill. "Not close enough . . ."

"The mon should be properly attended."

"What con ye do about what's happened?"

"Nothing, I reckon, but I con take the mon's body up onto the mountain. I know a proper place where he can be laid to rest." He said something more, his voice soft and tender, and then there was only the rustling of leaves in the maple and warblers singing.

Bletsung Macleod said nothing more. She was staring up at Dead Man's Mountain, tears streaming down her cheeks.

At ease with his departure, I fell back asleep.

"She loves him, Fagan," I told him when I awakened late in the afternoon. I'd gotten up and peeked outside, making sure Bletsung Macleod would not hear. She was in her garden, wearing a broad-brimmed straw hat, hoeing weeds.

"It ain't our business." He groaned when I sat on the bed, for even that slight movement hurt him. His face was a mess of purple and black, one eye swollen completely shut.

"Maybe not, Fagan, but it bears thinking on, don't ye reckon? He loves her, too. Ye should've heard the way he spoke to her, so soft and sweet." I felt melancholy just thinking about it. "Papa used to talk to Mama that way."

Fagan lay still as he could to keep the pain at bay. "My pa ain't never talked to my ma like she meant summat to him, but I've seen her look at him as though the sun wouldn't rise without him. Don't see how she can feel that way . . ."

"It ain't hard," I said, thinking of my own situation. "Ye con love people without 'em loving ye back. Especially if ye know the reason they can't bear the sight of ye."

He turned his head and opened his good eye. "Maybe ye're wrong about your ma, Cadi."

I shrugged, sure I wasn't. "It don't matter anymore. I'm used to the way things are."

"No ye ain't."

I bit my lip and worried it until I could answer without my voice trembling. "It's my own fault things are the way they are. I may not have pushed my sister into the river, but I wished she'd fall."

"I've wished ill on my pa and my brothers, too, Cadi. That ain't why things happen. It weren't your fault Elen died."

"I know that now, Fagan, but don't ye see yet? Fault don't matter. I know what I am. I'm a sinner. Even when I tried to do good, it turned out bad."

"No more than anyone else. Some worse than others."

"Your father, you mean."

"Yes, my father. And my brothers. I hated 'em, Cadi." His good eye teared up. "So where's the difference between me and them, I ask ye? If I hadn't accepted Jesus and been washed clean down there in the river, I'd be the same. I was the devil's own and thought I always would be. And now, everything's changed. We're not the same, Cadi. Ye gotta believe what the mon told us."

"I want to believe, Fagan, but where's accepting Jesus gotten you? I should never have gone."

"Why not?"

"Look what happened!"

"Ye found hope, didn't ye?" He was still aflame with it, even hurting as he was.

"It dinna last long, did it? The mon's dead."

"He told us the truth, Cadi. Didn't ye feel it right into the heart of ye? Couldn't ye hear God's own voice in every word he spoke?"

"Everything the mon said made perfect sense while he was saying it. But maybe because I wanted so badly to feel I was forgiven, I'd have believed anything."

"You were happy, Cadi. Ye should've seen your face. You were aglow."

"Aye, I was so filled up with happiness I was fair bursting with it," I said, tears coming. "And then your pa comes with your brothers and beats the life out of that poor mon and the spirit right out of me. Where was God then, Fagan? I keep thinking and thinking about it, and I can't put it to rights with the way things are. Nothing's changed. Nothing ever will."

"That's because we've been doing things all wrong, Cadi."

Angry and frustrated, I glared at him. "Aren't ye listening to me, Fagan? Everthing's the same as it ever was."

"No it ain't."

I was trembling inside because of my own weak faith. I had walked away unharmed and terrified, and there was Fagan, battered and broken and ready for a holy war.

"He done nothing but tell the truth and got killed for it," I said.

"It can't end there."

It hadn't, though I didn't want to tell Fagan that the man had laid the burden heavy upon me. Most unfitting, to my way of thinking. I was a child, an outcast. What could I do?

Yet the hand of God squeezed my heart. All that was within me clung like ivy to the trunk of that great tree I'd been grafted into. Me, a sprout and not a branch. Not yet, anyway. I'd opened my heart and God had come pouring in. God with his forgiveness. God with his mercy. God with his love. I didn't deserve any of it!

"I believe, Fagan. I do, but I'm terrible afraid. Your pa spoke to Miz Elda and he's gone to my folks, too. If he did this to you, he'll do worse to me."

"God will protect you."

"He dinna protect the mon by the river. He dinna protect you."

Fagan grasped my wrist tightly. "God was there. I won't pretend to understand why things went the way they did, but I know this. Ye've got to tell people the truth."

I gave a faint laugh, jerking my wrist from his grasp. "The Kai, ye mean? Ye think I should go and tell your pa?"

Grimacing in pain, Fagan closed his eye again. "No. I'll tell him myself when the time comes to do it."

I felt ashamed. After all his pa had done to him, Fagan wasn't losing courage. "I told Miz Elda," I said, wanting Fagan's approval.

"That's one."

I shuddered, thinking of Brogan Kai looking for me. I was bringing grief to my family again, now more than ever. Yet, even now, I yearned to share what I had heard. Telling the old woman the word of the Lord had been easy because she'd been waiting to hear what God had to say. I could tell my brother, Iwan, but he'd be quick to take Mama and Papa's side. And if I were to show up now, they wouldn't likely let me open my mouth before Pa'd be using his belt on me and lock me in the woodshed for causing trouble with the Kai.

"Maybe Miz Elda'll tell Gervase Odara."

"Maybe," Fagan said softly.

"I've been thinking, Fagan. It would not make people happy if I was to tell them what the mon said."

Turning his head slowly, he opened his good eye and looked at me. I felt like Peter denying Jesus.

"I mean, think about it," I said softly. "All our folks believe the sin eater's taken their sins away so they could be clean before God. You think they're going to be happy hearing their loved ones've all gone to the grave with their sins still on 'em? Ye think they're going to want to know their folks are probably burning in hell?" I thought of Granny. "Who'd want to believe a thing like that?" I hoped the Lord would see all the good in Granny's heart. She'd loved me when I wasn't worth loving and had been kind to the sin eater when no one else cared what happened to him so long as he did his duty. She set out food for him when all the rest gave him only their sins to eat.

"The mon said God sees the heart," Fagan said, more certain than I. "We gotta trust him, Cadi. We can't be looking back at the dead. We gotta look to the living."

"What if we tell people the truth and they won't listen, Fagan? What then? They ain't listened up to now. The mon was speaking to all of us, but we were the only ones to go down to the river and cross over."

"That don't change nothing, Cadi."

"So the same thing could happen to us that happened to that poor mon by the river."

"We can't think about what could happen. We gotta think about what God wants us to do. We're going to face him someday, Cadi. You and me, standing before the Lord Almighty. You want to tell him you knew his Son died for everyone in this valley and ye dinna tell anyone but one old woman?"

I hung my head in shame. I kept thinking about the blows Fagan had taken while I hid in the darkness.

"Jesus knew what it'd cost him, Cadi. And he knows what it's gonna cost you." Fagan took my hand again. "The fear ain't coming from Jesus, Cadi. It's coming from my pa. Ye can't let him hold ye back from doing what ye know we have to do. Ye can not withhold the truth. If ye do, it ain't God ye're serving, it'll be the Kai. And there's no hope for any of us if ye let him lead ye."

My stomach quivered as I thought of my promise to the sin eater. He was the first one I needed to tell. If not for him, I'd never have gone down to the river and heard the word of the Lord at all.

How was he going to feel when I told him everything he'd ever done had been for nothing?

"Please, Cadi." Fagan tried to sit up. Groaning, he lay back and closed his eyes.

I leaned over him. "Your head aching?"

He grimaced at my touch. "Hasn't stopped."

I eased myself off the bed so as not to shake him and went to fetch a cool damp rag for his forehead. "Thanks," he said. He felt for my hand. When I slipped mine into his, he squeezed it tight. "We're in this together." He fell asleep again. Still holding his hand, I lay down atop the quilts and watched him until I could no longer keep my eyes open.

It seemed God was going to have his way with me after all.

The way of Jesus and the cross.

SIXTEEN

I WENT AROUND THE HOUSE NEXT MORNING AND found the place where the sin eater sat beneath the window. It was worn smooth, a narrow pathway leading away toward the forest at the base of Dead Man's Mountain. I was following it when Bletsung Macleod leaned out the window and called to me. "Where ye going, Cadi?"

"To find the sin eater."

"Why don't ye wait a day or two. He'll come down. Ye can sit on my stool and talk to him through the window."

I shook my head, knowing if I waited a day or two, I'd lose my courage. "I have to go now, ma'am."

"Well, then, let me give ye something to take to him." She disappeared inside the cabin, and I retraced my steps to the barren spot below her window, waiting there until she reappeared above me. Leaning out, she held a basket down to me. In it were raisin scones and a jar of honey. She dropped an empty gourd with a long string and a cork in it. "Keep to the path, Cadi, and ye'll find a spring a mile up the mountain. You'll be thirsty by then."

It was a hard climb up Dead Man's Mountain with the temptation of Bletsung Macleod's scones and honey. The path wound its way upward between towering tulip trees, sugar maples, yellow birch, and red spruce. I found the spring and knelt down, cupping my hands and raising the water to my lips. Birdsong was all around me, and feeling safe, I rested there awhile, listening to the water trickling from the rocks. A yellow tanager fluttered to the ground not far away, pecking at the ground before flitting swiftly to the trees. Filling the gourd, I looped it over my shoulder, lifted the basket, and walked around the spring until I found the path again.

The day grew warm, the air heavy with moisture. The path went through a forest of waist-high ferns growing beneath a canopy of spruce and fir. I could hear the soft rush of water and came to a misting falls. Panting, I stood near the spray that hit the rocks, thankful after the heat for the refreshing shower. A rainbow arched in the stream of sunlight. There was a small pool at the base of the falls, and I wondered if the sin eater bathed here.

Picking my way carefully across the stream, I kept to the path winding ever upward until the rich smell of earth gave way to the smell of hot, sun-drenched stone. Pausing, I looked across the stretch of granite. My legs were tired from the long climb. Had I come so far just to lose my way? Sipping water from the gourd, I sat a few minutes beneath the shade of a pine that grew from cracks in the rock plateau. Then I walked across the layered stones, like giant steps, to a sparser forest beyond.

Walking between an outcropping of granite, I entered a thick forest of birches. The white trunks were stark against the green foliage, some of it already turning brilliant yellow and orange in the cooling air of the heights. There, on the other side, I found the home of the sin eater, a cave in the mountainside.

"Hello!" I called, my heart drumming. No one answered. I came a few steps closer, seeing a circle of stones where a fire had burned. An iron spit had been dismantled and left leaning against the cave entrance. Pausing, I waited, then called out again, louder this time, my palms sweating. "Hello!"

Still no answer.

Curious, I approached cautiously. "Sin Eater?" I called softly. Gathering my courage, I peered inside. "Sir, I've come to tell ye what the mon by the river said."

As my eyes adjusted to the dimness, I saw a pile of furs near the back wall of the cave. Other than a rough-hewn open cabinet in which were several small cooking pots, two clean glass jars like the one I carried in my basket, and some chipped crockery, the poor man had no furnishings. A lantern hung from a root that had grown through a crack in the granite. A thin stream of sunlight pierced the darkness from above.

Entering, I looked up and saw the cave was large enough for a man to stand straight. One area of the cave's wall that ended in a crevice, which I reckon opened to the outside, was blackened by years of smoke.

At least it was dry and cool after the heat of the late-summer day and would likely be warm enough during the cold winter months. Yet I felt sad thinking of the man living in this dark place for so many years.

I put the basket with the scones and honey on the pallet of furs and went back outside.

Had I come all this way for nothing?

"Sin Eater! Where are you?" Wind rustled the birch leaves. Was he close by, hiding and watching? "I've come to keep my promise!" I walked along the face of the mountainside, wondering what to do. Should I wait until he returned? And when would that be? What if night fell and he still didn't come? What if he did and was angry that I'd entered his home? A hundred dire possibilities raised their heads.

The wall fell away and the world stretched out before me, row after row of deep green and blue-purple mountains troughed by puffs of white mist. An eagle cried above me, riding the wind currents. Awestruck, I turned, gazing all around me at the majesty of it all. I had never imagined the world being so vast, so beautiful. I kept climbing, eager now to stand at the top and see all around. The sin eater and my promise were forgotten in my quest for the heights. It was steeper now. I had just paused to sit and rest when I heard the crack of rock against rock. Rising, I walked along a ledge.

And it was then I saw him and remembered why I'd come.

Hunkered down before a long, narrow shelf of stone, the sin eater stacked stones, encasing the man of God, who was now tucked into a crevice at the top of the mountain. The dead man lay upon a bed of pine beneath the shelf, hands folded upon his chest, his eyes held closed by white pebbles. Hunkering down, hand to mouth, I watched.

The sin eater placed the stones with great care, shifting and moving them until they fit together tightly, sealing the man of God into the mountain. When he was finished, he stood for a long moment, head bowed in respect. Then he climbed the short distance to the top. He stood with his arms raised to the sky as though wanting to grasp hold of something. Sinking to his knees, he bent over, holding his head—and I could hear his broken sobs.

Climbing down from the rocky heights, I returned to the cave of the sin eater, sitting outside and waiting for him to return. Despairing, I wondered what more grief I would bring the poor man when he knew the truth. An hour passed and then another. When the sun began the arc toward the west and he still had not returned, I knew I had to start back down or I would not be off the mountain before dusk fell.

"Didn't ye find him?" Bletsung Macleod asked when I entered her cabin, tired and dusty.

I sank wearily onto the chair, putting the empty gourd on the table. "Did ye know he lives in a cave?"

A frown flickered across her face, and she shook her head. "No, I didn't."

"He hasn't got much."

"Ye went inside?" Fagan said, pushing himself up so that he was sitting on the edge of the bed.

"Just for a minute. I called out, but he dinna answer." I told them about the sin eater entombing the man of God.

"He said he'd see to the mon," Bletsung Macleod said, "but I dinna think he'd carry him clear to the top of the mountain."

"Seems a fitting place," Fagan said solemnly.

She smiled sadly and sat on the stool by the window, gazing out at the mountain. "Poor Sim." A tear slipped down her cheek. "He had such hope . . ."

"Sim?" I said, approaching her. When she said nothing, I touched her arm lightly.

She turned her head and looked at me, distracted.

"Did ye say *Sim?*" At the look on her face, I knew she had spoken his name unwittingly. "His name is—"

She stopped my words with her fingertips and shook her head. "Ye must not speak it aloud. I wasna thinking, child."

"Hello!" a man called from outside, startling both of us. Bletsung grasped my wrist, yanking me quickly away from the window. Releasing me, she gestured for me to move back to the far side of the cabin. Fagan's face was ashen gray, for he knew that voice very well. It was his father.

"Bletsung! Helllooo!"

She went to the door. "Get down behind the bed," she hissed. "I'm leaving the door open or he'll know something's amiss." She went out onto the porch and called out, "Well, if it isn't Brogan Kai come again, hat in hand. And after all these years."

Fagan shut his eyes. I could see the pulse pounding in his neck.

"I'm looking for my son, Bletsung."

"Why would ye come to me?"

"Fagan was last seen with the Forbes girl." His voice was closer. I moved restlessly, wanting to dive beneath the bed, but Fagan caught my wrist, putting a finger to his lips as his father spoke to Bletsung from just below the steps. "The Humes boy said he'd heard she'd been up this way a time or two."

"That so? Well, ye've made a long walk for nothing. What happened to make them both run off?" My heart pounded at her question, for I was afraid it might rouse his suspicions.

"Ye seen the girl or not?"

"Ain't gonna answer, are ye?"

"It don't concern ye, Bletsung."

"Not much does, it seems. I've lived alone, Brogan. More than twenty years now. I don't know what goes on among the rest of you. Nobody comes to call unless they need the sin eater."

Neither said anything for a long moment. We didn't dare move, for Bletsung hadn't taken a step toward the door. We knew Fagan's father was still there, though not what he was doing or what he might be thinking.

"It dinna have to be this way, Bletsung." His tone was strangely tender and filled with regret.

Fagan tipped his head, frowning.

"Oh yes it did." Bletsung's voice was firm.

"I would've had it otherwise." The Kai's tone took on a hard edge. "And well ye know it."

"Aye, I know how ye wanted it. Ye just dinna understand it could never be any way but this."

"Things would've been better for ye if ye hadna been so stubborn!"

"It wasn't stubbornness that kept me here, Brogan Kai. It was love." Her footsteps moved away from the edge of the porch, coming back toward the open doorway. She stopped when he shouted at her.

"The lot fell to him! He's been the sin eater for twenty-two years. When will ye give him up for lost?"

"Never!" she said defiantly. "Never," she said again, her voice breaking as she turned away. She came back inside. "Never, never, never . . ." Closing the door firmly, she dropped the bar into place. Closing her eyes, she stood for a moment, her forehead pressed against the door. When she opened her eyes again, I saw a hint of fear in the blue depths before she turned away and walked to the front window. She lifted the curtain aside just enough to look out. She held her breath and then let it out softly in relief. "He's going away." She moved away from the window.

Needing to see for myself, I hurried to take her place, peeping out cautiously. The Kai walked slowly across her small meadow, his shoulders stooped, a gun tucked firmly beneath his arm, barrel down.

I jumped slightly when Bletsung put her hand on my shoulder. "Best stay away from the windows, Cadi."

I felt lighthearted at the reprieve. "He's gone, Fagan. We're safe."

"For now." Fagan sat on the edge of the bed. He stared solemnly at Bletsung Macleod. "He'll come back, won't he?"

She lifted her shoulder, her expression showing nothing.

His eyes narrowed slightly. "What's between you and my father?"

"Nothing."

"Then why're ye so red?"

She sighed. "It was a long, long time ago, Fagan, before you were born." She sat down at her table, looking weary and sad. Resting her elbows on the table, she put her face in her hands and rubbed her forehead as though it ached.

Fagan got up and came over, sitting in the chair opposite her. That determined look was on his face. He folded his hands on the table, never once taking his eyes from her. "I want to know."

She lowered her hands and looked at him. She looked at him a long time. I reckon she saw he wasn't going to give up until she answered. "He wanted to marry me."

"Ye mean he loved you."

"Once, a long time ago, he thought he did. Or maybe he just felt bad about what happened and it being his father's doing and all. I don't know anymore, Fagan. It don't matter now anyway. It was years ago. The truth be told, Brogan Kai could've been the king of England come to call on me and it wouldn't've mattered. I loved another. I love him yet and will always."

I came closer. "The sin eater."

She raised her head and looked at me. "Aye, my dear," she said with a sad smile. "I love the sin eater."

"Ye must hate my father," Fagan said. "You and the sin eater both."

Bletsung leaned across the table and put her hand over his. "It was Laochailand Kai who demanded a sin eater, not your father. Some said no, but in the end everyone gave in out of fear. The old man told Brogan he'd walk these hills sure if his sins wasn't taken from him. And we all believed he would."

"He was so bad?"

"Cold cruel. He let it be known to everyone in these parts that he'd left Scotland for good cause. Summat terrible, we knew, but not what. And there're stories of how this highland valley came to fall into our hands. He was a bloody Scot if ever there was one and proud of it. Everyone feared him." She withdrew her hand. "But there were others as bad."

"My father," he said grimly.

She shook her head and rose from her chair. She went to the

stool by the window and sat, staring out at the mountain as she often did.

"So how did it happen?" Fagan said. "How was the sin eater chosen?"

"Pieces of bone were used, a mark for each man placed on each one. They were put in a mazer bowl and stirred and one drawn out by Cadi's grandmother, Gorawen Forbes. She cried when she saw whose marker she held, but she turned her back to him just like all the rest."

"And you?"

She turned the stool, looking back at us. "I would've stood against the old Kai myself if Sim'd let me, but he said God himself had drawn his name from that bowl of sorrow and there weren't nothing we could do to change it. So I ran away and came back here. I ain't never had much to do with the people of this valley since, and only a few ever came by."

"The Kai," I said.

"Aye, and Gervase Odara comes a couple times a year for my honey, and when the sin eater's needed," she said bleakly.

"They just left ye alone all these years?" I said, saddened.

"Not all of 'em." She smiled at me. "Your granny came years back before she began ailing. She and Elda Kendric both. I always knew I'd see them ladies in the fall when the leaves turned red and gold, and again around Christmas, and in the spring." She laughed at the pleasurable memories. "Your granny always came when the summer flowers were in bloom, and she'd have a basket of bluets for me. They never came empty-handed. They'd bring chestnuts or a jar of melon-rind pickles or apple butter, and I'd send 'em home with honey. Elda came once by herself and gave me that flowered quilt you're sitting on, Fagan." She frowned, perplexed. "I never did understand why she give it to me, especially since Iona had just given birth to Cleet, but she insisted I have it."

"Miz Elda ain't never given my mother nothing that I know about," Fagan said, frowning slightly. "They've never had nothing to do with each other that I know about. Why would she?"

"Summat must've happened to put up a wall between 'em," Bletsung said. "It's a sorrowful thing to be cut off from loving kin."

"Must be so," I said. "Miz Elda sent all her kin over the mountain years ago."

"Not all of 'em."

"What do ye mean?" Fagan said, studying her.

Bletsung Macleod looked between us. "Don't ye know?"

We looked at one another and then back at her. "Know what?" Fagan said.

"What've ye been told about Elda Kendric?"

"Pa said to stay clear of her. Said once she's worse than the plague. Only time I ever heard him mention her was when he was cursing her, and he won't have her mentioned in the house."

"And your mama?"

"She's never said a word about her."

Bletsung's eyes filled with tears.

Fagan searched her face. "What about Miz Elda?"

She shook her head, tears slipping down her cheeks. She looked away again.

"Tell me!"

She looked back at him, her blue eyes tear washed and fierce. "Don't use that tone on me, boy. It ain't for me to say more than I have. Miz Elda must have her own reasons for keeping silent. Maybe I'll go and ask her about 'em. Lord knows, I've missed talking with her." She looked away. "Time passes and we look to the things that won't hurt us, like the work that needs doing in the garden and the bees and putting up food for the winter. And all the while, people grow old and pass on, breaking off a piece of our hearts and taking it with 'em until there ain't nothing left but a hollowness inside."

"Ye could go visit Miz Elda," I said, feeling her misery as though it was partly my own. "She'd welcome ye sure. Ye could sit on her porch and visit with her all day long if ye liked."

Bletsung laughed sadly and shook her head. "No, I couldn't, Cadi."

"Why not?"

"Because she'd have to cross Kai Creek to get to there," Fagan said grimly.

"That ain't why," Bletsung said. "Ye mustn't think your father's the only reason I've stayed to myself all these years."

"Why then?" I asked.

"I know my place."

But Fagan was set in his mind. "I've got to leave here. I'll bring more trouble on ye if I don't."

"Your father won't bother me."

"He will if he thinks I'm here."

She smiled. "We'll make sure he doesn't find out."

Fagan scraped the chair back. "How ye plan on doing that? I can't stay cooped up in your house for the rest of my life, ma'am. It ain't right for me to stay here and soon as I can, I'm leaving!"

She stood, facing him across the room. "And go where? Back home to your bloody-minded kinfolk? I fear for you, Fagan. Ye think anything will've changed now your pa's killed that preacher? I con tell ye it won't. It'll be worse than ever. Ye go against the man and who'll stand with ye? Your ma? No. Your brothers? Never! Ye'll stand alone, and he'll lay into ye worse than before and maybe kill ye this time. Is that what ye want to happen?"

He just looked at her, his eyes bleak.

Her face softened. "Ye're safe here and welcome to stay as

long as ye like," she said more gently. She rose from the stool. "I've chores to do."

Grimacing in pain, Fagan rose as soon as she was gone. He jerked his arm away when I tried to help him. "I can manage to make it to the bed by myself."

I stood in the middle of the room, hands at my sides, watching him. He eased down onto the bed, wincing as he stretched out. Where could he go and not be found?

"There's a place where he'll be safe, Katrina Anice," Lilybet said, standing at the end of the bed where Fagan lay. "You know where."

It came like a flash of insight. "I know."

Fagan turned his head and looked at me. "You know what?"

I cocked my head, looking at Lilybet, wondering at her. "Should we go now?"

"No, but rest assured. You will know the proper time."

"I thought I'd have to go alone."

She smiled. "The Lord sent his disciples out two by two."

"Are ye talking to yourself again?" Fagan said, annoyed. "Why do ye have to act so crazy?"

I grinned at him. "I ain't crazy. I know where we can go and no one will follow."

"Where?"

I strode across the room and tugged the quilt up over him. "Go back to sleep, Fagan. When the time comes, I'll show ye the way."

There was plenty of work for me to do around Bletsung Macleod's place, and I didn't mind pitching in. Sometimes she'd stand and watch me, smiling as she went back about her own chores. We didn't say much to one another, but it was an easy silence, the land itself filled with sounds aplenty. A stirring of air rustled the leaves in the oak, hemlock, white pine, and red spruces while birds swooped, soared, and sang. Bees hummed with busy contentment while insects cricked in the tall grasses of the nearby meadow. And there was the creek with its melody of water on rock.

I didn't think much about Mama until I saw her standing near the curtain of mountain laurel. My heart jumped at the sight of her so silent and mournful, watching me work beside Bletsung Macleod. When I stopped and straightened, looking back at her, she turned quietly away and disappeared among the green tangle of vines. My throat closed so tight, I thought I'd choke. Part of me wanted to run after her. Part was glad she'd gone away.

"What is it?" Bletsung said, looking toward the forest near the creek.

"Nothing," I said and started hoeing again, my eyes hot and gritty. I'd never known Mama to walk so far. She must've gone to Miz Elda's and heard I'd come here, then come all the way to the end of the valley to see for herself. I wondered if Miz Elda had told her the Kai had killed the man of God. Did she care that he was gone?

Feeling a trickle of moisture, I wiped my cheek with the back of my hand and kept at the hoeing. What had Mama been thinking when she was standing there watching me? That she was well rid of me? Why had she wasted so much of the day just to look at me and turn away again?

"You all right, Cadi?"

"Just sad is all." I'd made up my mind not to lie anymore.

Bletsung watched me a moment and then looked toward the woods. "I don't know a soul in this valley that ain't sorrow filled."

We worked in her garden until the heat of the day was heavy upon us and then went back into the house. "Oh," Bletsung said, smiling, and headed straight for the window where two dead rabbits lay on the sill. She peered out and then drew back in dismay. "He's been and gone already. I wonder why he went away. He's been so eager to hear what ye heard from the man down by the river."

"He must've had a reason." He'd probably seen Mama.

Fagan dressed the rabbits, and Bletsung stewed them. Then we three waited all evening for the sin eater to come back, but he didn't.

"Sometimes he goes up to the mountaintop," Bletsung said, tucking me in for the night. "He'll come down again when he's ready."

Fagan insisted he sleep on the floor. He argued so long and hard, she gave in and let him sleep on the pallet she'd made before the fire.

The winds came up that night, keening the advance of fall. I awakened once to rain pounding on the cabin roof. The night was so black it even doused the stars. Only the embers in the dying fire glowed. Shivering, I tucked myself closer to Bletsung Macleod's warmth. Even then, I could not sleep. I kept thinking of the sin eater sleeping in that cold cave in the side of the mountain. The grieving lay like a heavy burden on my heart. What must it be like living up there all alone when the savage winds of winter were blowing over the rocks and through the trees, and there wasn't another living soul around to keep him company.

"There's God," Lilybet said.

I sat up, but it was too dark to see anything. "Aye, but does the sin eater talk to him?"

"His heart has cried out to God for a long, long time, Katrina Anice. God hears those who seek him. He embraces the rejected. He is father to the fatherless, light to the blind, a path to the lost . . ."

My heart burned within me. I knew it was the word of the

Lord I was hearing, and I was filled to overflowing with hope. Sim's salvation was at hand; God would come to him. "I thought it was all over when the Kai killed the man," I said in a hushed voice. "I was so scared."

"You've only just begun, Katrina Anice. Never fear. God is with you."

Excited now, not feeling the cold at all, I crawled out from beneath the covers, careful not to brush against Bletsung Macleod and awaken her. I crept carefully to the end of the bed and sat cross-legged at the end of the bed, eager to hear more. "Begun what?"

"You've begun your walk with the Lord. You opened your heart to Jesus Christ, and you were baptized at the river. Your eyes and ears are open now. Your mouth will be opened, too."

"I'll go up on the mountain again and tell the sin eater everything the man told me."

"Yes."

"Will it grieve him?"

"Yes."

"Oh," I said slowly, thinking. "Can I only tell him a wee bit at a time so he takes it in easier and it won't hurt so much?"

"No."

"What if I don't remember everything I'm to tell him? What if I say it wrong and he won't believe?"

"God will give you the words to speak. Trust in him, Katrina Anice. He loves you. You are very precious to him. The Lord has counted every hair on your head. He has all your tears in a bottle. He has written you in the palm of his hand. He has called you by name."

My whole body was covered with goosebumps at her words. "The Lord loves *me*?"

"Oh, yes." She came closer, so close I could feel the warmth radiating from her. "And the Lord loves Sim, too. You mustn't worry about what you're to say to him. You mustn't hold back when the time comes."

"Should I go now?"

"You'll know the time."

"Will it be soon?"

"Soon, Katrina Anice. Soon you will go forth in the name of the Lord."

"Cadi?" Bletsung put her hand on my shoulder, and my eyes popped open. I was lying on my back in bed, not sitting at the foot of the bed as I'd thought. "You're talking in your sleep, darlin'." I was trembling violently and she drew me close, pulling the quilts up more snugly around us. "Was it a bad dream, Cadi?"

"No."

"You're shaking like a leaf in the wind. Are ye cold?"

"No."

"Can ye tell me about it?"

The Spirit within me stirred. "Yes, I can." Turning to her, I sat up. Drawing the corner of Elda Kendric's basket-of-flowers quilt around me, I talked. Oh, how I talked. All the rest of the night, I kept on, telling Bletsung Macleod everything I'd been told down by the river.

And then the sun came up over the mountains, a spear of brilliance coming straight through the window where she always sat looking up at Dead Man's Mountain, up where the sin eater lived. Oh, how Bletsung Macleod wept. She wept and wept and grasped me close, and then I knew.

The Lord had saved her, too.

SEVENTEEN

We'd only just arisen from bed when someone helloed the house. Fagan came fully awake of a sudden and held his arm around his ribs as he struggled up in haste. "It's my mother!" He panted against the pain that was so clearly etched on his disfigured face.

I clambered from the bed and ran to peer out the window while Bletsung yanked her dark skirt over her head and buttoned it over her nightgown. "She's coming up," I said, heart racing. "She's coming!"

"Stay back from there, Cadi! She'll see ye."

"She's alone. Leastwise, I canna see anyone with her."

Fagan raked his fingers through his hair. "Pa never gets up this early. She must've come of her own. It ain't like her. Summat's terrible wrong."

"Stay put," Bletsung told him. "Ye'd better sit, Fagan. Ye look ready to keel o'er."

"*Hellllooo* . . ."

Bletsung took her shawl from the back of a chair and threw it around her shoulders, her face tight and withdrawn. "I never thought to see Iona in my part of the valley again," she said grimly. Opening the door, she went out. Iona Kai didn't stop when she appeared, but kept on until she was close enough to throw a stone through the window.

"What do you want, Iona?" Bletsung called out. She stood at the top of the steps, back straight, chin up in challenge. "What're ye doing here?"

"I'm lookin' for my son!"

"Brogan's already been here looking for him!"

There was a heavy moment, and then Iona Kai said derisively, "It ain't the only time he's been here, is it, Bletsung Macleod?"

"Ye always did have a nasty mind, Iona. And an even nastier tongue."

"Ye know where my boy is, don't ye?"

"And if I did, why would I be telling the likes of you?"

"He's *my* son, not yours. Ye'd understand if ye'd ever had children of your own."

"You and all the rest saw to it that'd never happen, didn't ye?"

They was stinging one another with words, dredging up hurts from years past. I kept listening, trying to make sense of it all.

"Come away from there," Fagan said.

"I will not."

"It was God's doing, not mine," Iona Kai said with less belligerence.

"Don't be looking at your feet when ye say it, Iona. Look me in the face. It was God's doing? Ye sure about that?"

"I had nothing to do with it!" the woman shouted angrily.

"Did I say ye did? The part ye had was turning folks away from me afterwards."

"Never did I do such a thing as that."

"Ye did and well ye know it! You and your vicious lies. I ain't never cast a spell in my life!"

"I dinna come to talk about the past, Bletsung."

"Maybe not, but it's there between us, ain't it, Iona? High as a stone wall, and ye built it yourself. Brogan married ye, didn't he? Ye got what ye wanted. Why did ye add to my misery?"

"I hate you, Bletsung Macleod! The devil take ye! I hate you so!"

"Aye, I know ye do."

Iona Kai began to cry, her face fierce in humiliation. "Where is my son, you witch! Where is he?"

I'd always thought Iona Kai a quiet, down-pressed woman, yet here she stood, spewing words so filled with hate it fair scorched the house. When I looked back at Fagan, I saw his face was pale as ashes and grievous shamed.

Bletsung stood on the porch, the shawl pulled tight around her, her chin held high in grave dignity. "Ye dunna deserve a boy like Fagan, Iona."

"You've no right to speak to me so!"

"Right or not, I'm speaking my mind. A mother ought to protect her own son."

"It ain't a woman's place to stand against her own husband, but ye wudna understand these things, not having one."

"Even when the mon's doing wrong? What sort of a wife and mother are ye to stand aside and watch your man sin and your son pay the price for it? I'll tell ye this, Iona. I'd stand against hell itself to protect Fagan, and he ain't even mine."

"Fagan! If you're in there, lad, *come out!*"

Weary and hurting, Fagan walked toward the door.

"He's safe, Iona. Or don't that matter to ye? He's mending from the beating Brogan give him because he stood up for the man by the river. A man of God! Did ye not know?"

"He shouldn't've stood against his da. He shouldn't've done it! If he'd listened to his father, none of this would've happened. He should've stayed away like he was told."

"Fagan done what was right!"

"He belongs with his own kin!"

"And what'll happen to him if he goes home now, do ye think? Has Fagan's da changed his mind? Your son took every word that man said into his heart, Iona. He ain't going to follow in the Kai's footsteps anymore. He belongs to the Lord now."

"I want him back!"

"Why?"

"You can't have him! He's my son! I'll not leave him here."

"There's the truth of it, aye? Ye're still blind with jealousy after all these years, so jealous ye'd rather put your own flesh and blood in danger than let him be with me?"

"*Fagan!* Come out here, boy. Come out to your mama."

Fagan looked at me sadly and then, resigned, opened the door. Steeling himself against the pain, he walked out and stood in the shadow of the porch. I knew it weren't only the pain of the cuts and bruises from the blows and kicks he'd taken. He was heartsick. And so too was I. My heart ached so, I went out and stood beside him. He didn't know I was there until I took his hand firm in mine.

"You there, girl! Get away from him!" Iona Kai's face was mottled red. "This is *your* doing!" I'd never seen a woman look more twisted and ugly. She scarce looked at Fagan, so intent was her hatred against Bletsung and me. She was casting blame left and right and not keeping a particle for herself. "I knew ye had him! I knew it! Soon as I get home, I'm telling Brogan how ye hid his son away from him. Then he'll see ye for what ye are!"

I went cold at her threat, remembering what he done to the poor man by the river. Would he do the same to us? It had been clear enough then that he had no great love for his own flesh and blood.

Bletsung stepped forward, her face pink. "You tell him, Iona. Ye do that because if ye don't, the *next* time he comes here, I'll tell him *myself.*"

The words struck hard and Iona's mouth worked. "Come on, boy. Ye're going home where ye belong."

I held tighter to his hand. "Ye don't have to go, Fagan. Stay here with us."

"Let go of me, Cadi. I have to go."

"They don't love you! They don't love you the way we do! Tell him, Bletsung."

"He knows, Cadi."

"Let go, I say."

Biting my lip, I did as he said and fled to Bletsung in my grief, grasping her around the waist. She put her arm around me, holding me close. "Ye can stay, Fagan," she said in a wobbly voice. "Ye can stay with me as long as ye like."

"She's my mother, ma'am. The Lord says to obey, don't he? I got to hold to that. I gotta hold to God or I ain't got nothing." He took another step and looked back at her. "Whatever hurt she's caused ye, I'm truly sorry for it."

Bletsung reached out and cupped his cheek briefly.

"Get away from her!" Iona screamed at her son.

Fagan winced at the awful sound of her rage. Turning away from us, he went down the steps clumsily, holding to the railing for support. Iona Kai walked toward the house, shoulders back in defiance and challenge. When Fagan reached the bottom, he straightened and let go of the rail. Raising his head, he looked at his mother. She stopped and her face went terrible white. Her hands went to her mouth. He walked toward her, hurting with every step, and she just stood there, staring and staring at him, her hands pressed over her mouth. When he stood before her, she didn't move.

"It's all right, Mama."

"Oh." Reaching up, she touched his bruised and battered face in disbelief. "Ohhhh." Turning away, she bent at the waist. "Ohhhhhh," she wailed, dropping to her knees and rocking.

Fagan put his arms around her. "Mama . . ." He drew her up. Turning, she clung to him, sobbing against his bloodstained shirt.

Bletsung put both her arms around me and looked away. I could feel her body trembling violently.

I listened to Iona Kai's keening, and the Spirit within me stirred. "It's coming to right. It's coming to right."

"I'd drag him back if I thought I could make him stay," Bletsung said in a broken voice. "They don't deserve a son like him. They don't deserve a son at all."

"Hush now. If ye can forgive her in your heart, it'll come to rights for ye, too. Ye'll see." I didn't know how I knew, I just knew. God had lit a lamp in me, and it was burning brightly.

Bletsung Macleod gave a soft, broken laugh and looked down at me. Cupping my face, she smiled. "Ye've ever been a strange one, Cadi Forbes. Stranger than I ever was. I could forgive her a month of Sundays, and it wouldn't matter a whit to how she feels about me. I learned a long time ago not to put much hope in people, especially Iona Kendric."

My lips parted in surprise. "Kendric? She's a Kendric?"

"Aye. Elda's daughter. Didn't ye know?"

"No, ma'am. Never heard tell of it." That meant the old woman was Fagan's granny. Did he know it? No, I knew he didn't. Yet, in the very heart of him, he'd known her for a kindred spirit and been drawn to her. Why had the old woman never told him so herself?

Iona drew back from Fagan, looking up at him again. The shame was clear on her face and the sorrow, too. She touched him again and spoke to him too soft for us to hear, standing where we were on the porch. Fagan stood still beneath her touch, saying nothing. Lowering her hand to her side, Iona stepped around him and walked slowly up to Bletsung's house. She stood at the foot of the steps, eyes downcast, mouth working. Letting out a shaky sigh, she raised her head.

"I reckon there's truth in what ye say. He canna come home."
The cost of her admission was there to behold. She looked old
and worn and hopeless.

Bletsung looked down at me in faint surprise and then back
at Iona. "He can stay here as long as he likes, Iona." She hesitated and then added with deliberation, "And ye're welcome
here, too."

Iona Kai's eyes flickered in surprise. She lowered her head
briefly, staring at the ground. Then she raised her eyes once
more and shook her head. "He canna stay here either, Bletsung."

"Will ye hold your bitterness forever?"

"It ain't that. I heard Brogan saying last night he was coming
here." Color flooded her cheeks. "I dinna know he'd come already. It bodes no good. I thought the most he'd do is whip him,
but I can see now he's past reason. No, the boy's got to leave.
He's got to hide somewhere Brogan canna find him. I dunna
know where that could be, but I'm terrible afeared what Brogan'll do if he finds him."

"So he's coming sure?" Bletsung said, clearly wishing it was
only a thought in Iona's head.

"He's coming. I don't reckon he'd harm ye," she said, the
poison still in her veins. "His feelings toward ye ain't much
changed, even after all these years."

"Ye never had reason to worry."

"He's a mon strong of mind and set on a path. He called Fagan a Judas and Cadi the goat who led him. I thought it was the
whiskey speaking, but it ain't. He said last night if Fagan'd been
there, he'd have pinned him to the wall with his hunting knife.
He's been talking and acting crazy since he went down and
killed that man by the river. He says he's gonna put an end to
the mon's lies."

"They weren't lies, Mama," Fagan said, coming to stand beside her. "He spoke the gospel truth."

"It don't matter if it was truth or no." She looked up at Blet-sung, beseeching her. "Ye know him as well as I, Bletsung. When he gets summat in his head, it's fixed forever. He doesn't know when he's gone too far. I canna bear to see more harm done to the boy, and I don't want Brogan having more blood on his hands." She turned to Fagan and grasped his arms. "Ye've got to go, Son. Ye've got to go now." She wept bitterly. "And ye'd best take the girl with ye."

Bletsung released me and came down the steps. "Ye canna go back to him, Iona. He'll know ye've warned the boy, and he'll kill ye sure as shooting."

"Where else can I go? Back to Mama? We ain't spoke a word in eighteen years."

I saw the question flicker across Fagan's face. "What're ye talking about, Mama? Your mama died years ago. Ye said—"

"Stay here with me, Iona," Bletsung said.

Iona drew back from her. "I canna stay with *you!* I've loved Brogan Kai all my born days, and it's 'cause of you I ain't even had a corner of his heart."

"He married ye, didn't he?"

"He needed sons." Her face was ravaged by warring emo-tions—love, bitterness, despair. "Truth have it, if I died today, it wouldn't make one whit of difference to him." She looked at her son, her mouth trembling. "The reason you and your pa've never gotten on is ye take after my father. Donal Kendric was the only man who ever stood against Laochailand Kai."

"Miz Elda?"

Iona Kai's eyes were awash with tears. "I'm sorry, boy. Your pa made me promise never to tell ye."

"If that be the way of things, dunna sacrifice yourself to the devil!" Bletsung said.

Iona turned and glared up at her. "He ain't a devil! He ain't! He's just a man who'd do anything to get what he wants, and it's all coming back on his head to roost!" She covered her face and wept bitterly.

Bletsung looked at Fagan and he shook his head, bewildered. He put his arms around his mother; she leaned into him, her fingers grasping at his shirt. He looked over her head at Bletsung, shocked at what had poured from her. He clearly didn't know what to do or say to protect and comfort her.

"Bring her inside," Bletsung told him quietly. "I'll keep her here with me. I'll hog-tie her if I have to, but she ain't going back to him. One look at her face, and he'll know what she's done." She stood back for them, following them up the steps. "Ye and Cadi get some things together and go hide in the root cellar. It's cut into the mountain just back of the house."

"That won't do," Iona said, hiccuping with sobs. "It won't do at all. He'll look there. He'll look everywhere. He knows Cadi's here and reckons Fagan ain't far away. He says there's a bond between 'em and he means to break it. They'll have to go o'er the mountains to Kantuckee."

"They're children, Iona! Would ye send them to their deaths? There's painters and bears and snakes. There's Indians as well, some with long memories of the things done 'em. And if that ain't enough, fall's coming, winter soon to follow."

"If they go, there's a chance. If they stay, there ain't no hope for either one of them."

"The easier way is through the Narrows and down the river to the Blue Ridge . . ."

"I've kin in Kantuckee, remember," Iona said. "One of my brothers would take 'em in, I'm sure." Her mouth trembled as she looked at Fagan's stricken face. "Ye've more kin than ye've ever guessed. I'm sorry. I'm so sorry."

"We can make it," Fagan said, giving an air of boyish confidence and bravado.

I knew a better place to go, but said nothing. Not yet. One

word of it and Iona Kai would come undone again and make matters worse trying to hold us back.

"The Lord is with you, Katrina Anice," Lilybet said and beckoned me from the doorway. "Go now."

"We have to go." I grasped Fagan's hand. When I pulled at him, he gasped in pain. "I'm sorry, Fagan, but there's no hope for us if we do not obey the Lord."

Iona looked from me to Bletsung. "What's the girl saying?"

"It's too soon," Bletsung said, distressed and wanting to detain us. "Ye'll need food and something to keep ye warm at night. Ye can hide in the forest and come back when ye know it's safe. Wait a few more days."

I looked into Fagan's eyes. His fingers tightened around mine. "We're going now," he said.

"I know the way," I told him softly.

We were at the foot of the steps when I saw Brogan Kai coming up from the creek. "That way," I said, pushing Fagan toward the sin eater's path.

"Fagan! You *Judas!*"

"Don't look back and don't stop!"

"Run, Cadi," he gasped. "I'm not going to make it."

"*Brogan!*" Bletsung came down the steps.

"Keep going! Keep going!" I urged Fagan, slipping my arm around his waist and giving him as much support as I could. He stumbled once, almost taking both of us down. As I helped him straighten, I glanced back and saw Bletsung struggling with Brogan, trying to hold him back. He flung her aside and came after us. The look of death was upon his face.

"Oh, God," I prayed. "Oh, God, help us! Please help us!"

We had reached the trees, but I knew Fagan would never make the climb. He was already winded, rasping from pain, pale and sweating.

"*Fagan!*"

Strength poured into my arms and back as I held him up and kept him moving. A heavy mist came down, seeping through the tops of the trees until it lay heavy around us. It swirled softly about our legs as we followed the path upward. I kept expecting the Kai to burst upon us. My heart drummed wildly in my ears. "Don't give up! Keep on!"

"Fagan!" The Kai's voice came eerie through the mist. "I'm going to find you, boy!" I could feel the blackness of his wrath. "And when I do, ye're going to be sorry you was ever born!"

Fagan tripped over a root and fell hard. "Go on, Cadi. I can't make it."

"You have to!"

"You're safer without me. Go on."

"I'll wait until ye've your breath back." I looked back down the path, my heart pounding in my ears. Any second, the Kai was going to come through the mist and do to us what he'd done to the man of God.

"Go on, I tell ye! My father's the best tracker in these mountains." He shoved me roughly away from him. "Go on!"

"I won't! I won't leave you!"

"I'm going to find ye, boy!" The Kai's voice was further off, coming at us disembodied through the mist. How long before he found us? I dashed the tears from my eyes and tried to get Fagan up again.

"Ye don't listen worth nothing, do ye?"

"If ye've got breath enough to talk, ye can walk. Now, get up! *Come on!*"

"What do you think ye could do if he finds us, aye?" he said, managing his feet. "Ye're no bigger than a mite."

"Save your breath." I grunted when he stumbled against me.

We kept to the path as we climbed. We were both parched when we reached the waterfall. Fagan sank to his knees, white-faced and exhausted. He drank his fill of cool water and lay back on the moss-covered ground, eyes closed, unmoving. My thirst quenched, I let him rest briefly while I stood guard, watching the trail. I hadn't heard Brogan Kai call out in a long while, but that didn't mean he'd not found our trail. I could only hope his wrath would give way to his fear of the sin eater.

There was no mist where we were, but I could see it still thick among the trees below us. I could see no further than the trees just below us it was so dense.

"We have to go on, Fagan." It was harder to get him up this time. He was tight-lipped, saying nothing now, and I knew it was taking all his determination to put one foot in front of the other. At the rate we were going we'd never make it up Dead Man's Mountain by nightfall.

We weren't even a quarter mile up the path from the water-fall when Fagan's last bit of strength gave out completely. He sank to his knees again. He gave a gasp of pain when I tried to help him up. "Can't . . . ," he said, his head drooping against my shoulder.

"Fagan?"

When he didn't answer, I knew he'd fainted. Easing him back, I held his head in my lap. "Fagan?" He was so white, I thought he'd died. "Fagan!" Laying my hand on his chest, I could feel his heart beating slowly. He was still breathing. "Fagan, I canna do it alone. I've got to get help." He made no response.

I heard a branch crack not far away and caught my breath. I couldn't leave Fagan on the path for his father to come upon. Looking around frantically, I wondered what to do.

"Hide in the cleft of the rock."

I recognized the voice, though it was like the sound of many waters. I knew it and obeyed. Grasping Fagan under the arms, I dragged him toward the rocky side of the mountain. The fallen leaves rustling beneath him sounded loud in my ears. Could the

Kai hear it, too? I reached the rocks and pulled Fagan into a wide crevice. If his father came upon us there, we'd be trapped and easy prey for his wrath, for there was no escape. Stone rose above and around us. When I had Fagan all the way into the cleft, I stepped around him and pressed myself against the stone so that I could peer out and watch the woods.

The Kai appeared on the path below. Head down, he was following our trail like a hound to the scent. My heart stopped, for I could see how dragging Fagan had left a clear path straight to our hiding place in the rocks. I knew the Kai would soon be upon us like a mad dog ready to tear apart its prey.

He came to the spot where Fagan had fallen and stopped. My heart fluttered frantically within me, like a flapping bird, wings beating to escape its fate. The Kai stared at the ground as though he could not make sense of the signs. Straightening, he looked around slowly, his head lifting as though taking scent from the air. He frowned, perplexed. When he looked toward the rocks, I pressed back further and held my breath.

God, please, help us! I don't want to die! I don't want Fagan to die!

Silence. Nothing but the soft puff of wind high in the trees. Not even the insects moved.

He was waiting.

And watching.

I breathed shallowly, mouth open, straining to hear.

A twig snapped.

I could hear heavy footsteps approaching the rocks. The closer they came, the harder and faster beat my heart. The Kai came so close I could hear him breathing through gritted teeth, like a beast hunting its prey. My heart thundered in my ears. He began to move away again, passing so close to me I could smell his sweat.

Silence again.

I peered out cautiously. He was looking around the area,

finding nothing. I could only wonder, for even I, poor tracker that I was, could've found our trail easily from the path across the leaves to the rocks where we were hidden. Had God put scales over his eyes so that nothing made sense to him?

Glaring around the woods in frustration, the Kai gave a black curse. He looked up the path, and something flickered across his face, stripping away the wrath and giving me a glimpse of the fear that held him from going further up the mountain. Kicking the dirt angrily, he turned and headed back down the mountain trail, slapping leafy branches out of his way. The mist closed behind him, and the forest sounds began once more.

I slid down the rock and hunkered there in the cleft. Gratitude filled me until my throat closed with tears. God had made the mist. I knew he had, though others later tried to convince me it was a coincidence. I knew the Lord God Almighty had protected us. Fagan and I had been in the midst of desperate trouble, and the Lord himself had stretched out his hand and covered us so that the Kai with all his tracking skills could not find us.

I leaned against that cold stone, my hands pressed against my heart, and knew I was loved. "Oh, Jesus, Jesus . . ." My heart was bursting. I longed for the Lord to be right beside me so I could throw my arms around him, so I could clamber onto his lap and stay there safe forever.

Fagan groaned softly, and the ecstasy of the moment evaporated like the mist that had been a wall against our enemy. Fagan could not make the climb up the mountain, nor could we go back. I knew from whence would come our help, for the Spirit of the Living God was whispering to me: *Run. You will not grow weary or tired. Run . . .*

And so I did, not the least worried about leaving Fagan alone. Surely God would put angels all around him. I ran the rest of the way up the mountain to the sin eater's dwelling place.

"Sin Eater!" I cried out, coming to the mouth of his cave without calling out a hello first. "Sin Eater!"

"Don't enter in! Stand where ye be."

Never one to listen much, I entered in anyway and heard a scrambling. It was a moment before my eyes adjusted to the dimness and I saw him huddled against the back wall, covered over with a worn blanket.

"Ye canna come into this place, Cadi. Go back!" Edging to the right, he felt the bed and found his leather hood, snatching it beneath the blanket covering.

"I need your help, Sin Eater."

"I canna help ye, child! I told ye before. Now, go away and leave me alone!"

"Fagan's fainted. He's just down the mountain, hidden in a cleft in the rocks just past the waterfall."

"What've ye done, girl? Wait and take him back down. Neither one of ye should be here. This is the mountain of the dead."

The Spirit stirred within me. "Get up, mon! Stop cowering in the darkness! Ye will no longer sit like a pile of dry bones. You will *stand up and live as you were meant to do!*"

He rose, the blanket dropping away as he quickly pulled the leather hood over his face. "Are ye mad? Think what you're doing. What put it in your mind to bring your friend to me, knowing what I am?"

"Aye, I know what ye are. Ye're a man like all the rest!"

"Not like the rest. I've eaten sin twenty years past! I *am* sin now. Dunna ye understand yet? It's overtaken me. And it will overtake you if ye do not go back where ye belong."

I stepped forward, hands at my sides, chin jutting. "Have ye forgotten ye sent me to hear the word of the Lord? Well, I heard it!" I went out into the light.

Hungry and thirsty for it, he followed. "And?" he said, his

very stance speaking his eagerness to receive the word of the Lord as well.

"I'll not speak to you again until Fagan's safe inside your cave."

He uttered a frustrated cry. "Trouble hovers over ye like a black cloud!"

I didn't argue. I simply led him down the mountain, glad my back was to him and he couldn't see the smile on my face.

Fagan was where I'd left him, still unconscious. The sin eater did not come inside the cleft, but stood gazing in at the boy. I could see his eyes fill with compassion, but he made no move to do anything.

"Ye'll have to carry him," I said.

"I'll not touch the lad and bring more sorrow on him!"

"Then what? Leave him here? There's thunder in the distance. It'll be raining soon. He'll get wet. He'll get sick. Maybe he'll die. Ye want that on your head along with everything else?"

"I thought ye said ye'd not talk to me again until I had the lad safe inside my cave."

My face grew hot and I pressed my lips together, glaring up at him.

"Easy, lass. I'll make a stretcher. Ye've only to get him on it so I can drag him the rest of the way to shelter."

EIGHTEEN

*F*AGAN CAME ROUND WHEN WE WERE SAFELY INSIDE the cave. "What happened?" he said weakly. I told him, seeing how his gaze moved about the strange environs. The place smelled of cool earth, wood ash, and stone. Somewhere deep inside the cavern water dripped softly.

"Is this where he lives?"

"Aye."

"Then where is he?"

"Gone awhile. Down the mountain to see about Bletsung, I reckon." It was long past sunset, the crackling fire our only light and warmth.

"It's raining," Fagan said, the wet rush pounding the earth outside the cave opening. I added another stick to the fire. Fagan was shivering, and I was about to take one of the fur coverings from the bed, when a voice behind me stopped me cold.

"Don't touch that!" The sin eater stood just inside the entrance of the cave. Fagan sucked in his breath, staring up at the tall, thin man wearing a leather hood. In one hand was a large, dressed rabbit. "Look away, boy." Fagan did so quickly.

"He's cold."

"These'll warm him." The man swung a large bundle on a pole from his shoulder and set it down before me. "From Bletsung. She said ye'll have to stay awhile." He nodded toward the bundle. "Put the blanket around him. It's all right. I've not touched it."

I untied the bundle quickly and handed Fagan the dry blanket folded inside. Bletsung had also sent three loaves of bread, a jar of honey, a small sack of dried apples, a larger one of dried beans, and a dozen long strips of dried venison jerky tied with some string.

Setting up the frame, he spitted the rabbit and set it over the fire to roast. Then he broke the pole over his knee. Taking one half, he broke it again and tucked the two pieces into the fire. Breaking the other half, he set the pieces aside for later.

"What about the Kai?"

"He must've gone back another way."

"And my mother?" Fagan said in a tense voice, shivering.

The sin eater cocked his head slightly toward Fagan, careful not to look at him. "She's at the cabin. Long as she stays with Bletsung, she's safe."

"Thank you, sir," Fagan said.

The sin eater went to the back of the chamber and sat. The wind blew outside the cave, rustling the dark woods round about. Thunder rolled in the distance. The fire crackled, filling the cave with a soft, warm glow and the smell of roasting meat. My stomach cramped, and I knew it would be a long time before the rabbit was cooked enough to eat. Tearing off some bread, I dipped it in the honey and gave it to Fagan. Breaking off a larger piece, I poured honey on it and rose. "It must be cold back there, Sin Eater. Come sit by the fire with us?"

"It's better I stay here."

"Ye're soaked through from the storm."

"I have to keep my distance from ye."

Some feeling stirred within me, melting away my fear of him, and I rose. Dragging the fur covering from the sin eater's bed, I hauled it toward him.

"Leave it be!" The man half rose and yanked the cover away from me. "You know not what ye do!"

I stood my ground and held out the bread with honey. "You're hungry. Eat."

"Ah, Cadi, dunna be so rebellious, child. Ye must shun the sin eater or be tainted by the blackness I carry."

"I won't shun you!" I stepped closer. "Now, take the bread and come sit with us."

He grew frustrated. "If anyone ever finds out you've been here with me, touching my things, you'll be an outcast like I am! I will not have it so!"

"I don't care what they say."

"Nor do I," Fagan said simply, gazing now without fear at the man.

The sin eater groaned in despair, sinking down onto the earthen floor near the stone wall of the cavern. He held his head in his hands. "Ye canna stay here! Ye canna!" He raised his head, his eyes tormented. "There's no hope for me. I thought there might be, but with that poor man laid to rest on the mountaintop, all hope is gone. I am the sin eater and will be until my days are done. There is no deliverance for me."

"But there is," I said, aching for him, feeling his anguish as though it were my own.

"Nothing ye can tell me will make a difference. I've sins past bearing upon my soul, and when my time comes, God's going to cast me into the outer darkness where there'll be nothing for me but torment and the gnashing of teeth."

Fagan leaned forward, his face intense in the firelight. "Not if another sin eater takes away your sins."

The sin eater raised his head, cocking it slightly like an animal listening intently. "Is that what's in your heads? I'd sooner die with the sins upon me than see another man suffer the same fate."

"When you die, they'll choose another. Like it or not, that's the way of our people," Fagan said. "You know it's so."

"Aye, but that's a long time off yet. I'm strong and healthy. Ye've nothing to worry about. And besides that, ye've never done anything so bad the lot would fall to you."

"How would ye know that?" Fagan said.

"I know because I've watched you. The lot always falls to the one deserving of it." He hung his head. "God pierces and divides the soul and spirit like joints and marrow. He knows a man's thoughts and intents of his heart. There is no creature on earth that can hide from God's sight. I know that, too, for there was great evil in my heart that drove me to commit a terrible sin. I didn't think what I did wrong, but then the Lord brought me to face myself and I saw the darkness in me. He made known to me the motives of my heart, and they were evil."

He raised his head slightly, but kept his eyes averted from us, staring instead into the flames. "I asked God to forgive me and poured out reasons for what I'd done. But, you see, I fooled myself. My heart and soul were naked before God Almighty, and he saw into the blackness of my soul. When the lot fell to me, I knew the Lord God had cast judgment upon me."

I hunkered down, wishing he would look at me so that I could see into his eyes. "What did you do that was so terrible?"

"It doesn't matter now."

"You matter."

"No. Our people matter. Ye've got to understand. I have work to do and it's important work. Someone has to be the living sacrifice. Someone has to take their sins away. Who can stand before God on the Judgment Day with their sins still upon them?"

"No one," Fagan said simply.

"Just so," the man said softly. "That's why I do what I do. I've sorrow aplenty, 'tis true, but no regrets. It's nobody's fault but my own I am the sin eater. And in a way, the Lord has blessed me in it. For each time someone dies, I know I'm part of seeing them safely on. Your granny understood, Cadi. She stood in the graveyard once knowing I was there in the woods watching and said loud enough for me to hear that there's no greater love than for a man to lay down his life for his friends. And I do love my people. And from a distance, I've been a small part of their lives. I'm willing to stand forfeit for their sins. Better that one man be cast into hell so that the others will have a chance of heaven."

"One, yes," Fagan said, "but not you."

"Ye dunna understand, lad. It's been done this way in Scotland and Wales since time immemorial, and it'll be done just the same. The lot is cast into the lap, but the whole disposing thereof is of the Lord. It was God's will I am what I am."

"It was the will of men, not God."

"Ye know not of what ye speak."

"I know the truth, and you will have it! Do ye think ye can take the place of God?" Fagan asked.

"Never was it so! Not in all my born days."

"And yet ye've tried. All these years you've been the sin eater, thinking to take the sins of others upon yourself, and ye've done nothing but stand in the way of the Lord."

I cringed, for Fagan's words, though true, were like a hot iron on an open wound. I could see the man recoiling in pain.

"How can ye say that to me, lad? Someone's had to be the living sacrifice. It's ever been my desire to serve God."

"Of myself, I'm saying nothing. I'm telling you what the man of God told us. There is only one Lamb of God, and he is Jesus Christ. We've no need of a scapegoat anymore. We need *him*."

"I've eaten the sins of my friends so that they can have salvation." I heard the anger in his voice. "Have I not done as God called me to do? Was it not my lot that was chosen?"

"It was Satan who cast the lot, and ye've served him well."

"I've never served Satan! It's only been in my heart to serve God and make up for what I'd done!"

"Then confess and repent! Be free of it!"

"To you, a lad? Not likely!"

"Do you really believe God needs you to fulfill his purpose?"

"Fagan, dunna be so cruel," I pleaded, seeing the hurt in the sin eater's eyes. His heart was tender and already broken. Wasn't there a gentler way?

"Get behind me!" Fagan said to me, his eyes blazing. "He will know the truth, and the truth will set him free!"

"What is the truth?" the sin eater said. "Tell me! I want to know the truth! Before God, I swear it! Dunna spare a word of what the man told ye!"

"So be it," Fagan said. "Hear it and be set free of sin and death. Hear and know the word of the Lord. In the beginning was the Word, and the Word was with God, and the Word was God. And the Word was made flesh, and dwelt among us, (and we beheld his glory, the glory as of the only begotten of the Father,) full of grace and truth."

The firelight danced upon the walls and my skin tingled as he spoke, for the voice of the One who spoke through the man by the river now spoke through Fagan as well.

"Our Lord Jesus is full of grace and truth. Jesus of Nazareth was God's anointed sent to take the sin of the world upon *himself* so that we might be saved. *He* performed miracles of healing. *He* cast out demons. *He* raised the dead. And *he* was put to death, nailed to a cross because *he alone* is the Lamb of God. Only he, the Holy One, can wash away the sins of the world. And Christ did that day on Calvary. He died to set men free. And God raised him up on the third day and granted that men might see him so that they would know without doubt no power could hold him in the grave. And Jesus told those who believe on him to preach to the people and testify that *he* is the one, the *only* one appointed by God as judge of the living and the dead. For it was of this Jesus Christ that all the prophets of old bore witness that through his name everyone who believes in him receives forgiveness of sins and eternal life. And even now, Jesus Christ sits at the right hand of God."

My heart exulted and I rose, the Holy Spirit loosening my tongue as I raised my hands to heaven. "Surely our griefs he himself bore, and our sorrows he carried; yet we ourselves esteemed him stricken, smitten of God, and afflicted. He was pierced through for our transgressions, he was crushed for our iniquities; the chastening for our well-being fell upon him, and by his scourging we are healed. All of us like sheep have gone astray, each of us has turned to his own way; but the Lord has caused the iniquity of us all to fall on him."

The cave was filled with light and warmth, and Fagan stood and spoke forth the word of the Lord that had been put in his mouth by the Holy Spirit. "God made Jesus who knew no sin to be sin on our behalf, that we might become the righteousness of God *in him.* There is now no condemnation for those who are in Christ Jesus. For the law of the Spirit of life in Christ Jesus has set us free from the law of sin and of death."

The Spirit stirred within me. "Neither death, nor life."

"Nor angels, nor principalities."

"Nor things present, nor things to come."

"Nor powers, nor height, nor depth, nor any other created thing . . ."

"Can ever separate us from the love of God, which is in Christ Jesus our Lord."

Trembling violently, the sin eater hunched forward and covered his head with his hands. *"I am undone!"*

"You can be saved," Fagan said. "You've only to accept Christ."

I came around the fire and knelt close to him. "God loves you."

"Get away from me!" He reared back from me. "This is the truth I've longed to hear? That in twenty-two years, I've never saved a single soul from damnation?"

"Only God can save a soul," Fagan said.

"The man said we've only to believe and open our hearts to Christ to be saved," I told him. "Why will ye not confess his name?"

"How can I? Now that I know—"

"You've longed for the truth, and ye have it now," Fagan said.

"Too late! Too late!"

"All these years ye've lived an outcast, ye've cried out to God. Well, he is come. Receive him!"

"I canna! I canna!"

"Let him into your heart, mon," Fagan cried out, "and it'll no longer be you who lives, but Christ living in you."

"It can never be!"

"He loved you so much he delivered himself up for you," I pleaded. "Can ye not love him back?"

The sin eater raised his head. "I thought I was serving him. How can he undo what I've done? They've all been lost *because of me!*"

"Deliver yourself up to him and see what God will do," Fagan said.

"All those people. My people . . ." He fled from us, rushing out into the storm.

"Wait!" I said, running after him. I stood outside in the pouring rain, crying out to him to stop. I ran back inside the cave, drenched and chilled. "Oh, Fagan, why won't he listen?"

"He did. He knows, Cadi. He believes!"

"Then why is he running away?"

"He's not." Lightning flashed so close the hair on my arms and head rose. "He's running to God for judgment."

"But he'll be killed!"

"Oh, ye of little faith."

"Lightning always strikes the high places!" I bolted from the cave.

"Cadi, wait!"

I didn't stop.

The thunder rolled like the mighty voice of God calling the sin eater to his mountaintop. I raced after him, dashing the rain from my face as I ran, afraid for him. The wind had come up, whipping the branches of the trees and whistling through the rocks. I felt each roll of thunder in my chest. Lightning flashed, and above me was the sound of a tree cracking. I smelled burning wood. As I clambered up the wet, slippery rocks, I saw the sin eater leap to the high point that jutted out above the purple mountains and night-cast valleys beyond. He stood straight and tall, head thrown back, arms outstretched, fingers spread.

"God! Oh, Lord God!" he shouted to the heavens. "They trusted me to take their sins away!" he cried into the wind. "They turned to me for salvation! And I am nothing! Oh, Lord, it's because of me they've gone to their graves with their sins still upon them!"

"Come down from your high place!" I called out to him. "Come down before you're struck dead!"

"Leave him be!" Fagan said from behind me. He set me aside as he moved past. "Not all have been cast into hell!" he called to the sin eater.

"Oh, God, they didn't know!"

"The Lord is a God of mercy who judges the heart!"

The sin eater turned. "What of them?"

Fagan walked forward and stepped up to the stone shelf.

"You know the wrath of God is revealed from heaven against all unrighteousness. So did they! All are without excuse."

"No one told them!"

"Those who have a heart for God have the eyes to see and the ears to hear! Not by *your* will, but by the will of *God* whose Spirit moves over the whole earth looking for those who love him. God has made himself known since the creation of the world! God himself has set eternity in our hearts! Have you not seen? Have you not heard? You are witness to his eternal power and divine nature in the heavens and the mountains and valleys round about you! Have you not known his death each winter and his resurrection every spring? You saw! You knew! You hungered. You thirsted. You cried out. And he has answered."

"Would that I could remain acurst for the sake of those I love."

"Oh, Lord, forgive him," I prayed feverishly. "He doesna know what he did."

Lightning struck the shelf of rock at his feet, shattering it in a splash of sparks, and the sin eater and Fagan tumbled down. Scrambling over the rocks, I reached them. *"Fagan!"*

He sat up, hardly dazed, and raked the wet hair back from his face. "Where is he?"

"There," I said, sure he was dead.

The wind died down. The rain softened. Fagan and I went to him and knelt down. "Sin Eater," Fagan said gently.

"No more," the man said softly, broken. Curling on his side, he gripped the leather hood that covered his head and wept. "God, forgive me. I'll never stand in the way again."

"What did you do?" Fagan said.

"I killed a man. I struck him down in anger."

Fagan sat back upon his heels and looked toward the valley. I saw the grief in his face as the lightning flashed again, and I knew he was thinking of his father.

"Do you believe Jesus is the Christ, the Son of the Living God?"

"Yes!"

"And do you accept him as your Savior and Lord?"

"Yes."

"Then rise up."

He did so. He stood still for a long moment and raised shaking hands to his covered face. He slowly drew the leather hood from his head and held it tight against his chest. Eyes closed, he raised his head so that the rain poured down over his face. I looked up at him with the faintest trepidation, thinking to see some kind of monster as we'd all been led to think he was.

He was an ordinary man.

"Jesus," he said softly, mouth trembling. "Jesus, my life is yours. Do with it as you will."

The three of us stood on the top of the mountain in the rain, waiting for something momentous to happen to him. Another flash of lightning. A roar of thunder. An earthquake. Instead, the storm lessened. The wind ceased to shriek and whistle.

"What's your name?" Fagan asked.

"Sim," he said after a slight hesitation. He lowered his hands to his sides. "Sim Gillivray."

Wet and shivering, I took his hand. "Can we go back to your cave now, Sim Gillivray? I'm cold."

He made an odd choking sound and didn't move.

"What is it?" Fagan asked, stepping closer. He took the leather hood from the man's hand and tossed it away. "What's wrong?"

"Nothing," Sim's voice was hoarse. "It's just that . . . no one's touched me since the day my name was drawn from the mazer bowl."

NINETEEN

SIM GILLIVRAY AND FAGAN TALKED FAR INTO THE
night. Sim was hungry to know every word the man by the river
had said, but I wore out and fell asleep to the lull of their conversation, the crackling fire, and the rain pounding outside. It
was a good sleep, sound and deep, all through the night and
much needed after days of wondering and worrying about too
many things beyond my control. In it, I imagined Lilybet stroking my hair and telling me God loved me and was watching over
me. I didn't know then that the Lord was preparing me for what
was coming next. Peace dwelt in my heart and soothed my soul.

But outside that cave in the valley below, a storm was brewing
the likes of which I'd never seen before nor would ever see again.

When I awakened, the rain had stopped. Light seeped in
from the split in the leather curtain Sim Gillivray had hung long
ago to keep the weather out of his cave. A thin brilliant line of
light speared the dimness so that I could see dust particles dancing in it. That stream of sunshine ended at a wide crack in the
back wall of the cave and darkness beyond as though it was a
target. I'd never noticed it before.

Curious, I rose, stepped across Fagan sleeping curled up in a
blanket, and crept over to see if anything lay beyond that crack.

There was cooler air, but I could see nothing beyond a few feet of narrow stone corridor. The blackness was so deep and so thick, it was like a wall. Far back, I could hear the slow, steady *drip, drip, drip* of water. I had heard it before but thought not much about it, too curious about other things. Yet now, the questing spirit Granny had talked about came up in me so strong everything else was forgotten in my desire to venture back and see what lay inside that darkness.

First I needed to make a torch. Creeping across the cave, I ducked outside and into the woods. I collected long twigs and sticks and a strong vine and sat down to make a fagot. It seemed large enough to last me a good bit of time, time enough at least to get a look. Hurrying back, I set it afire from the hot coals.

The narrow passageway wound back and forth like a snake down a rabbit hole. I'd just about lost my courage when it opened into a chamber several times bigger than the one Sim Gillivray had made into his home. Toward the back were rock formations coming down from the ceiling and up from the floor. They looked like giant fangs, and I imagined myself standing inside the mouth of a dragon. The floor of the cavern was slick, smooth, and damp, like a monster's tongue might be. I had to stop my fanciful thinking, for my heart was pounding its way right up into my throat.

Drip, drip, the drops of water fell, the sound louder now to my ears. The columns of stone shone with moisture.

I kept telling myself to think of something other than a dragon, but the mind of a child is a fixed thing at times. I needed something to distract me and held the fagot higher looking for it. It was a strange place with an oppressive feeling about it. Like something terrible lived inside. Shaking, I turned slowly round about looking from ceiling to floor, wondering if there were eyes watching me.

Drip, drip, drip.

One area on the curved wall was blackened by soot. Beneath the dark stains on a dry dirt surface was a circle of rocks and the gray ash of a long-dead fire. As I turned more, I saw painted figures all along one side of the cavern. The stick figures seemed to dance in the flickering light of my small torch. Dance and tumble . . .

A piece of burning twig dropped onto my hand. Hissing in pain, I dropped the fagot. As it hit the rock floor, the small flame went out, leaving only small glowing embers. Hand shaking violently, I picked the fagot up quickly and blew softly on it, desperate to revive the flame. One by one, the embers died. Darkness enfolded me and pressed in tight.

Drip, drip, drip.

My heart pounded in my ears. I could hear my own rasping breath. I held the fagot up to my face and could see nothing, nor feel even the smallest hint of warmth. It was dead out, and I didn't remember where the corridor was. I'd turned myself around. I turned again, slowly, straining my eyes, desperate to see some small dot of light that led back to Fagan and Sim Gillivray.

Nothing.

I had never been in such darkness before. It was utterly devoid of all light. And that blackness was heavy, pulsing, and full of terrors to my child's mind.

Drip . . . drip . . . drip.

I imagined those white, glistening teeth.

Drip . . . drip . . .

Was it saliva trickling as the dragon thought about chewing me up and swallowing me?

I screamed. The sound swelled as my own panic-stricken voice surrounded me, echoing back from all directions. A sudden swift flapping of wings and high-pitched keening sound came rushing and swirling. Terror filled me so that I was paralyzed. When something brushed my hair, I screamed again, dropping to my knees and covering my head. I imagined all the demons of hell coming at me, intent upon grabbing hold and taking me down into the black pit. *"Help me!"* I screamed again.

"Cadi!" Sim Gillivray shouted from a distance. "Don't move! We're coming, honey. Stay where ye are!"

"Where are you?"

"Sim's gone to make a torch!" Fagan called.

"Hurry! Oh, please, *hurry!*"

"Hold still, girl!" he shouted back at me.

"They're coming for me!"

"Who's coming?" Fagan called, alarmed.

"Demons! There's demons in here."

"No demons. Sim says there's bats. He says to hold your peace, and they'll return to their roosts. Stay low! For crying out loud, Cadi! Stop your caterwauling! Sim's back. He's lighting the torch."

Curled on the cold floor of the cave, I listened to the rushing sound above me. It grew fainter as light flickered from the narrow corridor down which I'd come.

"Cadi, where are you?"

Looking up, I now saw the last few bats swoop between the stone columns and disappear into the darkness beyond. Clambering to my feet, I ran toward the light in the narrow corridor and straight into Fagan. He gave a grunt of pain and fell back. He would've fallen had not Sim caught hold of his shoulders and steadied him.

"What do ye think ye're doing?" Fagan said, gasping in pain, trying to pry me loose of him.

I clung like lichen to a tree trunk. "There's ghosts in there."

"Ghosts?" Fagan whispered, eyes brightening.

"On the walls round about. Everywhere! I swear. Don't go back in there!"

"They're just pictures, Cadi," Sim said quietly, holding back. "Nothing to be afeared of."

"Pictures?" Fagan said. "Pictures of what?"

"People."

"I want to see."

"We ought to get Cadi out of here, Fagan."

"Just for a minute. Stay here, Cadi. We'll be right back."

"No! I ain't staying here!"

"There's only one torch, and we'll be wasting it taking ye back. Now, buck up and don't be such a coward."

His words stung, for I wanted Fagan to think well of me. "What about the bats? They was coming down on me by the hundreds, maybe thousands."

"Not so many as that," he said, glancing at Sim.

"There's plenty of the beasties, but I reckon they're back in the other chamber by now. They keep to it unless something startles them."

"Like Cadi screaming her head off."

"I'd like to see what you'd do without a torch in that cave!"

"They go out by another way, farther along," Sim said. "There's a narrow cut in the mountainside that opens to the sky. It's far back from here."

"How far back have you gone?"

"About as far as a man can go, I reckon."

I was in awe of his courage. Who would be brave enough to go deeper into this dreadful place, the home of bats and who knew what else?

"I've had twenty years to explore this cavern. I know near every inch of it. Even the places only big enough for a man to crawl into. Some places are better left alone. That big chamber back and east of us is one. It's where the bats live. Thousands of 'em landing upside down on the ceiling. I stay clean out of that place."

Fagan looked intrigued. "What's it like?"

"Has scat knee-deep on the floor and a stench so bad ye can hardly breathe. I reckon the bats laid claim to that place more than a few lifetimes ago."

Fagan took the torch from Sim and went on ahead.

He was going right on in just like I knew he would. "Fagan!" I whispered after him.

"I'm going to see the pictures ye was talking about is all. Ye can come on along or wait there. Your choice."

"It's all right, Cadi," Sim said. "Ye can wait right here and be fine."

Filled with consternation, I followed them, hoping Fagan hadn't set his mind on seeing that bat cave as well. The cold air hit me again, sending a chill up my spine as we stood in the center of the chamber.

Fagan moved closer, holding the torch high. "Did you paint 'em, Sim?"

"No. They was here long before I was. I spent a few weeks in this chamber the first winter I was the sin eater. Couldn't sleep much for looking at 'em."

The people were stick figures, simple to draw. Even I could've painted them, and maybe done a better job. "Ye think a child painted 'em?"

"Too high up," Sim said.

"What are those humps supposed to be?" I said. "Hills or something?"

"Indian hogans, I think," Fagan said, studying them.

"That's what I reckon they are," Sim said, moving no closer.

"Men, women, and children playing." Fagan moved on to the next. "Look at that one. They're dancing and playing. And the next one, there's a man wearing a hat."

"A white man," Sim said, his voice soft and grim.

"They're shaking hands, ain't they? The white man and the chief."

"I think so."

"More whites, two women with them. What's this one?"

I stood beside him. "Looks like fire."

"You're right. The hogans are burning," Fagan said. "That's what's happening, isn't it, Sim?"

"Reckon so."

Moving closer, I looked up at the painted sticklike figures scattered about. The man wearing the hat held a stick pointing toward another line of figures. A line of black went from neck to neck, linking them one to another. Some of the stick figures were bent over. Were they wounded or old? Some stood straight, but were smaller. Women? Three held babies. The next picture showed the people standing in a linked line above six thick black lines straight up and down and two wavy lines beneath. The man in the hat stood behind them pointing his stick.

I looked to the next. Then small lines came out in all directions from the stick the man held, and the people tumbled, arms and legs out, down into the wavy lines. The last picture scene showed stick figures lying still beneath three vertical lines ending in swirling circles.

The only sound around us was the *drip, drip, drip* of the water.

None of us moved. We just stood staring at those pictures. I looked behind me. Sim Gillivray looked grim and sad. Fagan stared up at the cave wall, his eyes filled with horror. I looked from them to the last scene. All those people, old men and women and babies. Their bodies seemed to float in the swirls. I wasn't sure I understood what the pictures were telling me. Shaking, I knew in the heart of me but didn't want to face it.

"He shot the first one in line, and the rest fell with him," Fagan said. "The man in the hat murdered 'em."

"It's the Narrows, ain't it?" I said. "They fell into the Narrows and went over the falls."

"Not all," Sim said, stepping forward and pointing to one

stick figure hiding in the woods in the third picture. "He escaped and lived long enough to come up here and hide. He's the one who painted these pictures."

"What happened to him?" Fagan said.

"He died. I found his bones over there behind those two pillars."

"Is he still there?" Fagan said, heading for them.

I'd seen Granny laid out for burying, but I'd never seen human bones before. The skeleton, still clad in decaying leather leggings and shirt, was stretched out flat, one leg bent up to the side. The skull was tipped toward us, jaws open. I could imagine the eyes of his soul staring up at me from those black empty sockets and drew back behind Fagan.

"He can't hurt ye, Cadi," Fagan said.

"What's that beside him?" I asked.

Fagan leaned down and picked up a small wooden bowl while I drew back, moving closer to Sim Gillivray.

"His paint bowl," Sim said.

"There's still some encrusted in it."

"Put it back where ye found it," Sim said gently. "It tells the end of the story."

"The end?" Fagan put the bowl down. "What happened to him?"

"Near as I can figure, he was wounded and dying when he come in here. What I know for sure is he was determined to leave the truth behind."

I looked up at the pictures on the cave wall. "That's why he painted those pictures."

"Aye, that's so."

"How do you know he was wounded and dying?" Fagan leaned over the skeleton and studied it.

"Either that or he killed himself."

"But how do you know?"

"Because he didn't use clay or soot and ash to paint those pictures. He used his own blood."

"I'd like to know when it happened and who done it," Fagan said when Sim had gone out to check his traps.

I wasn't sure I believed it. "I ain't never seen an Indian in all my born days, Fagan. Only heard of them."

"That may be so, but as far back as I can remember, I've heard people talking about 'em like they was a terrible threat. Pa's said more than once they'd as like to kill ye as look at ye. And now, I reckon I can see why they'd feel that way."

"*We* didn't do 'em ill. We wasn't even thought about when all that was happening, Fagan. It ain't our fault."

"Don't matter. Don't ye understand, Cadi? We're blood kin to whoever done it."

"No kin of mine would do such a thing as murder women and children. I won't believe it!"

His mouth tightened as he looked at me. "But ye can believe it of mine, can't ye?"

The heat came up into my face and lingered there. It was terrible true. Having seen Fagan's own da beating on him with the face of the devil and swearing to kill him, I could imagine 'em all capable of anything. The Kais were a bloodthirsty lot, except for Iona and Fagan. "I'm sorry," I said, eyes downcast. I was sorry to believe as I did and even sorrier Fagan was born a Kai.

"I know my kin have a lot to answer for," he said, grim faced, "but there were others in the third picture. Remember? The man in the hat wasn't alone."

"I don't want to think about those pictures anymore." And I didn't want to think about the man who'd used his own blood to paint them. I didn't want to think about who else might have been with the man who'd fired the gun and sent all those people to their deaths. "Can't we talk about summat else?"

"No. I've got to know."

"Why? What good'll come of knowing?"

"I can't just forget what I saw back there! It's like a knot in my chest. I have to find out when it happened and who did it."

"Why?"

"Because I think the Holy Spirit's telling me to go looking for the answers."

"God already knows who done it, don't ye think, Fagan? He don't need us to find out for him."

"Course God knows, Cadi. That ain't the point."

"What is?"

"God wants us to know."

I chewed on my lip, wondering what path God was sending us down this time. Would it be one with more heartache for Fagan and more disillusionment for me?

"What do ye say, Cadi?"

I was not eager to seek the answers, but felt it was the stirring of the Holy Spirit that was urging Fagan ahead. I wasn't going to be the one to tell him to rebel against the leading of the Lord, even though I felt safe inside Sim Gillivray's cave. Long as we stayed where we was, Brogan Kai wouldn't come after us. I'd seen the look on his face and knew it was fear kept him away. But it was dead certain that man had nothing to fear in the valley. He was waiting down there for us. I'd had scares enough for one day being caught in darkness, surrounded by bats and seeing a dead man's bones. I didn't feel brave enough to face the living.

"It's all right," Fagan said gently. "Ye don't have to come. I can take care of myself."

Blinking back tears, I saw Lilybet through the blur of them, sitting across the fire from me, beside Fagan. She smiled at me tenderly. "Remember the night by the river, Katrina Anice. Remember when Brogan Kai was beating Fagan. Who threw the stone?"

"I did."

"You did?" Fagan said, cocking his head slightly, bemused. "Did what?"

"I threw the stone."

"What stone?"

"God has not given you a heart of fear," Lilybet said. "And ye shall go two by two."

I sat up straighter, the fear and hesitance washed away, and looked across the fire at him. "I'll go."

"Go where?"

"Wherever you go, I'll go."

The troubled expression dissolved. "That's my Cadi." A smile spread across his face as he stood. "We'd best go now before Sim comes back. He'll only try to talk us out of going."

"He'll worry when he finds us gone."

"We'll leave word with Bletsung."

"Where are we going?"

"Miz Elda's the oldest living soul in our valley. Maybe she can give us some answers."

We were watchful but not afraid as we came down Dead Man's Mountain and stood at the edge of the woods behind Bletsung Macleod's house. Bletsung was at one of her hives, opening it.

"She's gone clean out of her mind," Fagan said. "She's robbing that hive in broad daylight! She's trying to kill herself."

"No, she ain't." I caught his arm before he could barge out into the open. "She does it all the time. The bees don't mind."

We watched as the swarm rose like a cloud and then draped her like a shawl while she drained the amber honey into the jar. As she walked slowly away, the mass drifted away like a soft gray mist floating behind her. She saw us as she neared the cabin. Waving, she ran toward us. We met her on the path Sim Gillivray had worn going to his sitting place beneath her window.

"Is there no one with ye?" she said, eyes bright and eagerly glancing toward the trees.

"We're alone."

A faint frown crossed her face. "But where's . . . where's the sin eater? I have not talked with him in two days."

"He went out this morning to check his traps. He'll likely bring ye summat for supper this evening," I said.

"I don't care about him bringing me something. Is he all right? Did ye not tell him what the man told you?"

"Aye, we told him," Fagan said.

"And?"

"He knows the truth."

"What did he say? What did he do?"

"He accepted Jesus Christ as his Savior and Lord, ma'am."

"Then where is he? Why hasn't he come down off the mountain?" Deeply troubled, she looked between us. "What's he going to do?"

"He didn't say, ma'am," Fagan told her. "Maybe he just needs more time to think."

She couldn't hide her disappointment. Forcing a smile, she patted Fagan's shoulder. "Well, at least you look better than the last time I saw you."

"Feeling a sight better, too. How's Ma?"

"Not so good."

"She sick?"

"At heart, I reckon. I told her everything you told me about Jesus, and she's been crying off and on ever since."

"Why?"

"She won't say." She looked from him to me. "Ye need a good hot bath and hair brushing, Cadi. Ye're a sorry sight for such a pretty little girl."

"I was in a cave and bats were a swooping down on me and we found—"

"We'd best get going." Fagan drew me away. "Would ye tell Sim when ye see him that we're all right? We're going to my grandmother."

"Elda? Ye'd best be careful."

"We'll keep an eye out for Pa."

"Maybe you should wait a few more days."

"She's probably worrying about us, and we've things we need to ask her."

Bletsung looked greatly perplexed, but asked no questions. She looked up at the mountain again, troubled. "I wish there was something I could do."

I knew the answer plain as day. "Ye can pray."

She looked ready to cry. "I've prayed long and hard over the years, darlin'. Maybe I've been doing it wrong."

"Ye done it right," Fagan said, grinning. "You and Sim's saved, ain't ye?"

"Reckon so, though it don't feel like it yet."

I tugged her sleeve. "Just tell Jesus ye trust him and ye're waiting on him to tell ye what to do."

She looked down at me and smiled faintly. "From the mouth of a babe I'm taught, eh?" Something flickered in her eyes and she grew still, tears surging. "So be it," she said softly. I didn't know what I'd said to bring that look of pain into her eyes.

"Come on, Cadi," Fagan said and walked away.

I followed after him, though I kept looking back at her. We'd gone clear across the meadow, and Bletsung was still standing in the path where we'd left her, looking so forlorn, my heart ached. "Wait up," I said and ran back to her. "I love you."

She ran her knuckles lightly down my cheek. "I love you, too."

I hugged her tight. "God loves you, too, Bletsung. I know he does."

"I'll hang on to that," she whispered brokenly. Kissing me on the top of the head, she set me back from her. "Ye'd best go on now. Fagan isn't waiting, and I've a strong feeling he's going to need you."

I wished he wasn't in such an all-fire hurry to find the truth about everything. I couldn't help wondering if some secrets were best left in darkness and some deeds done best forgotten.

Yet, something inside urged me to catch up to Fagan and press on.

TWENTY

Fagan and I followed the path on the north side of the forested stream. The rhododendrons had lost their clusters of rosebay and white, and the last of the summer cardinals, jewelweeds, and purple thistles were blooming along the bank and tucked into rocks and woodlands. A dozen swallowtail butterflies flitted from bloom to bloom. We reached the spot where the creek joined the river and followed along the bank to the stepping rocks. Fagan went first, and I stood watching him and wondering what he thought he was doing. We were heading across the river just east of Kai land. He paused on the table rock in the middle. "Come *on*."

I came ahead, hopping from rock to rock, careless in my haste. I slipped once and sat hard on the rock, feet and legs getting wet.

"Careful!"

I glowered at him as I picked myself up, rubbed my backside, and kept moving. "I thought we was going the long way around." He was taking us back by way of Kai Creek.

"We're safe."

"We'll be going right by your place."

"Take my word for it."

"It's too pretty a day to die," I grumbled.

"Hush now. I can't put the feeling into words. But Pa ain't gonna see us. I just know it." We made it to the other side. "Besides," he said, watching me make the last jump, "Pa'd expect us to go the long way round. If he's waiting, that's where he'd be. Over there, on the north side where he can watch the trail along the river."

"I hope you're right."

We headed up the hill into the hazels, holly, dogwood, and huckleberry with the canopy of great chestnuts spreading above us. It was cooler in the forest shade. A burst of flapping near stopped my heart as a turkey took flight from the leafy floor, startled from its foraging. Fagan grabbed his sling from his back pocket, loaded a stone, and stopped its flight.

"What're ye doing?" I said, heart flapping within my chest like an echo of those wings before he wrung the bird's neck.

Fagan picked the limp turkey up by the feet. "A beauty, ain't he?"

How could he be so calm when I was expecting Brogan Kai to come charging out of the woods any second with those ham-sized fists of his? "What're ye going to do with it?"

"Dress it."

"Now? Give it to me." I yanked it out of his hands with both of mine.

"Hold up, now. Miz Elda don't like me bringing anything round to her unless I've dressed it first."

Stopping, I turned round and glared at him. "We gonna hunt round and find a pot to scald it and then pluck its feathers, too?" Swinging around, I marched up the path, holding the bird by the feet while its head and body bounced against my back. "While we're about it, why don't we collect chestnuts and crack 'em so's we can make stuffing?"

Fagan fell in alongside me. He was laughing! I wanted to swing that turkey and clobber him with it.

"Got yourself a turkey, did ye, Cadi?" Miz Elda said, sitting in her rocking chair beneath the porch shade. I'd seen the look on her face when she saw Fagan and his bruises. Something dark and fierce came into her eyes until she banked it.

Heaving the bird from my back, I whumped it down on her porch. "Fagan kilt it. Just like ye said, Miz Elda. A Kai can't go anyplace without killing something." I was sorry as soon as I said it, ashamed into my bones.

"And he wasn't up to carrying it?"

"I was up to it." Fagan just looked at me.

"He wanted to dress it first." I sat down glumly on the bottom step, too tired and hot to go up yet. "I figured we could do the chore here and maybe live to eat it."

"Stop grumbling," he muttered under his breath. "I forgive you."

"Well, now, I do thank ye for the bird. I ain't had turkey in a month of Sundays. Go on in and stoke the fire, Fagan. There's water in the barrel. Ye con fill up the pot while ye're about it."

"Yes, ma'am. Ye want him dressed?"

"Easier if we scald him first."

Fagan lifted the turkey, went up the steps and into the house. I followed him part way, wishing I'd said I was sorry before he'd forgiven me. I sat down near Miz Elda and leaned against the post in the shade. She leaned around, looking after Fagan. "Ye can cut off those wings and spread 'em out good in front of the fire to dry. They'll make right good fans."

"Yes, ma'am."

She settled into her rocking chair again, tipping it back and forth for a minute, saying nothing, watching me. I was too tired to speak. The yellow-brown thrushes, purple finches, and juncos were singing in the trees.

"Ye're in dire need of a bath, Cadi Forbes. If your mother got a look at ye, there'd be an end to your visits."

"Ain't been time."

"Did ye find what ye was looking for, child?"

"Yes, ma'am, and more. We mean to tell ye all about it and ask ye some questions."

Miz Elda leaned forward in her chair and put her hand on my head. "I was beginning to wonder if you and Fagan had been done in."

I took her hand in both of mine and held it against my cheek. "Near abouts." When I let go, she leaned back with a tender smile and rocked some more.

A hawk flew over, and three purple martins took wing so fast the gourds Miz Elda had hung from the barn swung back and forth. There was nothing like a family of martins to keep the hawks away from the barnyard chickens. Miz Elda didn't have a one to spare.

She leaned around her chair again. "Don't put that turkey in until the water's boiling!"

He came out onto the porch. "Water's on and the wings're drying. I'm going to wash up." Passing her by with a shy look, he went down the steps.

"Where ye going to?"

"The creek."

"Stay here. There's a wash pan inside ye can use," Miz Elda said with decision. "Take some water from the barrel. When ye're done, toss the water out the side window there. The black-eyed Susans'll take it kindly." Gripping the arms of the rocker, she rose with difficulty. "Come on, now, Cadi. We'll do our talking inside where there's none to see us."

First thing she asked us was to repeat every word the man by the river said all over again. It was our pleasure to do so, though we was eager to ask our own questions.

"I ain't never gonna get tired of hearing about Jesus," she said, nodding. "Never in a million years." The roiling water and steam drew her attention. Rising from her chair, she took up the turkey by its legs and eased it into the boiling water. "Now, what's the question that's so important ye'd risk life and limb to get an answer."

"We was wondering about Indians, ma'am," Fagan said, easing into it.

"Indians?" Miz Elda kept her back to us. "What do ye want to know about Indians?"

"Was there any living here when our people first come."

"Well, now, boy, that was a mighty long time ago," she said, still not looking at us. She kept dipping that turkey up and down so's I figured she wasn't going to tell us nothing unless we asked straight-out. So I did.

"We want to know about the Indians who was murdered." Fagan shot me a look I'm sure he hoped would wither my tongue. I looked back at him. "We ain't got all day." And we had her full attention now.

"Who told ye such a story as that?"

To my mind, she didn't look shocked or angry, just wary.

"No one told us, Miz Elda," Fagan said gently. "Not in words leastwise."

I leaned forward, resting my arms on her table. "There was pictures painted in a cave up on Dead Man's Mountain, painted in blood."

"Blood, ye say?" That did seem to shock her.

"Be quiet, Cadi. Let me do the talking."

I ignored him. Next, he'd want us to pluck the turkey before he got to the point. "In the cave behind the one where Sim's been living nigh on twenty years." Let him roll his eyes in frustration. Sooner we got our answers, the sooner we could hightail it back to Dead Man's Mountain and out of reach of his raging pa.

"Sim?" Miz Elda said.

"Sim Gillivray," Fagan said. "The sin eater."

She smiled at me. "So, he finally told ye his name. Or was it Bletsung done it?"

"He told us soon as he accepted Jesus as his Savior."

"Glory be," she breathed, eyes bright, and then, just as suddenly, a look of anxiety came down over her face.

I leaned forward. "What about those Indians, Miz Elda?"

"Ye've a fixed mind, girl," she said, irritated. She lifted the turkey out of the boiling water, carrying it by its feet to the table. She took a basket and laid it and the scalded bird on the table and started working at it.

"I'll pluck feathers, ma'am," I said, grabbing the bird by the feet and dragging it closer to me. "You tell us what happened."

"What makes ye think it's summat I'd want to talk about?"

"Are ye saying ye won't tell us the truth?"

"I dinna say that. Just don't be in such a hurry. It ain't a pretty story and it was a long time ago. I need to collect my thoughts." She looked at Fagan and then closed her eyes and turned her head away. "I can't tell it without speaking ill of the dead."

"It's all right, ma'am," he said gently. "Don't hold back on my account. I ain't deaf and blind to the things my kin've done over the years. If they was part of what happened, it won't surprise me none."

"And it don't mean Fagan'll turn out like 'em, neither," I said, yanking a handful of feathers and putting them in the basket.

"Never thought he would," she said quietly.

"I'm hoping I take after Mama's side of the family."

Miz Elda raised her head and looked at him. "So ye know." He nodded. "Did Sim Gillivray tell ye?"

"I knew from Mama."

"Oh."

I'd never heard one word so heaped up with pain. Pulling a few more feathers, I glanced at her as I put them in the basket. A tear was running down her weathered face as she looked at him.

All the longing and loneliness she must have felt for all those years showed plain.

"I never dared hope . . ."

Fagan leaned forward and put his hand over hers. "I don't understand why she never said nothing."

"Reckon she couldn't. Your father hates me."

"But why? What'd ye ever do to him?"

"It ain't got much to do with me, but I reckon it's everything to do with those pictures ye found in the cave." She patted his hand and then left her own on top of his as though she didn't want to let go of him. "The truth ain't gonna be easy for ye to hear."

"The Lord is my comfort."

She nodded and then let out her breath slowly. "It was your own grandfather Laochailand Kai who killed those Indians, Fagan. But he didn't do it all alone. Though I'm loath to tell of it, my own darlin' Donal was part of it, except for the women and children. He was never the same after that day. Sick into his soul, he was, grieving like. So was the others, too. We thought to put it behind us and forget what happened, but I reckon it ain't to be. Things done in dark come to light eventually."

"Start from the beginning, Granny," he said gently. "I don't understand how it came to be."

"I hate to speak of the dead, boy, especially when he's your own blood kin, but Laochailand Kai was the hardest, coldest, and cruelest man I ever knew. First time I knew it for certain, we was already on our way up here to the mountains, and there was no turning back. He was sitting at the fire one night, drinking, and he boasted of taking vengeance on a landowner back in Wales. He said the man told him he wasn't good enough to court his daughter. So he ruined the poor girl."

"What do ye mean 'ruined'?"

"I mean he took from her what she was only to give to a husband." She looked at me and I looked back, still not under-standing. "It don't matter, Cadi. You're too young to understand these things, but it was like this. Laochailand said if he wasn't good enough for her, then she wouldn't be good enough for anyone. And he made sure of it. When the deed was done, she begged him to bring her with him to America, but he said he'd had all of her he wanted."

"Didn't her father do nothing?" Fagan said, his face like thunder.

"The girl wouldn't tell him where Laochailand Kai had gone. She loved him, ye see, and was afraid her father would kill him for what he'd done. I reckon she lived in the hope he'd change his mind and come back for her. It took her father two years to find out Laochailand had come across to America, and by then, the girl was dead."

"Dead?" I looked up from my work on the bird. "What hap-pened to her?"

"She bore Laochailand Kai's child and then drowned herself and the wee bairn in a lake on her father's estate. Her father promised two hundred pounds to any man who could bring proof Laochailand Kai was dead. One by one, four men hunted him down and tried to kill him, and all four died by his hand. Donal and I reckoned that was one of the reasons Laochailand Kai was so set on heading east and settling into these high mountains, that and wanting to be a landowner himself with power over other men."

"Why would ye follow after a man like that, Miz Elda?"

"Because we dinna know any better, Cadi dear. We dinna recognize him for what he was. Ye see, child, Laochailand Kai had great charm and presence. He was a handsome man and well spoken. He deceived us. Oh, there were times when he made me uncomfortable, but I never could put my finger on what it was about him that didn't seem quite right. So I suppressed the spirit within me that was telling me I was in the presence of such corruption. Laochailand Kai was a liar and a murderer." She withdrew her hand from Fagan's, hanging her head in shame. "And when we put ourselves in his charge, we became just like him."

Fagan was pale and still, saying nothing as he waited for her to tell the rest, the whole of it, no matter how deep it hurt.

Miz Elda looked from him to me. Leaning forward, she began working at the bird as though she desperately needed something to do with her hands. "When we come up into this valley, I thought I'd never seen nothing more beautiful. Splashes of color everywhere. Yellow tulip trees, the orange-red maples, and puffs of white dogwood and serviceberry along the river, the lavender of the Judas tree against the brown forest floor where new leaf growth was coming up. Gorawen called it the God-green of spring."

"Granny Forbes was with ye?"

"Aye, child, Gorawen was among the first, and your grandfather Ian with her. And your mama's mother and father, too, darlin'. God rest their poor souls. Seven families in all come up with Laochailand Kai. We came up the trail past the falls and along the Narrows into the valley. It took our breath away, it did. I remember feeling so happy. I was filled with such a feeling of hope. And then we reached the Indian village and the children came running toward us, greeting us."

She withdrew her hands from the work and clenched them until her knuckles were white.

"The chief came out and walked right up to Laochailand Kai, hand extended in welcome. For ye see, Laochailand Kai had been up here before and made friends with them. They was all happy to see him come back. For he had charmed them, too. They didn't know—" Her voice broke and she stopped.

Fagan reached out again and put both his hands over hers,

caressing them gently, encouraging her, though his expression was filled with sorrow. "If we confess, the Lord is faithful and just to forgive us our sins and cleanse us from all unrighteousness."

She opened her mouth as though in surprise. Tears filled her eyes and poured down her cheeks. And she went ahead swiftly and told the rest. "Laochailand Kai shook the chief's hand with one of his hands and drew a gun with the other. He shot the man square in the face. He had a second gun tucked in his belt and drew it, killing another, all the while shouting for our men to burn the hogans. All hell broke loose around us. The women and children were screaming. Men fell dead or wounded. Some nights I can still hear 'em screaming. And Donal and Ian and all the rest were fighting for our lives.

"When it was over, Laochailand Kai sent the men out hunting for the women and children who'd run off to hide. Then he went round and clubbed the wounded to death. All but one, the chief's own son. When the men brought the others back, Laochailand Kai wanted them shot dead. Donal refused and so did the rest. None of them had the stomach to murder women and children in cold blood. So Laochailand Kai tied them together, one after another and took 'em to the Narrows. He shot the chief's son to death there, and when the young man fell, he took the rest with him down into the river. They all went over the falls."

I didn't want to believe her. With everything in me, I fought against it. Yet a still quiet voice within my soul said it was true. Every word of it was true.

"It's all right now, Granny," Fagan said gently. "It won't have the power over ye it did."

"I've been so afeared of God knowin'."

"God always knew. He saw."

"I reckon he did," she said brokenly. "There ain't never been a single moment's peace since that day. For all the beauty of this place, what we done has been like a terrible ugly scar upon the land. None of us has prospered. Many have fallen by the way. Two families are all dead and gone, wiped out by sickness. And the melancholy has run down into the blood of our children."

I thought of my mother. Had I been the only cause of her sorrow?

Fagan looked at me, and I could almost see the thoughts in his blue eyes. We had become like that, he and I, our minds moving in the same direction. Or maybe it was the Lord within us giving us like minds as he taught us the truth and brought us through it. For the thing I'd dreaded most had come to pass. *All* had sinned. Not just Fagan's kin, but my own as well, and others besides. No one was better than another. All shared the legacy of murder.

But I knew something else. I knew it so deep within me, my soul sang with the knowledge and thanksgiving of it: Jesus Christ had redeemed me. Without him, I would be the same as they, locked in a prison of guilt and shame, afraid of death, terrified of being buried with my sins still upon my head. "But for Jesus, but for Jesus . . ." I said and could say no more.

"Ye believe what we told ye about Jesus, don't ye, Granny?" Fagan said.

"Aye, I believe ye, every word."

"And do ye accept him as your own dear Savior and Lord?"

"I do, though I'm unworthy to speak his name."

"Say it, Granny."

"I can't."

"None of us are worthy. He died for us, Granny. He was nailed to the cross for everything ye just told us."

"Oh, Jesus," she said softly and wept. "Oh, precious Savior, my Lord."

Fagan rose and put his arms around his grandmother. "Ye can lay your burdens down now, Granny. Ye can give them all to him, and he'll give ye rest."

"Oh, I'm tired, so tired," she said softly. "I could sleep a month of Sundays."

"I'll help ye to bed."

"Shouldn't ye baptize me? Ye said the man did so with you."

He helped her to her feet. "There's time enough tomorrow."

"She could be dead in the morning," I said.

"Cadi!" Fagan looked at me as though I'd grown horns.

"Well, it's the truth! Besides that, she can't walk all the way down to the river. She ain't strong enough to make it."

"Will you shut up?!"

"I reckon the good Lord's called her to tell things as they are," Miz Elda told Fagan. "There's a bucket there by the door, lad. Might as well baptize me now as take a chance I won't be breathing come morning."

"She didn't mean it. Did ye, Cadi?"

I went for the bucket.

"Go on now," Miz Elda said. She sat down again and folded her hands in her lap. "Douse me good. We'll all feel better for it."

"Ye're sure?" Fagan said.

"She said so, didn't she? Do it!"

Her frail body shuddered as Fagan turned the bucket. She was having some kind of fit, sputtering, gasping, choking. For a whole minute we both thought she was dying of the shock of all that water being poured over her poor old head. And then I realized she wasn't dying at all. She was cackling. No, not cackling, *laughing!*

"Well," she said when she could get her breath back. "That woke me up."

Fagan and I hugged her as we all three laughed together, joyous in our newborn freedom. We had the feeling of wings and tongues of fire upon our heads. Our souls sang with exultation.

All the while, outside, the darkness gathered.

We'd come down off Dead Man's Mountain to learn the truth, and we had. But just a part of it. We'd only just taken hold and pulled the tail of the beast.

And as the first thread in the tapestry loosened and came undone, the dragon awakened.

TWENTY-ONE

$\mathcal{M}$IZ ELDA STUFFED THE TURKEY WITH DRIED BREAD, crumbled herbs, and roasted chestnuts while I washed the floor with the water puddled from her baptism—though most of it had seeped through the cracks, dripping down beneath her cabin. Fagan went outside to chop and tote firewood, stacking it on the porch next to the front door where it'd be easier for Miz Elda to fetch. It was nightfall before we sat down together to give thanks to Jesus for seeing us through the day and giving us a fine turkey for supper. It was a far sight from Miz Elda's usual repast of chicken soup and biscuits from Gervase Odara. "A pity she ain't come today," Miz Elda said. "She could join us. The last time I seen such a fine meal laid out was the day of Gorawen's funeral, and I had no stomach for it then."

I lowered my head, feeling the grip of loss again and wondering about the fate of my poor Granny who'd never heard the gospel.

Miz Elda leaned over and tipped my chin. "Don't ye go worrying yourself about her, chile." She brushed my cheek tenderly and patted my hand. She leaned back again, smiling. "The last few years we was able to get together, yer granny and I talked about what might happen. Neither of us thought Sim Gillivray could do nothing to save our souls from our sins, no matter how willing the poor lad was."

"But she never heard the gospel."

"Maybe not in so many words, but thinking on it now, I feel a peace about her. Gorawen said more than once she cudna see how a God who had created so much beauty could not offer us a way back to him no matter what we done. And he did, didn't he? Jesus is the way back. Yer granny sensed it, for she was one to sit on her porch and look out and see the wonder of it all, wasn't she? And she had a thankful heart."

I thought of Granny sending me off to find the wonder for myself up on the outcropping of rocks overlooking the valley, in the fields of wildflowers, down by the river where the dogwoods bloomed. All through the years she'd appealed to what she called my questing spirit. And I wondered now if she hadn't been sending me out to find the miracle of God's works round about me.

"Oh, will ye look at that, now?" she'd say, and I'd look up to see the flocks of passenger pigeons like smoke on the horizon heading south. "Every year, they head south. Ye can set time by 'em. I wonder where God sends 'em?"

On a warm day when I'd be bone-deep in my sorrows, she'd say, "I'd love to have a few smooth stones from the riverbed. Ye think ye've got time to go for me since I can't make it myself these days?" And I'd go—and I'd watch the rainbow trout with their white fins and bright red-and-pink sides as they spawned in the tail of a pool and in the side riffles away from the current. Life, it was, being renewed year after year.

In spring, Granny would send me off to pick bluets, violets, and windflowers. As the weeks passed, she'd ask for yellow lady's slippers and bleeding hearts, then roses and white rhododendron clusters that grew along the stream. She'd always seem to know the day when the mayflies danced and died. When I'd come back from whatever venture she'd sent me on, she'd talk about how life was precious.

"Don't let a day go by without seeing some wonder in it, Cadi. Stop moping around the house wishing for things to change between ye and yer mama. Go out and see what's there for ye."

God was there.

God was everywhere.

It dawned on me then that that was why I could never find comfort from the sin eater. It wasn't for him to give. The gift I needed had already been given; the evidence of it was all around me, everywhere I looked, even in the air I breathed. For hadn't it been God himself who had given me life and breath?

I kept thinking about Granny. I remembered how we'd sit on the porch, melting and waiting for the hot summer day to end in the relief of nightfall. In the thankful cool, we'd stare up into the infinite black sky with glitters twinkling while the lightning bugs sparkled like fallen stars in the woods round about us.

In the fall, Granny'd send me off to capture one monarch butterfly from the thousands that migrated. She'd hold the jar a long while just looking at the pretty thing. "From a worm this came. Don't that beat all?" And then she'd take the top off the jar and watch it flutter away.

First frost had been an event to Granny Forbes, for with it came the high mountain gold and the soft winds that stirred up blizzards of red, pink, orange, and yellow leaves swirling. "The maple's always last to give up its color," she'd always say. The maple that grew near our cabin was like a red blaze against the encroaching winter gray skies, its leaves like crimson sparks on the dead brown ground.

Granny would sit by the window during winter and look out at the snow heaping or watch the icicles' slow growth from the eaves of the front porch. They'd catch the sunlight and cast a rainbow radiance. Granny was ever hoarding bread crumbs and sending me out to toss them about near the window so that she could watch the towhees, titmice, red cardinals, and mourning doves foraging for the bits of food in the vast white. During the ice storms and long bleak nights of winter, she'd tell me the mountains were like sleeping giants that'd come awake again soon. "God'll see to it."

And God did. Those mountains always did wake up, without fail. Year after year, the earth came back to life again with what Granny called "God-green." She always said no matter how much you watered, you couldn't get the same color that came with a single rain of the life-bearing water of heaven.

Now I knew why it happened that way, what Granny was trying to show me in words she didn't have. It was no accident, no coincidence, that the seasons came round and round year after year. It was the Lord speaking to us all and showing us over and over again the birth, life, death, and resurrection of his only begotten Son, our Savior, Jesus Christ, our Lord. It was like a best-loved story being told day after day with each sunrise and sunset, year after year with the seasons, down through the ages since time began.

I knew after hearing the word of the Lord, I'd never walk anywhere again without seeing Jesus as a babe in the new-green of spring. I'd never see a field in all its glory without thinking how he lived his life for us in the royal robes of every summer wildflower. I'd ever see the greatness of his love in the beautiful sacrifice in the brilliant reds, oranges, and yellows of fall, and winter white would always speak to me of his death. And then spring again, his resurrection, life eternal.

Lo, I am with you always.

You are, Lord. You are. The quickening in my soul told me so.

"She saw, Cadi," Miz Elda said. "I'm going to believe that the Lord who can do anything he pleases opened her mind and heart and showed her the way home."

Peace filled me, a peace not coming from Miz Elda's consoling words or of my own feeble, childish reasonings, but a gift from God himself—God who is just, God who is merciful, God who can do the impossible. I just knew I didn't need to worry about Granny anymore. It was all taken care of, whatever become of her. For the Lord is God, and Jesus knew her heart. No, I didn't have to worry at all.

We finished our eating, cleaned up the dishes, and went to bed. Once or twice I awakened to the hoot owl outside and Miz Elda's snoring beside me. Fagan, who was sleeping on the floor, got up just before dawn and went outside to sit on the porch steps, his head in his hands.

Miz Elda roused when I got up. We didn't say much. We was all heavy, thinking about what was ahead.

"We'd better be going back soon," Fagan said, but I could see something else was troubling him. I guessed I knew what it was and was proved right when he finally talked about it as we was eating porridge Miz Elda made us.

"Seems like some have the eyes to see while others are blind," Fagan said.

"Your pa, ye mean," I said, seeing his hurt. It's strange how a person can take such a beating from someone and still love him so much. Fagan hated what his father was, but he still loved him. I reckon that's the way God is. Loving us enough to send Jesus, but hating the way we live. Hating the sin, not the sinner.

"Pa. And others. Why don't they wonder? Why can't they see it round about the way ol' Miz Forbes did?"

"Why couldn't ye?"

He turned and looked at his grandmother. "But I did!"

"Aye, ye did, lad, but don't be too proud about it. It weren't hunger and thirst that took ye down to the river. Ye went because yer father told ye not to go, pure and simple." When he looked down and didn't answer, she looked at me. "And why'd ye go, Cadi?"

"I went 'cause Sim Gillivray made me promise. He said he wouldn't even try to take away my sins unless I gave my word first."

"So there ye have it, aye? It weren't humble reasons that made either of ye go. It wasn't 'cause either of you was any better than anyone else. Even later, aye? Fagan, you wanted to be different from your father, and Cadi, you wanted to be relieved of your terrible guilt."

"What was your reason?" Fagan said.

"I'm facing death and don't want to burn in hell." She gave a laugh. "Seems to me, it's pure selfishness that brings us within hearing distance of the truth, and then God has his way with us, don't he? He knows the ones already that'll come looking for him, and he even lights the way. It all begins and ends with him. So I reckon God's going to get done with us whatever he wants done."

I felt the portent of her words. She'd been thinking a long time, and it all seemed clear and laid out straight ahead in her mind. But not in mine. "What do ye think God wants us to do?"

"Speak the truth, do what's right, and take what comes."

"We will," Fagan said, "Soon as my pa cools off, we'll come back down from Dead Man's Mountain and start telling people what the man by the river said."

Miz Elda shook her head. "Nope. That won't do."

"What do ye mean?" he said. "We have to tell them."

"That ye do, but ye won't say nothing if ye go back on the mountain. Not now."

"I give ye my word."

"Ye already give yer word to God, boy. The minute ye went into the river with that man ye knew things would never be the same. Didn't ye? What'll happen if ye go back on that now?"

"I ain't going back on it!"

"Not yet. But don't ye see? Just going back up on that mountain's breaking your word. Ye go back and the truth will end right here."

"How ye figure that?" he said, eyes hot.

"Well, now, think about it some. Don't ye reckon it was God opened the way for ye to come down here to me in the first place? He led Cadi into that cave so she'd find the pictures telling of the blackest sin that's held this valley in darkness all these years. Why do ye think he did that?"

He looked away from her piercing stare. "We can't do anything now."

"Oh yes ye can! Ye've already started doing the Lord's work. And ye'll keep right on with it!"

Fagan turned, agitated. "We've got to wait awhile! Pa's too riled. Ma says he ain't thinking straight. Ye can see what he did to me. What d'ya think'll happen to Cadi if she stands with me against him? One blow and she'd be dead."

"Maybe, but that don't matter."

I gulped, staying well out of it. I was hoping Fagan would win in this battle of wills and yet feared Miz Elda's words and reason would sway him.

"How can ye say that, Granny? Ye love her as much as I do."

My mouth fell open as I looked at him. He *loved* me? He loved *me*?

"Listen to yer granny now, boy. Yer thinking's askewed. Ye ain't alone anymore, are ye? It ain't ye against yer pa now, is it? If God can raise Jesus, don't ye think he can look after ye and Cadi, too? Ain't he already looked after ye? Ye two have been *chosen* to be his witnesses, and *this* is the day the Lord made. Not tomorrow or the day after. Not next week or next month or next year. *Now!*"

Fagan was pale. "Maybe you're right, but Pa wouldn't give us time enough to tell more than a few."

I was learning to recognize when it was God speaking

through someone. He repeats himself. He says it over and over because we're so stubborn and stupid and unwilling. And scared. Even when he tells us not to be afraid, we set our mind about it, worrying and fretting about every little thing. I was shaken by what God expected us to do.

"Cadi could tell her folks and Iwan," Miz Elda said. She probably thought that would be easy, but I reckoned telling those I loved most about the Lord would be the hardest of all, especially considering they'd most likely thought I'd been bad enough to be cast into hell. How were they going to understand the goodness and love of God from the likes of me? And if they refused to listen, what then? It'd feel like I failed 'em again and sent 'em straight to hell. Because they'd know the truth and have no excuses.

"We've already told Bletsung and Ma." Clearly Fagan was thinking about it, just like I feared. I thought he'd give a bigger fight against Miz Elda's proclamation. But *no*. He heard the Holy Spirit in what she said, and he was going forward no matter the cost to either of us.

And seeing how he said he loved me, I knew I'd follow him to the death, if need be.

"One by one, we'll tell 'em," Miz Elda said. "I can start with Gervase Odara today. She's due to bring me some more medicine."

I sighed. "I wish there was a way to get 'em all together in one spot so's we could tell 'em all at once."

Miz Elda gave a soft gasp of surprise. "Why, of course!" She looked at me, her eyes bright. "Out of the mouths of babes." She laughed.

"What?" I wondered what trouble I'd brought on myself now.

"We can get 'em all together in one spot." A broad grin filled her face, and her eyes were lit with excitement.

"Where?"

"Why, right here, child!"

"How?" Fagan said.

She chortled. "That's the easiest part. All ye have to do is fetch the bell from my trunk and ring it eighty-five times."

"But they'll think ye've died!" I protested.

"She's right, Granny," Fagan said grimly, and then his eyes lit up as well. "Yes, they will. They'll think ye're dead!"

"Aye, and they'll come, won't they? Every last one of 'em in our valley. They'll lay down whatever they're doing and come right on up here to pay their last respects and lay me out for burial." She laughed again, enjoying the thought.

"Even my father," Fagan said slowly.

"Oh yes, him, too. Probably sooner than some others. He's been waiting a mighty long time for me to pass on. I'll bet it's been the one prayer he's said in all these years. And won't he be surprised!"

We never even thought about Sim Gillivray.

Or the trouble he might bring.

TWENTY-TWO

M Y BROTHER, IWAN, WAS THE FIRST TO COME AT THE ringing of the bell, Gervase Odara following soon afterward. Uncle Robert came on horseback with Aunt Winnie riding behind him. The Connors, Humes, Byrneses, Sayres, Trents, and MacNamaras hurried up to Miz Elda's cabin. Soon to follow them was Pen Densham with his son Pete, whose broken leg still hadn't yet mended. The O'Sheas arrived, Jillian holding her new baby to her breast, and Aunt Cora and Uncle Deemis and their young'uns, who were tearing about the place like foxes after the chickens.

Sad to say, no one was too happy when they saw Miz Elda sitting hale and hearty on the front porch in her rocking chair. They was plumb *mad* about it. Not that it was anything against her. She was respected in our valley, if for no other reason than she'd lasted longest. They just didn't like being interrupted from whatever they'd been doing for no cause at all. So they thought, at least; so within minutes of arriving, they all started in shouting questions at Fagan, who was ringing that bell for the whole world to hear.

"What in Hades is going on here?"

"Why're ye ringing the bell with the old woman sitting there in her rocker like always?"

"Your pa's going to skin your hide, boy, calling us out for nothing! And dang if I won't help him do it!"

"What're ye calling us up here for?"

"'Cause I told him to, that's why!" Miz Elda hollered at 'em. "Ye think we'd be ringing the bell if it weren't a matter of life and death? Now, hold yer peace and wait! When everyone's gathered we'll tell you what's going on in this here valley!" She was enjoying herself. "I'd think ye'd be pleased to know I'm still breathing. Fact is, I ain't felt better in my entire life."

Brogan Kai came with his two older sons. When he saw it was Fagan ringing the bell, his face got all red and tight. I thought he'd come charging up, but he didn't. He kept his distance, asking others in a low voice what was going on. But his eyes, oh, his eyes were so black with rage and hate, I knew something terrible was going to happen, if not now, then later in the day or tomorrow or whenever he could get his hands on us.

"Where's Fia?" Miz Elda asked my pa when he come alone.

"In bed. Ailing."

I didn't think much about it then because she had been ailing off and on ever since Elen died.

"Well, then, Angor, ye'll be taking the news home to her, I expect."

"Yes, ma'am, whatever the news be." He glanced at me in question. I could see he thought I'd done some terrible sin, something worse than they already thought I'd done. It made me sad my own father thought so little of me. But then, I hadn't given him much reason to think better.

The last two to arrive were Bletsung Macleod and Iona Kai. Everyone went quiet when Fagan spotted them. He stopped ringing the bell for a few seconds, and people turned around to see why he was staring so. He started ringing the bell again as they came up the hill path together, each with a bouquet of flowers. Iona was so pale, she looked like death. She looked at Brogan Kai and paused. Everything about her pleaded for his understanding, but he just stared back at her, lip curling in a sneer. He spit on the ground by her feet, right there in front of everyone. Bletsung reached out and took her hand, drawing her away.

They kept on walking toward Miz Elda's cabin. People moved back for them as they came up to the cabin and then closed in behind, whispering.

Miz Elda watched them come. The laughter had died in her when she saw Iona. She went all still and quiet. I saw her hands shake as she clasped them in her lap and knew she was reining in her emotions. So I moved closer, putting my hand on her shoulder. She was trembling all over, so filled up with feelings at seeing her daughter come to her after eighteen long years. But what sort of feelings were they? And what would she say after so much hurt?

I thought of my own mother and how I longed for her to forgive me, and I prayed. I prayed hard.

Iona Kai stopped at the foot of the steps. She stood for a long moment beside Bletsung Macleod, her head down. Bletsung leaned close and whispered something to her, and then let go of her hand and moved back a step. Iona Kai slowly raised her head. When her mouth jerked, she pressed her lips together tightly and stood silent of a moment.

"It's nice to see ye well, Mama," she said finally, her voice thick with emotion. She looked at her mother, and in her face was a question, unspoken but clear. And all about her, people watched and waited to see what the old woman would do, the old woman who had the well-known reputation of being hard and unforgiving.

Miz Elda sat silent for a full minute, and I knew it wasn't for lack of words to say but for being unable to say them. "I never dared hope to see ye again in this lifetime," she said finally. And then she smiled and opened her arms. "Welcome home, darlin'."

Iona flew up the steps. Dropping to her knees, she put her head in her mother's lap and wept. Miz Elda wept, too, all the while stroking her daughter's hair gently and looking out at the others. Her eyes fixed upon Brogan Kai. He glared back at her, a muscle jerking in his cheek. There was hate in his look, a black pit of it.

"Ye can stop ringing the bell, lad," Miz Elda said. "We're all gathered together now, except for those who canna come. It's high time for ye to do yer talking."

Looking out at all the people, I had strong feelings of doubt about what was coming. They was not in the best of spirits for hearing anything, let alone something so different from what they believed. What one of them would listen to Fagan, a lad in rebellion against his father, or to me, reputed to have killed my own sister? I was plumb shy and hung back, hiding behind Miz Elda.

Fagan took a deep breath, squared his shoulders, and walked to the front steps. He stood there, looking at his father first, then round at all the rest. "I've got good news to tell ye!" he called out in a strong voice. "News that will bring ye tidings of great joy!"

"Shut your mouth and stand down, boy!" Brogan shouted.

Fagan stayed where he was, undaunted, and spoke the word of the Lord. It flowed out of him, straight, clear, ringing louder than the bell, just like the man by the river had told us. Fagan told the who, the what, the when, the where, the how, and the why of it all in simple words any child could understand. For we had, hadn't we? Surely they would, too. Oh, surely the goodness and mercy of God would speak to them. . . .

It was all said and done before Brogan Kai reached the space before the front steps of the cabin.

"You're crazy!" he shouted up at us. "You've gone out of your mind just like I warned ye would if ye listened to the madman. He was filled with lies and clean out of his mind!"

Fagan looked at him. "Is that why ye killed him, Pa?"

There was a collective gasp, and people turned to stare at the Kai.

He faced them, shoulders back, head high. "Aye, I killed him! And I'd do it again! I did it for all of us. It's my duty to protect our valley. Look at the damage that man done in even the short time I let him alone. What right did he have, a stranger, to come up here from God knows where, spilling out lies and turning our own children against us? I should've killed him sooner!"

"God made us witnesses," Fagan said loudly. "He's chosen us to be his servants so that we'll know him and believe him and understand he *exists.*"

"You ain't telling us anything we don't already know for ourselves, boy," someone shouted, taking Brogan's side.

"Hear the word of the Lord!" Miz Elda called out in a strong voice.

"Everything around us testifies to the glory of God," Fagan said. "Even the stars above us show his handiwork. God made the world and all things therein, seeing as how he is Lord of heaven and earth. He's the giver of life and breath. It's in him we live and move and have our being. Forasmuch as we're his children, we oughtn't think that we can be saved by a man's devices."

"He's speaking against the sin eater!" Brogan Kai shouted. "That's what he's doing. Don't ye see? All these years, we've trusted in him, knowing from centuries past that we've needed a sin eater to make us ready to meet God. And ye stand here listening to him?"

"Our salvation depends upon God's only begotten Son, Jesus Christ!" Fagan shouted.

"He's a boy. What does he know?"

"This is the truth! It's Jesus who was nailed on the cross. It's

Jesus who shed his blood to atone for our sins. It's in Jesus we must believe, for he is the resurrection and the life!"

The Kai's face was feral as he glared up at Fagan. "Ye're a fool!" He turned and spoke to the others. "Don't listen to him! He's been poisoned by lies."

"I'm telling the truth and you know it. That's why ye're so set against it. Before Christ there was no other, and neither shall there be after him. He is the Lord and there's no Savior except Jesus!"

"Who here will risk going before God with his sins still upon ye?" Brogan asked. "Will you, Angor Forbes? What about you, John Hume? Or you, Hiram Sayre? Who wants to be the first to die and not have the sin eater come? Who wants to be first to burn in hell forever?"

They looked afraid, confused, like sheep without a shepherd. Brogan came through them and stood before the cabin. It was as though he wanted to put himself between them and Christ, blocking their way to the safety of the fold.

"You're dead in your sins," Fagan said into the terrified silence. "And dead ye will remain if ye put your hope in a sin eater! Only God can take away your sins, and Jesus is the Christ, the Anointed One, the Lamb of God."

"*Lies! All lies!*"

"Listen to the boy, people!" Miz Elda said. "For our clan is destroyed for lack of knowledge!"

"God dinna send his Son into the world to condemn us! He sent him that we might be saved. Believe on him who died for you. Whoever believeth in him shall not perish, but have everlasting life," Fagan continued.

"He's saying our ways are evil!"

Fagan came down the steps and faced his father. "Those who do not believe are condemned already. And this is the condemnation, that light is come into the world, and you love darkness because of your evil deeds!"

Brogan hit Fagan hard, and he fell to the ground.

"Brogan!" Iona cried out. "Don't!"

"Don't? I should've taken care of this long ago. And don't open your mouth again, woman!" he warned her with deadly calm. "Ye've spoiled the boy, and this is the result of it."

There was a stirring in me, a rush of fire in my blood. I came around Miz Elda's chair and stood at the front steps. "It's not the work of any man that makes us presentable to God! Jesus is the one who took our sins and nailed them to the cross! It's been done. *It is finished!*"

"Ye'd like that, now, wouldn't ye?" Brogan seemed to have forgotten Fagan, seeing me as his enemy now. "You who pushed your own sister into the river and watched her drown!"

The attack was like a spear through my heart. I looked at my father and saw he was ashamed. His face reddened in anger—but it was an anger roused by the telling of family sins in a public place.

"I didn't push her," I said with a calm past my understanding. "Elen came across the tree bridge and fell into the river."

"You little liar!" Brogan said. "Everyone knows you did it. Everyone's talked about it ever since. Everyone knew how ye were jealous of her."

"Aye, 'tis true I was jealous. 'Tis true I sometimes wished she'd never been born." I saw Brogan Kai's eyes light with triumph and satisfaction, but I didn't hesitate. "And that day when I saw her coming across to find me in my special place, I wished she'd fall. But I *dinna* push her. And I have mourned the passing of my sister ever since."

Papa just stood there staring at me, saying nothing. When he lowered his head, I reckoned he thought the worst of me still.

It was my brother, Iwan, who stepped forward. He looked back at Brogan Kai and then up at me on Elda Kendric's porch.

"I believe ye, Cadi. And I believe what Fagan's telling us is the truth."

"So do I," Cluny Byrnes said and pressed forward from behind her parents. She smiled across at Iwan, eyes radiant.

The Kai's look was malevolent and mocking. "No doubt ye both would. Two who'd like to be forgiven for what they done in secret. Tell 'em, Cleet. Tell 'em all how ye seen Iwan Forbes and Cluny Byrnes tangled together up in the woods. Go on and tell 'em all what these two been doing behind her father's back."

With a sneer, Fagan's brother came forward and did just that in gleeful detail. Cluny tried to run away, but her father grabbed her and swung her around. Grasping her arms, he shook her. "Is it true?"

"It weren't the way Cleet's saying," Iwan shouted, but when he tried to move, Pa grabbed him and held him back.

"You harlot," Cluny's father said, shaking her. "Shaming me before everyone."

"Let her go! I love her. I want to marry her!"

"And ye think that makes it right?" Brogan said.

"Pa! We dinna mean it to happen." Cluny was crying. "I swear!"

"We *all* sin!" Miz Elda stood. "We all fall short of the glory of God. These two have confessed and repented, and they are forgiven."

"No, they ain't!" Brogan shouted. "Not unless her father says so, and they'll still carry that sin on 'em until the day they die! That's why we need the sin eater."

Cluny's father was weeping in shame and disappointment, pushing her away from him now, turning his back on her. And the poor girl was torn between pleading for his forgiveness and going to Iwan, who was holding out his hand to her.

"The sin eater is not the way to salvation!" Fagan cried out as he straightened to his feet once more.

"You all know what we have to do, people!" Brogan said, turning on them. "You've always known! It's the way things was done in the old country! And so they shall be done here!"

"And if it is so done, then we'll go on doing evil as we did the first day we set foot in this valley," Miz Elda said. She toddled forward, leaning heavily upon her cane. "For I will tell you the truth of how this land came to be ours."

And she did so, not sparing a single detail. I could tell by the downcast eyes of some that they'd already heard the terrible story from their own kin who'd been part of the massacre. Others looked sick at the revelation.

"They were savages! They'd've scalped us in our sleep!" Brogan said, defending his father before him.

"If that were true, Laochailand Kai would not have felt the need of a sin eater, now, would he?" Miz Elda said. "He'd've not been afeared for his immortal soul. But he knew he was a man with blood on his hands, innocent blood! That's how this whole wretched business of the sin eater started!"

"It will not end!" Brogan Kai snarled. "Not until I draw my last breath!" He turned, challenging one man after another, all of whom were aware of the Kai's two sons with their loaded muskets. "Who's got the guts to end it? Aye? You, Angor? You, Clem?" He turned and looked contemptuously at his own son. "You, Fagan?"

I saw the desire in Fagan's eyes to strike back at the one who had struck so often at him.

"Be not caught in the wiles of the devil, boy," Miz Elda said quietly.

"The devil, you say," Brogan mocked. "I'm not the devil. *He* is."

"Ye shout lies at us, Brogan Kai," the old woman said. "Ye speak words brewed in yer foul mind. Ye've set your heart against God, and it's Satan ye serve. He who would make Jesus Christ a stumbling block is of the devil!"

"May God strike you dead, old woman," he said, head down like a charging bull.

She stood firm, and Fagan came to stand beside her. She nodded. "I reckon he will, but it'll be in his time, not yours."

The strength of faith shone forth from her and from Fagan, so that even the Kai had to see it and feel it. For just an instant I saw a flicker of doubt and fear in his eyes. And then Bletsung Macleod spoke.

"There's no need for all this fighting. It's over anyway."

Brogan glanced at her. "What do you mean, it's over?"

"Si . . . the sin eater. He's gone."

"Gone where?"

"I don't know."

People began talking all at once. "What're we going to do? Who'll we turn to? God'll never forgive us. . . ." They were agitated and afraid, confused and looking for someone to tell them what to do.

Had they heard and understood nothing? Were they all deaf and blind?

"I'll show you how deep I care about our people," Brogan said. "I'll prove it to you. I'll give you my own flesh and blood. Fagan's brought this grief on us, and Fagan will be our new sin eater!"

"*No!*" Iona screamed. "No, not Fagan!"

"Shut up, woman. *I* decide."

"Brogan, ye canna do this to him!"

"I'm the power in this valley, and I'll do whatever I want."

"You'll not do it, Brogan! Not after all I've suffered. Ye'll not take him from me!"

"I'm the one who says who it will be. Not you! Not anyone!"

"What about the lottery?" someone called out.

"Yes, what about the lottery?" another cried.

Brogan's face went red, for he could smell the scent of rebel-

10

7

lion. "Ye've heard Fagan speak against our ways. Ye've heard him speak against his own kin. We don't need the lottery!"

"There never was a lottery to begin with, you Judas, and well ye know it!" Iona screamed at her husband. "It was a lie from the beginning, a lie, I tell ye!"

The color was ebbing from Brogan's face as he stared at his wild-eyed wife. "She's crazy. She doesna know what she's saying."

"I knew. I knew all about what you'd done years back when I found the lots ye hid underneath the house." Her knuckles were white on the porch post as she looked out at the friends she'd lost in their fear of her chosen husband. "Fagan had hidden from his father after a beating, and I'd gone looking for the boy after Brogan went out hunting. I found him back in a corner under the house. He was playing with some bones. Chicken bones, they were. And then I saw the markings on 'em. All of 'em were the same, every last one of them."

"She *lies!*"

"Does she?" Miz Elda's eyes blazed. "I dunna think Laochailand Kai ever cared what God thought of him. I knew the man. I knew the man better than anyone else in this valley. It was my husband, Donal Kendric, who stood against him. And my darlin' Donal died for it, right there where Brogan now stands. Had I a gun in my hands, I'd have killed him for it, and he knew it. He told me if I ever said anything about it, he'd come back and take the only thing I had left in the world, my daughter, Iona."

Iona Kai pressed her forehead against the post, her shoulders shaking as her mother kept on.

"He said he'd smash her head against the rocks just the way he had the Indian children." She looked down at Brogan Kai. "And you are of his blood and of the same mind."

"Then so is Fagan," he said, blatantly unashamed of his inheritance.

"I'll prove what I say is true!" Iona said, letting go of the post and tearing at the buttons of her worn dress.

"She's gone mad," someone cried.

Brogan laughed. "Get your mother, boys," he told his other two sons. "Take her home where she belongs." They began to shove their way between people.

"I'll show you!" Iona said over and over. "I'll show you!" She unlaced what looked like a corset and tugged at it, yanking and pulling at it until it slipped out from the front of her dress. "See! Look!" She held it out for all to see. Stitched carefully in neat rows like a bone corset were the lots with their markings.

Stunned silence fell over the group as they studied the bones. Some moved forward to see more clearly, then turned back to the others, their stricken faces telling the tale as clearly as could be.

"Why did ye do it, woman?" Uncle Deemis called out. "Why did ye keep silent all these years?"

"Because I love him, God help me. I've loved Brogan all my born days. And I was afraid for him. I was afraid of what all of you would do to him if ye knew what he'd done." She bunched the corset with the lots in it against her heart. "And I was afraid if I told, the sin eater would come down off the mountain and kill him sure."

"And he'd have the right, wouldn't he?" Though Bletsung spoke quietly, her tone was bitter and furious. I looked at her, startled. Tears hung in her blue eyes, and her expression made my heart feel like it was breaking. "He done it 'cause of me, didn't he? Didn't he, Iona? That's why ye hated me so much all these years."

"Aye." That one word, so full of grievous hurt and sorrow, hung in the air between the two women. After a moment, Iona drew a trembling breath and went on. "Aye, he did it because of you, Bletsung, and I'm sorry for my mean-spiritedness. It weren't your fault how Brogan wanted ye. He done it because he's loved you, you see, only you, all these years. He's never loved me for a single minute, even after I give him the sons he wanted. Though I lived in hope, it didna make a difference. He could never forget it was you he wanted. That's why he made sure your beau was the sin eater. To get rid of him. So he could win you for himself after the poor mon was gone up to Dead Man's Mountain."

"I only ever loved one man in my whole life," Bletsung said. "Sim Gillivray."

"I never thought ye'd throw your life away, waiting for him."

At Brogan Kai's bitter words, Bletsung turned to him. "Though he's never touched me in all these years, I'll wait," she said. "I'll wait and I'll love him until I draw my last breath."

Brogan's face darkened. "Or he draws his!"

"Even then," she said, defying him. She threw back her head. *"Sim!"* she called out. "Sim Gillivray is the man I love." She proclaimed it for all to hear and then looked at Brogan Kai again, her tears spilling over and streaming down her face. "And next to God, there will *never* be another so loved in my life."

Iona wept on the porch, her corset still pressed against her breast. Brogan looked at his wife in disgust and turned on Fagan. "Ye've done this, you Judas! You're fatherless, boy. Ye hear me? Fatherless!"

It was a cruel blow, for despite him, Fagan still loved the man who had begat him.

"That's where ye're wrong, Brogan," Miz Elda said almost gently. "Though ye've cast him out, he's got a Father. His Father reigns in heaven and on earth. Fagan belongs to the Lord!"

"Amen!" came a deep voice from the heart of the woods just above Miz Elda Kendric's house.

People looked up, startled and afraid. Brogan's dark eyes

went wide, and his face paled as a tall man in worn leather clothing appeared at the edge of the forest. He came down the hill with purposeful strides, and all who dared look could see his face.

Sim Gillivray, the sin eater, had come back among us.

TWENTY-THREE

"WELCOME, SIM," MIZ ELDA CALLED OUT TO HIM. "It's been a long, long time."

"Yes, ma'am, it has."

People moved back from him as though he carried a deadly plague, but I'd never seen a man with such strength and humble dignity. And purpose.

Bletsung Macleod seemed to melt at the look of him. "Sim," she said, her heart revealed in that single utterance. Brogan's head snapped around when she took a step toward the sin eater. Without even glancing at her, Sim put out his hand, warning her back. He didn't take his gaze from Brogan Kai as he kept on coming.

Most of our kin and friends had turned their faces away so as not to look at Sim. A few had turned their backs. Even Brogan had stepped back at first sight of him, but now he stood his ground, his eyes black fire.

"You don't belong here, Sin Eater." He thrust his arm out. "Douglas! You, there, boy! Give me your gun!"

"No, Pa!" Fagan put himself between them. "Don't do it!"

"Stand back, Fagan," Sim said quietly. "This is between me and your pa."

"Ye're right about that," Brogan sneered. "Ye've no business coming down off the mountain unless ye been called."

"He was," Miz Elda said loud enough for all to hear. "Same way ye all was called. We rung the bell."

"To no good purpose, old woman."

"The best purpose, I'd say. Sim Gillivray's coming home."

Brogan glared up at her. "The devil, ye say. He canna come back to us! He's been eating sin twenty years and more." He appealed to the people. "Ye all want him living down here among us, him and his blackened soul?"

People were drawing back from both of them, turning this way and that, whispering among themselves, afraid and torn.

Sim spoke with a quiet nobility of manner. "As much as I've wanted to save our friends and neighbors, all I was ever able to do was eat the bread and drink the wine. It was nothing but an empty ceremony. It accomplished nothing."

"That can't be true," someone cried out. "It canna be."

"It *is* true," Sim said, looking round at the stricken faces. "I knew in my heart while I was doing it, but I hoped. That hope was pure in vain. I hope now in Jesus Christ!"

"But we've been taught ye could take away sins!"

"I can't. We've all been deceived. Every last one of us." Sorrow filled his face. "Ye've all been looking to me for your salvation all these years, and I ain't nothing but a man like any other."

"Your name was drawn because ye were the worst sinner in this valley!" Brogan declared.

"What'd ye do, boy?" Miz Elda said. "What was so bad ye went up on that mountain without a word of protest?"

"Don't tell them, Sim," Bletsung said. "Ye don't owe 'em nothing after all these years."

"It needs the telling, beloved," he said tenderly and then faced his peers. "I killed Bletsung's father."

"Murderer!" Brogan shouted. "Ye hear that! He's a murderer!"

"No more than you, Pa," Fagan said, sorrowful shame on his face.

"I dinna kill one of our own. I killed a stranger come among us to stir us up and lead us into lies. This man murdered one of our own! That's why he's the sin eater."

Bletsung's face flushed with anger. "Ye want to know the whole truth of it?" she shouted at them. "You want to know *everything?*" Her face contorted in anguish, and of a sudden I wanted to stop her. I knew not what she had to say, but if it was as awful as the look on her face, I knew it would pain her in the speaking.

Sim beat me to it. He stepped toward her, raising his hand in protest. "Bletsung, no——"

But she cut him off. "As you said, Sim, it needs the telling." She faced the crowd, her shoulders straight, though her lips trembled. "My father's cruelty drove my mother to kill herself. She ate foxglove just to get away from him, for a day never went by that the man did not abuse her with hand and word." She looked around at them all. "Some of ye knew what he was like. Ye knew and ye did nothing to help us." Tears coursed down her cheeks, and her voice went quieter. "Sim did. Sim saved me from him."

"By murdering one of our own!"

"Aye, one of *your* own," she said bitterly, "if ye want to claim him as such."

"That's not the whole of it, is it?" Elda Kendric said. "What else was going on?"

Bletsung looked up at Miz Elda, her stricken face going white.

"Tell 'em, child," the old woman said. "Tell the whole truth once and for all. Lay your burden down."

"Ye don't have to say nothing about it, darlin'," Sim said. "It was my sin, not yours."

"It's secrets that's got this valley into darkness, Sim Gillivray, and secrets that'll keep it so." Miz Elda looked at Bletsung again and spoke gently. "Would ye have it ever thus, child?"

"No, ma'am," Bletsung said in a little-girl voice. She turned slowly and lifted her head, looking round at them all. "A few years after Mama killed herself, Pa took it in his head that it was his right to use me like a man uses a woman."

I didn't understand what she was saying, but I saw from the faces of those looking at her that they did. It must have been something terrible, for I saw shock, disgust, and pity. Bletsung covered her face and turned away again.

"Tell 'em the rest, Sim," Elda said gently. "Be done with it."

Sim's eyes mirrored Bletsung's anguish. "I was coming up from the meadow when I heard Bletsung screaming. I ran into the cabin. When I saw what he was trying to do to her, I took hold of him and—" He shut his eyes at the memory.

"Ye smashed his head into the hearth," Brogan said. "That's what ye did. Ye crushed his skull against the stones."

"Yes," Sim said quietly, looking at him. "Yes, I did."

"And then let Bletsung lie for ye, ye coward. Ye let her say her pa fell when he was drunk."

"I did," Sim said quietly.

"My father *was* drunk!" Bletsung said. "Drunk on whiskey and the power he had over me. And God forgive me, I was glad when he was dead!"

"And no wonder," Miz Elda said, tears coming to her eyes.

"Ye wasna glad the way it happened," Sim said. "For all he done and for all he was, he was still your father. He was still a human being." He turned his head away from her and faced those now looking at him. "I want ye all to know that. Bletsung had no part in what I did."

Bletsung reached out a hand to him. "Ye didna mean to kill him, Sim. Ye was so mad ye wasna thinking."

He made no attempt to take her hand. "Dunna matter. He was a man and I killed him. That's why I thought God put the finger on me to be the sin eater. That's why I agreed to go up on

Dead Man's Mountain. And now I've come down from there to tell ye what I've found out. The *truth!* I ain't never been able to give ye or yer loved ones what ye needed. The fact of it is I've stood in yer way." Tears ran down his face. "God forgive me, I've been the Judas goat leading our people to slaughter without even knowing that Satan was using me to do it. And it's gotta stop!"

"Don't listen to him! He's just looking for a way out of his duty to us!" shouted Brogan.

"Fagan speaks the truth," Sim said. "You don't need a sin eater. You need Jesus Christ!"

"Don't listen to him, I tell ye! We've lived this way as far back as we can remember, and we ain't changing our laws now."

"It stops now, here and now!" Sim cried out in a voice of authority. "The work was done on the cross of Christ!"

"This is *my* valley!" Brogan's rage was out of control. "No one stands against me and lives!"

"No, Pa!" Fagan cried out.

"Ye speak of God. Well, let God be the judge between us!" Brogan Kai raised Douglas's gun and aimed at Sim's heart. Fagan threw himself between his father and the sin eater, but Sim moved faster. He caught hold of Fagan's arm and dropped him to the ground out of the way as Brogan pulled the trigger.

The gun exploded. I heard a scream and realized with a shock that it was the Kai. He dropped the musket, his right hand half blown away, his face black with powder burns and red with blood. Falling to his knees, he shrieked in terrible pain. Douglas looked on in terror.

"Brogan!" Iona screamed, tearing down the steps. "Brogan! Oh, Brogan . . ." She fell to her knees, drawing him close. Fagan came and knelt down, crying as his father wailed in agony while his mother rocked him.

"Ye fool!" Cleet said to Douglas. "Ye loaded too much powder again! Dinna Pa tell ye a hundred times?" Douglas shoved past his brother and ran, disappearing into the woods.

Sim looked on in pity. He came forward, hunkering beside the fallen man and the woman who held him. He grasped the Kai's wrist tightly to stop the bleeding.

The Kai's screaming stopped as he went limp in his wife's arms.

"He's dead! Oh, he's dead," Iona said, weeping.

"No he ain't, dear," Sim said. "He's just unconscious."

"Let him die!" an angry voice shouted. "We'd be well rid of him!"

Sim raised his head and looked around solemnly. "Would ye curse a man who's down? He ain't no worse than any of the rest of us."

Gervase Odara came forward. "We'll need some clean cloths."

Miz Elda pushed herself up from her chair. "Bring him on inside."

Sim Gillivray, the man who'd been tricked in the lottery and cheated out of twenty-two years of his life, lifted Brogan Kai from the dirt and carried him into the cabin. And it was the old woman that Brogan had so wronged who helped her forsaken daughter and the mountain healer tend him.

People milled around, waiting for news and mumbling of what should be done. Sim came out after a long while. "He'll make it, folks. He won't have no use of his right hand, and he's blind in one eye, but he'll live."

I gave a start when my father, Angor Forbes, came forward. "We've been talking among ourselves, and we figure if any man's deserving to be cast out as a sin eater, it's Brogan Kai himself. He done ye wrong, Sim. He ought to pay for it."

Sim frowned, looking from my pa to the others. "Ye all agree with him?"

"Aye!"

"Ye think I was the one wronged?"

"Yes!" they called out loudly.

"We'll abide by whatever ye want to do," my father said.

Sim stood on the porch looking down at him. "It's what ye're hoping I want, ain't it, Angor? Revenge."

Color seeped into Pa's face. He looked ashamed but spoke out in his own defense. "He's held us all in fear all these years. Me as much as any man here. We'd live easier if we never had dealings with the man again."

"Ye need not fear Brogan Kai anymore," Sim said simply. "He's never had power over ye but what ye've given him yerselves. And I'll tell ye this. Ye say you'll abide by whatever I want to do? Then here it is. I forgive him. I ain't gonna judge the man. What right have I to judge anyone? What right have any of us?"

Fagan had been standing in the doorway, tense, listening to them discussing the fate of his father. I could not take my eyes from him, for at Sim's words his eyes caught holy fire. He came forward and stood at the railing, looking out over the men who'd wanted to make his father the sin eater.

"Judge not, lest by your own measure will ye be judged, sayeth the Lord!" he said in a loud voice.

"Amen," Sim said quietly. He smiled. "If I've anything to say about it, I'm the last sin eater this valley will ever know. Ye heard God's truth from this lad and this girl. Jesus *is* the way, brothers and sisters. Jesus is the truth. *He* is the life."

I felt the nudging and leaned on the railing, looking out among our people. "Ye've all heard the truth now. Life and death are before ye. Which will ye choose?"

TWENTY-FOUR

ONLY A FEW FOLKS WENT DOWN TO THE RIVER TO BE baptized that day. Sim carried Miz Elda 'cause she was too old to walk herself and said she wanted to be a witness to what was going on. Bletsung walked beside Sim, touching his arm tenderly every now and then. And my brother, Iwan, went. Cluny Byrnes broke away from her father's hold and ran after us, him shouting after her that she was no longer welcome home and no daughter of his.

All in all, there were only seven of us that praised the Lord for what he'd done. Seven who asked him to reign in our lives. Only seven out of so many.

Even Pa turned away and went on home. It near broke my heart in two when I saw him go. I ran after him, clinging to him and pleading with him to come with us to the river and be baptized.

"I got work to do and your ma to see to. She took to her bed four days ago. She ain't been up or et nothing since."

I let him go then, weeping as he walked away. The sadness of it stayed with me at the river while I watched Iwan and Cluny be baptized. Even the laughter and rejoicing could not dispel the feeling inside me that things was left undone, that God wanted me to do something more. As Sim carried Miz Elda up the path

315

once more, I followed with the others. Fagan took my hand. He knew how I was feeling.

When we reached the cabin, we found it empty, Brogan Kai having been carried home by Cleet and Cluny's father.

Miz Elda was fit to be tied, she was so happy. She looked shriveled and ancient, but her eyes were sparkling with life like never before. She kept smiling like all her cares had been washed away. And well they had.

If we could all just let them go.

"What's troubling ye, Cadi?" she said to me.

"Pa didn't come."

"He will, given time. I'm sure of it."

"It's Mama I'm worried about," Iwan said. "She come home four days ago after a long walk and took to her bed. Pa and I both tried to find out what's wrong with her, but she just turned her face to the wall. She's just given up on living, and nothing we can say makes a difference. It's like she don't care anymore."

The wind in the valley had stirred Miz Elda's white hair so it stuck up in all directions like a porcupine. "Four days ago, ye say?" She raked some back from her forehead.

"Yes, ma'am," Iwan said.

"She come by here four days ago asking after Cadi. I told her she'd gone to Bletsung's place." She looked around. "Where's my brush? Land sakes, I can't see for this straw. Stop laughing, Fagan. It ain't respectful to laugh at your poor ol' granny."

"Here it is, ma'am," Bletsung said, stifling a grin. "I'll brush your hair for you."

"Well, someone better."

"Mama come by and seen me," I said, remembering how she'd stood at the edge of the meadow by the mountain laurel near the creek. "She didn't come up to the house or call out or nothing. She just stood looking at me. Then she turned her back and walked away."

Miz Elda grew thoughtful. "Then maybe it's you she's mourning, child."

"It's Elen she loved. Not me. She'd be happy if she never had to look at me again."

"That ain't true, Cadi," Iwan said, leaving Cluny to come hunker before me where I was sitting. "She loves you. I'm sure she does."

I shook my head, the ache inside hurting worse than it ever had before. Why now? Oh, God, why now? This should be a time of joy, not sorrow.

"Ye ought to go and talk to her, child. Find out what's ailing her."

Everyone was looking at me, and I felt stripped naked and vulnerable. "I can't!" My throat closed up like someone was choking me. I fought the tears, but they came anyway, burning hot, searing right down into my heart.

"Yes, ye can, darlin'," Sim said. "Ye had courage enough to come looking for the sin eater, didn't ye, when all around ye lived in fear of me? And because ye sought a Savior, ye found the one who takes sins away, Jesus Christ our Lord. He showed ye the way to salvation. Now show your mother."

"I reckon it was your prayers brought that man of God to bring us the truth up here into the mountains, Cadi," Fagan said.

I wondered. I had a strong feeling there had been someone else crying out to God long before I was born. Sim Gillivray.

"The Lord answers prayers," said a familiar voice and I glanced up. Lilybet stood in the doorway. "Let love lead ye home, Katrina Anice. All ye need will be given. Ye've only to ask."

I got up and went out the door, thinking to follow her, but she was nowhere to be seen.

"Cadi?" Bletsung said, leaving Miz Elda. She came to me and put her hand on my shoulder. "What is it, honey?"

317

I was shivering violently. "I'm going home now. Only would ye all do summat for me?"

"What, darlin'?"

"Pray for me. And pray for Mama. Pray real hard."

I ran all the way home because I knew if I walked, I'd have time to think and change my mind. I had to do it while whatever it was within me was impelling me to go home. My side ached and my lungs burned, but I didn't stop. I came up the steps and stood in the doorway.

Papa was sitting on the edge of the bed, his hand on Mama's shoulder. When he glanced up, I saw he was crying. "Cadi's here, Fia," he said softly. I saw her body tense. Papa got up slowly and left her. "She won't listen to me. She's just plain given up." He looked at me beseechingly and then went outside to sit on the front porch, leaving me alone with my mother.

Panting, I stood in the doorway until my breath eased. "Mama?" I said softly and came forward. She kept her back to me as I came close. "Mama, I'm sorry for what happened to Elen. I was jealous of her."

"I know."

"That day I said such terrible things to her. And you."

"I remember."

I didn't want to say it was because I missed my mother's love and attention. I didn't want to make excuses for myself. "I saw her coming across the tree bridge, and I was still so mad I wished she'd fall. And when she did, I tried to see her. I wanted to undo it. I knew when she fell I didn't hate her or you, Mama. Not deep down. But it was already too late. I didn't push her, Mama. I swear on my life, I didn't."

"I know you didn't," she said hoarsely. "I never thought you did, even for a minute."

"Ye didn't? I thought . . ." I didn't want to hope.

She turned over slowly. Her face was so thin and ashen and drawn with grief. "I never blamed you for what happened to Elen, never, not once." She touched my dress, pinching a little of the worn cotton between her fingers and rubbing it. "Is that what ye thought? It's ever been the same in my mind since it happened."

"What, Mama?"

"It should've been *me*," she whispered brokenly.

A feeling swept through me, like a warm spring breeze, clearing all my misunderstanding. "Oh, Mama, why?" I said gently, though with sudden insight, I knew.

"Because I sent Elen to find ye." Her face convulsed. "I sent her." She gave a ragged sob. "I knew I'd done wrong when I took your doll away and gave it to her. It meant so much to ye. It was a cruel thing to do, and I sorely regretted it. Before I could put things to rights, you'd run off. Granny said you thought I favored Elen more than you, and I knew it must seem that way at times. She was little for her age, and we'd near lost her when she was a wee bairn. She was sickly and needed me more is all. Ye had spunk right from the beginning and an independence that tested me at times."

"Granny called it my questing spirit."

Mama smiled sadly. "Aye, she did, didn't she?" She touched my hair. "She understood you so well, Cadi. Better than I ever did. There were so many times when I was envious of the way you could sit with her by the hour, talking, while we hardly ever had a word to say to one another."

"Oh, Mama . . ." How I'd longed for her to sit with me and Granny and pass the time with us even for a few minutes. I thought she'd stayed away because she hated me, because she blamed me for Elen's death.

"I never meant for ye to blame yerself, Cadi. It was my doing. I told Elen to go and find you and give your doll back. And she went. And she died."

"Ye dinna know I'd gone to the river, Mama. Ye dinna know I went to the Narrows."

"I should've been the one to find you." Her mouth trembled. "I should've been the one to follow after ye. Not Elen. It should've been me hunting for ye so I could tell ye I was sorry for what I'd done. It's my fault she fell down into the Narrows. It's my fault she died, Cadi, not yours."

"It was an accident, Mama."

"An accident that never would've happened if I'd been a proper ma." She withdrew her hand from me, clutching the sheet over her. Her heart was breaking all over again. "I lost ye both in the river that day. Ye wudna get near me after that day, and I didna blame ye. Oh, and when ye'd look at me, I'd see that terrible grief in your eyes and know it was my fault it was there. Ye were suffering so, I thought I'd lose my mind. I'd lost both of my girls that day. Both of ye." She closed her eyes and turned her face away.

Aching for her, I brushed my fingertips lightly over her wan cheek. "Ye dinna lose me, Mama." I stroked her hair the way she used to stroke mine when I was small. Her muscles relaxed. Perhaps she was remembering, too. Turning her head slowly, she looked up at me again, her eyes awash with tears.

"Ye looked happy with Bletsung Macleod. There seemed to be an understanding between ye."

"Aye, there is."

"I know what people say about her, but they're wrong. She's kind and loyal. She's lived all these years close to that terrible mountain, hoping, I guess."

"Yes." I laid my palm against her cool cheek. "Bletsung's all those good things, Mama, but if you'd opened your arms to me that day ye came and stood beneath the mountain laurel, I would've run into them."

She blinked, searching my face. "Ye would? Truly?"

I smiled shakily and nodded, for I couldn't speak.

Hope flickered in her eyes, the tiniest spark of it—and fear, too. A fear I recognized only too well. She lifted one arm. It was all I needed. I leaned down to her. When I felt her arm slip around me in a firm embrace, I let out my breath. "Oh, Mama, I love you so much!"

She pulled me close then, holding me tight so that I was lying next to her on the bed. We clung to one another, weeping.

"Oh, Cadi," she said, kissing me. "I love you, too." I drank in the sound of her tender voice.

And then she called me the name she had when I was very small. "You're still my wee l'il bit of heaven. . . ."

※

Lilybet. Little bit of heaven. They do sound some alike. And it's raised questions over the years, though whether Lilybet was an angel or no ain't for me to say. Fact is, I don't rightly know what she was. I've thought about it from time to time, and what's come to me is this: some things we'll never know until we face the Lord and ask him. Granny Forbes told me that as a child, and Lilybet said it again in her own way. She was ever pointing the way to God's high path.

I can't tell ye rightly whether Lilybet was real or not. All I know is she was there when I needed her most. I never saw her again after the day of the new covenant. That's what we came to call it. A new beginning, it was. I didn't need Lilybet after that, ye see? I had the Lord.

I like to think God sent Lilybet to me and she wasn't someone I made up in my own mind, though I had a surefire imagination. I can tell ye this, though, if God'd come himself in a burning bush the way he did with Moses, I'd've died of fright on the spot. No question about it. Instead, I'm thinkin' the Lord gave me a little girl who looked like my sister, Elen, and spoke like Granny Forbes. And I'm pure thankful for his tender mercies in my regard.

Those tender mercies extended to many of us in ways too many to count. Light came into our highland valley that day so long ago, and it's been shining bright ever since. What started with seven of us grew with each passing day. Soon more joined us at the river. Some took months, even years, to believe in the truth and make the journey to be baptized.

I'm sorry to say some never went at all.

Iona stayed by Brogan Kai, taking the blame for everything that happened, making guilt her mantle. The Kai stayed proud and bitter to the end of a long, miserable living, and then fell into the hands of almighty God.

Douglas was never seen again after that day. Everyone figured he headed over the mountains, wanting to get as far away from his father as possible. His brother Cleet was killed the following spring when he got between a she-bear and her cubs.

As for the others in our valley? Well, some was just too proud to believe they'd ever sinned bad enough to deserve hell. Gervase Odara was one who said so. She held to that conviction right up to her last day on this earth. She helped others hold to the same way of thinking, and no amount of talking and praying swayed or softened their hearts. I reckon they put all their faith in her medicines and their own good works. And though it made 'em feel right good during this life, it grieves me to know it didn't do much to save 'em in the next.

Some of the folks who went down to the river later was driven there, like I was, by guilt over sin, by shame and despair. They longed for forgiveness and peace. And by God's grace and mercy, they received it and rejoiced in it all their livelong days.

I kept up praying, from that day forward 'til now, that every last one of our folks in our highland valley would make the decision to pursue the Lord rather than serve the devil. Sadly, some never made a choice. Some thought living as they had was armor enough against Satan. So they just walked on through life, mortally wounded and never even knowing it.

But to those of us who opened our hearts, God Almighty gave us peace and joy beyond any we'd ever known. And ye know the rest of the story, for I've told ye young'uns the tale often enough.

We renamed Dead Man's Mountain for the man of God who brung the word of the Lord to us. Prophet's Peak it is to this day.

Sim Gillivray took Bletsung Macleod as his bride, and they had a fine son the following spring. Morgan Kerr Gillivray. Your father.

Fagan Kai left our valley for a time. He went down into the Carolinas and worked so that he could get some schooling. When he learned to read well enough, he came back to the mountains and brought a Bible with him. First place he come was my folks' house to see how I'd growed up. Guess he liked what he saw, 'cause he asked me to marry him not a month after he come home to stay. The Lord blessed us with a baby girl two years later, Annabel Beathas Kai. Her name means beautiful and wise, and so your mama is.

Since your grandpap and I've gotten too old to walk over these mountains much, your mama and papa have carried on for us, preaching the gospel from New Covenant House. 'Course it's bigger now, ye know. It ain't the mean little cabin Miz Elda Kendric lived in all those years ago and gave to your grandpap Fagan when he come home.

It's sad but true, there're still people in our mountains who ain't seen the light or accepted the good news of Jesus Christ. Not yet, anyway. We're still aworking on 'em and praying for 'em. But as for our house, we serve the Lord who brung your grandfather, the last sin eater, down off the mountain and back among the living.

Now then, darlings, it's long past your bedtime. Your mama's standing at the door, waiting to tuck ye in. Give your old Granny Cadi a hug and kiss good night. I love ye so.

Sleep well, now, and dream dreams of the Lord.

For ye are my own little bits of heaven.